D1431469

The Trouble with

WHISKEY

The Whiskeys

MELISSA FOSTER

ISBN-13: 978-1-948004-18-3

Cover Design: Elizabeth Mackey Designs
Cover Photography: James Critchley Photography

WORLD LITERARY PRESS
PRINTED IN THE UNITED STATES OF AMERICA

A Note to Readers

I am thrilled to bring you another Whiskey family series. The Whiskeys: Dark Knights at Redemption Ranch have had a special place in my heart since I first wrote about them in SHE LOVES ME (Harmony Pointe), and I have been excited to write Dare and Billie's story, since I met them in SEARCHING FOR LOVE (The Bradens & Montgomerys). Dare and Billie are one of the feistiest couples I've ever written, and their story was both heartbreaking and fun to write. I have fallen hopelessly in love with Dare and Billie, their families, and the rest of the crew at Redemption Ranch, and I hope you will, too.

If this is your first introduction to my Whiskey world, all of my books are written to stand alone, so dive in and enjoy Billie and Dare's fun, sexy ride to their happily ever after. When you're done, you can go back and read my other Dark Knights series. The Whiskeys: Dark Knights at Peaceful Harbor and The Wickeds: Dark Knights at Bayside.

The Whiskeys and Wickeds are just two of the series in my Love in Bloom big-family romance collection. Characters from each series make appearances in future books, so you never miss an engagement, wedding, or birth. A complete list of all series titles is included at the end of this book, along with previews of upcoming publications.

Download Free First-in-Series eBooks

www.MelissaFoster.com/free-ebooks

See the Entire Love in Bloom Collection

www.MelissaFoster.com/love-bloom-series

Download Series Checklists, Family Trees, and Publication Schedules

www.MelissaFoster.com/reader-goodies

If you prefer sweet romance, with no explicit scenes or graphic language, please try the Sweet with Heat series written under my pen name, Addison Cole. You'll find many of the same great love stories with toned-down heat levels.

Remember to sign up for my newsletter to make sure you don't miss out on future releases:

www.MelissaFoster.com/News

WHISKEY/WICKED FAMILY TREE

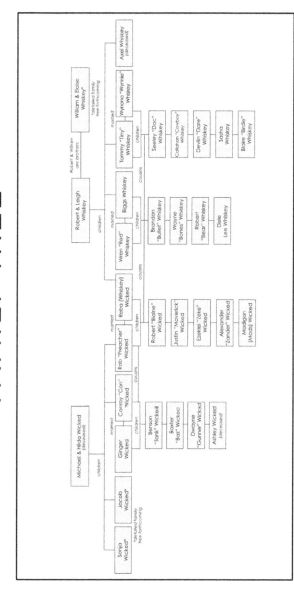

New York Times Bestselling Author

MELISSA FOSTER

Chapter One

BILLIE PUSHED THE tray of drinks she was carrying high over her head as she weaved through the crowd, skirting the packed dance floor at the Roadhouse, her family's biker bar, where she'd worked since she was old enough to earn a buck. She and her younger sister, Bobbie, had grown up in the rustic dive, hanging out while they did homework and washing dishes when they were shorthanded, because that's what the Mancinis did. They got shit done and had one another's backs. Much like the sea of guys who were there every night wearing black leather cuts—vests with the Dark Knights motorcycle club patches on them. Her father was the vice president of the club, and the bonds of that brotherhood were unbreakable.

She approached the group of good-looking out-of-towners wearing khakis and dress shirts by the pool table who had ordered the drinks and was acutely aware of their slick-looking buddy eyeing her up as he waited for his turn at pool. They grew 'em big and strong around Hope Valley, Colorado, where ranches and livestock paid the bills for most families. Billie had a thing for calloused hands, scruffy faces, and no-bullshit men who had no use for suits and ties. But summertime brought all kinds of mountain-loving tourists to their small town.

"*Drink! Drink! Drink!*" a group of women chanted.

Billie looked toward the commotion and saw three busty women standing shoulder to shoulder, each cradling a shot glass between her breasts. Devlin "Dare" Whiskey licked the swell of one of the giggling blonde's breasts, and she shook salt onto the wet spot. *You've got to be kidding me.* As the girl handed the shaker to the girl beside her, Dare licked the salt off her breast and wrapped that big ornery mouth of his around the shot glass. He tipped his too-frigging-handsome face back as he downed the shot hands-free. Well, his hands weren't actually free. As the girls whooped and cheered, he hauled that blonde into a kiss, then made his way to the next giggling girl and repeated the whole damn thing.

Fucking Dare.

Billie and Dare had been best friends when they were growing up, along with their other best friend, Eddie Baker. The three of them were inseparable. They'd earned the nickname the Daredevils by the time they were seven years old because they were always racing or trying to do risky stunts on their skateboards, dirt bikes, and anything else they could find. They drove their parents crazy, but instead of dissuading them, their parents made sure they learned how to do those things safely. Their stunts got riskier as they got older—skydiving, cliff diving, drag racing, and just about anything else that would give them an adrenaline rush. Even though the Daredevils' motto was "The *right* person always wins, not the *best* person," because they considered themselves equals on all levels, she and Dare had still always tried to one-up each other with new challenges, while Eddie's love of technology had taken over. They all had their *thing*. When Eddie became enthralled with making videos and movies, opting out of many of their stunts in lieu of videoing them, they supported his love of movies in every way they could, doing anything he asked. Dare was into classic cars and motorcycles, so they went to all the classic car shows, and motocross was Billie's passion. She'd become a pro racer at eighteen, and Dare and Eddie had cheered her on at nearly every race.

They'd had a lot of laughs, despite Billie and Dare fooling around one time the summer before he left for college. There had always been something dark and electric between them, as if they were twin flames. Even back then he was rugged and muscular, cocky as hell, and *boy* could he kiss. But that'd been a one-time thing, and although their relationship had gotten a little awkward for a while, they'd moved past it and had remained stunt besties into adulthood, when she and Eddie, who had always been a grounding force in her life, began an ill-fated year-long relationship.

They'd remained the Daredevils—unbreakable and unstoppable—until six years ago, when Eddie was killed during a stunt gone wrong, and their lives had never been the same. Dare had begun taking his stunts to terrifying levels, and Billie had let go of that dangerous lifestyle and everything that reminded her of it. Including Dare. The trouble was, Dare was always around, and just the sight of him rattled the chains that kept her skeletons in the closet.

A round of cheers pulled Billie from her thoughts as Dare did the third shot. He glanced over, his eyes locking on Billie as he plucked the glass from his mouth. A cocky grin curved his lips, and he raised his brows in that way he had that said, *Come here, sugar, and I'll do you so good you'll never forget me.*

She rolled her eyes and turned away, focusing on giving the

customers their drinks and trying not to think about how spot-on that arrogant biker's silent message was. He was the only man who had ever ignited a fire deep inside her. They hadn't even gone all the way that hot summer night all those years ago, and she *still* got turned on just thinking about his hands on her.

Irritation climbed up her spine, and she spun around to head back to the bar, but Mr. Slick-Out-of-Towner was *right there*.

"Anyone ever tell you that you look just like Bridget Moynahan?"

Only every swinging dick in this place. "I've heard it a time or two." She tried to step around him, but he blocked her path, stepping closer.

"You're a lot hotter than she is." He put his hand on her hip. "What're you doing later?"

Billie quickly sized him up. She was five seven, even taller with her boots on, and this douchebag was *maybe* six feet. She narrowed her eyes and lifted her chin, catching movement in her peripheral vision as she said, "Not *you.*" She shoved his hand away as Dare closed the distance between them, looking like a bull ready to charge. She got right in Mr. Slick's face, her voice deathly calm. "Touch me, or any other woman in here without her permission, and you'll be lucky if you can crawl out the door tonight."

"Come on, baby, you know you want me." Slick ran his hand down her arm.

"*Really*, dude?" She sighed, as if bored, and in the next second, she grabbed his hand and twisted his arm inward, while bending his hand back. He doubled over in pain.

"Jesus, *fuck.*" His knees buckled, and he sank toward the floor.

Every Dark Knight in the place was on their feet, and Dare was at the head of the pack, as Billie glared down at the kneeling jerk with a smile. "Aikido. It does a body good." She seethed, "Now get your sorry ass out of my bar. You hear me?"

"Get the fu—"

She bent his wrist further, and he cried out. "Yes, ma'am. I'm leaving right now," she said calmly. "Let me hear it before I break your wrist."

"*Fine*," the guy gritted out, and she wrenched his arm higher. "Yes, ma'am! I'll leave!"

She let go of his hand and blew past him, glowering at Dare as several Dark Knights followed the guy toward the door.

Dare fell into step beside her. "You okay?"

She scoffed. He knew better than anyone that she could take care of herself, and if she ran into trouble, Bobbie knew how to use the shotgun they kept behind the bar. "Fucking fantastic. You can go back to the girls who get off on being saved." She strode behind the bar and put the tray away.

Bobbie sidled up to her with a teasing smirk. "You'll never get a man if you keep hurting them."

Billie gave her younger, fair-haired sister and roommate a deadpan look. Bobbie laughed and went to deliver drinks to a table. Billie turned back to the bar as cheers rang out by the mechanical bull. She looked across the room and saw Dare climbing onto it, eating up the attention, but his gaze skirted over those eager women's heads, and he winked at Billie.

"Did you two ever hook up?" Kellan grabbed a bottle from behind her and started making a drink. He was a part-time bartender and law school student, with deep dimples and a sunshine-and-whiskey personality—always in a good mood but tough when he needed to be.

We're not going there. "What is this, Gossip Central?"

"I'm just curious. I think you'd make a great couple. You're both badass."

"I hope you make a better lawyer than matchmaker." She nodded toward his customer, who was watching him intently, as if he could make him move faster. "I think he wants that drink you're holding."

As the night wore on, the bar got even more crowded. Billie went into the stockroom to restock the liquor, and when she came out, Dare's groupies were waving money, egging him on as he climbed onto the bar and began dancing to "Save a Horse, Ride a Cowboy." The man was two-hundred-plus pounds of hip-thrusting, tongue-wagging sex on legs. Bobbie and Kellan were dancing behind the bar as they served drinks, and while most customers were enjoying his show, there was a handful who looked shocked and slightly appalled.

"Are you freaking kidding me?" Billie mumbled as she set the bottles down and scanned the crowd for Dare's brothers, who could usually help wrangle him in. But Doc and Cowboy were nowhere to be found. She spotted his cousin Raleigh "Rebel" Whiskey and held her palm up, giving him a *Do something* stare.

Amusement rose in Rebel's eyes. He shouted, "Good luck," and took a swig of his beer.

Was she the only sane person in the bar? She stomped over to Dare. "Get off my bar!"

He grinned down at her, cupping his ear. "What's that? You want me to shake my ass?" He turned his butt toward her and shook his infuriatingly hot ass, causing an uproar of cheers and laughter.

"Take yourself to the strip club down the road!" Billie hollered.

That cocky grin widened. "You want me to *strip*?" Hoots and whistles rang out as he whipped off his shirt and swung it around his head.

Billie put her hands on the bar. "*Off*, Dare! And I don't mean your pants!"

A collective squeal rang out from the women he'd been with all night. Dare grabbed Billie's arms, hauling her onto the bar. He wrapped his thick arm around her waist, gyrating against her, those piercing dark eyes reaching into her soul, reminding her of all the years they'd done shit like this and laughed all night.

"Come on, Wildfire, you know you want to cut loose with me."

Her chest constricted at the nickname he'd called her since they were kids and had rarely used the last few years. But on the heels of that warmth came the sharp, painful truth. Her feelings for Dare were the reason Eddie was dead. *She* was the reason Eddie was dead. She stuffed those warm feelings down deep and sneered. "I want to cut *something*, all right. Put on your damn shirt, get off my bar, and take your showboating ass onto the dance floor."

"Only if you'll dance with me." He tightened his hold on her, hips grinding, broad chest brushing enticingly against her, as women yelled, "I'll dance with you," and "Damn, look at those hips go!" Some guys had puppy-dog eyes that got them special favors. Dare Whiskey had about a hundred ways of looking at a woman to get what he wanted, and as he tilted his head, brow furrowing, eyes pleading, a seductive smile playing on his lips, Billie's mind spun back to the last time she'd been sucked in by that look.

The night they'd hooked up—and he'd broken her heart.

She leaned closer, putting her mouth beside his ear, and promised, "One dance."

The elated grin on his face *almost* made her feel guilty as they climbed off the bar, much to his entourage's chagrin, and he reached for her. "Let's dance, sweet darlin'."

She tossed him a clean towel. "The only dance I'm doin' is tending to customers while you wipe down that bar." She felt the heat of his stare as she strutted into the stockroom with Bobbie on her heels.

"Why are you like that to him? He's just having fun."

Billie turned on her. "Because this is a *business*, and if someone gets hurt, we're liable. Do you want everyone thinking they can come in here and do shit like that?"

"No, but it's *Dare*. He's always done it. I don't get it."

"There's nothing to get. This is our family business, and it's about time we stopped running it like it's a playground." Bobbie was an elementary school teacher, and she only worked part-time at the bar, while Billie managed it full time and took the business more seriously.

Bobbie crossed her arms with a pinched expression. "Can you just tell me *why* you're such a jerk to him lately? I know things changed after Eddie died, but it's like you've suddenly got no patience for him, and I've never seen him do anything but be your friend."

Because grieving without him was more terrifying than any stunt, and every time I look at him, I remember the betrayal in Eddie's eyes right before his fatal accident. But the more I push Dare away, the stronger he comes at me to rekindle our friendship, and that makes it harder for me to keep that wall between us. Basically, I'm messed up, because I want to tear down that wall as badly as I want to bolt in the other direction. She clamped her mouth shut before any of that escaped, letting the ugly truth continue eating away at her like a ravenous rat trying to gnaw its way out.

She grabbed two bottles of alcohol and headed back to the bar, catching sight of Dare dirty dancing with his groupies. *I need to get out of this town.* She'd told herself that forever, but she'd never leave. Traveling over the summers for her motocross races when she was younger had proven what she'd always known. She belonged in Hope Valley, even if it meant being around Dare Fucking Whiskey.

Pushing that thought away, she escaped to the one place she didn't have to think—behind the bar. Unfortunately, Bobbie followed her *again.*

"Billie...?" Her sister lowered her voice, and a challenge rose in her eyes. "You're not *jealous* of those women with Dare, are you?"

"Are you insane? Do you think I want to be a notch on his belt? It's a wonder the damn thing hasn't shredded."

DARE SAT AT a table with his older brother Callahan, who went by the road name Cowboy, and their cousin Rebel, listening to them shoot the shit, while he chewed on thoughts of Billie. She hadn't looked his way in more than an hour, and that pissed him off. He was so damn tired of missing her—the *real* her—he was sick with it. If he were one of his therapy clients, he'd give himself a list of tools to sever those ties, starting with the obvious—stop showing up at the Roadhouse. But he could no sooner do that than he could forget how it felt to finally have her in his arms again on that fucking bar, her fierceness and bullheadedness be damned. That woman had owned his heart since they were kids.

Dare had wanted *three* things for as long as he could remember, and Billie was at the top of that list, followed by becoming a Dark Knight and being a therapist at his family's ranch—Redemption Ranch—where they rescued horses and people, giving ex-cons, recovering addicts who had gone through rehab, and people with social or emotional issues, and other lost souls, a second chance.

Some might say two out of three wasn't bad. But as Dare looked across the bar at Billie, his heart said otherwise.

He never should have made that stupid pact with Eddie in high school, but they were two kids crushing on their best friend. They'd agreed neither would make a move, but if *Billie* made the move, they could act on it. Dare had gotten lucky when she'd made a move the summer before college. But his luck hadn't lasted. Moments after making out, she'd kicked him to the curb.

He'd been knocked on his ass, and had gone down a bad path after that, partying hard and doing some scary shit just to try to get her out of his head. His father had tried to straighten him out more times than he could count. There was no one tougher than Tommy "Tiny" Whiskey. He was six four and three hundred pounds of badass biker and rancher. But Dare didn't scare easily, and while he was wild, he wasn't stupid. He'd gone to college and had kept his grades up despite his partying so his parents would have no reason to pull him out of school. It wasn't until his sophomore year, when Billie had told him she didn't even know who he was anymore and that he didn't have what it took to become a Dark Knight that he'd finally cleaned up his act. He'd gotten his shit together, interned in his field during school and at the ranch when he wasn't in school, where his mother, Wynnie, a psychologist, led a staff of therapists. He'd prospected the Dark Knights, and after graduation, he'd come home determined to get his girl.

He'd gone straight to Eddie's house to tell him he was done respecting the pact. But before Dare could get a word out, Eddie dropped the bomb that he and Billie were seeing each other. Dare had fought the urge to drink himself into oblivion, and instead had poured everything he had into becoming the best therapist he could be and living a damn good life, because he'd been sure that Billie and Eddie would realize they weren't right for each other, and when that happened, he'd be there to show her the light. He'd gotten his master's degree and had since earned a strong reputation for his unconventional therapy style.

He hadn't counted on Eddie proposing to Billie or Billie saying yes, which had gutted Dare anew.

He should have fought for her that summer before college. Maybe then she wouldn't have ended up with Eddie, and Dare wouldn't have said the shit he'd said when she'd gotten engaged, and ruined their friendship.

"I can't believe how late I am!" Birdie, their youngest sister, said as she breezed up to the table, jerking him from his thoughts. She was wearing black-and-white checked shorts with ruffled hems, a cropped black T-shirt, and red high heels. Her wild dark hair had a red-and-yellow polka-dot ribbon braided into a lock running down the left side of her face. She wore two bracelets with enormous red and white beads and white-framed glasses—cosmetic, not prescription. Her style was as quirky as her personality. She slid into a chair at the table, talking a mile a minute. "The shop was crazy busy, and Quinn and I got to talking after we closed up. You know how that goes." Birdie was co-owner of Divine Intervention chocolate shop, where she worked with her bestie and their aunt. "Quinnie will be here later, by the way..."

As Birdie rattled on, Dare looked across the room at Billie leaning over the bar in that skimpy red leather halter top. She looked hot as sin in cutoffs, cowgirl boots, and that sexy black choker she wore like a brand. She'd always dressed edgy and sexy, reeking of confidence and a don't-fuck-with-me attitude. He'd seen her ice people out of her life, but he never thought he'd be one of them. Until Eddie died, and the world as he knew it failed to exist.

"This place is packed. Who's Dare looking at?" Birdie scrambled up to her feet on the chair, drawing Dare's attention as she looked over the crowd. She was a tiny thing, which was why Dare had coined the nickname Birdie when she was just two years old. It suited her better than her given name, Blair. "It's Billie!"

"Who else?" Rebel said as Birdie sat down. "If he keeps staring at her like that, people are going to think he's a stalker."

"He's right, man," Cowboy agreed. "Give her a break."

Dare looked at his fairer-haired, bearded, and *formidable* older brother, who along with their oldest brother, Seeley, who went by the road name "Doc" and ran a veterinary clinic at the ranch, were always trying to rein him in. Cowboy was naturally bossy, and while that was perfect for managing the ranch hands, it had never gone over well with Dare. "Think I give a shit what other people think? I'm just making sure nobody gives her a hard time."

Cowboy arched a brow. "Nobody but you? I think she's made it more than clear that she doesn't need your protection."

"Who are *you* to talk?" Birdie chimed in. "You're overprotective of everyone we know, and you're always busting my balls about how I dress and what guys I talk to."

"That would be *all* of your brothers," Rebel pointed out.

"I don't need help from the peanut gallery, thank you very much," Birdie said.

Dare loved Birdie's take-no-shit attitude.

"Sorry to break this to you, Bird," Cowboy said. "But you don't have balls."

"Oh yeah?" She sat up straighter. "You always say it takes brass balls to ride the mechanical bull. Who holds the record for the longest mechanical bull ride two years running?" She pointed to herself with both thumbs.

Dare chuckled, Cowboy shook his head, and Rebel high-fived Birdie.

"Thank you very much." Birdie reached for Dare's beer.

He put his hand over the bottle. "You driving?"

"Yes, *Daddy*, which is why I'm only taking a sip of yours and not drinking my own." She yanked the bottle away and took a drink, then set it down in front of him. "Are *you* driving?"

"Yes, but I've got about a hundred and twenty pounds on you, and this is my first and only beer."

"Sometimes I wish I were heavier. *Now...*" She tapped her chin, looking around the room. "I need to find a woman for Cowboy." She'd gotten a hair up her ass a few months back about marrying Cowboy off, and she was always trying to find him a woman. Birdie lived for her made-up *missions* as much as their sister Sasha lived for their paintball games.

13

Birdie reached across the table and patted Cowboy's arm. "There's a cute blonde. The one in the blue top."

"No thanks," Cowboy said. "Dare had his mouth on her a couple of hours ago."

Birdie gave Dare a disapproving stare. "Do you have to make out with *all* the women in this town? Geez."

There was only one woman he wanted to get his mouth on, but she'd like to run him over with her truck. "Just sharin' the love, darlin'."

Birdie rolled her eyes. "You guys would lock me up if I did that."

"Damn right we would," all three of the men said at once, to which Birdie went off on them.

Dare zoned out, thinking about Billie. She had a right to hate him. The last thing he'd said to her before Eddie died was not to marry him. She'd lost the man she loved, and Dare had lost both of them. As a therapist, he understood her grief and everything she was going through, but as her friend, he wanted to help her deal with it and bring back the fun-loving, fearless girl who would have sold her soul for a career in motocross and a lifetime full of adventures. But she'd buried that part of herself right alongside Eddie, leaving Dare to sit in that bar year after year, watching guys hit on the best friend he loved and the woman he couldn't help but adore, despite the giant chip on her shoulder and those beautiful eyes shooting darts at him every chance she got.

She was waiting on tables, flashing that gorgeous smile, and tossing her long dark hair over her shoulder, getting hit on and doing as much flirting as she was shutting down. But *that* was Billie, confident as the day was long. She knew how to earn tips and how to protect herself. At least physically. But that tender heart of hers was all kinds of broken, and *Dare* was just the man to fix it.

She glanced over, catching him staring. Her eyes narrowed, and she turned away, wasting that stunning smile on the four badass Transom brothers, who looked like starving dogs salivating at their next meal.

Fuckers.

The blonde and her friends sidled up to Dare. "You want to get out of here with us?"

"Hell yes." Anything to distract himself from thoughts of Billie.

"Um, *hello*? Nice introduction, brother dear," Birdie chirped at him.

He leaned down and whispered in her ear, "No need for you to worry your pretty little head with introductions. I don't know their names, and even if I did, I'd forget them by tomorrow."

He followed the three women to their apartment and spent far too long listening to bad music, ridiculous conversations, and inane questions about being a biker—*Do you, like, trade women? Have you ever killed anyone? Have you ever been in jail?*—to which he could have responded, *Hell no, not directly, and no. Thanks to Billie pulling my head out of my ass the summer after my junior year of college, I managed to stay out of jail, and now I help other people see the errors of their ways.* But he didn't waste his breath, because it was closing time at the Roadhouse, and as he dodged enticing offers for *group play*, which he'd totally be into if Billie hadn't stirred up shit in his brain, those lovely women reminded him of all the reasons he wanted to leave.

He was done wasting time with women he didn't care

about. He'd lost Billie because he hadn't fought for her. *Well, guess what, Mancini. It's time to knock that chip off your shoulder and face this shit head-on before our whole lives pass us by.*

DARE DROVE HIS motorcycle around the bar to make sure the asshole Billie had given shit to wasn't hanging around, and then he parked out front to wait for her and Bobbie to leave, just as he'd done hundreds of times before. The parking lot was empty, save for Bobbie's Jeep, Kellan's car, and Billie's old truck. There was a time when the only things she'd drive were fast cars, motorcycles, and motocross bikes. Back then, she'd have hauled his ass up on the bar and laughed when her parents told them to get the hell down. Man, he missed that wild streak.

He looked up at the neon orange ROADHOUSE sign above the front doors and the wide front porch that spanned the length of the building. He could still picture fourteen-year-old Billie standing on the steps in her cowgirl boots and cutoffs, with a dirt bike helmet tucked under her arm and sass pouring out of her mouth. When they were growing up, he'd thought that bar was the coolest place around. It was pretty great and full of amazing memories, but now he knew it wasn't the place that was the coolest. It was Billie, with her larger-than-life personality and that arrogance that had always gotten under his skin. *It was Eddie, too,* he thought with a stab of longing. He'd been the calm to their storms, and Dare missed him every damn day.

The front doors of the bar opened, and Kellan and Bobbie walked out, locking the door behind them. Dare climbed off his motorcycle as they descended the stairs.

Kellan nodded at Dare and said, "Have a good night," as he headed to his car.

A concerned smile *almost* reached Bobbie's eyes. Her blond hair fell to the middle of her back. She was more sweetness than sass and was a few inches shorter than Billie, but she could definitely hold her own.

"Hey there, darlin'."

Bobbie crossed her arms. "Billie's not going to be happy to see you out here."

Tell me something I don't know. "After the shit she pulled with that asshole tonight, do you really think I'd let you two walk out of here alone?"

"I know you better than that, and so does she. But Kellan was here."

"And he left with you, which means she'll be walking out alone," he said as Kellan drove out of the lot.

Bobbie sighed. "You're right. Thanks for watching out for her. I know my sister doesn't make it easy, but I'm glad you do it."

"I've been doing it our whole lives, darlin'. It'll take a lot more than her smart mouth to stop me."

"I know that, too." She headed to her Jeep, calling over her shoulder, "Watch yourself. She keeps a knife in her boot."

She always has. "You know I like 'em feisty."

A little while later, Billie came out the front door. Her keen eyes swept the lot, getting hung up on Dare. He could practically feel the earth move with the roll of her eyes as she came off the porch.

She headed for her truck, not slowing down when he fell into step beside her. "What're you doing here?"

"Same as always—keeping you safe."

She stopped in her tracks, the air chilling. "You've been showing up here for as long as I can remember. Have I ever *once* needed your help?"

"Do I really need to remind you of all the times you've needed my help right here in this parking lot?"

"Did all that partying you did after high school mess up your brain? Because I can't remember *ever* needing your help."

"Last year. The prick from Wisconsin with the eyebrow ring."

"I could have handled him."

"No doubt. But you shouldn't have to. And the two guys who were passin' through town a few months before that, who you flirted with so damn much they followed you home?"

Her eyes narrowed. "What're you talking about? Nobody ever followed me home."

"Who do you think stopped them from fucking you up?"

"What…?" She shook her head.

"*Yeah.* Those stitches I got in my cheek? They weren't from a fight with Cowboy."

Her brows knitted.

"That's right, darlin'. I see you doubting it. But you know I don't lie. You're tough as nails, but two guys against one unsuspecting woman? You wouldn't have had a chance."

"Why didn't you tell me?"

"Because I took care of it and made sure they left town."

"Thanks, but I'm not *your* responsibility."

Maybe not in your eyes, but I'm loyal to the bone. "You became my responsibility the day you poked me in the chest and said, *You're my new best friend. Let's go get into trouble,* and made me pinkie swear on it."

"I was *six* and obviously had very poor judgment."

"No doubt. Johnny Petrone was proof of that." That earned him another eye roll.

"I was *fifteen*."

"And bawling your eyes out on those very steps." He pointed toward the bar. "Because he broke up with you. He was *never* worthy of a single date. What the hell were you thinking?"

"Is that why you gave him a black eye?"

"He made my best friend cry. I'd have done more than that if Doc hadn't stopped me."

Her jaw tightened, a war raging in her beautiful hazel eyes. "You were always out of control."

"And you weren't?" He held her gaze.

"Not like you."

He stepped closer. So close she had to tip her face up to see his, burning off the chill she tried to wear like a shield. "You're *exactly* like me. Always have been. Always will be. You lived and breathed for the next adrenaline high, and just doing it was never enough. You *had* to excel, just like me. You worked your ass off to become a pro motocross racer. I don't know how you walked away from it and turned your back on everything else you loved except the damn bar."

Her eyes narrowed, her chest rising with her heavy breaths, brushing against him. "I grew up."

"You got *scared*." He let that sink in, and if he hadn't been looking for it, he'd have missed the slight twitch in her eyes, the *tell* that gave away when she was thinking about something or lying. "It's time to stop pretending to be someone you're not, Billie. I know you love the bar, but that's just a piece of who you are, like the ranch is part of who I am. You're like a caged tiger in there. I see it in your eyes and feel it every time I'm around you. That's *not* you, Billie. You used to shine like the fucking sun, and now you're like a thunderstorm waiting to happen. I hate seeing you like that, and so would Eddie."

"If you don't like what you see, then stay the hell away from me. Stop coming to *my* family's bar." She took a step toward her truck, and he moved in front of her, blocking her way.

"That's not happening, and I don't believe you want me to."

"You don't care what *I* want," she seethed. "This is about what *you* want."

"You're damn right it is, because what I want is to stop you from throwing your life away."

Her eyes twitched, but her jaw tightened again. "Go find someone else to save."

"You're so damn frustrating," he gritted out. "I don't want to *save* you. I want to help you get back to living the life you deserve. The life you *really* love."

"Save your psychobabble for someone else. Why do you care what I do, anyway?"

"Because I fucking *love* you, and I loved Eddie, and now he's *gone*, Billie. But you're still here, and acting like someone you're not *isn't* going to bring him back."

Anger flamed in her eyes, and she pushed past him and headed for her truck.

"We *both* lost him, Billie, and you haven't talked to me about what happened to him even *once*," he said as she climbed into her truck. "I get that you hate me for what I said the day he died." Her hand stilled on the door. "I'm sorry I opened my mouth. I wish I could take it all back, but fucking *yell* at me. Beat the hell out of me. Do *something* to get that anger out of your system, because he was a piece of us, and you're the *only* other person on this earth who knows what that truly means."

She swallowed hard, her eyes downcast.

"Come on, Billie." He softened his tone. "Hasn't this gone on long enough? I just want my best friend back. I want to talk and hang out and do fun shit with you. I fucking *miss* you, Billie. I miss us."

She lifted sad, angry eyes to him. "Well, I'm not that girl anymore, so get over it."

She slammed her truck door, and he watched her drive away. She was so damn stubborn, getting her out of the armor she'd worn like a shield would require finesse. He might have once been a bull in a china shop, but he'd had six long years to learn patience, and he was ready to put that patience to the test and face his biggest, most important challenge yet—showing the woman he'd always loved that some *dares* are worth the risk.

Chapter Two

AFTER A FITFUL night's sleep spent overthinking every word Dare had said to her, Billie drove to Elk Mountain Park for her morning run. She'd never been a great sleeper, but her inability to shut her mind off had gotten even worse after Eddie died and she'd given up her adrenaline-driven lifestyle. She'd had a hell of a time finding safer ways to get rid of her excess energy. She was still struggling with that, but running helped to clear her head and calm her mind.

Or at least it usually did.

This morning, as the sun beat down on her shoulders, she couldn't get lost in the serenity of the grassy fields and scenic mountains. Instead, Dare's freaking voice was echoing in her head. *You got scared…You used to shine like the fucking sun, and now you're like a thunderstorm waiting to happen. I hate seeing you like that, and so would Eddie.*

She kicked up her speed, trying to outrun the truth in his words.

All she wanted was to be in control of her life, and she'd never felt more *out* of control. *I just want my best friend back…I fucking miss you, Billie. I miss us.* She pushed herself harder, sweat pouring down her neck and chest, but there was no outrunning the bone-deep ache of missing every damn thing she'd lost or given up. Most of all, being part of their trio and their exciting, carefree days, easy friendships, and crazy, fun nights. It never mattered that Dare and Eddie were opposites in every way. In fact, it made the three of them better. Dare was big, burly, and wild, while Eddie was lean, fit, and careful. Dare kept his dark hair short and his scruff trim, while Eddie's blond hair was always in need of a cut and he shaved only under duress. Dare was bullheaded, had several piercings in his ear, septum, and nostril, and was tatted from neck to pecs. Lord only knew how much ink was in the danger zone, but she'd seen the tattoos on his thighs and calves. Eddie was full of boyish charm and had not a speck of ink on his body. God, she missed being with them. The way Dare pushed her and how Eddie always knew the right thing to do and say, as if he'd been put on earth because the universe knew they needed someone more rational to rein them in and be their sounding board. She missed their banter as much as she missed their fights, and she missed the person she'd been with them.

But how could she ever go back, when it hurt so bad?

She looked up at the clear blue sky, as she'd done thousands of times before, and pictured Eddie's handsome face, his blue eyes glittering down at her, shaggy blond hair falling in front of them. She imagined him laughing, because imagining anything less always brought tears. Every time she talked to him, she thought she'd said everything she could ever want to say. She'd apologized for not loving him the way he deserved to be loved more times than she could count, but still when she looked up, that was the first thing that came out. "It's me again. I'm sorry for not loving you the way you deserved. I wish I were wired differently. You were *always* there for me." She gulped in air, thinking about how he'd encouraged her and cheered her on at motocross races—*What're you waiting for, Billie? Get out there and show the world what you've got*—and recorded even the most ridiculous of stunts.

"That should've been enough." *But you were too easy, and I don't do well with easy. But you knew that, didn't you?* That brought a wave of guilt that nearly bowled her over, but it was as true as the sky was blue. "I could really use your words of wisdom right now, Eddie." She took a few deep breaths, trying to calm her racing heart. "I don't know what to do, but Dare's right. Most days I feel like I'm going to explode. It *hurts*, Eddie. I wish you were here to tell me what to do." She heard an airplane in the distance and wished she were on it. Scratch that. She wished that she *wanted* to be on it, because going away would make things so much easier, but she didn't want to leave the place or people she loved. "Can you just give me a sign, Eddie? A hint about what I should do?"

She ran faster, wishing she'd never started dating him, because she'd known even then that her heart had already been spoken for. But she'd thought she could get past her feelings for Dare. Oh, how she'd tried, year after year, but he was so deeply rooted in her soul, she didn't know where she ended and he began. She didn't even know when she'd fallen in love with him, but she'd known she was in too deep the summer after high school, when she'd had a bit too much liquid courage at a party and had gone in for a kiss—and had come out the other side consumed by sensations more powerful than any thrill she'd ever experienced, more addicting than the adrenaline rushes that had ruled her life, and it had terrified her. She knew at that moment that loving Dare Whiskey was dangerous, and she'd told him it could never happen again. It was a good thing, because he'd gotten so out of control that summer, drinking too much, toying with drugs, and tempting fate with treacherously dangerous stunts, she'd been sure she'd stop wanting him. But here she was, ten-plus years later, asking her dead ex-fiancé for help.

Her lungs stung, her clothing was soaked, and her heart hurt like a bitch. She slowed to a walk and bent over, resting her hands on her thighs as she tried to catch her breath. The breeze felt good on her face.

"Maaaaanciiiiiiniiiiii!"

She whipped around just as Dare parachuted to the ground on the other side of the field. *Are you freaking kidding me, Eddie? He's your sign? Either you've got a wicked sense of humor, or I'm in trouble.*

She headed across the grass toward Dare as he unhooked his equipment. Most people wore flight suits, but Dare and Billie had always hated them. He wore a T-shirt, cargo shorts, and sneakers, and he had a small backpack strapped to his chest. His cocky grin brought a smile, despite her annoyance.

"Hey, girl. Great morning, huh?" He shrugged off the pack that was strapped to his chest and plopped onto his ass as he unzipped it.

"It *was*. What're you doing here, Dare?"

He pulled a plastic bottle of orange juice out of the backpack and set it on the grass. "Having breakfast." He withdrew a plastic container and took off the top, revealing two sandwiches. "PBJ and banana. Wanna share?" He patted the grass beside him.

She rolled her eyes as she sat down. "Am I supposed to believe you went skydiving armed with my favorite breakfast and just *happened* to land in the field where I run practically every day?"

"I figured you missed me."

"I just saw you last night."

"*Exactly.* That was a long damn time ago, and I know you're dreaming about me and shit."

"There's that ego we all know so well."

"You don't know it nearly well enough anymore, and you run *three* days a week, not seven." He leaned his shoulder against hers, lowering his voice. *"Embellisher."* He held the plastic container in front of her. "Go ahead—you know you want it."

"Not hungry, thanks."

"Bullshit. You're always hungry. I mean, I know you'd rather have some of this." He waved to his body. "But I don't fool around with women who want to scratch my eyes out. Now, dig those nails into my back…" He winked.

"Dream on, *Devlin.*"

"Pullin' out the big guns, are ya?" He lifted the container again. "Eat the damn sandwich, and don't worry, *Wilhelmina*, I won't take it as an olive branch."

Ugh. Why had her parents saddled her with her great-grandmother's first name? She reluctantly took the sandwich and bit into it, further irritated that his sandwiches still tasted better than anyone else's. The raspberry preserves and bananas were sweeter, the peanut butter chunkier, and the bread was as soft as a cloud. "Thanks."

"I lied. I'm totally taking it as an olive branch." He shoved half his sandwich in his mouth and reached into his backpack, handing her a bottle of water, amusement shining in his eyes.

She yanked it from his hand. "You're a pain in my ass."

"Good. The day I stop being one, I'll know I mean nothing to you."

As if that could ever happen. She chugged the water. "Did you come here to give me more shit?"

"I haven't decided yet."

"Great." She pushed to her feet.

He yanked her back down. "Chill out, Mancini. I'm just having breakfast with my bestie."

"I'm not your bestie anymore."

"You'll always be my bestie. Those bonds don't break just because you get a hair up your ass for a few years."

"Lucky me," she said sarcastically. "Whose butt do I have to kick for flying you out here?"

"Flame gave me a lift. Good luck kicking the ass of a guy who jumps into fires for a living."

Flame was Dare's friend Finn Steele's road name. He was a smoke jumper and a Dark Knight, and now he was on Billie's shit list. "Freaking Finn. You can bet I'm going to give him hell."

"Good luck with that. Hey, maybe I'll go running with you sometime."

She scoffed. "You couldn't keep up."

"Wanna bet?"

"Yeah. I win, you stop coming around. You win, you stop coming around."

He ate the rest of his sandwich in one bite, eyes narrowing as he chewed and swallowed. "You'd be lonely without me."

"I've been without you for a long time, Dare, and I'm not lonely." She took another bite of her sandwich and gazed out at the field, hoping she'd pulled off the lie.

"Twitch, twitch."

She tried to stifle a smile as she turned to look at him. "You think you know me."

"Besties for life know each other's tells."

"Just like I know you're here to get me to talk."

He leaned back on his palms and crossed his ankles. "Is that so bad?"

"Why *now*? After all this time?"

"I never stopped trying to talk to you."

That was true, even after she'd tried to cut him out of her life, he'd been persistent, coming back day after day, calling, texting, showing up when he knew she'd be home, trying to talk to her at the bar after she'd gone back to work. Weeks later, when he'd finally taken the hint and those check-ins had tapered off, she'd been as relieved as she was devastated. But he'd never stopped trying.

"But as I told you last night," Dare said thoughtfully, "I miss you, and you never let me apologize for what I said that day. It was selfish of me to tell you not to marry Eddie. If I could go back and do it over—"

"You'd say the same damn thing," she said sharply. "We both know you always speak your mind, regardless of the ramifications." It was one of the things she admired most about him, because she'd always done the same thing. But holding everything in for all these years was exhausting.

"Not as much anymore."

"Did your professors knock that out of you when you were in school?" She'd never talked to him about his career, but she knew all about the ranch. It had an excellent reputation for its live-in therapeutic programs, and Billie had heard that Dare was an exceptional therapist. He'd always been curious about what made people tick. She was curious about the work he did, but she wasn't ready to go there.

"Yeah, I guess you can say that. Or you could say I've grown up, too." He looked at her for a long moment, those dark eyes holding her captive. "But I hate the way you look at me like you wish it'd been me that died that night. I get it, and I'd switch places with Eddie in a heartbeat just so *you* wouldn't have lost him."

Her throat thickened. "Is that what you think? That I wish you were dead?"

"Sure feels that way." He sat up, taking a swig of his juice.

Emotions stacked up inside her. "Well, I *don't*, and I never have." She pushed to her feet and paced. "I wish *nobody* had died. It didn't have to happen." She couldn't keep her voice from rising. "Eddie *never* did flips. He was too uncoordinated, and he knew it. He never should've gotten on that bike."

Dare stood up. "We both tried to stop him, remember?"

"Of course I remember! How could I forget? The whole thing plays out in my mind like a horror movie every night, and I don't hate you for what you said, either. So stop thinking I do." She stomped back to him, hands fisted, remembering what he'd said when he'd seen the ring. *You're not going to marry him, are you? I love Eddie, but he's not your forever guy, Billie. He's not the man who sets your soul on fire.* "You didn't say anything that I didn't already know. I'd already broken up with him when you saw the ring and told me not to marry him. He wouldn't take the ring back, but we were already done. *That's* why he and I were fighting before he grabbed the bike instead of filming us. That's why he *died.*" Tears spilled from her eyes. Dare looked shocked by her confession, but she was too upset to slow down. "Because of *me.* Because I couldn't love him the way he loved me. It's my fault he's dead, Dare. *My* fault!"

"*No*, Billie, you are *not* taking on that responsibility." He pulled her into his arms.

"Let me *go*." She beat her fists on his chest, crying out of anger, frustration, and so much hurt, it was inescapable.

"*Never.*" He held her tighter, despite her struggles. "It wasn't your fault. It wasn't *his* fault. It was a stupid stunt gone wrong."

"But he never would have done it if I'd loved him the way he loved me." Her confession broke open the floodgates, and she clung to him, powerless to stop the tears and grief she'd been holding back for years. She braced herself for him to get angry that she blamed herself, because that's who Dare Whiskey had always been. Her great protector. The man who refused to let her suffer and had always built her up so she felt indestructible. All that fortifying had taught her to be strong, and until this very moment, she'd believed she was a master at hiding her suffering.

But Dare didn't get mad.

He didn't say a word.

He just held her as she cried, running his hand down her back, the muscle in his jaw clenching against her temple. He was more muscular than he'd been years ago, when he'd haul her into his arms after they'd nailed a great stunt or she'd won a motocross race, but he still felt familiar and safe. *Despite years of battering you with my attitude, like an iceberg ramming into an unchillable mountain.* That brought a stab of guilt, and she drew back, but he tightened his hold on her again, speaking low.

"I'm not done with you yet, Mancini."

She closed her eyes against the rush of emotions that came with the words he'd said to her all those years ago after their tipsy tryst, to which she'd responded, *Yeah, you are, 'cause I'm done with you.* She'd thought she was so tough then, not giving in to being another notch on his belt. Little had she known she was biting off her nose to spite her face.

"Yeah, you are," she choked out, and pushed from his arms, wiping her eyes, wondering if she could bolt and whether he'd chase her this time.

"Sit down, Mancini." He didn't wait for a response, grabbing her wrist as he sat, pulling her down beside him.

Here comes the anger. She sat up straighter, readying for an onslaught of fortification.

"Breathe," he said soothingly, and handed her the water bottle he'd given her earlier. "Take a drink."

His jaw was tight, dark eyes serious but not angry. Who was this calm impostor?

"Or don't." He put the water bottle on the grass between them and opened his orange juice. He finished what was left in the bottle and pulled one knee up, lazily resting his arm on it and gazing out at the field, as if he had all day to sit there with her. "You really broke up with him? You went out for so long, when you accepted his proposal, I thought I was wrong, and he was the love of your life."

"Not everyone who dates for a long time is meant to be married." It was hard to process this serious side of Dare. It was so new to her and it was hard to talk about something she'd kept off-limits for so long, but he deserved to know the truth. At least this piece of it. "I loved Eddie, but no matter how hard I tried, you were right; he didn't set my soul on fire. That's why I couldn't marry him."

HOLY SHIT. DARE'S mind sped back in time, to when she or Eddie had made comments about their relationship. It hadn't happened often, but there were a few times when one would mention maybe they should take a break or they'd hit a rough patch. Now Dare saw those times as missed opportunities to fight for her. But she hadn't wanted *him*, and he wasn't a glutton for punishment. At least not that type of punishment.

She met his gaze. "Now do you understand why it's my fault?"

"No, but I can see why you would lean that way. You pissed him off, and then he did a stunt he shouldn't have."

"Because he was mad."

"Because he was a *dude*, and our egos are bigger than our dicks. We have a visceral need to save face. You hurt his heart and his pride, and he was out to show you that you didn't break him. He was *still* a man who could do cool shit, even if he shouldn't have tried."

"I want to roll my eyes at that, but the whole ego-dick thing rings true."

"Except for mine." He waggled his brows, and she shook her head with a small smile. He'd take it. "You know, you were always pissing one of us off, and we both tried plenty of stupid stunts while we were angry, and we didn't die any of those times. Eddie's death was tragic, but it wasn't your fault."

"When I hear you say that, I want to believe you, but then late at night, it all comes rushing back, and…"

"Then maybe I need to be around you late at night to remind you that it's not your fault." That earned a half-hearted eye roll. "I get it, Billie, and what you remember might never change. But what it means might change someday, and that's what I hope for. Do you remember my sophomore year of college, when I was partying way too hard and you were trying to get me to stop being an idiot?"

"Yeah. You told me to back off, and I told you if something happened to you, it would be my fault for not stopping you. I was so angry at you. I swear you are the *most* stubborn person I've ever met."

"It's like looking in a mirror, isn't it?"

Her eyes narrowed.

"Remember what Eddie told you when you said that to me?"

She looked down and plucked a piece of grass. "He said I can't be responsible for your choices, no matter how much I hate them."

"That's right, darlin', and Eddie sure as hell wouldn't want you to carry the burden of guilt because he was pissed off for a few minutes. You know that, don't you?"

She shrugged.

"Somewhere way down deep, beneath the hurt and guilt, I think you know it. And lucky for you, *I* know it, and I'll keep reminding you until you dig out from under the muck and mire enough to see it."

"You're not some kind of magician who can change people's views."

"Unfortunately, I know that all too well. I also know how long you've carried this burden and how stubborn you are, and I know it's not going to go away with one conversation."

"Or fifty."

Challenge accepted, sweet thing. "I guess we'll see. Is that why you pushed me out of your life? Because you thought I'd blame you for Eddie's death if I knew you'd broken up with him?"

She fidgeted uncomfortably, and he had a feeling she was

done talking about it.

"Every time I see you, I remember that day and that it was my fault he died." She stood abruptly. "What do I owe you for this session, because I've got to go?"

As badly as he wanted to go with her, he remained sitting, knowing the harder he pushed, the faster her walls would go back up. "Dinner tonight."

She scoffed. "Just because we talked doesn't mean we're besties again."

"We'll see about that." He winked.

She shook her head and headed back to the running path.

Billie didn't just *walk* anywhere. She strutted determinedly, her gorgeous ass swaying in those skimpy running shorts. When she picked up her pace to an easy jog, he hollered, "You're moving like that gorilla on your back has lost some weight."

She didn't miss a step as she flipped him the bird without turning around and ran faster.

He watched her growing smaller in the distance, and that noose he'd been wearing for years, the one he'd've bet would be making it hard for him to breathe until the day he met Eddie on the other side, loosened the tiniest bit.

Chapter Three

TUESDAY EVENING, AFTER a busy day spent working on the ranch and seeing clients, Dare showered and dressed, then put on his cut. He had church tonight. That's what the Dark Knights called their meetings, and after dinner, he'd head over to the clubhouse with his father, brothers, and the other Dark Knights who lived on the ranch. He grabbed his cowboy hat on the way out of his cabin and was greeted by the familiar scents of the ranch, horses, hay, hard work, and family. The sun peeked over the mountains in the distance, casting shadows on the ranch where his roots ran deep. He and his family all lived and worked on the property, with the exception of Birdie, who lived by her chocolate shop in Allure, a neighboring town.

He climbed onto an ATV and headed up to the main house for dinner, passing the pastures and barns he'd worked in all his life. The ranch had been in his mother's family for generations as a horse rescue. His father was from Peaceful Harbor, Maryland, where his grandfather had founded the Dark Knights. He'd ended up in Hope Valley when he and his brother Biggs had taken a cross-country motorcycle trip and had happened upon the Roadhouse. His mother had been there with her girlfriends, and his father had taken one look at her and told Biggs he was going to marry her one day.

Biggs headed back to Peaceful Harbor alone that summer, and Dare's father began working on the ranch. A few years later, his parents married, and his father continued on at the ranch while his mother pursued a career as a psychologist. Dare's father had begun hiring ex-cons and recovering addicts, hoping to give them a leg up, but he'd been sorely disappointed when many had ended up back in jail or on drugs. He'd eventually realized that while they'd served their time or overcome their demons, they hadn't had the ongoing support they needed in order to rebuild their lives while remaining clean, sober, or out of trouble. It hadn't taken long for his parents to come up with the idea to extend the ranch's mission to include a therapeutic environment where people could learn new and better ways to cope with difficult situations while living and working on the ranch and attending group and individual therapy sessions. Giving them the support they needed, as well as a purpose. At the time, Tiny had been itching to start another chapter of the Dark Knights, and he'd finally found its mission, working hand in hand with the ranch in giving people second chances and helping them stay away from addiction and trouble. Over the years, many of the people who had gone through their programs had become Dark Knights, and several still worked on the ranch.

Decades later, his father oversaw the ranch, which spanned a few hundred acres, with several houses, barns, outbuildings, indoor and outdoor riding arenas, eleven cabins for live-in clients, a host of offices with living quarters for staff and newcomers, and a full veterinary clinic. They'd helped hundreds of ex-cons and recovering addicts find a new lease on life, and they now employed four therapists, including Dare and his mother, one equine rehabilitation therapist—Sasha—who often worked with interns, several dozen ranch hands managed by Cowboy, a residential manager/cook, two on-call physicians, a director of therapeutic services, and a handful of other personnel.

He passed the paintball field, which Sasha and Cowboy had expanded a few months ago, and cruised up to the main house, where offices for traditional therapeutic services were located, as well as residences for several staff members and any clients who were younger than twenty-one. Having always been intrigued by human behavior, growing up around tough bikers whose mission was to help everyone in their path and witnessing firsthand how the ranch's programs had helped people with difficult or checkered pasts, Dare had known early on that he wanted to be a therapist on the ranch. But Dare's methods weren't traditional. He found it easier to connect with clients when their hands were busy and they were thinking about work rather than baring their souls. Instead of holding therapy sessions in an office, he held them outdoors while they worked on the ranch together.

As he parked the ATV, the front doors of the main house opened, and four-year-old Gus Moore ran out, followed by his father, Ezra. Ezra's father was a Dark Knight, and Ezra had gone through the program as a troubled teenager. He'd later interned with Dare's mother during school breaks and summers while he earned his degrees. He'd become a Dark Knight and was one of the ranch's well-respected therapists.

Gus spotted Dare climbing off the ATV and ran toward him in his tiny cowboy boots and shorts, dark curls bouncing around his adorable face. "Dare! Take me for a *wide*?"

Dare scooped him up. "Hey there, little man. I think we'd better ask your dad about that." He lifted his chin to Gus's tall, dark-haired single father. "You're not hanging around for dinner?" The people who came through their programs were often estranged from their families, and the Whiskeys did everything they could to help alleviate the feeling of being alone, including eating with staff and clients, hanging out at bonfires, going on trail rides, and playing paintball. His parents were true believers in the work hard, play hard mentality, and their well-rounded approach helped. They'd become the only family some of their clients had.

"Not tonight. I promised to drop Gus off with his mom a little early." Ezra shared custody of Gus with his ex-wife.

"Do you have time for us to take a quick spin?"

"*Please*, Dad?" Gus begged.

"Sure, buddy. A quick one, but listen to Dare."

"I will!" Gus beamed at Dare as he carried him to the ATV. "Can I wear your hat?"

"You remember the rule?"

Gus nodded. "Hold on to the ATV even if the hat comes off."

"You've got it, buddy." He put Gus on the ATV and plunked his hat on his head as he climbed on behind him.

"Can we see *Sasha*?" Gus had a major crush on Dare's younger sister.

Dare and Ezra shared an amused glance, and then Dare headed across the field toward the rehab barns. Sasha was walking out of the barn when they drove up. Her dirty-blond hair was pulled back in a ponytail, and she wore jeans, a T-shirt, and her favorite maroon barn boots. Everyone in their family had their quirks. Doc was a deep thinker who kept his rascally side so tightly locked down, Dare wondered if he'd ever set it free again. Cowboy was fiercely responsible and overprotective of everyone, but he had a touch of scoundrel in him, and Dare was the rebel. Sasha was two years younger than Dare and as calm and centered as he was adrenaline-driven, but she had a sassy streak a mile wide and the quiet strength to back it up, while Birdie was their chameleon. She had a little bit of everyone in her, and she was whatever she wanted to be on any given day.

Gus waved wildly. "Hi, sugar!"

Dare laughed as he cut the engine.

"Hi, *Gusto*. I think you've been hanging out with Dare too much." She peered under the big-brimmed hat. "How's the cutest guy on the ranch?"

"Doing well, thanks." Dare smirked.

Sasha gave him a deadpan look. "I heard you *dropped in* on Billie's run the other day. You don't have a shiner, so I guess she didn't deck you."

"Where'd you hear that?" Dare hadn't seen Billie since Sunday, and it had taken every bit of his willpower not to stop by the bar last night or reach out by text. But he was biding his time, letting her get past her irritation from their impromptu chat.

"I was texting with Finn, and he mentioned it."

"Who's Finn?" Gus asked.

Dare narrowed his eyes. "Someone Sasha should be careful texting with."

"Why?" Gus asked.

"He isn't exactly known for being a gentleman with the ladies," Dare answered.

"And you are?" Sasha shook her head. "Dare's just being

silly, Gus. Finn's a really nice guy. Did you come to pick me up for dinner?"

"*Uh-huh!*" Gus motioned to the ATV. "Climb on, *darlin*!"

"You *are* the cutest boy around." As she climbed on behind Dare, she said, "What happened with Billie?"

"We're not done talking about Finn."

They drove back to the main house, and Ezra was sitting on the curb waiting for them.

"*Well*, look who's here," Sasha said a little *too* appreciatively.

Dare turned, glowering at her, and she rolled her eyes. Women were always checking out Ezra, but his ex was a bit of a nightmare, and he was all about his son and work. Dare couldn't remember the last time Ezra had even mentioned going out with a woman.

"Watch yourself," Dare warned. They'd instituted a strict policy against fraternizing at work years ago, after Doc had fallen for the daughter of a powerful politician while she was working at the ranch and had gotten in a heap of trouble, which Dare swore had changed his brother forever.

Sasha rolled her eyes and turned a smile on Ezra. "Hey there, Ez."

"How's it going, Sasha?" Ezra asked as Dare climbed off the ATV and lifted Gus off the seat.

"Our latest rescue is eating well and gaining strength, so it's a good day." She started to climb off the ATV.

"Wait!" Gus ran over and offered his hand.

Sasha glanced at Ezra. "Did you teach him that?"

"Dare taught me!" Gus exclaimed as she climbed off, and Dare's hat tumbled to the ground. "He said to help girls and animals before I help myself."

"That's right, little man." Dare ruffled his hair, and picked up the hat.

"Maybe he could've left out the part about calling them *sugar*," Sasha said.

Ezra chuckled. "Let's go, buddy, before Dare gets his butt handed to him." Ezra took Gus's hand. "See you tomorrow, Sash. Enjoy dinner. Dare, I'll see you at church."

"What the hell was that?" Dare asked as he and Sasha headed for the doors.

"I have no idea what you're talking about," Sasha said with amusement.

"You're going to get yourself into trouble. What's the deal with Finn? Are you two hooking up?"

"Is Billie finally speaking with you again?"

"*Sasha*," he warned.

"*No*, okay? Finn's a friend. What about you and Billie?"

"Your guess is as good as mine." But he hoped to tip the scales in his favor.

They went inside the main house, which boasted high ceilings with exposed wooden rafters, a large two-story gathering space with couches, chairs, bookshelves, craft tables, and a massive stone fireplace. To their left were meeting rooms and offices, and to their right, the kitchen and dining area, a movie room, and more offices. The staff residences and rooms for younger clients were upstairs.

Savory smells and the din of conversation came from the dining room as Dare's family, the ranch staff, and their clients worked together, setting the large farmhouse-style tables and bringing the food out from the kitchen.

"Smells like Dwight made your favorite barbecued chicken," Dare said. Dwight Cornwall, their residential manager and cook, lived in the main house and oversaw their younger clients.

He'd worked there since Dare was thirteen, and as a retired navy commander, he ran a tight ship.

The dining room was bustling with activity, and several men and women who worked on the ranch and a few of their clients turned to greet Dare and Sasha. Dare put a finger to his lips and snuck up behind his mother as she set napkins on the table and hugged her.

She let out a little gasp and spun around, a warm smile brightening her eyes. "*Dare*. You startled me, sweetheart." She hugged him, looking as well put together as always, from her makeup and necklaces to her neatly combed blond shag and peach blouse. She preferred jeans and boots to anything else, and she was kindhearted, strong, and always had the best interest of their clients and family in mind.

"Sorry, Mom. I didn't mean to startle you."

"Get your hands off my woman," his father growled from across the room as he set a platter of chicken on one of the tables.

He was a bear of a man with a pendulous belly, a bushy gray beard, and longish gray hair that was currently trapped beneath a red bandanna tied around his forehead. His leatherlike skin was covered in faded ink, and not a day passed when he wasn't wearing boots and jeans. He'd been raised by a hard-ass, misogynistic biker, and he was gruff. He didn't smile often and didn't give a shit how many people crossed the road when they saw him coming. But if those people who judged him on physical appearance alone ever took the time to get to know him, they'd realize that while he could crush a man's skull with his bare hands, he'd built a life around helping others and treated women like queens.

Dare met his father's steady gaze. "I'll do what I want, old man."

Several of the guys eyed them. Dare and his father had gone head-to-head more times than he cared to admit, and as an arrogant, drunk teenager during spring break of his freshman year of college, Dare had even gone after his father physically. He'd never forget the look in his father's eyes when he'd grabbed Dare by the front of his shirt and had lifted him off his feet with one hand and said, *We can throw down as often as you'd like, boy, but whatever you're running from will still be there, and so will I. This ain't the way to handle your shit, so pull yourself together before you get yourself killed.* Dare had been too headstrong to hear the meaning behind those words at that time, but they'd since become words he lived by. His father was the best and strongest man he knew.

"Not if you want to live to talk about it," Cowboy said as he came in from the kitchen with a tray of food.

"And we all know how much you like to talk." Hyde Ledger, a heavily inked ex-con, smirked.

Dare had been Hyde's therapist when he'd gone through the program a few years ago. Hyde had gone from being a belligerent bastard to a downright cool guy. He'd prospected the club and had become a patch-wearing member. He'd stayed on to work at the ranch, as the Whiskeys had become family to him. So much so, that Hyde ribbed Dare about always wanting to talk things out, just like his siblings did.

"Talking is a good thing," his mother said. "Besides, I think Dare could give Tiny a run for his money if he wanted to."

"Tiny would squash him like a bug," Darcy, another of Dare's clients, said. She was a recovering addict who had come to the ranch four months earlier after completing ninety days at a rehab program and having trouble acclimating to her drug-free lifestyle. Her ability to joke about Dare was a sign of how great she was doing.

His father laughed. "You got that right."

"You wish, old man," Dare teased.

As the guys started joking around with his father about each of them taking him on, his mother touched his cheek and said, "Maya told me that you got your tickets to Spain." Maya Martinez ran the offices of the ranch, but she didn't live on site. "I hate to think of anything happening to my beautiful boy. Are you sure you want to go there?"

He'd been planning this trip to run with the bulls for more than a year. "I'm going, Mom. But I'll be fine."

Sasha sidled up to him and lowered her voice. "Maybe you *shouldn't* try to get on Billie's good side in case you get trampled. She's already been through enough heartache."

"Jesus, Sasha. I'll be *fine*," Dare snapped as Doc came through the front door with his black Lab, Mighty, one of his many dogs. Mighty scampered over to Sasha, who knelt to love him up.

"Are you and Billie talking again?" his mother asked with surprise as Birdie burst through the front doors and sprinted into the dining room wearing bright yellow shorts, a billowy purple top, and platform sneakers. She skidded to a stop between Dare and their mother.

"I can only stay for fifteen minutes, but I'm starved." Birdie looked Dare up and down. "You look good, and you *smell* good. Got a date? Wait, it's Tuesday. *Church.*" She petted Mighty on her way to the table, slid into a chair between Hyde and Darcy, and began piling food onto her plate. "Fill me in on your lives, but do it quick."

Dare looked at his mother, and she shook her head, smiling.

"So?" his mother urged. "Are you and Billie talking again?"

"*I* never stopped talking. She finally gave me a few minutes of her time the other day." *And it was fucking awesome.* He hoped she'd continue opening up to him. He worried about her. He'd felt Eddie's loss, and the loss of his friendship with Billie, like the world had crumbled beneath his feet. But while he'd talked about his feelings for years, he knew Billie had chosen to keep hers to herself, and he knew all too well how that kind of heartache could destroy a person.

"A few *minutes?*" Doc scoffed as he strutted over to them. He was tall and fit, with short brown hair somewhere between the color of Dare's and Cowboy's. "If that's all you got going on, it's no wonder women never call you back."

"Hey Dare, you could always slip her my number," Taz, a crazy motherfucker and the fastest ranch hand Dare had ever met, chimed in.

Dare gave him a *touch her and die* stare as the others joined in with more banter, and before he knew it, even their mother and father were cracking jokes.

Dinner as usual…

AFTER A DELICIOUS meal with fun conversation, Dare climbed on his motorcycle and followed his father, brothers, and the other Dark Knights who worked at the ranch off the property toward the clubhouse. But when the others turned right off the main road, he kept going, heading straight to the Roadhouse.

He blew through the front doors, and Billie looked over

from behind the bar, a reluctant smile tipping the edges of her lips. "Now, *that's* more like it!" He threw his hands up and did a backflip, causing gasps and applause from the customers.

"Nice, Whiskey!" someone hollered.

Dare took a bow, eyes locked on Billie, who was scowling as he strode over to her.

"What was *that*?" she snapped.

"A celebration. You didn't cast daggers at me when I walked in."

She tried to stifle a smile, eyes narrowing. "What're you doing here, Dare?"

He crossed his arms on the bar, leaning over it. "Just letting you know that you and I have plans tomorrow afternoon." He knew she had Wednesday off.

"No." She began wiping down the bar.

He put his hand over hers, stilling it and bringing her eyes back to him.

She arched a brow. "You aiming to lose that hand, Whiskey?"

"Be ready at noon, and dress comfortably."

"I can't. I have to…" Her eyes skirted around him. "Bathe my cat."

A slow grin stretched across his face. "I can think of a far better way to get your pussy wet."

She yanked her hand free, glowering at him. "I'm not going anywhere with you. I told you, just because we talked doesn't make us besties."

"If that's what you've got to tell yourself to get through the night, go right ahead, Mancini. I'll see you tomorrow at noon."

As he strode toward the door, she hollered, "Dream on, Whiskey!"

He looked over his shoulder to see her eyes were blazing with fury. "I'll be dreaming, all right, about your hands on that pussy."

Dare turned to leave, nearly barreling into her father. His arms were crossed over his leather cut, his dark eyes trained on Dare. Manny Mancini wasn't a large man, but his Italian lineage gave him an authoritative presence, with strong features, tan skin, short salt-and-pepper hair, and pitch-black brows, which gave his dark eyes a menacing stare. "What the hell did you just say to my daughter?"

Dare had nothing but respect for his fellow Dark Knight, who had been like a second father to him all his life, but he wasn't about to sugarcoat anything. "Manny, I asked her to do something with me tomorrow, and she said she can't because she has to *bathe* her *cat*."

Manny's gaze darted to Billie, then back to Dare. "She doesn't *have* a cat."

"No shit. She's been allergic since we were kids." Dare clapped a hand on Manny's shoulder. "You raised a tough woman, and I'm just giving the shit she doles out right back to her. No harm, no foul. Come on, we've got church."

THE DARK KNIGHTS' clubhouse was located in an old firehouse on the edge of town. They'd renovated one bay to expand the meeting area, and Rebel rented the other bay for his classic car restoration business. When Dare's father had founded the club thirty-plus years ago, he'd purchased the firehouse with the hopes of his younger brother, Axel, a mechanic, putting down roots there in Hope Valley and using the bay Rebel now rented. But Axel had a wandering soul and a homegrown heart. He'd ended up settling down in their hometown near Biggs. He and Biggs had run the Peaceful Harbor chapter of the club together, and Axel had owned an auto shop there before they'd lost him to cancer a little more than a decade ago. Biggs continued to run the Peaceful Harbor chapter of the Dark Knights, and Dare's cousins now ran the auto shop.

Dare sat at a table with Cowboy, Doc, Rebel, and Hyde, surrounded by a roomful of tough men, many of whom Dare had known for decades. Some tatted and bearded, others clean-shaven without a speck of ink, and all wearing black leather cuts proudly boasting Dark Knights' patches. He looked at the sun-weathered faces of his fellow bikers, many of whom worked at the ranch—Ezra, Dwight, Hyde, Taz, and a handful of other ranch hands—and those men whose family members worked there, like Ezra's father, Pep, and Otto, whose wife, Colleen, was a therapist at the ranch, and felt the familiar warmth of brotherhood. Many of those men had been there for him when he'd had those rough couple of years in college and when they'd lost Eddie. Eddie's father wasn't a Dark Knight, but the whole club had shown up for his funeral, because Eddie had been like a son to Tiny and Manny, which made the Bakers family to the entire club. Dare would give his life for any of the men in that room, and he knew they'd do the same for him.

Everyone's attention was riveted to his father and Manny sitting at the head table going over club business. His father was a strong leader, and the men in that room, and in the community, held him in high regard for his groundbreaking endeavors to help others. Not only did their chapter keep the residents and businesses of Hope Valley safe by patrolling certain neighborhoods and keeping their ears to the ground about seedy operations that were connected to deleterious activities, but they also made it their mission to raise awareness about mental health issues and drug and suicide prevention.

Normally, Dare would be solely focused on every word said during church, but tonight his mind was down the road with the stubborn dark-haired beauty who tried to ditch him by claiming to have a freaking cat. Did she really think he'd let it go that easily? As if he hadn't noticed the kink in her armor when he'd walked in the door? He'd wanted to slam his hands into that fissure and pry that armor off.

"The next order of business is Festival on the Green, which is only two months away," his father announced, drawing Dare's attention. "As always, Redemption Ranch will have a table set up to raise awareness about our services and collect donations, and the Dark Knights will have a table to educate people about who we are and what we do. Wynnie, Alice, and our daughters are coordinating volunteer efforts." Alice was Billie's mother. "Many of you have already signed up to take a turn at the table and to help with security at the event…"

Festival on the Green was a weeklong event in Allure, with live music in the park and businesses and crafters setting up booths. Local businesses held sidewalk sales, and at the end of the week, there was a big fireworks display. Dare had been going since he was a kid, and he looked forward to it as much for the fun as he did for spreading the news about the ranch and the club. But Billie hadn't helped coordinate or attended the events in years. She used to love hanging out at the festival with him and Eddie, helping at the tables, checking out the local shops, and watching the fireworks from *their* spot on a hill in the park. He missed those times, and with the festival on the horizon, he realized this just might be the perfect time to start reminding her of how much fun they used to have together.

"The last business on our docket is our fall Ride Clean campaign. Manny, do you want to take this one?" his father asked.

Ride Clean was the name of their anti-drug efforts. Every September they kicked off the campaign with a club ride and rally and a day of fun and fundraising at the ranch, where kids could go on hayrides, pony rides, and trail rides and learn to groom horses and care for them in other ways. They played yard games and paintball, and Dare and his siblings gave talks about their jobs and answered questions. The goal was to show kids that there were ways to have good, clean fun and to introduce them to the world of horses and to the Dark Knights as members of the community they could turn to in times of trouble. The Dark Knights' families provided food and baked goods to be sold at the event, with proceeds going to the campaign efforts.

"Sure. Our wives and daughters will be coordinating volunteers, activities, and refreshments for the event. And yes, Birdie is donating chocolates again." There was a round of cheers. "We're still looking for volunteers to speak at schools and youth clubs. Sign-up sheets are open online and here at the table."

Dare had already signed up. He liked to party as much as the next guy. Okay, maybe more. But he wasn't a kid anymore, and he got his thrills in other ways. He knew and respected his limits, and he was passionate about helping people, especially teens, learn healthier ways to deal with their issues and emotions.

As their father wrapped up the meeting, Cowboy nudged him, speaking quietly. "Want to hit the Roadhouse after this?"

"You know it." He eyed Doc, Rebel, and Hyde. "You guys

up for a drink?"

Rebel cocked a grin. "When am I ever *not* up for a drink?"

"I'm in as long as your sisters don't try to drag me onto the dance floor," Hyde said. He didn't dance, but Birdie and Sasha didn't care, and they always tugged him to his feet.

They all looked at Doc. He was four years older than Dare, two years older than Cowboy, and a quiet charmer. He had an affable personality, but he'd always been more private than his brothers, and he usually kept his thoughts to himself, which was why when he did give an opinion, it was worth mulling over. That hint of mystery annoyed Dare at times, but it reeled in the ladies. "Can't tonight. I'm seeing Mandy."

"Wasn't that the same chick you were seeing on Valentine's Day? This must be some sort of record." Rebel smirked.

Dare and Cowboy exchanged a curious glance. Doc was particular about the women he went out with, but he never saw them for more than two or three months, leaving a trail of broken hearts in his wake. Dare knew better than to give anyone hopes of a real relationship with him. How could he, when he compared them all to Billie?

Doc turned a serious stare on Cowboy and Dare. "*Don't* say a word."

"Who *us*?" Dare said with feigned innocence. "We'd never say she must be into pity fucks to have hung around this long."

"Or that we'd heard there was a bet going around Hope Valley. Five hundred bucks to any woman who could last four months with you without losing their minds," Cowboy added.

"We'd never say that shit." Dare chuckled.

Doc glared at them. "Assholes."

Dare and Cowboy laughed.

The meeting was over, and the room came to life with loud

conversations and guys milling about, getting drinks and playing pool. Dare and his brothers' phones chimed with texts. Dare looked at his phone and saw the SOS group text from their mother. That was how she contacted them during church if there was an emergency at the ranch. If the meeting was still going on, one of them would step out to call her back. If not, their father made the call. They looked at their father, who was standing with Manny by the head table. He already had the phone to his ear, brows knitted.

"Rebel, looks like you're on your own for that drink." Dare pushed to his feet. "Tell Billie I know she's thinking of me."

Rebel grinned. "You mean when she's not thinking of me? That woman is one *fine* piece of—"

Dare shut him up with a dark stare, and Rebel held his hands up in surrender, chuckling. Dare and his brothers headed over to their father as he finished the call and pocketed his phone.

"What's going on?" Dare asked.

"A seventeen-year-old took the neighbor's BMW, and their fifteen-year-old daughter, out for a joyride," their father said. "The kid's name is Kenny Graber."

"Shit. Did they get hurt or hurt anyone else?" Cowboy asked.

Their father shook his head. "No, they got lucky."

"Anything happen between them?" Doc asked.

"The girl swears nothing happened and that it was her idea to take her parents' car."

"We'll find out about that." Dare knew all too well about covering for others. He, Billie, and Eddie used to do it all the time.

Their father nodded. "I know you will. You're taking the

lead on this one, Dare. The boy's father convinced them not to press charges and to let him come to the ranch instead."

They had several safety measures in place for teens. They lived, ate meals, and did schoolwork in the main house under Dwight's watchful eyes, and when they worked on the ranch, it was under the guidance of Dare, Cowboy, or one of their senior barn managers. Dare was currently working with two other teens.

"What else do you know about Kenny?" Cowboy asked.

"This is his second offense. Legally he has a license, but his parents took it away last month when he took their car out at three in the morning and got pulled over. He's a smart kid and was doing fine in school before they moved here about three months ago for the old man's job. About a month after they moved, his grades went south, and he started skipping school. They aren't sure if he's doing drugs or drinking, but they suspect he might be," their father explained. "Your mother said they're at their wits' end."

Dare knew a little something about driving his parents mad with worry. "I'll swing back to the ranch and get the company truck." If they were picking a kid up at a detention center or an adult from jail or prison, the Dark Knights would go with them, but when they were picking up someone from a home, they tried not to overwhelm the family. "Where should I meet you?"

"At the corner of Millhouse and Western. We'll follow you in." His father gave them the Grabers' address and told them the parents' names were Carol and Roger. "I'm bringing Rebel in case the kid runs."

Perfect.

AFTER PICKING UP the truck with the Redemption Ranch logo on the side and the child lock on the door, Dare headed out to meet the others. During the years he'd interned while he was in college, he'd gone with his parents to pick up a few teenagers. At the time, he'd felt like an impostor, which had been partially true. He'd cleaned up his act, but he hadn't been ready to be a role model by any means. The more times he'd accompanied them, the more things he'd noticed, like how the kids would look at him in one of three ways. With detest, pleading for him to get them out of that situation, or with carefully veiled hope, because they'd gotten themselves into a situation they couldn't find a way out of, but they wanted to. He'd been there once himself, and those looks had twisted him up inside, made him question his every decision and his future. But they also made him realize he was on the right path. They'd inspired him to work harder to be a person who *could* turn the hatred and those pleas around and earn the respect and knowledge to bring that hope to fruition.

His parents had later told him that they'd known he'd either fold under the pressure and realize he didn't want to be the person bringing those kids in, or he'd step up to the plate and become the role model and therapist those kids deserved.

He pulled up next to his father's motorcycle and watched the man who'd doled out tough love and mucked stalls with his sons while teaching them what it meant to be part of Redemption Ranch and, more importantly, to be well-respected members of the community climb off his bike and come to his window. Dare could only hope he was half the man his father was.

His father put a hand on his shoulder and said, "You've got this, son. We'll be right behind you."

The confidence in his father's voice brought a rush of pride. He waited for his father to climb onto his bike before heading to the Grabers'. They parked out front, and Rebel headed around to the back of the house in case the kid tried to bolt. Teenagers could be fast, but Rebel ran like the wind.

As they made their way up the front walk, a woman peered out the front window. Dare recognized the fear in her eyes. He'd seen it many times from parents hoping for a miracle with their troubled kids, husbands, wives, sisters, significant others, and friends who had called the ranch as a last-ditch effort to help the people they loved.

Dare knocked on the door, with his father and brothers behind him. The door opened, and the worried faces of a woman who looked to be in her late forties, with red-rimmed, teary eyes and blond hair that brushed the shoulders of her blouse, and a balding man wearing a dress shirt and glasses who looked to be closer to fifty peered out. "Mr. and Mrs. Graber?"

"Yes," she said softly.

Dare's heart went out to her. "I'm Dare Whiskey from Redemption Ranch. I believed you called for some help with Kenny."

Her gaze swept down the length of him, those worry lines deepening.

Dare was used to the surprise rising in her eyes as she looked over his shoulder at his father and brothers in their leather cuts, jeans, and boots, his father's red bandanna firmly in place, tattoos on display. Everyone knew the ranch was owned and run by the founder of the Dark Knights, but knowing it and seeing a bunch of six-feet-plus tatted bikers up close and personal were two very different things.

To ease her mind, he said, "Part of what we do at the ranch is to strip away the idea that *good people* have to look a certain way."

What he didn't say was that a little intimidation went a long way to earn respect from wayward kids, and those that weren't intimidated tended to see a tatted biker as someone who could get down with their behavior. Dare always set them straight, but that initial connection didn't hurt. And troubled adults didn't give a damn what they looked like. They were either their enemy or their savior. And oftentimes they were both.

"I see. Please, come in."

She stepped aside, and Dare offered his hand to Roger. "Dare Whiskey, sir." As he shook his hand, he motioned to the others. "This is my father, Tiny, and my brothers, Doc and Cowboy."

As they introduced themselves, Dare spotted the suitcase by the door, which their mother would have requested they pack for Kenny, and he saw the lanky teen sitting in the living room to their right, his leg bouncing nervously, forearms resting on his legs, hands clasped, head bowed. He was wearing jeans, expensive sneakers, and a black hoodie.

"Mind if I speak with your son directly?" Dare asked, bringing Kenny's eyes up to his. Dare lifted his chin, holding Kenny's stare. The boy's gaze hit the floor again, his leg bouncing faster.

"Yes, of course. We didn't want him going to jail, and we didn't know what else to do," Roger explained. "My friend is an attorney, and she suggested we try the ranch."

Carol said, "We tried to explain why we're doing this—"

"I'm not going to any damn *ranch*," Kenny interrupted,

rising to his feet.

Dare walked into the living room. "Hi, Kenny, I'm Dare. You probably should have thought about that before you stole a car, endangering yourself, the friend you took with you, and everyone else on the road."

"I didn't *steal* it," he said, full of piss and vinegar. "We *borrowed* it, and I didn't hurt anyone. I'm a good driver."

"You didn't have the owners' permission, which makes it theft. You got lucky you didn't hurt anyone. If you had, you'd be in jail right now."

"This is bullshit," Kenny barked.

Dare stepped closer. "Watch your language—there's a lady present. This is what's going to happen tonight. We're going to take you back to Redemption Ranch, where you'll be staying for the next few weeks."

"Few *weeks*?" He glared at his parents. "Are you kidding? What about school?"

Dare doubted he gave a shit about school, especially since there was only one week left in the semester. But kids who were involuntarily brought to the ranch often grasped at straws to remain in control of their lives. "You'll be finishing school at the ranch this year."

As Dare said it, his father stepped between him and the boy's parents, and Doc and Cowboy led them into the other room. Their mother would have already explained to them that this was how things would go down. Making parents unavailable allowed their child to realize they had no friends left in the room and established control being handed over to the ranch.

"Mom! *Dad!*" Kenny hollered.

"They tried to help you, Kenny, and now they've asked us to help. They love you too much to change their minds."

"I don't want your help," he snapped.

"I get that," Dare said. "When I was your age, I didn't want anyone's help, either, but as I was saying, tonight we'll go to the ranch, where you can get a good night's sleep, and in the morning you and I can talk about what happened and try to figure things out."

"I'm calling the police! You can't do this. It's *kidnapping.*" Kenny dug his phone out of his pocket.

"You go right ahead and make that call. Joyriding is a felony in this state, and once the police are involved, the law is the law, and they're required to seek punishment." Dare crossed his arms, nodding his approval. "Go ahead. We'll wait."

Kenny's gaze darted to Tiny. "He's lying, right?"

"Whiskeys don't lie, son," Tiny said. "You can make that call, or you can come with us and we'll help you through this."

"I don't *need* help. I won't do it again." Kenny's voice cracked with desperation.

"We're going to make sure of that. Now, we can sit here and debate all night, or you can come with us and deal with this head-on. Show everyone what you're really capable of."

Muttering angrily more to himself than anyone else, Kenny skulked to the foyer and reluctantly grabbed his suitcase.

Chapter Four

DARE LIKED TO make the most out of every day and was regularly up before dawn, tinkering with one of his many classic cars, riding his motorcycle, or doing whatever else he woke up with a hankering for. But this morning he had only two things on his mind—getting into Kenny's head and spending time with Billie. Last night, after introducing Kenny to his family and the rest of the staff, Dare and his parents sat down with him to explain how their program worked. He was ornery and resistant and not at all happy about losing his cell phone, but they were used to that. He settled into his room sullenly, but they were used to that, too, with teenagers.

He spent the early hours jotting down notes about how the pickup went and made a brief action plan for Kenny's therapy. Dare never spent too much time on initial action plans, as he needed to get to know his clients before he could determine what they really needed and what tactics would work to help them. Though he was up early, he wasn't in a rush to get up to the main house. They allowed all new clients to sleep in their first morning to ease into their new environment, while the staff and other clients were already busy working and undergoing therapy. He leisurely enjoyed his coffee, replaying his conversations with Billie in his mind. *Bathe your cat my ass.*

When it was time to see Kenny, he stopped in one of the barns and grabbed a pair of extra work boots for him. He waved to his father, driving a UTV away from one of the rescue barns, heading for Doc's vet clinic. They'd gotten three rescue horses in last week, and one of them had been so badly abused, it couldn't walk. His father spent as much time as he could with the rescue horses, and Dare had noticed that he was with that one every morning before sunrise. All of the horses who came to them received tender, loving care and the promise of a good life. When they were healthy and rehomed, they left with a plaque for their new stall with their name on it. Sasha had come up with the idea years ago. She called it their badge of dignity. Their family liked the idea so much, they made something similar for the people who went through their programs. They didn't get plaques, but they got gold cards for their wallets that read MEMBER OF THE REDEMPTION RANCH FAMILY on the front, and IF LOST, PLEASE RETURN TO along with the address and phone number of the ranch, a gentle reminder that they always had a place where they belonged.

He headed up to the main house and entered through the kitchen door. He liked to get Dwight's two cents about new clients before seeing them on their first day. Dwight was pulling biscuits out of the oven, a deep V etched between his brows. He was as tall as Dare, thick and athletic. His head was as clean-shaven as his face, and because of his serious demeanor, he looked every bit the drill sergeant, but he had a softer side. Dare had seen it after they lost Eddie, and after Billie had pushed him away, he'd spent many long nights in that kitchen talking with Dwight over a beer or some delicious concoction he whipped up.

"Figured I'd see you come through that door." Dwight set the tray on the top of the stove and motioned in the direction of the pass-through between the kitchen and dining room. "Your mother's with the new kid. He's as tight-lipped as a virgin, but he did as I asked—made the bed and showered."

Dare watched his mother talking to Kenny as she ate breakfast, while Kenny stared at the food on his plate. "Has he made any eye contact with her?"

"Nope."

"How long has he been sitting there?"

"Fifteen minutes or so. Hasn't taken a bite."

"Then I'd say it's time to start our day." Dare shoved a biscuit in his mouth and grabbed two more on his way to the dining room.

His mother looked up as he walked in, giving him an empathetic look he'd seen many times but had only recognized as an adult. The look that said the poor boy was a little lost. His mother had raised five rambunctious kids. She could demand obedience with one swiftly spoken sentence or a stern glance, but she liked to ease it out of a person. That was probably one of the things that made her a great mother and therapist. Dare had learned a lot from her, but he had his own way of easing compliance from disobedient teens. As a kid who had often done the opposite of most of what he was told, he knew kids like Kenny needed a firmer stance at the get-go. He didn't mollycoddle or try to ease anything out of them. He set up expectations, kept them busy, and tried to relate to what they were going through. He didn't sugarcoat things, but he joked around when it was appropriate and gave them the respect he felt people deserved, regardless of the trouble they'd gotten into, and eventually, they all opened up.

His mother stood and patted Kenny's shoulder. "I'll see you later, honey. Enjoy the morning."

Kenny's eyes remained trained on his plate.

"Kenny," Dare said sharply, bringing the boy's angry eyes to him. "In this house, we acknowledge the people who take time out of their days to talk to us."

"What am I supposed to say?" he snapped.

"Something kind. *Thank you* works, or, *You too.*" Dare put one hand on the back of Kenny's chair, the other on the table beside him, leaning in. "The more respect you show, the more you'll be given."

He looked at Dare's mother. "You too."

"Thank you, Kenny. I intend to."

"And so do we," Dare said as she picked up her dishes and carried them to the kitchen, giving him an approving smile on her way. He returned his attention to Kenny. "You've got five minutes to eat that meal."

"I'm not hungry."

"A'right. Take your plate into the kitchen, thank Dwight for cooking, wash your dishes, hit the bathroom, and meet me out front." Dare headed out the front door without looking back, showing Kenny that he trusted him to do as he was told. He believed in giving enough rope for the kid to get tangled up but not to hang himself.

Dare stepped onto the porch and gazed out at the horses grazing in the pastures and the guys unloading hay by the hay barn. Sasha was walking a rescue horse in one of the corrals, the sun kissing the ground beneath their feet. He didn't know how Birdie could prefer living in town to being surrounded by *this*.

Simone Davidson came around the corner of the house.

"Hey there, big guy. I heard there's a new kid in town. Let me know if I can help."

Simone had completed rehab in Peaceful Harbor and had come to the ranch a year and a half ago after her ex, a drug dealer, had posed too much of a threat for her to remain in Maryland. Biggs had made the arrangements, and another Dark Knight, Diesel Black, who had grown up in Hope Valley and was like a brother to Dare, had brought her out. She'd been a nervous wreck and painfully thin, which had accentuated the scar running down the left side of her face from her ear to her chin, ending just below her lower lip. A gift from that asshole ex. But she'd thrived at the ranch. Her eyes were bright, her cheeks full, and her auburn hair was thick and shiny, its natural waves and curls billowing around her face. She was even taking classes toward becoming a substance abuse counselor.

"I appreciate that. I hear you're acing your classes. We're all really proud of you." His phone vibrated, and he pulled it out, glad to see the thumbs-up text from Dwight, indicating Kenny had thanked him and done his dishes. Dare took that as a win, because half the kids didn't make the effort.

"Thanks." Simone's smile reached her eyes. "I'm proud of myself, too. I'll catch up with you later. I have a session with Wynnie."

She went inside, and Kenny came out a minute later with his eyes trained on the ground. Dare handed him the work boots. "Let's get this show on the road. Put these on, and leave your sneakers over there by the door."

"Why?"

"Because those are nice sneakers, and I don't think you want to get horseshit on them."

Kenny sat on the porch steps to change into the boots. "I

can't believe I have to do this crap."

"It's better than being locked up in juvie or tried as an adult and stuck in jail." Dare stretched his arms out to the sides, inhaling deeply. "You might not appreciate it now, but eventually you'll realize how lucky you are to have all this at your fingertips."

They climbed into a two-person UTV, and as Dare drove away from the house, Kenny spun in his seat. "Is that a *paintball* field?"

"Yup."

"Can I use it?"

"You can earn the use of it, sure."

He slumped back in his seat.

"Remember what we said last night? You're not in prison. But you don't know us, and we don't know you, so until we get to know and trust each other, I think we'll both be treading carefully. I mean, you stole a car. How do I know you won't try to steal this UTV?"

"This thing sucks."

"Works all right around the ranch."

"I wouldn't steal it."

"That's good to know. How about a horse?" he asked as they drove past a pasture.

"I don't even know how to ride them."

"Then maybe I'll ask Cowboy to teach you. But you hurt a horse, and you'll be on my shit list. Got it?"

Kenny nodded.

"You gonna try to steal my ATV?"

"You have an ATV?" he asked almost excitedly, but must have caught himself, because in the next breath that brooding look returned.

Dare noted his reaction. "Yeah, a few of them. Do I need to lock them up?"

He rolled his eyes.

"I'm serious, dude. This place can be a hell of a lot of fun, or it can be grueling, and that's pretty much up to your attitude. But if you try to steal anything from this ranch, we're going to have trouble."

"I'm not *stupid*, despite what my parents probably told you."

"Actually, your parents think you're very smart, but I like to form my own opinions." Dare let him chew on that as he gave him a tour of the property, then parked by one of the smaller barns. "Let's go." He headed over to the toolshed. "Grab a wheelbarrow and a manure rake."

"What's a manure rake?"

Dare showed him the tools, and with a wheelbarrow and manure rake of his own, he motioned for Kenny to follow him into the barn.

Kenny dropped the wheelbarrow handles and covered his nose. "*Ugh*. It smells rancid in here."

"That's the smell of horses, and you'll learn to love it."

"Not in this lifetime."

"I guess I don't need to ask if you've ever mucked a stall." Dare parked his wheelbarrow next to the first stall and pointed to the stall next to it. "Park your wheelbarrow in front of that stall. We're going to clean them out."

"I thought you said this place was fun." He parked the wheelbarrow and looked into the stall. "Gross. This *blows*."

"It's a lot more fun than being locked up in juvie. Now, get busy filling up that wheelbarrow, like this." Dare showed him how to fork the manure and soiled straw bedding into the wheelbarrow.

Kenny followed suit. "What's the point of this? To show me I'm not worth shit?"

"Dude, I'm mucking the stall next to you, and I'm worth a hell of a lot more than shit."

"Yeah, about that. What kind of therapist shovels shit?"

"The kind that doesn't want to sit in an office all day." Dare didn't care that Kenny was trying to demean him. He was just glad he was talking. "We rescue horses from all sorts of bad situations, and I like helping to take care of them. They rely on us to keep them safe and get them healthy. A dirty stall can lead to several types of health problems."

"Well, I doubt it's healthy to feed them hay on the floor with their piss."

"That's straw, not hay, and it's used for bedding, not food. A thick bed of straw helps keep moisture levels down and acts like a protective barrier between the horse and the urine."

"How?"

Dare was glad he was interested, or at least inquisitive. "Urine soaks through it and settles on the floor." He kept his explanation short, wanting to give him enough information that he was learning, without getting too sidetracked from the conversations that mattered more. "Have you ever held a real job?"

"No. My parents have money. I don't need to work."

Dare looked at him. "Must be nice. What about after you turn eighteen? Are you college bound?"

"No way. I hate school."

"So, what'll you do to earn a living? Or are your parents going to fund the rest of your life?"

He shrugged. "I'll figure it out." He tossed manure into the wheelbarrow, nearly tipping it over, but caught the handle.

"Need a hand?"

"No." He loaded up the rake and tossed another load of straw and manure in, nearly knocking it over again.

Dare grabbed the handle before it tipped. "It's okay to ask for help."

"I could've caught it."

"A'right, but if you dump it, you clean it up. Or you can ask for a hand. It doesn't matter to me. Try not to pile everything up on one side like that. Keep it even and it'll be harder to tip." They worked in silence for a few minutes. "What do you like to do?"

"Drive fast." He tossed a rake full of manure into the wheelbarrow. "But I guess you know that."

"I like to drive fast, too, when it's legal."

"Whatever. Were you in prison? Is that where you got all those tattoos? That eagle on your neck had to hurt."

"It's a phoenix, and I've never been to prison, but if someone didn't step in and straighten my ass out, I definitely could have ended up there."

"What'd you do?" Kenny asked.

"Whatever I wanted, and it was stupid."

"That's what all old people say."

Dare cocked a brow. "I'm only twenty-nine."

"That's old. You're almost thirty."

Dare chuckled and tossed another load into the wheelbarrow. "I guess to you it is. If you're lucky, life is *long*, Kenny, and it can feel like every day is a prison sentence, or every day is a new chance to enjoy yourself at whatever you're doing. Keep stealing cars, and your life will literally become a prison sentence."

"Whatever."

"You say that a lot. But it's not *whatever*. This is your life, and next year you'll be old enough to do anything you want with it."

"I can't wait." Kenny tossed more straw and manure into the wheelbarrow.

"What're your plans?"

"Get the hell out of Hope Valley."

"You hate it here that much, huh? Is that why you took your parents' car shortly after you moved? To go back to where you used to live?"

Kenny gritted his teeth as he worked.

Dare took that as a yes. "I bet you miss your friends. Did you have a girlfriend there?"

He shoved the manure rake harder into the straw and dropped the load into the wheelbarrow without answering.

Another yes. Things were starting to become clearer. "What about the girl you took with you on the joyride? Is she your new girl?"

"No. She's just a friend. She was bored and wanted to have some fun."

"And you suggested taking her parents' car out for a spin?"

"*No. She* said we should take it, and she kept bugging me to do it, so I did."

"So she wouldn't think you were boring?"

He shrugged.

"But you took it early in the evening. You had to know you'd get caught."

Kenny didn't respond and put another load in the wheelbarrow.

"Hold on. We need to dump these in the compost heap

around back." They set down their rakes and wheeled the manure out of the barn.

"How long do we have to do this?" Kenny asked. "I'm sweating."

"Yeah, I can smell you from here," Dare teased, earning a reluctant smile. "We'll do it for as long as it takes to get through all the muck that's settled into the cracks, until we can see our way clear to start fresh."

BILLIE WAS FIT to be tied.

She'd gone for a run, washed her truck, and cleaned the whole damn house, trying to get Dare off her mind, but *nothing* worked, which was why she'd power washed the deck. She figured blasting and destroying dirt might do the trick. But her clothes were soaked, and she *still* couldn't stop thinking about him, hearing him call her name as he parachuted to the ground, seeing that big-ass grin on his face last night at the bar, hearing him gloating in celebration. *You didn't cast daggers at me when I walked in.* She was beginning to see how addicts fell off the wagon years after going through rehab. Letting him in for just that short time at the park had her missing their friendship, missing *him*, fiercely.

Music blared from her earbuds as she put away the power washer. She still couldn't believe she'd told him the truth about the day Eddie died. She'd thought she'd locked that truth down so tight, she'd take it to her grave. But she hadn't counted on Dare being so different. He never used to *deal with* problems. He was just ornerier than them. He'd bully them away, building her up until she believed she was indestructible and better than whatever she was battling, making it so she could move on without fear.

She headed inside, trying to figure him out. He still had that edge she loved, challenging her without hesitation, making her *think* and *feel* and get all fired up inside. But he was more thoughtful now. A listener *and* a talker. When did that happen? Was it new, or had she just become so adept at not really seeing him, she never noticed? The old Dare would have followed her home Sunday morning after her run, trying to convince her to have dinner with him.

As much as she hated to admit it, a tiny part of her wished he had.

She guzzled a glass of water and went to take a shower.

She stood under the warm spray, thinking about how sure she'd been that Dare would show up at the bar Monday night to try to coax her into hanging out with him again. As much as she hated to admit it, she'd watched the door all night, *hoping* he'd walk in. But she hadn't heard a peep until he'd burst into the bar last night and had done that damn backflip.

Okay, she secretly thought it was awesome, because it was so very *Dare*, and *that* was the problem. She'd always liked who he was, and this new part of him, the calm, thoughtful listener, made him even more attractive. She pictured his rugged face as she washed herself, the heat in his eyes as he'd held her on top of the bar last weekend, his hard body grinding against her. He'd felt so good, she closed her eyes remembering the feel of his thick thighs and the monster in his pants pressed against her. She could still smell his rugged scent, feel the heat of his bare chest burning through her shirt. His voice growled in her ear. *I can think of a far better way to get your pussy wet.* Picturing his hands in place of hers, her fingers slid between her legs. Her mind reeled back to the summer after high school graduation, his thick fingers working their magic as they ate at each other's mouths. She could still taste him. Her fingers quickened, the same way his had, and she cupped her breast with her other hand, rolling her nipple between her finger and thumb, pretending it was his mouth on it. She could still hear the guttural, appreciative sounds that had escaped his lips as he'd made her come, still feel his thick, hot cock in her hand. Her hips and hands moved in sync, her breathing quickened, and behind closed eyes it was Dare's face she saw as his name screamed from her lungs like a curse. She continued the torture, bringing herself up on her toes and pressing one hand to the cold, wet tile, her eyes tightly closed as she imagined Dare on his knees, his mouth between her legs, sending herself spiraling over the edge again—*"Dare!"*

She leaned her forehead against the slick tile, warm water raining down her back, her body trembling as she came down from the high and the lust slowly cleared from her brain.

Freaking Dare. He was like a tick, growing bigger and more annoying until she had to do something about it.

She finished showering and dried off, wrapping a towel around herself and swearing that was the *last* time she'd come to thoughts of Dare Whiskey.

She'd been swearing the same damn thing forever.

Cursing herself, she opened the bathroom door, barreling into a chest of stone in the hallway. She screamed, reflexively throwing a punch, connecting with a jaw as her towel fell to the ground...and Dare's face came into focus.

"What the hell are you doing, scaring me like that?" she shouted, scrambling for her towel as his gaze raked down her body, heat rising in his eyes, igniting the electrical charge that was always humming between them.

He rubbed his jaw. "Apparently missing out on a lot of fun. *Twice*, huh? Guess you weren't kidding about bathing your—"

"Don't you *dare* say it," she seethed with as much anger as embarrassment, pushing past him to go into her bedroom. Why couldn't they live in a house with a master bathroom?

He followed her in. "If it makes you feel any better, when I'm going for a *solo ride*, it's your face I see and your mouth I'm thinking about. And now that I know what's under that towel. *Mm-mm.* I'll be thinking about much more than your mouth."

"Ohmygod. *Shut up!*" Not only had he given Billie her first orgasm that summer, but she'd been about to blow him when they'd been interrupted. *Great.* Now she was thinking about his cock again. She scowled. "Why are you in my house?"

"The door was open. I figured you were expecting me, and when I heard you—"

She silenced him with a glare.

He held up his hands in surrender. "I was just going to say that when I heard you in the shower…"

She exhaled with relief.

"Calling my name in the throes of passion."

"Dare!" She shoved his laughing ass away, but he caught her wrist, tugging her against him, and *Lord*, he felt good.

"Twice."

She knew she'd never live that down. "*Forget* you ever heard that."

"Not a chance, darlin'." He lowered his voice, his hungry gaze drilling into her. "I like knowing you've been thinking about our unfinished business as much as I have."

"We don't *have* unfinished business." *You've been thinking about me?*

72

"Come on, Mancini, I heard that plea in your voice. You were thinking about *my* hands on your body." He palmed her ass, and she gasped in surprise, heat scorching through her. "*My mouth pleasuring you, my c—*"

"Devlin Whiskey, do *not* make me get my gun." *Lord have mercy.* She'd like to get her hands on his *gun*. No. No she would not.

He chuckled, but it did nothing to lessen the heat between them as he gave her ass one hard squeeze and stepped back. "Get dressed, Annie Oakley. We've got plans."

Her traitorous body cried out for his touch, and she tried to beat those needs into submission. "No, we don't."

He put his hand over his heart. "Aw, Mancini, that stings. You forgot about our date already?"

She smiled despite herself. Damn him and his charming antics. "I never said I'd go."

"Come on, darlin'. You know you've got to fill up that bean-flicking bank with thoughts of yours truly."

His stupid grin made her smile harder. "You're an ass."

"No shit, sweetheart. But the cat's out of the bag. You *like* my ass."

She rolled her eyes. "Get over yourself."

"You know you want to come. Oh wait, you already did that."

She gave him a deadpan look.

"You know, I'm feeling a little behind the finish line. Maybe we should spend the day here instead and catch me up." He reached for his belt.

"*Fine*, I'll go. Just stop talking about *that*." She shoved him out the bedroom door and closed it behind him, wondering how she was going to get through the day.

Chapter Five

AFTER AN HOUR and a half of listening to Dare sing along to the radio and joke about Billie losing her towel, her embarrassment was long gone. They stopped at a roadside café for lunch, and when they got back in the truck, he had her laughing so hard her sides hurt. At least until they made their way up a mountain to the Cliffside Thrill and Aerial Adventure Park, a childhood favorite of theirs and Eddie's. Her nerves caught fire.

They used to beg their parents to take them there, but because it was a long drive and admission was expensive, they rarely went. Once they got their driver's licenses, she, Dare, and Eddie saved their money and went together, just the three of them. They'd stay all day, riding enormous ziplines, unfathomable roller coasters, a terrifying canyon swing, and souped-up go-karts and conquering a challenging aerial adventure course.

Her stomach knotted up as they followed a crowd through the gates. Kids were begging to go on rides, tugging their parents' hands, and chattering about everything they wanted to do. She glanced at Dare, remembering the cute school-age boy who had been all attitude and the cocky teenager who'd oozed nearly as much testosterone as the man beside her, bringing years of memories rushing back. *Good* memories. Memories Billie didn't want to forget, but she'd left that thrill-seeking lifestyle behind for a reason.

"Like what you see, darlin'?"

She realized she was staring at him. He was still so full of himself, which should be a turnoff, but it wasn't. "I'm trying to decide whether I want to slap you or hug you."

"Given what I heard when I walked into your house, I'd say you want to do more than hug me, and I'm not into slapping, but if that's your thing…"

She rolled her eyes but couldn't help her smile. "Shut up. I can't believe you drove all this way when you know I won't go on the rides."

"I don't know that, and who says I want to go on the rides, anyway? I thought we'd just walk around and talk about old times."

"You did *not*."

He laughed and slung an arm around her shoulders, tugging her closer as they walked through the crowded park, just like old times. "You're right, Mancini. Is it so bad that I hoped you might go on one ride with me and remember that life wasn't always just about the bar?"

"My life isn't just about the bar." *Who's the impostor now?*

"Really? I'm all ears. Fill me in on your hobbies."

"I have lots of them. The biggest one is avoiding you," she said sassily.

"Well, you suck at that one, so it's time for a new one. Seriously, what do you do for fun these days?"

"Nothing you'd find exciting."

"Try me, because I think your shower was pretty exciting."

"*Dare.*" She tried to shrug out from under his arm, but he

tightened his grip on her, guiding her in the direction of the go-karts.

"I'll stop giving you shit about that."

"No, you won't."

"Yeah, probably not. But what do you expect? It was the highlight of my year." He tugged her down a path to their right that she knew led to the aerial adventure area.

"You must've had a pretty lame year so far."

"Nice try. *Hobbies*, Mancini. Cough 'em up."

"I do lots of things. I go running and hang out with Bobbie and watch movies."

Dare feigned a yawn.

"Would you stop? I like my life just the way it is."

"If that's true, then I'm glad. But I can't imagine leaving everything I loved behind like you did. Don't you miss all the fun the three of us used to have?"

"Of course I miss it."

She was pleasantly surprised that he didn't push for more as they made their way to the aerial adventure course. Just the sight of the massive webs of thick ropes, cargo nets, and Burma Bridges spanning acres of ground and unimaginable heights made her blood pump faster.

A challenge sparked in Dare's eyes. "As I recall, I beat you the last time we raced across the multivines." Multivines were cable-and-rope courses between two platforms where they walked across a cable thirty-plus feet above the ground, using only strategically spaced dangling ropes for support.

"You beat me by *two* seconds," she reminded him.

He shrugged one shoulder. "It's still a win."

"Hardly."

"I seem to remember you rubbing my nose in my loss when

you beat me by *one* second on the alpine roller coaster."

She grinned. "That was pretty awesome, and I still hold that record."

"Care for a rematch on the multivines? Or does this little ropes course count as a ride you're not going on? We can start on the kiddie ropes until you're used to using your muscles again."

"Shut up. My muscles are just fine."

"I don't know. I mean, shower workouts don't use all the muscles rope climbing does." He laughed, and she swatted him.

"Put your money where your mouth is, Whiskey. Twenty bucks says I'll beat you."

He shielded his mouth, speaking into her ear. "Hear that, girl? My bestie's coming out, so you best beware."

"You're a fool," she said as they went to get their equipment.

They suited up with helmets and all the necessary safety equipment, and as they headed over to the course, Dare said, "I want to start small, on the spiderweb."

"Why?"

"I haven't climbed in a while and want to get my footing. You gonna give me shit about it?"

No, because I know you're doing it to protect me. "I always knew you were a little soft."

He swatted her ass, and she yelped and took off running toward the course. He was hot on her heels, but she scampered up to get hooked to the belay line.

Before their parents agreed to take them to the park the first time, Dare's father had built a small rope-climbing course in the woods at the ranch for them to practice on. Billie, Dare, and Eddie had used that course every day for months, and they'd come up with all sorts of plans to expand it, but they were always too busy to follow through.

Billie had a momentary flash of unease as they started climbing the massive spiderweb, balancing on wiggling ropes. She knew it was just because she'd beat into her own head that she was *never* doing these things again.

"You okay, Mancini?" Dare asked.

"*Yes*," she bit out, angry at herself for her unease. All around them, kids and adults were climbing and swinging. She felt ridiculous for hesitating and started to give herself a pep talk. But Dare moved behind her, caging her in with his big body. His rugged scent infiltrated her senses, and all those magnificent muscles pressed against her back.

"*What* are you doing?" *And why does it have to feel so good?*

"Making sure you don't fall."

His warm breath slid over her cheek, alighting tingles beneath her skin. "I don't *need* you behind me."

"Is that an invitation to come *inside* you?"

Her entire body flamed. She struggled against that delicious thought and managed, "When did you get so dirty?" *And why do I have to like it so much?*

"I've always been dirty, darlin'. You've just never let me get close enough to melt that layer of ice you've been wearing for far too long."

"Well, *stop* it! You're making me hot."

He lowered his face, his whiskers brushing her cheek, sending scintillating sensations slithering down her body as he said, "I've got the image of your naked body seared into my brain. Sure you want to talk about *hot*?" He leaned into her, her temperature spiking. "Or are you going to move that fine ass and start climbing?"

"If *you* move, *I'll* move."

"A'right, but I'm not sure this is the place for it." His hips gyrated.

"*Dare!* Ohmygod! Quit it!" She felt her cheeks burning, but that was nothing compared to the inferno he was causing inside her.

"I thought you were asking me to give you something else to think about."

Her heart was racing, her body was on fire, and she had a feeling she'd think of nothing *but* how good he felt for the rest of the day. "Get away from me!"

"That's not something I hear very often, but if you insist." He moved next to her, the king of all smirks plastered on his all-too-handsome face.

She scowled, her trepidation smothered by frustration, and focused on beating his cocky ass up to the top. As she scaled the rope web, her frustration fueled her determination, pushing her into that age-old zone in which she used to disappear when she climbed. She'd forgotten how freeing it was to be suspended high above the ground, her fingers gripping the rough rope, heart thudding against her chest. Dare climbed right beside her, matching her pace as she climbed faster or slowed to find her grip. Adrenaline coursed through her as they neared the top. She pushed herself to climb faster, and Dare's foot slipped, slowing him down enough for her to grab the top rope first.

Happiness like she hadn't felt in years whipped through her. "Yes!" she hollered, throwing one fist toward the sky as he climbed to the top beside her.

"Way to go, Mancini!"

"That was *so* fun!" She schooled her expression, leveling him with a stare. "Even if you did let me win."

He laughed. "You know me better than that."

No, she knew him *exactly* like that. "Race you down!"

They raced all over the ropes course, conquering catwalks, tube nets, swinging platforms, Burma Bridges, and climbing on, up, over, across, and through dozens of cargo nets. They tied on the multivines, but again, Billie was sure that was all Dare's doing. He probably could've beaten her one-handed. He was big and muscular, but he was lightning fast. He always had been. They egged each other on as they went from one course to the next, and for their big finale, they went on the free-fall simulator and came away cracking up. Billie was exhilarated. She felt younger and lighter than she had in years.

"I had forgotten how incredible this feels," she said breathlessly, leaning on Dare's shoulder.

"To fall off a platform?" he teased.

"All of it." *The air feels electrified, I'm breathing deeper, and my cheeks hurt from smiling!* She kept those details to herself. "From the climbing to the racing to just being with you and having fun."

He slung an arm across her shoulders, pulling her against his side. "I missed you too, Mancini."

Why did that feel so good to hear?

They headed out of the aerial park arm in arm, following the crowd to the alpine roller coaster, and stood at the wooden railing, watching the cars take off. Billie's pulse quickened with memories of taking that wild ride. Thirty-five hundred feet of heart-pumping thrills. Unlike normal roller coasters, the cars were affixed to the track, designed to take the downhill, winding hairpin turns at breakneck speeds. The track was built hanging over the sides of the mountain, and each car was separate. Riders could go alone or with someone sitting in front of them, and the rider controlled the speed of their car with the throttle. She and Dare used to go as fast as they could and compare times when they were done. As she watched wide-eyed thrill seekers climbing into the cars, the girl she'd been battled with the woman she'd become, egging her on, just like she and Dare used to.

"Do you remember the first time you rode this thing?" Dare asked.

"Kind of." She didn't know why she said that. She'd never forget that day. They were nine years old, and their families had come to the park together. Eddie's parents couldn't go, so he'd ridden with her family. Once their fathers had realized that parts of the track were built *over* the side of the mountain, they'd tried to talk them out of riding it, but they'd known even then that there was no stopping the Daredevils. Eddie had decided to hang back and watch the first two times Billie and Dare had ridden. Another thing Billie had always appreciated about Dare was that even as a kid he hadn't made Eddie feel bad for holding off on doing anything scary. He somehow knew she *really* wanted to do it and that it was okay to egg *her* on but not do the same to Eddie, like most boys would. Instead, he'd built Eddie up and told him he was smart to check it out first. When she and Dare were waiting in line, she'd been as nervous as she was excited. Dare had noticed that nervousness and had taken her hand and said, *You're the bravest girl I know. Thanks for doing this with me.* That was all it had taken to bolster her confidence.

It was quite possible that she'd loved him even then, because as she thought about that day, she remembered a different type of nervousness had settled in after he'd said that.

Butterflies in her belly.

The sounds of the roller coaster and riders screaming with fear and delight as they sped past pulled her from her memories.

Dare took her hand, just like he'd done all those years ago, and said, "You were the coolest that day, acting like you weren't scared when you must have been ready to piss your pants." He leaned on the railing, still holding her hand, forcing her to do the same.

This was who Dare had always been. The friend who took care of her, who presumed she'd want to hold his hand, and knew when she needed to even if she'd never admit it to herself. She'd missed these parts of him so much, it brought a wave of unexpected emotion.

A little while later he pulled out his phone and thumbed out a text.

"Hot date tonight?" She said it teasingly to hide the streak of jealousy she'd tried to ignore nearly every damn day of her life.

"Hell yeah. I'm with you, aren't I?" He winked.

A thrill skittered through her, and she told herself not to go there. She couldn't afford to get tangled up in the guilt *that* would cause. His phone chimed, and he read the message, then pocketed his phone with a pinched expression and leaned on the railing again.

"Everything okay?" she asked carefully.

"Yeah. We got a new kid staying at the ranch. I just wanted to check on him. It's his first day."

"Is he doing okay?"

"According to Cowboy, he's ornery as fuck, which is par for the course. The kid's got grit. I think he's in a tough situation. New to town and might have left someone special behind."

"That is rough. What's he there for? Drugs?"

Dare shook his head. "I haven't gotten that far yet, but I doubt he's done more than drink and maybe smoke some weed. He's just getting into trouble, and his parents want to straighten him out."

"Is that what you do? Straighten kids out?" She knew what the ranch was known for, but she was curious about Dare and what he did for the people who came there.

"It's not my job to straighten them out. Only they can do that. I talk to them and hopefully find the right keys to unlock the chains tethering them to their demons. If I'm lucky enough to figure that out, then I open a door and show them how to get there so they can leave those monsters behind. But it's up to them to muster the courage to get *to* the door, to walk through it, and not stumble back." He studied her face with a thoughtful expression. "You found those keys for me."

She was shocked. "*I* did? When?"

"When I was on the fast track to hell my first couple years of college." He smiled. "I kept my grades up, though."

"You always knew how to play to win. But I don't understand what you mean. What keys did I find?"

"The ones that mattered. You said you didn't know who I was anymore and that I didn't have what it took to become a Dark Knight. I don't know which one of those two things gutted me more, but you've always been the only person who knew how to get through to me."

He held her gaze for a second before looking out at the roller coaster zipping by, leaving her to mull over what he'd said.

"That's who I try to be for my clients," he said. "I try to see past what they want me to see and peel away enough layers so we can get to the heart of their issues and figure out what's going to make a difference."

She could see this calm-talking version of him helping people dig in to their issues and find a way to move forward. "The three of us, and this place, made a difference for me."

"I get the three of us. I mean, we were all part of each other. But why this place?"

"It was like our parents had finally trusted us enough to spend the money to take us here. Remember how big a deal it was?"

"I sure do. I wonder if they regretted it when Eddie threw up on the canyon swing the first time he rode it."

She laughed. "That was so gross. Thank God your mom had sent extra clothes for you. She always thought of everything." She loved his parents like her own. Tiny was gruffer than her father, and he wasn't particularly warm, but his love shined through that rough exterior in other ways. Like the way he protected his children and supported their dreams. In truth, he'd done that for all three of them. What Tiny lacked in warmth, Wynnie made up for in droves. Dare wouldn't be the caring, warm-hearted, protective, bullheaded beast he was without a tough father like Tiny and a loving mother like Wynnie, and for that, Billie would always be thankful.

They listened to the screams and watched kids coming off the ride, doing high fives and laughing hysterically, just like the three of them used to do. Billie got goose bumps remembering the fear and anticipation before the ride and the high as they came off.

"What do you say, Mancini? Take a ride with me? I'll go in your car, so you won't be alone."

"I'm not *afraid* to ride alone."

"Then why did you say you won't go on the rides?"

"Because I left all of that thrill seeking behind when we lost Eddie."

"I know, darlin'. But *why*? Remember, I know nothing about what was in your head back then."

"Because one second he was there with us, and the next he was gone." The confession brought an onslaught of emotions, and she pushed from the railing, freeing her hand. "*That's* what scared me, not the stunts or these kinds of rides. It was the reality of how quickly death can happen."

"That's a valid fear," Dare said compassionately. "It was devastating for all of us. I wish you hadn't shut me out so we could have gotten through it together, but we all have our own ways of grieving, and I guess you needed to be alone." He drew her into his arms for a quick hug. "But I'm really glad you're here with me now." He kissed her head and stepped back, while she tried to keep her emotions from swallowing her whole.

"Can we not talk about that? I don't want to ruin our day."

"Sure. Another time." A playful grin brightened his eyes. "I totally understand being fearful where dangerous stunts are concerned. But I *see* you looking at this roller coaster, Mancini, and I can *feel* how much you want to ride it." He nodded to a group of kids coming off the ride, and his lips tipped up. "I'm pretty sure we're safe on this one, but if you'd rather not, I won't push."

"Like that look in your eyes isn't a push?"

"What look?"

"That look that says, *Come on, Mancini. You know you want to.*" Her words came fast, frustrated, and more honest than ever. "And *yes*, I want to! But you *know* how I am. If I go on this, it's just the start. We're going on every ride in this place, and then you and I are going to compete, which will only make it more fun, and then I'm totally screwed."

He laughed. "That's what I'm counting on."

"God, you're *such* a pain. Nobody else *ever* pushes me like this."

"Because nobody else knows you like I do."

His ever-confident stare pissed her off because he knew he was right, and so did she. "*Ugh!* Why did you have to take me here? You knew I'd want to ride the stupid roller coaster. How can I look at it and *not* want to?" She grabbed his hand, tugging him toward the line. "Let's go, you big jerk. But just so you know, this park is where it ends, so don't think you'll get me to jump out of a plane or run with the bulls."

"I'd never dream of it."

"You're the worst liar I've ever known."

DARE WOULD DISAGREE. He'd proven himself to be the best liar all those years ago, when she'd kicked him to the curb and he'd acted like he hadn't given a damn. But he wasn't about to get into that when she was finally peeking out of the darkness. He could hardly believe she'd opened up to him as much as she had, and he hoped she'd one day trust him enough that they could talk about all of it.

The afternoon flew by as they raced on the alpine coaster at breakneck speeds. Billie lost the first time, which pissed her off, and she insisted on going again, thrilling Dare. She lost and demanded another race. This time she tied, and he was shocked that she was okay with that, but she dragged him to another ride.

They rode roller coasters with 360-degree barrel rolls, corkscrews, and some of the steepest free falls in the States. As the day wore on, Billie became less combative, less guarded, and a hell of a lot more like her old self, hanging on to Dare between rides and giving him hell in the playful, sexy way she always had, unleashing the sizzling heat between them. It was hell trying to keep himself in check, especially with the sound of her crying out his name echoing in his mind and having to look at her in those skimpy cutoffs and her tight black-and-gray tie-dyed shirt. The damn thing laced up the front, revealing the swell of her breasts and a hint of a black lace bra, making that sexy black choker she wore even sexier. He'd always felt that fire between them, but he'd had no idea how deep it ran on *her* side until today. How long had she wanted him like that? He wondered about that as they flew across ziplines and swung over a cliff on the massive canyon swing, going nearly vertical fifteen hundred feet above the ground.

They'd been there all day. The sun was starting to set as they waited in line for the go-karts. She hung on his arm, her sweet curves rubbing against him, those gorgeous eyes shimmering with excitement as she talked a mile a minute about the good old times. This was how easy it had always been between them—and how torturous. It was all he could do to try to pay attention to what she said instead of pulling her into the kiss he was dying to take.

When it was their turn on the go-karts, they sped around the track, racing neck and neck. Billie glanced over, beautiful as could be with the wind blowing her dark hair over her shoulders, giving him that narrow-eyed, seductive look she'd mastered in high school. But damn, it was even hotter now, more potent than any look he'd ever seen. He wanted to see it when she was lying beneath him and he was buried deep inside her, causing those desperate cries.

Her laughter broke through his reverie, and he realized she'd gunned her engine and was speeding ahead.

Fuck.

He put the gas pedal to the floor, swerving around the other go-karts, until he was on her tail. Every time he tried to pass her, she veered into his path. She lifted one hand, flipping him off, and he laughed. His girl was definitely coming back, and nothing could make him happier.

When they climbed out of their go-karts, there was an announcement about the park closing soon. Billie strutted over and hooked her arm through his, hanging on him as they headed away from the ride. "Guess you've lost your touch after all these years, Whiskey."

"Don't kid yourself. I was just distracted."

"Mm-hm. *Distracted.*" She giggled. "Can we grab a corn dog on the way out? I'm starved, and they have the *best* corn dogs."

"I've got a corn dog you can eat."

"Real smooth, Casanova." She bumped him with her body, grinning like she couldn't stop, and damn that looked good on her. "This has been the greatest day. Thanks for pushing me to have some fun."

"Want to have some more?" He waggled his brows.

"You're always pushing the envelope."

"Darlin', I push limits, not envelopes. I've got something to show you when we get back home."

"Is it in your pants?"

He arched a brow. "Do you want it to be?"

"Shut up." She tugged him toward a corn dog stand near

the exit, giving him a playful look as she spoke to the vendor. "I'll take the *biggest* one you've got, and he'll take the littlest."

What're you up to, Mancini?

She pulled a twenty-dollar bill out of her back pocket.

"Put your money away, Mancini. You're my date today." He paid the vendor, and as they headed for the truck, she took a bite of the corn dog, moaning like it was the best thing she'd ever had. The sensual sound seared through him, and he ate half his corn dog in one bite. She did it again, and he stopped in his tracks, uttering a curse.

"What's wrong?" She licked the top of the corn dog, making another appreciative sound.

He glowered at her. "If you don't stop that shit, you're going to get yourself in trouble." He ate the rest of his corn dog in one bite and started walking again.

"Wha—" Her eyes widened like she hadn't realized what she was doing to him, but that look of surprise quickly morphed into a challenge. "Who doesn't love a *thick, salty* corn dog?" She ran her tongue along the length of what was left.

He gritted his teeth as they neared the truck.

Amusement rose in her eyes, and she held his gaze, lowering her mouth over it, moaning louder. Her eyes closed, and she ran her hand down her chest, her nipples pressing against her tight T-shirt as she moved the remaining corn dog in and out of her mouth.

Fuck this. He grabbed her by the arms, pinning her against his truck. Laughter fell from her lips as he ripped the corn dog from her hand. "Buckle up, baby girl, because Big Daddy Dare don't play."

"Big Daddy my butt, you weirdo." She laughed.

"That's not what you said that night you were all over me. I believe it was *Oh, Dare, you're so big.*"

"I *lied.*" She smirked.

Nice try, darlin', but your beautiful eyes betray you. Holding her gaze, he slid his tongue around the edge of her corn dog, then flicked the center fast and continuously as he ground his hips against her. She felt so fucking good, and he knew she loved it, too, because desire simmered in her eyes, and she swallowed hard. He pressed his chest to hers, growling in her ear, "You like teeth *and* tongue, Mancini? Because I know how much you like fingers."

"I like it *all*," she said haughtily. "But I prefer battery-operated boyfriends who don't talk back." She flashed a victorious grin.

He'd waited so long to see her happy and to feel the connection he craved like a drug, the combination was like an aphrodisiac. He felt her heart beating faster, almost as strong as the electricity zinging between them. Her lips were a breath away, her gorgeous eyes gazing hungrily, *trustingly* up at him. His entire being ached to kiss her. But he'd only just gotten her back, and he didn't want to fuck this up, so he fought the urge, gritting out, "Lucky for you, I consider toys teammates, not competition."

Her eyes flamed, and a nervous laugh bubbled out.

Ah, my girl likes that idea.

In the next breath, her eyes narrowed. "Don't get your hopes up, Whiskey."

"I don't know, Mancini. Two hot singles and the night is *young*. Get your fine ass in my truck. We've got places to go."

Chapter Six

THEY DIDN'T GET back to Hope Valley until almost nine thirty. Billie couldn't remember the last time she'd had so much fun, but she was glad it was dark out, because her nerves were rattled, and she didn't want eagle-eyed Dare to notice. What the hell was she thinking, flirting with him? She'd stuck to her guns for six long years, maintaining distance to keep her guilt—and their ridiculously powerful connection—at bay, and in *one* afternoon she'd blown it. *This* was one of the reasons she'd shut him out of her life. She'd been an adrenaline junkie since she was a little girl, and Dare made her feel like she could do anything. He was her ever-enticing racetrack, and their explosive energy fueled every ounce of her—her brain, her desires, her *heart*. When they were together, her senses were sharper, her drive and determination stronger, and her happiness was off the charts, even when he was being a stubborn ass. She knew she could be just as annoying to him. They were made of the same grit.

Except Eddie's death had proved they had their differences.

She'd tried to bury her adrenaline-seeking self, while Dare had found new limits to push. He'd immediately begun training for death-defying motorcycle stunts: jumping over buses and riding the Wall of Death. Dare had jumped over *five* buses, and from what Billie had heard, he was training to jump over more. The Wall of Death was just as treacherous—driving along the vertical, wooden-planked wall of a barrel-shaped cylinder at high speeds, parallel to the ground. In both stunts, the slightest error in judgment could end in serious injury or death, and Dare wanted to beat *every* existing record. Most people rode the Wall of Death at about forty miles per hour for carnival shows and entertainment. But that wasn't limit-pushing enough for Dare. He'd wanted to beat the reigning champ, who reached speeds of seventy-eight miles per hour. Dare had gone to the UK to train with the best in the field, and three years ago he'd gone to the Sturgis Buffalo Chip and had beaten the world record. Billie had thought she'd shut down her feelings for Dare back then, but she'd felt like she hadn't taken a single breath while he'd been training and had nearly lost her mind when he'd gone to Sturgis. The fact that her feelings for him were unshakable had made her even more determined to keep her distance.

And now here she was, sitting in his truck wearing the cowboy hat he'd left on his seat, thinking of him flicking that damned corn dog with his tongue as he turned off the main road and into Redemption Ranch.

The ranch used to be like a second home to her. She'd often eaten meals with Dare and his family, their staff, and their clients, had attended every event, and had spent holidays bouncing between houses with Dare and Eddie. But after Eddie's accident, she'd stayed away for two full years, until her father had talked her into attending the events the Whiskeys hosted, because *That family loves you, and we don't turn our backs on love.*

Only she *had* turned her back on love. More than once.

She sat up straighter as they drove beneath the wooden beam with an iron *RR* across the top—the first R was backward. "What are we doing here?"

"I want to show you something at my place."

She hadn't been to Dare's cabin since before Eddie died. He'd always had his eye on the cozy three-bedroom cabin that was tucked away from the others, near the climbing area his father had built. It had an enormous pasture out back where they used to run around. But every time he'd asked his father if he could live there when he was older, Tiny had said he was afraid to put Dare where he couldn't see him.

"If you think I'm touching your *corn dog*, you've got another thing coming."

He grinned. "I've got you in my truck for the first time in years. I'm already counting myself lucky."

The sweet comment caught her off guard, chipping away at her resolve to try to reinstate a modicum of space between them. He winked, and she looked out the window as they drove by the pastures and corrals they'd grown up racing around and hiding in and the barn where she'd taken her first kiss.

She remembered that moment like it was yesterday. They were six years old, and Eddie had just gone home. She and Dare were crouched in a horse stall hiding from Doc and Cowboy, who were looking for her because her mother had come to pick her up. Dare had been whispering incessantly and wouldn't stop, so she kissed him to shut him up. He'd looked at her like she'd lost her mind and snapped, *What was that?* She'd said, *A kiss, stupid.* He'd scowled and said, *No duh. Why'd you kiss me?* To which she'd responded, *I felt like it.* He'd asked her if she'd kissed Eddie, and she'd said, *No. I kissed you, dummy.* He'd wiped his mouth with his forearm and said, *Well, don't do it again.* She had never liked to be told what to do, so she'd kissed him again, thrown her hands up like claws, and shouted, *I'm the kissing monster!* He'd sprinted out of the barn, and she'd chased him. Doc and Cowboy were on their heels all the way up to the main house. She warmed with the memory.

"You look hot in my hat."

She glanced over, catching a coy grin that made her stomach flutter. This open attraction he was sending her way was new. He'd held her hand and put his arm around her, but he'd never acted so openly attracted to her. She liked it. Too much. *I will not flirt with or touch Dare.* She repeated it like a mantra, wondering how she'd gone from staying away from him to needing to remind herself not to touch him.

He drove through the property, passing the other cabins, porch lights glowing in the darkness, and his parents' cedar-sided home set up on a hill. He wound down the gravel road they'd walked hundreds of times as kids to get to the climbing course. A sense of nostalgia tugged at her. She could still hear the three of them running on the gravel, making plans for their next big stunt. She felt a stab of longing for those carefree times, when life was easy and Eddie was still alive.

The headlights illuminated a massive four-bay garage in the distance, with two ATVs parked out front. "Wow, that's new. Whose is that?"

"Mine."

"I heard you were still tinkering with classic cars, but you could fit an entire showroom in there." He'd always had a love for the classics. His grandfather had left him his 1958 Ford F100 truck, and as a teenager Dare had saved the money he'd earned from working on the ranch and had bought an old Chevelle, the site of their tipsy teenage tryst. She'd been surprised when he'd gone from driving his grandfather's truck to the newer one they were sitting in, which he'd bought a few years ago. She'd wondered if his grandfather's truck had finally died, which would make her sad for him, because he'd cherished it. But part of keeping her distance was not allowing herself to ask others about Dare or what he was up to.

The rustic log cabin came into view on the far side of the garage. The porch light cast a golden halo over the deep front porch, which was only a few inches off the ground and had never had railings. She loved that he hadn't added them and imagined him sitting on one of the two wooden chairs sipping a beer or his morning coffee. But Dare wasn't the kind of guy who sat around sipping anything, and she quickly nixed that image.

As he parked in front of the cabin, she noticed the stone chimney hadn't changed. She used to tuck flowers between the stones only to have Dare tear them out and say they were stupid. When they were young, people had come and gone from all the cabins on the ranch as they'd bettered themselves. When Eddie died, she'd wished she'd had a place far away where she could go to heal. But even if she had, her heart had been staked to the man beside her, and she knew she wouldn't have left Hope Valley. She might not have been able to be close to him, but she liked knowing he was nearby.

"How'd you convince your dad to let you live here?"

"I guess he realized I was more trouble than I was worth, and it was easier to put me out of sight."

She pushed open her door. "I could have told him that."

Dare lunged across the seat, but she jumped out of the truck before he could grab her. She spun around, laughing and pushing his hat back on her head as he climbed out, a wolfish grin playing on his lips. "You're slowing down in your old age, Whiskey."

"Hardly. Be nice and I'll show you *my* toys." He winked.

She stood stock-still, her pulse racing.

"They're not quite as fun as yours, but I think you'll like them." He headed for the garage.

She hurried to catch up and swatted him, but she'd missed his sense of humor and was enjoying every second of it. "I can't believe you tore down the cute workshop that used to be here. I loved that place."

"I know you did. I didn't tear it down. It's around back."

He opened one of the bays, and when he turned on the lights, her breath caught at the sight of shiny classic cars, motorcycles, and trucks and an array of old weathered vehicles.

"*Wow.* You've been doing a heck of a lot more than tinkering. When do you have time to work on these? Other than finding new ways to risk your life, I thought you spent your downtime getting into the bed of any willing woman in town."

His eyes narrowed. "Is *that* what you think of me?"

She shrugged, not wanting to think about it, much less talk about it.

"You wouldn't be altogether wrong, but I'm not a man whore. You know how much I always wanted to do this shit. When I was getting my master's, I needed something to keep me busy and out of trouble, so I started with the two that had the most sentimental value."

He pointed across the garage at what she realized was his grandfather's fully restored two-tone blue-and-white truck.

"You finally did it!" She walked over, admiring how gorgeous it was. She reached for the door handle. "May I?"

He nodded.

She opened the door and climbed into the driver's seat. The interior was shiny and spotless. "Dare, this is beautiful. The seats were torn, and the dash was cracked. Now it looks brand-new. Did you do all this yourself?"

"Most of it. I rebuilt the engine with Rebel over at his place."

"I can't get over the difference. I bet your mother was floored to see her dad's truck look so good."

"Yeah, it makes her happy every time she sees it. That was my first project, and that one over there was my second." He pointed to the black Chevelle on the other side of the garage.

Butterflies swarmed in her chest. Was that car special because it was his first classic car or because it was where they'd made out the summer before he'd gone away to college? That was silly. He'd probably made out with dozens of girls in that car.

She walked over and peered into the window, remembering the night of that party at her parents' house. She'd heard girls bragging about making out with Dare throughout high school, and she'd been horribly jealous. She'd thought that summer might be her last time to try to kiss him, and she'd dragged him away from the other kids at the party on the pretense of wanting to show him something. When they were alone, she'd leaned in like she was going to tell him a secret and had taken the kiss she'd been dreaming about for what had felt like forever. Dare hadn't hesitated, as if he'd been waiting to kiss *her*, too, and at the time she'd gotten lost in that fantasy, forgetting about those other girls and all the rumors she'd heard. They'd stumbled to his Chevelle out by the road and had practically dived into the back seat, steaming up the windows, *and each other*, as they made out like they'd never get enough. His kisses had consumed her, and the friction from his erection grinding against her had made her tingle and burn with desire. His hands had been all over her, but she'd wanted *more*. She'd been the one to unbutton her shorts, and she'd never forget the way their gazes had collided, white-hot lust brimming in his eyes, matching the way she'd felt. He'd claimed her mouth as eagerly and possessively as his hand had pushed into her panties and claimed the very heart of her. She shivered with the memory of his electrifying touch. He'd known *exactly* how to make her feel like the grand finale at a fireworks show, and to this day, no one had ever made her feel that good. She could still hear the hunger in his voice when he'd said, *I want your mouth on me*, still feel the excitement racing through her at his confession. She'd unzipped his jeans and had palmed his erection just as a knock on the car window had sounded, and Cowboy's angry voice had cut through her tipsy, lustful state. Dare had moved fast, blocking her from Cowboy's view as she'd fixed her shorts. As they'd climbed out of the car, reality had hit her like a slap in the face. She'd been about to become a notch on Dare's belt, and from the death stare Cowboy had given him, he'd known it, too.

And here I am, more than a decade later, and my stupid heart is still all wrapped up in the same man.

"She came out great, didn't she?"

Billie startled as he came up behind her, and she tried to push those memories away, but it was like pushing water through a sieve. "Yeah. She's beautiful."

He leaned in so close, she felt the heat of his chest against the back of her shoulder, her pulse quickening as he said, "We made some great memories in her, didn't we, Mancini?"

Are you talking about all the times the three of us went out in that car? Or the night I broke my own heart?

"Want to take her for a spin?" he asked tauntingly.

Her nerves flared, conflicting emotions whirling inside her like bees. She knew if she got in that car with him, those memories would consume her, and she'd want to feel his hands on her and the ferocity of his kisses, and she knew they would be even more powerful now that he was a man. How many times had she relived those moments, wishing she'd never turned him away, then remembering how he'd gone off with another girl minutes later and hating herself for even thinking about it? *That* was the danger of them. The danger of loving Dare Whiskey. There was no turning off those feelings.

"No thanks," she finally answered.

"Come on. You love driving fast."

I love a lot of things, but it doesn't mean I should go after them. "Maybe another time. I should probably..." She hiked a thumb toward the open bay door.

"Not yet, you shouldn't." He draped an arm around her shoulder. "I've got something in the back I think you'll want to see."

They went through a doorway that led directly into the familiar rustic log-cabin-style workshop. It still smelled like oil, lumber, and *man*. Several dirt bikes were lined up against the wall to their left, tools, helmets, and other safety equipment hanging on the walls behind them. There was a workbench and shelves to the right littered with tools, extra bike parts, and more safety equipment. A half wall separated the rear of the workshop from the front.

"This way." Dare took her hand, leading her toward the back.

She admired the bikes as they passed, the thrills of riding pecking at her like a crow to roadkill. Her fingers itched to grip the handlebars, but her brain waved neon red flags. She shifted her gaze away from the bikes and realized there were pictures of her, Dare, and Eddie hanging between the other things on the walls. She looked around and found pictures of them *everywhere*. As little kids riding skateboards, snowboarding, and straddling dirt bikes, leaning in to drape arms around each other, their bikes at precarious angles. Their youthful faces beamed at the camera. Eddie's hair poked out from beneath his helmet, hers trailed over her shoulders and down her back, and Dare's was hidden completely. She took in pictures of them as teenagers, of her on Dare's shoulders, wearing his cowboy hat and Bobbie on Eddie's shoulders, playing chicken in a lake, and of her and Dare cliff diving and skydiving. There was a picture of her and Dare skydiving, nearing the ground, their parachutes billowing behind them. Eddie stood tall, lean, and shaggy-haired a short distance away, videoing them. He always had tripods and extra video cameras with him. He was always the most prepared, and he took care of them, too, bringing snacks for Billie and water for Dare, who guzzled it like he was a camel.

Her throat thickened, and she looked across the room at pictures of her in full racing garb, catching air on her motocross bike and straddling the bike on a track, hair a tangled mess, her helmet resting on the center of the handlebars, arms crossed over it, and a massive grin on her face. Tears stung her eyes as she took in pictures of Dare BASE jumping and the three of them goofing off and making faces at the camera. Her gaze lingered on a blown-up and framed video-chat screenshot of her and Eddie cheek to cheek and Dare in the small box in the upper right. She remembered that call. She and Eddie had gone to California for a race during her pro tour, but Dare'd had to stay home and work. She'd won the race, and they'd called him right away. She missed the girl in those pictures who didn't wear guilt and anger like war paint.

Dare touched her back. "Are you okay?"

She realized she was staring at the pictures. "Where did you get all these? Some are from when you were away at school."

"I collected them over time. Every time I came home during school breaks, Eddie would give me a flash drive with all the pictures he'd taken. I've got more in the back."

She glanced over the half wall and found a dozen or more pictures on the walls, but her gaze was riveted to one of her sitting on Eddie's lap by a bonfire with Dare, Doc, and Birdie. It was taken a few weeks before Eddie's accident at a Dark Knights' barbecue at the ranch. She remembered that night because she'd known she'd needed to end things with Eddie, but she hadn't wanted to hurt him. He was looking at her like she was the light of his life, and she was looking at Dare like *he* was hers. She felt the walls closing in on her and reached for the partition to steady herself, her eyes trailing south to the area behind the half wall, where her old racing bike was parked, apple red and shiny as new, MANCINI painted down the forks in black.

Her chest constricted. "How did you get my bike? I told my dad to get rid of it."

"I asked him for it. I've got your equipment, too. I thought you might want it one day."

Her mind reeled, conflicting emotions pummeling her. "Well, I *don't*." She hurried out of the shop but heard him coming after her.

"Billie, *wait*."

She spun around, unable to stop her emotions from spewing out. "Why did you have to do that? You make everything so much harder!"

"What are you talking about?"

"Those pictures, the bike, the park, the way you show up at my work at closing time after guys are jerks."

Confusion riddled his brow. "I care about you, and as for showing up, I just want to keep you safe."

"I *know*." She threw her arms up and paced. "Damn it, Dare. I have been a dick to you for years, and you're *still* here, coming around, being the good guy."

"I'm *not* trying to be the good guy, Billie," he said vehemently.

"No shit! *That's* the problem. All you have to do is be *you*, and I lose my mind. I can't fucking get you out of my head."

He stepped into her path. "Why do you want to? What have I done that's so fucking unforgivable?"

Tears welled in her eyes, years of hurt and anger roiling inside her like a volcano ready to blow. "You make it *impossible* to love anyone else, and Eddie didn't deserve that. He was *such* a good person, and I tried. *God*, how I tried to love him with everything I had, and I *did* love him. But no matter how hard I tried, I couldn't get *you* out of my head. You were always there, reminding me that something was missing. I never would have even *known* something was missing if not for you."

DARE TRIED TO make sense of what Billie had said, but it sounded a hell of a lot like she was blaming him for her not loving Eddie.

She started pacing again, and he grabbed her wrist, stopping her. "I *never* tried to come between you and Eddie until you accepted his proposal, and I *only* said something because I didn't want to see you make the biggest mistake of your life. But you told me the other day that you had *already* broken up with him, so why are you blaming me?"

"Don't you *get* it?" she seethed. "I broke up with him because my stupid heart has always wanted *you.*"

He tightened his grip on her wrist, her words clawing their way through his chest, and spoke through gritted teeth. "Define *always,* because the one time we were together, you booted my ass to the curb pretty damn fast."

"I didn't want to be a notch on your belt! And you didn't even fight for me, so don't pretend that's not what I would have been. You wasted no time finding another girl to hook up with that night."

"What the hell are you talking about? I *told* you I wasn't done with you, and you made it crystal clear that what I wanted didn't matter, because *you* were done with *me*. I was an eighteen-year-old kid who had *finally* gotten the *only* girl I ever really wanted, because I couldn't try to get with you before that. Eddie and I had made a pact that neither of us would make a move on you, but if you made the move, we could go all in. And *you*, Billie, my best friend in the entire fucking world, *used* me and threw me away. So you're damn right I found someone else to be with that night, because you crushed me, and it was either that or...I don't know what I would've done, but it wouldn't have been good."

She shook her head. "A *pact?*"

"*Yes*, and it was the stupidest thing I've ever done."

"You can say that again," she snapped. "Did it ever occur to you two idiots that I could make up my own mind about who I wanted to be with?"

"I don't fucking *know*. That was forever ago, and we were trying not to hate each other for both being into you. I wanted to fight him for you, but he didn't want any part of that. Why do you think I went off the deep end after that night? Because in my head you were *mine*, but you didn't want me, and I didn't have a *clue* how to handle that."

"I *did* want you. I just didn't want it to mean nothing to you."

"How could the first person I think of when I wake up, the pain-in-my-ass challenging girl who's just as crazy as I am, the girl I've been fantasizing about since the day I realized that what's up here"—he tapped his head—"translates into some awesome feelings down there"—he eyed his crotch—"mean nothing to me?"

She laughed softly and shook her head.

"I've been in love with you since we were six years old, when you kissed me in the barn and called me a dummy. It's *always* been you, Billie, and I have no fucking idea why we're arguing, but I'm *done* wasting time." He tugged her into his arms and crushed his mouth to hers, urgent and possessive, hoping she wouldn't pull away or clock him in the jaw again.

She was right there with him, clutching his shirt, rising onto her toes, kissing him feverishly, unleashing years of repressed desire. Their tongues battled for dominance, just as they had years ago. Her fierceness was so damn hot, he'd wondered if he'd embellished it in his memory, but every swipe of her tongue made him ache for more. He backed her up against the Chevelle, their bodies grinding together as he fisted one hand in her hair, angling her mouth beneath his, taking the kiss deeper. Her mouth was sweet and hot and so damn perfect, he wanted to kiss her forever. She moaned and arched, rubbing her soft curves against him. He wanted to touch all of her at once, his hands moving down her hips, over her breasts, earning more sinful sounds as he pushed his hand beneath her shirt, needing to feel her hot flesh.

He unclasped her bra and tore his mouth away as he tugged up her shirt, growling, "I need my mouth on you."

Flames flickered in her eyes. "*I* need your mouth on me."

God, he fucking loved that. He teased her nipple with his tongue and teeth, and she grabbed his head, holding him there as he sucked and licked, earning one addicting sound after another. He wanted to OD on those seductive sounds. When he tugged open her shorts, *she* pushed them down. *So damn hot.* He sucked her nipple to the roof of his mouth as his fingers slid into her tight heat. She gasped, and her head fell back, so sexy and trusting. He lavished her other breast with the same attention, grazing his teeth over the taut peak as she rode his fingers, and he teased her clit with his thumb, earning sharp, pleasure-filled inhalations. She clung to him, moaning and panting, her every sound making him ache to be inside her. Her legs tensed, and he quickened his pace, her fingers digging into him as her orgasm took hold, and she cried out his name, her body pulsing around his fingers. He rose up and captured her cries in another demanding kiss as she rode out her climax.

He slowed them down, kissing her softer, and gazed into her eyes. "Catch your breath, darlin', because we're not nearly done."

He dropped to one knee, removing her sneakers and socks, and stripped her bare from the waist down. He took his time kissing his way up her trembling legs. Her skin was silky, warm, and so damn sweet, when he reached her upper thigh, her glistening sex there for the taking, he kissed all around those sensitive lips. She writhed and moaned.

"Lick me," she panted out.

He slicked his tongue along her wetness, taking his first taste of her, and holy hell. She was sweeter than honey, more addicting than life itself. Fighting the urge to devour her, he tore off her shirt and bra and lifted her onto the hood of the shiny black Chevelle. His gaze moved slowly over her, drinking her in. She wore only that sexy black choker. Her hair tumbled over her breasts. Her skin was flushed, lips swollen from their rough kisses, nipples pink from his teeth. His gaze traveled lower to the slick sexiness between her legs. "Fuck, baby. You're even more gorgeous than I imagined."

Her lips tipped up. "What're you going to do with me now that you have me here?"

"Whatever the hell I want." He ran his hands up her thighs and squeezed, his cock twitching behind his zipper.

She reached for his belt, but he moved her hands to his chest.

"Not yet, darlin'. I'm still *hungry*." He spread his hands on her upper thighs, teasing her sex with his thumbs, one at her center, the other on that magical bundle of nerves that had her chest heaving with her ragged inhalations.

"*Dare*," she pleaded, arching toward him.

"I've waited a lifetime to do this to you *right here*, and I'm *not* going to rush." His mouth came slowly down over hers, kissing her sensually, still teasing her down below, adding more pressure where she needed it most as he intensified their kisses. Building her up until she was shaking with need. Then he bit her lower lip, tugging as he drew back.

"Get back here." She grabbed his shirt, yanking him into another passionate kiss.

He'd never been with a woman who could turn him on the way she could with nothing more than her take-what-I-want attitude and that smart mouth of hers.

He kissed his way down her neck, over the swell of her breasts, slowing to tease her nipples. She clung to his arms, alluring sounds sailing from her lips as he kissed, licked, and sucked his way down her body. She leaned back on her palms as he grabbed her hips, nipping at one, then kissing a path to the other, and hauled her to the edge of the hood. She went down on her elbows as he spread her legs wide and buried his mouth between them.

"Holy…Oh God…Don't stop." She clawed at the hood of the car.

She tasted sweet, salty, and so fucking good, he couldn't get enough. He spread her legs wider, licking, *sucking*, and taking his fill. He grazed his teeth over her clit, and she bowed off the hood. He slicked his tongue along her sex, bringing his fingers into play as he feasted on her, earning one plea after another. She writhed against his mouth, clinging to the hood of the car as he took her right up to the edge, then slowed his efforts, leaving her whimpering and begging for more. He knew he'd hear those pleas in his dreams and gave her what she needed. He pushed his fingers into her tight heat and brought his mouth to her clit, working her into a moaning, rocking frenzy. His name flew from her lips like a prayer as she surrendered all restraint, hips bucking, sex clenching as her orgasm ravaged her. He stayed with her, savoring every pulse of her body, every moan and rock of her hips. When she collapsed onto her back, he came down over her, cradling her in his arms, and kissed her breathless.

"*Jesus, Dare,*" she panted out. "You need to patent your mouth."

He laughed. "Wait until you ride my dick. Come on, darlin'. We're going inside for this ride."

She pressed her hand to her chest. "Give me a second. My legs aren't working yet."

"When I'm done with you, you won't remember how to talk, either." He lifted her into his arms, guiding her legs around his waist, and headed out of the garage.

"*Dare.* I can walk."

"How about putting that mouth to better use."

Her lips came hungrily down to his as he carried her into his rustic, three-bedroom cabin, across the scuffed and worn floors into his bedroom. He tore the blanket down to the foot of the bed and lowered them to the sheets. Their mouths fused together, teeth gnashing, tongues battling, bodies grinding, desire pulsing in the air around them. He needed to get undressed, but he didn't want to miss a second of kissing and touching her. Every swipe of their tongues drove his need deeper. Every sensual noise stoked the inferno inside him. When he finally broke the kiss, she pulled him back for more. He'd always known they'd be explosive together, but *this...*

Real life was far better than fantasy.

"I need to be inside you," he said between ravenous kisses.

"You need to *strip* for me." Her eyes narrowed. "I want to see that bar dance up close and personal."

"I've got you, baby." He pushed from the mattress, took off his shoes and socks, and pulled his wallet from his back pocket, tossing it on the nightstand. Then he queued up a playlist on his phone that started with "You Can Leave Your Hat On" by Joe Cocker and put his phone by his wallet. His hips rocked to the beat as he pulled off his shirt and swung it around over his head.

"*Woo-hoo!*" Billie sat up in all her naked glory, swaying her shoulders to the music as he tossed his shirt to the floor.

He tugged her up to her feet, and their eyes locked—and *smoldered.* He took her hand and put it on the button of his shorts, thrusting slowly as she opened and unzipped them. He moved her hands to his ass, gathering her against him, their hips moving in perfect sync as their mouths came together in a deep, passionate kiss. His hands slid down to her ass, and he held on tight, earning more sensual, eager sounds. He pushed his fingers between her legs, intensifying their kisses as his fingers entered her slick center. Her forehead fell to his chest with a sigh, her shoulders and hips still moving to the beat. So fucking sexy.

"Get your mouth back here," he growled.

She lifted her head, and her eyes flamed. She kissed him *hard* as he teased and taunted, masterfully sending her careening over the edge of ecstasy again. He held her mouth to his, her inner muscles clenching around his fingers. His cock throbbed with anticipation. When their lips parted, she clung to him, panting, and rested her forehead on his chest again. He'd wanted her to open up to him for so long, he could hardly believe they were finally here. He lifted her chin, kissing her softly, and held her there to watch as he brought his glistening fingers to his mouth and sucked them clean. "*Mm-mm.* So damn sweet. I just found my new favorite treat."

He kissed her again, and he didn't miss a beat, going right back into his striptease as "Somethin' Bad" by Miranda Lambert and Carrie Underwood began playing. Billie stayed with him, dirty dancing as he stepped out of his shorts and boxer briefs and kicked them across the room. She eyed his cock hungrily, her eyes widening.

"Damn, Whiskey. I thought I'd imagined that glorious creature." She grabbed his hips, kissing her way south.

Fuck yeah.

Her lips were soft and warm as they trailed down his abs, and she fisted his cock. His chin dropped to his chest, and her eyes flicked up to his, holding as much challenge as desire. He threaded his fingers into her hair as she dragged her tongue along his shaft. *Fucking heaven.* She licked around the broad head and wasted no time taking his cock into her mouth, working it tight and fast. He was big and thick, and women usually toyed with the head and maybe a few inches. Billie took him to the back of her throat, and his hips thrust involuntarily.

Her gaze flicked up again, a warning blazing in them.

"Sorry, darlin'." He gritted out, "You just feel so damn good."

She smiled around his cock and quickened her efforts, working him with her hand and mouth in quick, tight, *deep* strokes, taking him right up to the edge of madness. He clenched his jaw to stave off his orgasm, and she slowed her pace, licking and sucking, until he held on to his sanity by a fast-fraying thread. His fists tightened in her hair, and he couldn't help pumping his hips, but she didn't complain. She opened her mouth wider, taking him impossibly deeper.

"*Christ*, baby."

Her mouth was as soft as velvet and as hot as fire, but as much as he wanted to brand her from the inside out, he needed to feel her wrapped around him, and he needed it *now*. He hauled her up to her feet, taking her in a punishingly intense kiss, and lowered them both to the bed. He got lost in her mouth, kissing her rough and hungry, his cock rubbing against her wetness. *Fuck.* They were pure fucking magic. He reared up on his knees to snag a condom from his wallet, but he couldn't resist making her come one more time. He slid his fingers along her sex and brought them to her clit.

She writhed. *"Whiskey."*

"I hear your warning, darlin', but you're not driving this train. Touch yourself."

That warning turned to daggers, and her hand moved between her legs. "Touch *yourself.*"

God, he loved her. "Already planning on it." He rubbed his hand along her sex, getting it wet, and fisted his cock, giving it a few slow strokes. Her eyes widened, then narrowed, and she licked her lips. *Oh yeah, baby, our possibilities are endless.* He continued stroking himself and used his other hand on her. She worked her clit as he found that magical spot inside her that had her hips rising off the mattress and needful sounds spilling from her lips. When she spiraled over the edge, he squeezed the base of his cock to ward off his release. She moaned, trying to press her legs together, but his fingers were still inside her, reveling in her greedy aftershocks.

"Jesus, baby. I could come just watching you come." He withdrew from between her legs and came down over her, gazing into her lust-drunk eyes as he painted her arousal on her lower lip. He dragged his tongue along it and sucked it into his mouth, savoring her taste before reclaiming her mouth in another fiery kiss. When he couldn't take it a second longer, he snagged a condom from his wallet, tore it open with his teeth, and sheathed his length.

She reached for him, and he laced their fingers together,

pinning her hands on either side of her head. There was such a mix of emotions looking back at him, he answered all her unasked questions. "You're mine now, Mancini."

"For *tonight*, anyway," she said sassily.

He'd expected nothing less from the girl who hated to talk about her feelings, doing her best to remain in control. "Stop lying to yourself, Wildfire."

He held her gaze as their bodies came together, slowly and so damn perfectly, her eyes widened with pleasure. When he was buried to the hilt, her inner muscles tightened like a vise. "*Jesus*, Billie. Why did we wait so long to do this?"

"Shut up and kiss me."

Their kisses were rough and greedy as they found their rhythm. But he wasn't ready to let loose. She felt too good, and he loved driving her out of her mind. He thrust in deep, withdrawing excruciatingly slowly, wanting her to feel every inch as he stroked that hidden spot inside her that brought her knees up and sent her heels digging into the mattress. He continued the torturous pace, clenching his teeth against the mounting pressure inside him. He gyrated his hips, and her fingernails dug into the backs of his hands.

"*Dare*" came out as a plea, but it was followed by a demand—"*Faster*"—cutting through his restraint. He released her hands, and there was no holding back, no finesse or easing into a new rhythm. They pawed and clawed, devouring each other as their bodies took over. She wrapped her legs around him, and he shoved a pillow under her hips, taking her deeper, thrusting faster, harder, her pleasure-filled cries searing through him like lightning.

"*Don't stop*," she demanded.

He slanted his mouth over hers, his tongue thrusting to the

same rhythm as his hips. Her fingernails cut so deep, he was sure she was drawing blood, but he'd proudly wear those scars. Need pounded through his veins, and he lost himself in the taste of her mouth, the feel of her wrapped around him, and the sinful sounds of their bodies rocking and grinding.

She was a temptress, a goddess, and she was finally *his*.

He thrust faster, pounded deeper, *harder*, kissing her ravenously. She returned his efforts feverishly. Her legs tightened around him, and with the next thrust, she cried out into their kisses, her body clenching around his cock so exquisitely, he buried his face in the crook of her neck, surrendering to his own explosive release.

He lay holding her as the last tremors rumbled through them, and their breathing calmed. Billie's eyes were closed, and he'd never seen her look more peaceful. There was no fight left in the woman beneath him. No anger, no challenge, just his best friend. Only now they were finally *more*.

He kissed her cheek, the edge of her mouth, and brushed his lips over hers. "Still with me, darlin'?"

A long, sated sigh left her lips.

He couldn't resist teasing her. "No words? My job here is done."

Her eyes opened, and a devilish grin appeared. "Dream on, Whiskey. Once you recharge, it's *my* turn."

Chapter Seven

BILLIE AWOKE TO the scent of sex and man and something hard against her ass cheek. It took her fuzzy brain a minute to realize it was Dare's erection. His big body was wrapped around her like a mating snake. Memories of their amazing day—and insatiable night—came rushing in, bowling her over like a freight train. In *one* day, he'd reawakened the thrill seeker in her. She felt that piece of herself clawing its way toward the surface like a hungry beast, bringing rise to trepidation she didn't want to think about. But the only other place for her mind to go was to how incredible it felt to be in Dare's arms, their bodies tangled together in the throes of passion. She closed her eyes, seeing the unforgettable look in his when he'd said, *Jesus, Billie. Why did we wait so long to do this?*

A web of guilt engulfed her as their confessions rose to the surface. How could she have admitted all her darkest secrets to him *and* slept with him? Why *now*, after all this time? He didn't even have to *try*, and he'd stripped her of her defenses, obliterating her ability to keep him at arm's length. She *never* did things like this. She'd thought she'd severed her impulsiveness. How did she go from riding roller coasters to riding *him*?

Shit. Shitshitshit.

She couldn't even blame it on alcohol this time. They'd both been stone-cold sober. She squeezed her eyes shut against her confusion, but it didn't help, so she opened her eyes and revisited the things they'd said. He and Eddie had made a pact? He thought she hadn't wanted him? He *loved* her? Dare's voice whispered through her mind, as if he'd heard that question. *I've been in love with you since we were six years old, when you kissed me in the barn and called me a dummy. It's always been you, Billie.*

She rested her head back against his chest, filling with a new type of happiness she'd never felt before. *You love me.*

But they'd wasted so much time. *She'd* wasted so much time. She'd hurt Dare all those years ago, and she'd hurt Eddie by loving Dare. More guilt piled onto her already confused heart.

It was all too much. She needed space to breathe and think.

She tried to slip out from beneath his arm, but he tightened his hold on her. His scruff brushed her cheek, sending tantalizing sensations skittering along her flesh. Her neediest parts clenched with anticipation. *Down, girl.*

"Where do you think you're going?" he asked huskily, sleepily, and all too sexily.

Straight to hell for being a hoochie mama. She glanced at the clock. It was only 4:03. Where did he think she was going? "To the bathroom."

He kissed her neck, grinding against her butt. "*Mm.* Come back and get some rest. You need to power up. I'm not nearly done with you."

Her heart skipped and her body cheered, but she tried to rein that in as he lifted his arm and rolled onto his back. She hurried into the bathroom, catching a glimpse of herself in the mirror as she closed the door. Her hair was a tangled mess, her eyes were puffy, and she had bite marks on the swell of her breast and at the base of her neck. Why, oh why, did that get her all revved up? She tried to remember where her clothes were, and her eyes flew open wider. *The garage. Nonono. One night with Dare and I let him spread me out like a buffet on the hood of his car.* She never did things like *that*, either.

Then again, she'd never been with someone like Dare, who made her feel as animalistic as he was. She clenched her mouth shut. Dare hadn't just brought out the risk seeker in her. His magic tongue had scrambled her senses!

She leaned her palms on the sink, glaring at herself in the mirror, whispering, "What is *wrong* with you?" Apparently *everything*, because the sex kitten on her shoulder was purring, *But it felt so good*, while the guilt-laden girl rooted in her brain was chastising her for sleeping with Dare. She used the toilet and washed her hands, eyes trained on the sink because she was unable to look at herself for another second.

She opened the door as quietly as she could and found Dare fast asleep on his back. One beautifully sculpted, tattooed arm rested on his forehead, his other lay across the side of the bed where she'd slept, as if he were waiting for her. She knew he was, and that set those butterflies free again. Moonlight shimmered across his tatted neck and broad chest. Her gaze slid lower, and heat flared in her chest with the memory of how good it had felt to kiss her way down those rippled abs and trace the ink flanking them with her tongue to that wickedness tenting the sheets. The man was a master at loving her body. She'd never come so hard or so many times in her life. The urge to climb across the bed and ride him like a bronco was stronger than her need to breathe. But if one night with Dare swamped her with this much emotion, staying would only lead to trouble. He'd gone from being a tsunami who bullied her into his waves to sneaking up like a quiet storm, lulling her in with gentler winds, effortlessly gaining force until she was so wrapped up in him, she could think of nothing else.

She didn't move, taking one last look at his handsome face and the lips she wanted to kiss forever. The energy in the room shifted from trepidation and guilt to longing for what she hoped might be one day.

But today wasn't that day, because this new Dare, with all his goodness, was even more dangerous than the one she'd known by heart. This Dare liked to talk, and she knew he'd want to delve deeper into their confessions.

There was only so much guilt and confusion a woman could take.

I'm sorry, Dare.

She tiptoed over to his shirt, which dangled from a lampshade on the dresser where he'd tossed it during his delicious striptease. As she slipped it on, she noticed a picture on the other side of the dresser of her, Dare, and Eddie when they were kids. It was taken from behind, and they were sitting on a fence watching horses. Eddie was to her left, and Dare was to her right. She was wearing Dare's cowboy hat, and his arm was around her. Her hands were on the fence, and Eddie's hand covered one of hers. DAREDEVILS was scrawled across the sky in kidlike writing. Dare must have written it when they were young. A lump lodged in her throat.

Dare turned onto his side, reminding her of her escape. She dropped to the floor and crawled over to his shorts, quietly digging his key ring out of his pocket, then tiptoed out of the bedroom. She gave the living room a cursory glance. Gone was the cheap furniture he'd used right after college, replaced with leather couches, wooden bookshelves, and rustic coffee and end tables. It was very masculine. Very *Dare*. She slipped out the door and ran into the garage for her shoes and clothes. She pulled on her shorts and carried the rest to his truck, wincing as she started it up, hoping not to wake him, because *that* was another conversation she didn't want to have.

As she drove away from his cabin, she looked out at the pastures, remembering all the times the three of them had sat on the fences talking about their next big thrill, what they were doing that weekend, or what they'd be when they grew up. She was going to be the best female motocross racer the world had ever seen, Eddie was going to be a visionary filmmaker, and Dare had always wanted to work with the people who came through the ranch therapeutic programs. Well, that *and* defy death more times than Evel Knievel.

That was another thing she needed to figure out. Dare would always be an extreme thrill seeker. Could she be with someone who tempted fate every chance he got?

DARE FELT LIKE he'd been asleep for a month. He couldn't remember the last time he'd slept so hard. Smiling at the reason, he opened his eyes to see his beautiful girl. Billie wasn't lying next to him. He rolled over to look at the bathroom, but the door was open and the light was off. He climbed out of bed and stretched as he headed out of the bedroom. His gaze moved over the empty living room, dining room, and kitchen.

What the hell, Mancini?

He opened the front door to see if she was on the porch. His truck was gone. *Fuck.* "My truck? *Really?*"

This was not what he'd expected.

He stalked inside, realizing he *should* have expected it. Billie had never liked talking about her feelings, and between all the things they'd admitted yesterday and their amazing sexcapades, she was probably halfway to...

He gritted out a curse and strode into the bathroom to shower. He had no idea where she went when she was mad anymore. Well, *hell*, that pissed him off.

Twenty minutes later he pulled up in front of the main house and climbed off his motorcycle, chewing on his anger. *Fuck.* It wasn't just anger. It was hurt, disappointment, and a whole bunch of other shit he didn't want to think about.

He blew through the front doors, thankful that Kenny was starting his regular schedule today, working with Cowboy after breakfast and meeting with Dare later in the afternoon.

His father was sitting at the table with Sasha, Doc, Cowboy, Simone, Kenny—who was eating breakfast this time, thankfully—Hyde, Ezra, a number of other ranch hands, and the men and women who were currently going through the program.

Cowboy and their mother walked in from the kitchen. His mother was carrying a basket of biscuits, and Dare snagged one.

"Mornin'," he grumbled.

"Look who the cat dragged in." Cowboy lifted his chin in Dare's direction. "Who'd you piss off?"

Dare took a bite of the biscuit. "What are you talking about?"

"I think he means the bruise on your cheek," Sasha said. "It looks like you got in a fight."

Shit, he hadn't even noticed it. "It's nothing. I need someone to give me a ride to get my truck."

"You left your truck somewhere? How'd you get home?" Doc asked.

"I drove my truck home, but someone took it." He wasn't about to tell them who and listen to them give him shit about Billie stealing his truck.

Kenny threw his hands up. "It wasn't me. I swear it."

Dare smiled. "I know. Don't worry. Hey, Doc, can you spare a few minutes to give me a ride?"

"I can, honey," his mother said. "I've already eaten, and I'm on my way into town anyway."

Great. He didn't really want his mother to know who had stolen his truck, but he needed the ride. "Thanks, Mom."

"Do you know who stole your truck?" his father asked.

"Yes, I do."

His father grinned. "What's the sweetheart's name?"

Chuckles rang out around the table.

"A *girl* stole your truck?" Kenny asked.

"She's got big ones to steal your truck," Sasha said.

"She must be one hell of a woman to have laid you out so bad you didn't wake up when she left." Hyde eyed Dare. "I'll take her number."

Dare glowered at him and then at their father. "Thanks, old man." His father laughed, and Dare shook his head. "Mom, are you ready to get out of here?"

"I think that's a good idea." His mother patted Kenny's shoulder. "I hope you have a great morning working with Cowboy. I put a hat with your boots to keep the sun off your face."

When Kenny remained silent, their father said, "Son, that's

my wife speaking to you. She went out of her way to make sure you were taken care of, and I'd like you to show her some respect."

Kenny looked at Wynnie, his expression hovering somewhere between reluctance and regret. "Thank you."

"You're welcome, honey. I hope everyone has a great morning." As his mother walked around the table to his father, there was a round of *You too*.

Dare was glad to hear Kenny's voice in the mix.

"I left a few contracts on your desk for you to look over." His mother ran her hand over their father's shoulder and kissed his cheek.

"You've got it, darlin'. Drive safe." He peered around her at Dare. "Anything in that truck or on your key chain we need to worry about? Do we need to change any locks?"

"No, Pop. She's not a hardened criminal. She just took my truck," Dare said.

"In the state of Colorado, that's a felony," Kenny reminded him.

Another round of chuckles rang out, and his mother gave him the *from the mouth of babes* look she'd seen him give his father a million times.

"Maybe you should bring her to the ranch and teach her a lesson," Kenny suggested.

"I'm planning on it," Dare said, and followed his mother out the door.

Once they were in the parking lot, she said, "You want to talk about it?"

"I'd rather gouge my eyes out with a spoon."

"Oh, honey. Don't be so dramatic." They climbed into the car. "Where did you take off to yesterday? We missed you at dinner."

"Out with a friend."

"The same friend who stole your truck?" she asked with more than a hint of amusement.

He took off his hat and scrubbed a hand down his face, jaw clenching.

She smiled coyly. "Want to tell me where I'm taking you?"

"Billie's house."

Her brows shot up.

"I took her to the thrill park, and one thing led to another."

Her expression turned thoughtful. "And she snuck out while you were still asleep?"

"That's about the size of it, I guess."

"I'm sorry, honey. That hurts, doesn't it?"

"It's definitely not a cause for celebration."

She reached over and gently squeezed his forearm. "Sweet darlin', you know dealing with emotions has never been easy for Billie, and I think she's been running from her feelings for you since you were kids. Maybe you should give her a little time before you go in demanding answers."

"What makes you think she's been into me for so long?"

"Mothers know these things. The same way I know seeing her with Eddie tore you up inside."

His jaw clenched. He and his mother had talked many times about Eddie's death and Billie shutting him out of her life, but he'd never told her about his real feelings for Billie.

"I loved Eddie. You *know* that. I wanted him to be happy." He looked out the window. "Just not with my girl."

"She wasn't your girl, sweetheart, and please don't think I'm minimizing your loss when I say this, but while you lost one of your nearest and dearest friends, Billie lost a best friend *and* a lover. It's more complicated for her."

"I know. I get it," he said too sharply. "I wish you could have talked to her after Eddie's accident. I wish *someone* could have gotten through to her."

"We all wish that would have been the case. You weren't the only one begging me to talk to her back then. Alice is one of my closest friends. She and Manny would have given anything to see Billie open up to someone. I can't tell you how many times Bobbie came to me asking the same thing. I tried *so* many times, and I know you did, too."

"I never stopped."

"Clearly." She smiled as she turned down Billie's street. "You and Billie are cut from the same cloth. When you went through that rebellious stage in college, you wouldn't listen or talk to anyone, either."

She pulled up to the curb behind Dare's truck, and his chest constricted, thinking of Billie wanting to take off so badly, she'd snuck out. "Thanks for the ride."

As he opened the door, his mother touched his hand. "Dare, go easy on her. It took a long time for you to figure out *how* to take a step back from your feelings and try to understand them. Considering that Billie let you back into her life, even if for only a night, she might be standing on a pretty scary precipice right now. She needs you to help her figure out how to climb down, not scare her into jumping."

He'd lost Billie as a teenager by taking her at her word, and he'd spent the last few years letting her try to figure things out on her own. If he'd learned one thing from her confessions, it was that Billie Mancini's heart was at risk of drowning in a sea of guilt and love—because of him *and* for him. There was no way he'd let her try to find her way to the surface on her own.

But his mother didn't need to hear that. He nodded curtly and headed up to the house to set things straight.

The door was ajar, and when he knocked, it opened. Bobbie looked over from where she sat at the kitchen table in a pretty floral dress, hair and makeup freshly done. She'd probably be leaving soon for work, which suited him just fine.

"Hey, Dare." Bobbie's gaze darted across the kitchen.

He knew by her pinched expression and the slight shake of her head that she and Billie were doing that secret girl-talk thing they did. He strode into the house and found Billie standing with her butt against the counter, holding a bowl of cereal. She froze with the spoon midway to her mouth. She was wearing *his* T-shirt. Her legs were bare, one foot resting on the other, one knee slightly bent. He'd kissed every inch of those gorgeous legs last night, and he could still feel them wrapped around him as he was buried deep inside her.

Fuck. That didn't help his state of mind.

"Nice shirt, Mancini. Did you get it from the same place you ripped off that truck out front?"

Bobbie stifled a laugh.

Billie's eyes narrowed. "I *borrowed* your truck."

"I think I'd better get to work." Bobbie put her plate in the sink and grabbed a tote bag from the counter. "Unless you need a referee?"

Billie glowered, and Bobbie held up her hands. "Just asking. I wouldn't want Dare to end up with a shiner this time." She giggled as she left the house.

"What the *hell*, Billie? After everything we said to each other, everything we *did* to each other, you sneak out like I'm nothing but a cheap date?" He closed the distance between them, his heart refusing to be silenced. "You're finally *mine*,

Mancini, and I know you've got a lot of shit going on in that beautiful head of yours because of me, or us, but I'm not going to let you run from us anymore."

She lifted her chin, stormy, *pained* eyes glaring at him. "Just because we had sex doesn't mean you *own* me."

"I don't *want* to own you, but I sure as hell don't want to lose you again, so at least clue me in and tell me why you took off."

"Because keeping you at a distance kept everything I didn't want to think about at bay," she said angrily, setting down her bowl. "Being with you was amazing, and I wanted it as bad as you did, but now everything we did and said is *right there*"—she splayed her hand by her face—"front and center in my mind."

"I don't see how that's bad, darlin'." He put his hands on her hips, feeling the tension rippling through her. "We both want this."

"I know, but I *hurt* Eddie because I wanted it."

"And that's a hell of a thing to try to deal with on your own."

She looked away, and he knew she was picking through the attic of her brain, gathering guilt like parents gathered keepsakes. He needed to get her mind back to the present and went for levity.

"I know you don't want to talk about it, but let's give it some perspective. You were young, and you were trying to convince yourself *not* to want all this." He stepped back and motioned to his body, just to earn a smile, which he did, if only for a few seconds. He drew her into his arms and gazed into those troubled eyes. "Seriously, Mancini. Eddie would have wanted us to be happy."

She shook her head. "He was so mad when I broke up with

him. He said, 'It's Dare, isn't it? It's always been him.'" She shrugged half-heartedly. "What am I supposed to do with *that*? I never got a chance to explain it to him."

The pain in her voice brought his arms around her. He held her close, his heart aching for her and for Eddie. "Don't you see, darlin'? That means he saw what we were too stupid and stubborn to admit."

"Exactly."

"Baby, that doesn't mean it was a death sentence for him or a means for penance for you, but it is a hell of a weight for you to carry around."

She lowered her eyes.

"Look at me, darlin'." Her sadness sliced through him. "We knew Eddie better than anyone. He was a grounded, rational thinker, and I have no doubt that if he'd lived, we'd have had it out, and we would have come out the other side just as tight as we were before. It might have taken some time for the sting to wear off, but there's no stronger bond than the one the three of us shared."

"I want to believe that."

"Well, that's a start. You know he didn't set out to kill himself, don't you?"

She nodded. "I know. He would never do that."

"Good, because he'd never purposely hurt anyone, and I think he'd have a really hard time knowing you've been torturing yourself for all these years."

"I think about that a lot," she said softly.

"You can be sure of it. He hated when you were sad or mad."

She smiled a little. "He did, didn't he?"

He was so glad to see her smiling, it made him smile, too.

"Remember that time you got detention and he went with you?"

"Yes. You got pissed off that neither of us sat with you when you got detention." She laughed softly. "You were always so competitive."

"Says the woman who never backed down from a challenge. I think the best thing we can do to honor Eddie is live our lives to the fullest. He'd want that, and he'd have a hell of a lot to say about you giving up motocross. He was so damn proud of you. We both were. I still am."

"He was my biggest cheerleader when you were away at school, and I was his, doing whatever he asked for his videos and cheering him on as he talked about the *unforgettable* movie he always wanted to make. Before every race, he'd say 'What are you waiting for, Billie? Get out there and show the world what you've got,' as if I ever hesitated."

Emotions stacked up inside him. "He was a good man."

"Good ol' *Steady Eddie*." Sadness worked its way up her face. "He was always so safe and careful before that day."

"I think you've forgotten how many times he did stunts that were over his head because he was pissed at me or had a bug up his ass about something. Remember the time he was hell bent on doing a front flip on the snowboard?" Dare shook his head. "I thought that was going to end a whole lot worse than with a broken arm."

"Me too."

"So you can't blame yourself for his last stunt. Like I said before, guys do stupid shit for even stupider reasons. The thing you need to hold on to is that Eddie was an incredible friend, and you're an amazing woman. I'm glad he got to experience what it was like to be loved by you. Because I'm sure that was a hell of a lot better than anything else in this crazy world."

Her eyes dampened, and she pressed her lips together. "I can't talk about this right now."

"Okay." He hugged her and kissed the top of her head.

"Thanks for trying to help. I'm sorry I took off with your truck."

He squeezed her butt. "And my shirt."

"I'm keeping the shirt." She tipped her face up, and he was glad some of the shadows were gone. "I just need some space to work through this."

"I hear there are some pretty great therapists over at Redemption Ranch. I could probably hook you up with one."

"Thanks, but I'm not like you. I can't talk it all out."

"If you need to crawl into your shell to figure this out, that's okay. But know this. If you take too long, I'm crawling in after you." He lowered his lips to hers, wishing she'd ask him to stay and talk it all out, but that strong, stubborn streak ran deep in the pigtailed girl he'd fallen in love with, and it had only gotten more powerful in the years since. He didn't want to change her. He wanted to help her find peace, with or without him. But in his own stubborn heart, he knew that when that peace came, wild horses wouldn't be able to hold back the feelings he'd gotten more than a glimpse of last night.

"Next time take the Chevelle. It's almost as gorgeous as you." That earned a genuine smile. "Where are my keys, darlin'?"

She pointed to a bowl on the counter with both their key chains in it. He snagged his keys and took one last glance at the woman who was stronger than anyone he knew. She'd had to be to get through all these years while holding on to so much hurt.

"For the record, Mancini. You make it impossible to love anyone else, too."

Chapter Eight

BILLIE'S HEAVY FOOTFALLS competed with the chaos in her mind as she finished her run Friday morning and slowed to a walk at the end of the trail.

She headed for her truck, more irritated than when she'd set out. She'd gotten the crazy notion that Dare wouldn't give her space, but he didn't show up at the bar last night. She'd half expected, and maybe had even hoped, that he'd drop out of the sky again during her run, but no such luck. She should be thankful that he'd learned to back off, but she couldn't stop thinking about the things he'd said. She also couldn't stop thinking about kissing him and all the deliciously dirty things they'd done. When she was in his arms, the world had faded away, just like it had at the park. He'd always had the ability to make it feel like the two—or three—of them were the only people on earth, even when they were surrounded by dozens of others. But nothing compared to the way she'd disappeared into him Wednesday night.

She climbed into her truck, too keyed up to go home, and headed to the one place that always helped to clear her head. The Roadhouse.

When she pulled into the empty parking lot, she thought about how many times Dare had been there when she'd gotten off work, straddling his motorcycle or doing wheelies in the lot. He hadn't just been there for her as an adult. He'd shown up at closing time when she'd worked there as a teenager, too. She thought about what he'd said about the guys who had followed her home, and she realized he'd been looking out for her even when she hadn't known he was. That made her feel good.

She headed inside with his voice whispering in her ear. *I've been in love with you since we were six years old, when you kissed me in the barn and called me a dummy.*

She locked the door behind her and took a moment to look around the bar. Her grandfather had moved away and given her father the bar before she was born, and her parents had run it for as long as she could remember. She'd taken over managing it several years ago, but her father still kept the books, and her parents filled in when they were shorthanded and came in to hang out sometimes, but it was primarily Billie's domain.

In a way, it always had been. She could still see herself, Dare, and Eddie as little kids sitting up at the bar drinking sodas before they opened for the day, while her parents worked in the office or took a delivery in the back. They'd blast the jukebox and dance or sit on the mechanical bull and pretend to ride. She'd had the *best* childhood.

She sauntered over to the jukebox, thinking of all the times she'd dragged Dare and Eddie out on the dance floor when they were teenagers. Who knew that Dare would become such a great dancer? The man had moves that could make a stripper blush.

She put on "I Like It. I Love It," followed by a number of other songs they'd loved. As the song rang out, she closed her eyes, letting the music seep into her soul. She pictured the three of them as teenagers and let her body take over, moving as freely as she had back then, without a care about who saw her or what she looked like. Her heart thundered as she danced across the room, spinning around tables and shimmying into the ring with the mechanical bull. She ran her hand over the sleek leather saddle. *Man*, she loved riding that thing. She wasn't as good as Birdie, and she had no idea how someone so petite could ride so well, but she could hold her own. She'd given it up when she'd given up everything else that made her heart race. *Including Dare.*

She danced around the mechanical bull, belting out the lyrics of one song after another, trying to push past the emotions and memories she was wrestling with. She danced harder and sang louder, but they refused to budge. The song "Angel Eyes" by Love and Theft came on, bringing with it the image of Dare standing by the mechanical bull, egging her on. *This song's about you, Mancini. Get up there and show these lame cowboys how it's done.* She felt herself grinning, her old competitive streak blazing forth. She looked around, even though she knew she was alone, and hoisted herself onto the bull. Her legs squeezed without thought, and her upper body relaxed. She swayed to the beat of the music, but the draw was too strong. She threw her hand up and lifted her butt off the saddle, swinging her arm around as if she were riding, letting out a loud *"Woo-hoo!"*

"You want me to turn that thing on so you can go for a ride?"

Her head whipped to the side, and she saw her father walking over, his dark eyes smiling beneath his pitch-black brows. He must have come in the back door. He was wearing jeans, a button-down, and a hopeful expression. She scrambled off the bull, feeling a little embarrassed.

"Having a little party, Daredevil?"

Her heart squeezed. "You haven't called me that in forever."

"I haven't seen you on that bull in an awfully long time." He slung an arm around her, hugging her against his side and kissing her head. "It's nice to see you riding again."

"I wasn't *riding*." She went to turn down the jukebox. She loved her whole family, but she'd always been closest with her father. Her mother thought she was a wild child, and Bobbie was so even-keeled, half the time she didn't know what to make of her older sister. But her father just rolled with the punches. He understood the fire in her belly as much as he did her need for solitude. That didn't mean he liked the way she kept everyone at arm's length, especially these last few years, but at least he seemed to understand her need for it.

"You doing okay, sweet pea?"

"Yeah, just thinking."

"Most people blast music and get on the bull to *keep* from thinking." He went around the bar and opened the fridge beneath the counter. "It sounds to me like this is a root beer moment." He set two cans on the bar.

"Dad..." Root beer at the bar had always been their thing. When the cans came out, she knew she had his full attention, and he always seemed to know when those times were needed.

He nodded toward a stool. "Come on over here and talk to your old man." As she climbed onto a stool, he sat down beside her. "How was your run this morning?"

"Good but hard. I was tired."

"Not sleeping much?" He opened the soda cans and set one in front of her.

She shook her head and took a sip. It was funny how the combination of sitting with her father and the old familiar taste eased her tension.

"Anything I can do to help?"

"How good are you at untangling knots?" She could talk to him about anything, but she'd never told him the truth about what had gone down between her and Eddie on that fateful day. That had been her burden to carry alone…until Dare weaseled his way back into her life. Into her heart.

"Physical or emotional? With one daughter who insisted on learning every knot under the sun at eight years old and another who was always asking me to make impossible things, like hammocks for her dolls, I'd say I'm pretty darn good at the physical act. And, well, living with three females teaches a guy a thing or two about the emotional side, too." His expression turned serious. "What's going on with you, sweet pea?"

"*Dare*, that's what. When did he get so talkative?"

Her father chuckled. "It's been a while since you've spent time with him. He's been putting that education of his to good use for a while now and helping a lot of people. I take it he finally got your attention?"

"You could say that. We spent the day at Cliffside, and, Dad, he got me to go on the rides."

His face brightened. "Well, I'll be damned."

"I know, right? *Freaking* Dare."

"How'd he get you to go?"

"That's just it. I have *no* idea. One minute my guard was up and I was badass Billie, taking care of myself, and the next minute Dare was standing in my house telling me to get in his truck. And I *went*."

"Sounds like he got sick of you snubbing him, but you're a

strong girl, Billie. Some part of you must have wanted to go."

"I *did*. I've missed him."

"He's a good man, sweetheart. He's stuck by you through thick and thin, and I'm not just talking about these last several years. I'm surprised it took him this long. He has never liked to let you stew. I don't know if you remember this or not, but when you were eight, you got a bee in your bonnet and told him you didn't want to be his friend anymore because he called you a stupid girl."

"I don't remember that."

"Maybe because it didn't last long. That night he stole his daddy's ATV and drove over here. He used a pocketknife to rip a hole in your window screen and climbed into your bedroom. That boy woke you up and said he wasn't leaving until you were his friend again."

She laughed. "Wait, I *do* remember that, but I didn't re-member why he'd done it. He brought a backpack filled with Oreos, barbecue chips, and Capri Suns, right?" *Daredevil snacks.* Her favorite snack was Oreos, Dare's was barbecue chips, and Eddie's was Capri Suns. They'd lived on them, and their parents had always kept all three on hand.

"Sure did, and his favorite cowboy hat that you stole every chance you got. He said he'd give it to you if you'd be his friend again, even apologized for saying you were stupid."

"I remember that apology. He said he was sorry he called me stupid but that I'd always be a girl and there was nothing I could do about it." She smiled. "He was such a weirdo."

"Maybe so, but when you cut him and everyone off, that weirdo showed up every day, week after week, month after month, begging us to talk to you and convince you to talk to him. He said he'd do whatever it took. He'd work at the bar for free for the rest of his life if we could get you to talk to him. And you know Dare. I'm sure he'd have done it, too."

"Mom told me he came by, but she never told me he offered to work for free."

"I'm pretty sure he'd do anything to have you by his side. I still don't know how or why you broke that bond, but I figured that was your business, and you'd let me know if you ever wanted to talk about it."

Her chest ached at how many times her father had tried to get her to open up, but she'd been too broken. Or maybe too brokenhearted. "I hated keeping my distance from him, but I was afraid not to." She traced the letters on her soda can.

"What were you afraid of?"

Tears burned her eyes, and she didn't know where they came from. She took a drink, willing them away, and forced the difficult words from her lungs. "The truth coming out."

"Truth?" His brows slanted.

"There's a lot you don't know, Dad. I broke up with Eddie the day he died, and I did it because I had feelings for Dare. I didn't tell Eddie that. I just said I didn't love him the way I should in order to marry him. I tried to give the ring back, but he wouldn't take it, and he said…" She swiped at the tears that had broken free, trying to keep any more from falling. "'It's Dare, isn't it? It's always been Dare.' *That's* why he took off on the bike instead of just filming us like he'd planned. He was so angry, and then he was *gone*, and I never got to explain or say I was sorry. Dare and I got together after the park, and now I feel so guilty about being with him, I don't know what to do."

Her father stood and wrapped his arms around her, and in the safety of his arms, she gave in to the tears and the heartache that felt like it was lodged in her bones.

"Let it out, baby. It's okay."

"I'm awful, aren't I?"

"No, sweetheart."

She nodded against his chest. "Yes, I am."

He took her by the shoulders, his eyes as serious as she'd ever seen them. "Why on earth would you think that? Do you know how many people are married to spouses they don't love? If you'd married Eddie, *that* would have given me pause. But to be honest, Billie, I didn't expect you to accept his proposal, and neither did he." He handed her a napkin to wipe her eyes, and they sat back down.

"You knew he was going to propose?" She didn't wait for an answer. "What did you mean *he* didn't think I'd accept? And if *you* didn't think I'd accept, why'd you let him ask?"

"I didn't think he'd go through with it. I thought he'd man up and end things with you."

"*Man up and end things?* Was he unhappy?" How could he have been unhappy and she not know?

"No, he wasn't unhappy. He was confused. He came to see me a few days before he proposed. His love for you was big, baby, and he knew you loved him, so don't ever question that. But he also knew it wasn't as fiercely as he loved you. I suggested you two take a break, but he said he couldn't walk away from you. He needed to know where you stood. Didn't you guys *ever* talk about this?"

Her stomach clenched. "You know I'm not much of a talker. He'd ask me if I was happy, and I said I was, because it was true. It's hard to explain. I loved him, and I was happy with him, but something was always missing. I should have told him that, but I couldn't."

"It sounds like you both had your secrets. He had an inkling that things weren't right, and you had secret feelings for Dare."

"But why *propose*? Why not just ask me straight up if I loved him the way he loved me?"

"I suspect it was for the same reason you didn't just come out and tell him that you had feelings for Dare. The three of you were a love triangle waiting to happen. I can't tell you how many of our conversations with Dare's and Eddie's parents circled that topic over the years."

"*Great*," she said sarcastically.

"Honey, young love is never easy. Eddie had already bought the ring and made his decision. He just wanted my blessing. He said if you turned him down, he'd be devastated, but he'd be able to walk away. So I have to ask, Billie. Why did you accept in the first place?"

"I don't *know*. I loved him so much, and he tried so hard to be a great boyfriend. And he succeeded. He was a great boyfriend. I wanted to love him like he loved me, but it just never happened, and then he was down on one knee, holding an engagement ring that he'd chosen just for me, and he was safe."

"What does that mean? Safe?"

She shrugged. "I don't even know anymore. It goes back to when we were teenagers." She wasn't about to tell him about her and Dare's miscommunication after they'd made out when they were teenagers. "Accepting his proposal was a mistake, and I wish I could take it back."

"I understand how you feel, but you have to see it for what it was. That proposal was Eddie's desperate attempt to hold on to the girl he loved. Plain and simple. It's a wonderful thing to have been loved that much, and you should *not* feel guilty for not loving him back in the same way. We can't choose who we fall in love with. That's the beauty of love. It sneaks up when we're not looking, and when it's real, it never lets go. But for *most* people, that deep, desperate love is unrequited."

"Like Eddie's."

"His wasn't unrequited. You loved him. That's something, and he knew that, sweetheart."

"I wish you had told me he was going to propose. Maybe *we* could have talked like this, and you could have told me to turn him down. Then I wouldn't have been shocked and done the wrong thing."

"That sounds like it would have been an easy solution, doesn't it? But there's no right or wrong when it comes to love. You did what your heart told you to do at that moment. And that's okay. You need to stop trying to take the blame for what happened. Eddie was like a son to me. We all lost a great friend, but it's nobody's fault. Not even his. He didn't know what would happen. It sounds like he was so worked up, he believed he could pull it off."

"That's what Dare said, that he wanted to prove he was still a man and I hadn't broken him."

"Dare's a smart guy, and I think he's right. But just so we're clear, I'm your father, sweetheart, but you were an adult, and you're no wallflower. If you didn't want to marry him, I knew you'd tell him so. But if I had cautioned you against it, you might've just married him to show me you were *badass Billie* and could do what you wanted."

She rolled her eyes.

"You can roll your eyes all you want, but you know how you are." He smiled. "Parenting is not easy, and I never know if I'm doing the right thing. I just do what feels right at the time, and it's never been up to me to change the course of my daughters' lives. I never tried to change your love of doing outrageous things, or told you to find a better career than running the bar, or forbade you from wearing leather pants or baring your belly, because those are your choices, and all those things have helped to make you who you are. But I have tried to let you girls know that I'm here for you, and you can always talk to me."

"You're a great dad, and I've always known I could come to you. I just wish I had back then."

"We can't go backward, sweet pea, but I will say this. I raised you to make the right decisions for *you* and to deal with the repercussions that came from them. But I never anticipated this situation. In hindsight, I wish I'd had a crystal ball. I would have stopped you *before* you said yes, but not because I think it would've changed what happened to Eddie. You know I believe the universe gives and it takes away, and we have no control over the *when*s and *how*s of it all. But I'd have stopped you so that *you* wouldn't have blamed yourself, because Eddie *chose* to try that stunt. He *chose* to propose knowing you would probably say no. You need to let that guilt go, and maybe the best way to go about that is by doing exactly what you're doing."

"Going crazy?"

"You're not going crazy, honey. You're slowly letting people back into your life, and that stirs up new emotions on top of guilt and a hundred other emotions you've been bottling up for years. If there's one thing I learned in therapy, it's that things get worse before they get better, and even when you think everything's cool, it'll bite you in the ass again. But hopefully by then you'll have let enough of us in to help you when it hurts so much all you want to do is close those doors again."

She hoped she could do that, because it was *hard* and lonely staying behind those closed doors, and even though she was slowly opening those doors, she knew life outside them was so much better. "I didn't know you went to therapy."

"Your mother and I both did because we didn't just lose Eddie, we lost a big part of you, too, and that's not something either of us was equipped to handle. But Colleen, over at the ranch, was there for us, and we got through it."

Her heart ached. "I'm sorry, Dad. I had no idea my moods affect you and Mom so much."

"You girls are our hearts and souls. If you're sad or mad, we are, too. But there's no need to apologize to me. I'm your father, and that comes with the territory. I'm also not the one who suffered the most. That would be the young woman you see in the mirror every morning."

Her throat thickened.

"And as far as Dare goes, he didn't take away *badass Billie* by getting you to go to the park with him. He gave that strong-willed girl a kick in her butt, and it made you even more badass. It takes a lot of guts to face the things that scare you." He leaned closer, lowering his voice. "We both know I'm not talking about the rides."

Her phone vibrated, and she took it out of her armband. There was a text from Dare. Her pulse quickened as she read it. *Hey, Wildfire. Space sucks. I like mine better when you're in it. Hope it's helping you.* How could a single text make her feel so good? She wanted to respond with, *I miss you, too,* but even after everything her father had said and the relief it brought, being able to put her feelings into writing still felt out of reach.

"Everything okay?" her father asked.

She nodded. "You've given me a lot to think about, Dad, so I hope it will be. But I feel like sorting out all these feelings is going to be more challenging than any race or stunt I've ever taken on."

"That's because you're the fiercest competitor I know, and you're up against yourself. But we both know that once you put your mind to something, there's no stopping you."

He couldn't know how badly she hoped that was true.

"THIS IS A whole lot better than shoveling shit." Kenny ripped the last old screw from the wooden fence post they were fixing and tossed it into the bucket, squinting his slightly-less-brooding eyes from the afternoon sun. He didn't like wearing the hat Dare's mother had given him. He said it made his head hot.

They'd been fixing fences for the past forty minutes, and Kenny had proven to be a strong worker.

"There are always chores to be done on the ranch. Some suck, and others suck a little worse. But if we slack off, the horses can get hurt." Dare moved the bucket where he'd discarded screws from the opposite post, watching Kenny get the new fence rail from the truck.

"Then why do you work out here when you could sit in an office?"

Dare handed him the power drill and went to hold the other end of the rail. "I don't like to be confined." What he didn't say was that it was also easier to get kids like him to open up if they were distracted by other things. There was nothing worse than feeling like the opening act of a show, and to Dare, who had shown up in his mother's office dozens of times after Eddie had died looking to bend her ear, that's what normal one-on-one therapy in an office felt like. His mother had suggested they take a walk, and it had made talking about his feelings and fears a thousand times easier. *Do you have time for a walk?* had become code for *I'm having a hell of a day and can really use some help.* Once he started working with clients, he found that talking with his clients outside gave him a clearer picture of who they were, and that was a beautiful thing. But today the distraction was helping Dare, too. He'd texted Billie several hours ago and still hadn't heard from her. It was taking everything he had not to drive his ass over there and find out what the hell was going on in *her* head.

"Me too. I hate sitting around." Kenny *set* the screws, just as Dare had taught him, and got busy screwing the rail to the post. When he was done, he gave the drill to Dare. "When can I get my phone back?"

"When I think you're ready. Who do you want to call?"

He shrugged, watching Dare screw the railing into the post.

Dare eyed the boy who thought the world was his enemy, remembering how hard it was at that age. The need to be cool and accepted was almost as strong as the hormones pumping through his veins. Yesterday's session had gone well enough. Kenny wasn't a talker, but Dare was used to that, and he'd gotten a few nuggets of truth out of him about how angry he was that they'd moved away from his friends.

"How do I earn it? What'll make you think I'm ready?"

"Keep doing what you're doing. Work, talk, keep your nose clean, and together we'll try to figure out what makes you tick and how to keep you from wanting to steal a car."

Kenny scoffed as they put the tools and buckets in the truck. "I know what makes me tick."

"Yeah?" Dare spotted Cowboy riding toward them on Sunshine, a sweet palomino they'd rescued a few years back. She was one of Cowboy's favorites, although he had many. "Tell me three things about yourself."

Kenny walked backward, eyes full of fear as Cowboy approached. "I don't like horses."

Cowboy looked from Kenny to Dare. "Everything okay?"

"He doesn't like horses," Dare said with a shrug.

"Why not? Have you had a bad experience with one?" Cowboy asked.

"No, but they freak me out. They're huge, and they look at you like they know what you're thinking." Kenny stepped closer to the truck.

"They look at you like that because they don't speak our language. They're looking for clues about what you're thinking and what you expect from them." Cowboy petted Sunshine.

"Horses are affectionate creatures." Dare moved by Sunshine's head and made kissing sounds. She dipped her head, pressing her muzzle against his chest, and he kissed her head and scratched her jaw. "See? That's how they hug. You have to gain their trust, but once you do, they'll treat you with the same love and respect with which you treat them."

"Riding a horse is a heck of a lot more fun than driving a car," Cowboy added.

Kenny shook his head. "I don't know about all that, but they still freak me out," Kenny said.

Dare and Cowboy exchanged a knowing glance.

"Mark my words, Kenny," Cowboy said. "We'll make a cowboy out of you yet."

"Where're you heading?" Dare asked.

"Up to the main house to talk to Maya, but it's such a nice day, I decided to take the long route. The fence looks good."

"Thanks," Dare said. "Kenny's doing a great job. We're heading over to fix the other one now."

"Great. I'll catch you guys later."

As Cowboy rode off, Kenny breathed a sigh of relief.

Dare motioned to the truck, and as they climbed in, he said, "Are you sure you've never had a run-in with a horse before?"

"Yeah, man. I've never been around them."

"Maybe we can work on acclimating you to them slowly and see if we can break down that fear."

"Whatever." He stared out the window.

As they drove to another pasture to fix another broken rail, Dare circled back to finish their conversation about what made Kenny tick. "You were saying that you know what makes you tick. Can you tell me two more things about yourself?"

"I don't know," he said without looking at Dare. "This is *stupid.*"

"Why is it stupid to want to get to know you better?"

"Because it doesn't matter."

"Of course it does. I want to help you get past stealing cars so you don't end up committing worse crimes. There's a big world out there, Kenny. Maybe we can figure out where you belong."

Kenny remained silent as they made their way across the property, and Dare let him stew, taking mental notes about the things that made him shut down. When they reached the broken fence, they went around to the back of the truck to get the tools out.

"Come on, Kenny. Give me something. What else do you like or dislike?"

Kenny shrugged as he pulled a bucket out of the truck bed.

"How about girls? Do you like them?"

"Yeah, but they lie."

"So do guys, unfortunately. What girl lied to you that made you believe they all lie?"

He kicked at the grass. "It doesn't matter."

"You do that a lot, saying things that impact your feelings don't matter. But they do matter, Kenny. Your feelings are important to me, and to your parents, your friends."

"*Bullshit.* My parents don't give a damn about *me.*" His voice escalated. "They moved me away from everything I knew. They didn't care that I lost my friends and my girlfriend. And for what? So my father can work at some lame-ass job?" His hands fisted at his sides. "So don't tell me that my feelings matter to my parents *or* my girlfriend, because she ended up fucking my best friend." He turned his back on Dare, his shoulders rising with his angry breaths.

That was a tough pill for anyone to swallow and not an easy one to move past. "Well, that blows. I'm sorry you had to experience that."

"No shit it blows, and don't ask me how it makes me feel."

"Why would I, when I can see how upset you are?" He walked around Kenny so he could see his face, and as he suspected, there was a war raging in his eyes, but that war was engulfed in sadness.

Kenny scowled. *"What?"*

"I feel bad for you. I know what it's like to love someone and have them choose someone else."

"Yeah, right," he gritted out, turning away.

"It feels like you've been stabbed in the chest. Betrayed by the people you trusted most. It makes you question and doubt everything. It eats away your trust in others and makes you want to build a fucking wall around yourself so no one else can hurt you."

Kenny looked at him cautiously.

"I told you I've been there."

"Don't give me the load of crap everyone says about my best friend not being a real friend or that me and her weren't meant to be."

"I wouldn't do that, because I don't buy into every situation being the same." He held Kenny's gaze. "I also don't know enough about your relationship to give an opinion. Maybe you weren't meant for each other, or maybe you were a jerk to her, or she was bad for you. I can't make any of those judgment calls. I don't even know how long you were seeing each other or how things were between you two when you moved away."

"Six months," he snapped.

"That's a long time. Did you love her?"

Kenny nodded, jaw clenching. "She said she'd wait. I was gonna get a job and save money to take a train to see her over the summer."

"That's a solid, smart plan."

"Lot of good it did me. Three weeks later I got a text that said she couldn't wait and she broke up with me."

"Man, that's harsh." And it explained a lot.

"I don't wanna talk about it."

I wouldn't want to either, but one day we will. "Okay, then tell me something else about yourself."

"I hate being told what to do."

"That's a good one, and it wasn't so hard. Was it?" Dare got the rest of the tools out of the truck and carried them over to the fence. "Most people don't like being told what to do. What bothers you most about it?"

"I don't know. *Everything.* Teachers talk to us like we're

stupid. My parents look at me like I'm some kind of alien, and they talk like it's still the olden days. They're always saying stuff like, *When I was in school.* Well, guess what, old man. That was a hundred years ago."

"People tend to draw from what they know, and that's usually taken from their own experiences. You can't fault them for that."

"But they don't *get* it. I've told them a million times that school's *not* the same as it was when they were my age."

Dare knew that Kenny's grades had been solid before he moved, but if he'd learned one important thing working with teens, it was that when they brought something up, there was a reason. "Have you tried to explain to them *why* it's not?"

"What do you mean? It's just not."

"There have to be reasons. Lots of parents feel like they don't know their teenagers, and kids feel like their parents won't ever understand them—"

"I know mine *won't.*"

"They can't unless you communicate effectively with them. When I was your age, if my parents were talking to me, I was thinking about the next thing I wanted to do, like seeing my friends or riding dirt bikes."

His eyes lit up. "You rode dirt bikes?"

"Yes, but that's not the point."

"But it's *cool.*"

"Yeah, it is, and we can talk about that another time. The point is, if your father was here trying to talk to you, even though you're about to fix another fence, you're probably thinking about getting your homework done to keep Dwight off your back and playing video games tonight."

"Nope. I'm thinking about dirt bikes."

Dare laughed, earning a genuine smile from Kenny. "I like your honesty, but here's the point. When your parents are trying to talk to you, your mind might wander, so you probably give them stilted answers like *it's not the same*. But your parents probably aren't sidetracked. They're solely focused on *you*, so while you're arguing about school being *different*, they're looking for answers about the son they love and trying to figure out how to help you."

"Well, they're not going to help by asking the same stupid questions a hundred times."

"Believe it or not, you're in control of that."

"No, I'm *not*," he snapped.

"Hear me out. It's up to your parents to ask the right questions and listen when you say your piece, right?"

"Yeah, and…?"

"This is where the control comes in. It's up to *you* to try to explain with more than a cursory answer, so they can fully understand where you're coming from. Let me give you an example. You fail a test, and your parents say you don't study enough, and they back that up by drawing on their own experience and saying they used to study for hours."

"They say that *all* the time."

"And how do you respond?"

"I tell them that I study enough, and then we fight because they don't *get* it. School is *harder* here than it was back home."

"Then you need to tell them that."

"They'll just say study longer."

"Maybe they will. But if you feel like that's not going to help, you could answer their study-time comment with reasons, like how the internet has made it easier to do research and learn different subjects, so it takes less time. But then you have to *also* tell them that the classes are harder and you need some extra help."

"I don't want *their* help."

"Why not?"

"Because they talk down to me. They treat me like I'm stupid."

"I'm sorry you feel that way. Unfortunately, a lot of parents don't realize how things come across to kids, and vice versa." He thought about his miscommunication with Billie when they were teenagers and wished he'd known then what he knew now. "We can work on fixing that together by finding a respectful way to tell them how you feel."

Kenny stole a glance at him, as if he was thinking about it, but said nothing.

"In the heat of the moment with friends, parents, and teachers, instinct drives us to defend ourselves any way we can, as fast as we can. But if you take a few seconds before responding to think about what the other person really needs to know in order to understand your side, and instead of arguing *yes, I do*s against *no, you don't*s, you communicate the real issues, things just might come out in your favor. Everything doesn't have to be an argument. But if you want them to respect your opinions, you have to communicate effectively and show them respect, too."

Kenny lowered his eyes.

"Showing respect starts with looking at the people who are talking to you, even when it's difficult."

Kenny met his gaze.

Dare gave a curt nod of approval. "Your parents deserve respect. I know it feels like they made decisions just to spite you, but moving was not an easy decision for them."

"How do you know?"

"Because I talked with them the other day when they called to make sure you were okay." He saw something in Kenny's eyes that looked a lot like he was glad they'd checked on him. "Did you know your father had tried for months to find work closer to your old home after he was laid off?"

Kenny shook his head. "I didn't know he was laid off."

"That's not surprising. Your father's job is to take care of his family, and he couldn't do that where you used to live, so he did what he had to. I know it sucks, especially given what happened with you and your girlfriend, but I would hope that if you ever become a father, you'd make sure you could support your family, too."

"I'd find another way. I'd never make my kid move away from all his friends."

Dare understood his point of view, but he also knew the harsh reality that life didn't always turn out the way one hoped. One day Kenny would understand that, too. "Have you talked to that girl since you broke up? What was her name?"

"Katie. She won't talk to me."

"I'm guessing that's why you stole the car the first time?"

"I just wanted to see her so I could *talk* to her," he said angrily.

"Did you think you could win her back?"

He shrugged.

"We can talk about that more when you're ready, and maybe after you've figured out a few things, you can call her so you can get some closure there."

His brows slanted. "You'd let me do that?"

"When you're ready."

"I'm *ready*," he said hopefully.

"Slow down, buddy. I mean when *I* think you're ready."

Kenny rolled his eyes.

"Believe me, you'll want to be prepared for that call. It probably won't be an easy one, and losing your cool won't do you any favors."

"Losing my cool with you or with her?"

"Both. But don't worry. I've got faith in you. We'll find better ways to communicate and safer avenues for all that fury you're carrying around."

Kenny grabbed the bucket. "Can we fix the fence now?"

"Absolutely." As they worked on taking out the old screws and removing the rail, Dare said, "You're done with school this year, but in the fall, if you're still having trouble, it'll be up to you to ask for help. You're too smart not to try. If you don't want to ask your parents, you can ask your teacher for help at lunch or after school, or ask a friend to give you a hand, or ask your parents to get you a tutor."

Kenny didn't say a word until they were done fixing the rail, and he spoke quietly. "The schoolwork isn't too hard."

I figured. "No? So why'd your grades tank?"

"Because of what happened with Katie. I couldn't concentrate."

Dare wanted to do a fist pump with that breakthrough, and he wanted to explore it further, but he knew when to bide his time, and he kept his cool. "That's understandable. Maybe tomorrow we can talk about that."

"Are we *done?*"

"Sure are. Unless you want to talk some more?"

"Heck no. Dwight and Simone are making cinnamon buns for a snack today, and I'm starved."

"Cinnamon buns? What're we waiting for? Let's get outta here."

When they got to the main house, Kenny climbed out of the truck and looked at Dare before closing the door. "Thanks."

"For what?"

"For not saying I was a dick to my parents when I was."

"I'm not here to make you feel bad about yourself. I'm on your side."

"Will you teach me to ride dirt bikes?"

"That's up to you."

Kenny's brows knitted in concentration, and he gave a curt nod, which he undoubtedly had learned from Dare, and headed inside. Dare was proud of him. He'd shared some heavy stuff today. They had a long way to go, but at least they were on the right track. Dare started driving toward the lower barns, where he was meeting up with Darcy for her session. His phone vibrated, and he saw Billie's name on the screen. "Finally."

He pulled over to read her message. *Space helped.* "Really, Mancini?" he grumbled. "I don't hear from you for twenty-four hours and I get two words?"

Another text bubble popped up. *Kind of.*

Grinning, he thumbed out, *You miss me, don't you, Mancini?*

Her response was immediate—an eye roll emoji.

That woman was going to drive him mad.

Another message rolled in. *Maybe a little. It turns out I like my space better when you're in it, too.*

"Now, that's more like it." He typed, *Sounds like someone wants to get frisky with their Whiskey.*

She sent a laughing emoji.

"Go ahead and laugh, Mancini. We both know you want me." He thumbed out, *Gotta head into a session with a client. Stay frisky.* He added an eggplant emoji and flames, hit send, and headed to the barn to meet his next client with thoughts of his Wildfire dancing in his mind.

Chapter Nine

FRIDAY NIGHTS WERE always slamming at the Roadhouse. Between the cheers around the mechanical bull, the din of the crowd, and the blaring music, Billie couldn't hear herself think—and she *loved* it. It wouldn't be a biker bar without rowdy guys knocking chests like fools and the girls who drooled over them. She didn't even mind putting guys in their places or telling people they'd had enough alcohol and refusing to serve them. She was always up for a challenge, and tonight she needed the distraction. She'd felt so much better after talking with her father and thinking about everything he and Dare had said, she wished she'd been honest with them ages ago. She'd been on such a high, she'd let those feelings come out in her text to Dare, and she'd been left with butterflies swarming in her stomach.

She put a napkin on the bar and set a drink on it in front of a tall dark-haired guy. "What else can I get you?"

He smiled, and panty-melting dimples appeared. "How about a date with a beautiful bartender?"

Bobbie had just come behind the bar, and she gave Billie a look somewhere between *Go for it* and amused.

Billie leaned on the bar in front of the dimpled stranger. "Aren't you sweet? Sorry, but I'm *taken*." The proclamation came without thought and brought a rush of happiness. "But the kitchen is open till ten, and we have some sweet wings that are sure to leave you satisfied." She handed him an appetizer menu and turned around to grab a towel.

Bobbie was *right there*, wearing a ROADHOUSE T-shirt and a goofy grin. "*Taken*, huh? And you didn't bite that guy's head off like you usually do? Well, that explains a lot."

"Why?"

Bobbie lowered her voice. "Obviously Dare got rid of all that pent-up anger you've been lugging around. Go *Dare*."

"Shut *up*." Bobbie was taking all too much pleasure in teasing her, and Billie was surprised she didn't hate it. But she didn't want her personal business to become the talk of the town.

"What's next? Will you be wearing his ID bracelet?"

She would have given anything to have worn that in high school. "Don't you have customers to help?" She took a step toward a group of guys hanging over the bar, but Kellan stepped up to serve them.

"Why, *yes*, I do. My favorite smokin'-hot Greek god of a single daddy is here." Bobbie pointed across the bar to Ezra, sitting at a table with Rebel and a few other Dark Knights.

"He's not even Greek. His last name is *Moore*."

"His mother is Greek."

"How do you know that? We've never even met his mom."

"People might be afraid of you, but they trust me with their secrets." She giggled and strutted out from behind the bar just as the front doors opened, and Dare strode in, followed by Doc, Cowboy, and Hyde.

Billie's pulse kicked up, and as customers' heads turned to check out the four leather-cut-wearing badasses blocking the doorway, she was pretty sure every other woman's did, too. But she didn't give them another thought, because as Dare led the pack toward the bar, his eyes never left hers. God, he was gorgeous, all those hard muscles inked to perfection. Her chest got fluttery, and she didn't love that out-of-control feeling when she was at work, with dozens of eyes on her.

A wolfish grin curved his lips as he planted his hands on the bar, leaning over it. "Hey, darlin'. Give me some sugar."

Her breath caught in her throat. *Are we doing this? Here? Now?* His brothers, and every customer sitting near them, were watching them with curious, amused expressions, and Dare was looking at her expectantly. *Jesus, Dare, give a girl a minute.* She couldn't think straight. She grabbed a handful of sugar packets from beneath the bar and slapped them down in front of him.

The guys cracked up.

Dare put his hand over his heart, leaning back as if he'd been shot. "Damn, Mancini, that *hurt*. Guys, is there a knife in my chest? Am I bleeding?"

She laughed. "Idiot."

"Dude, she shot you down good," Doc said with a laugh.

The guy who had just asked for her number said, "She's taken, man. I already asked."

Dare's eyes narrowed, but they were still locked on her. "Yeah, by a big-dicked biker, from what I hear."

She needed to sidetrack this conversation and looked at his brothers. "You want a round of beers?"

Cowboy's gaze moved curiously between her and Dare. "Holy shit. Tell me it ain't so, Billie. Tell me you're not the truck thief."

Her eyes flew open wider, and she looked at Dare, who wore a shit-eating grin. *What did you tell them?*

"I thought you had better taste than that," Hyde teased.

Shit. Shitshitshit. As much as she didn't want to become the talk of the town, she didn't want them thinking he'd been with someone else. "Yeah, I took his damn truck, but I gave it back. Y'all want beers or not?"

Hyde nudged Cowboy and held out his hand. "Pay up, dipshit."

Cowboy dug his wallet out of his pocket, and Billie rolled her eyes.

"Guys, really?" Dare snapped, and Hyde and Cowboy laughed.

"Yeah, we'll take those beers, Billie," Doc said. "Thanks."

She served them, then hiked a thumb over her shoulder. "I've gotta grab something from the back." She escaped into the stockroom.

Dare blew through the doors behind her, closing the distance between them.

"Dare. What was *that?*"

His arms circled her waist, and he was still smiling. "That was me saying hi to my girl."

"But *why* with a kiss, in front of everyone? I don't need the whole town knowing we're knocking boots."

"Why the hell not?"

"I don't *know.* Because we weren't even *in* each other's lives for years, and now we are, and—"

"We were always in each other's lives. I've always been in your heart." He touched his lips to hers. "And in your head." He kissed her again, longer this time, chipping away at her irritation. "I was here damn near every night you worked."

He kissed her neck, backing her up against the shelves, and his possessiveness sent her body into a frenzy of want and need.

"And we both know I was in your shower fantasies." He trailed kisses down her neck, igniting sparks beneath her skin.

"But this is *new*, and we still have stuff to work through," she said breathily.

He brushed his lips over hers. "You take all the time you need, darlin'. You're mine and I'm yours, and I'm not going to hide that. But we don't need to make a big thing of it. When you're ready, I look forward to letting the whole world know."

"I don't want to hide it, either. I just don't want to make out at my bar. I need people to respect me here."

"I get it, Mancini, don't worry. I've got your back." His eyes turned volcanic. "And now I want your *mouth*."

His mouth came coaxingly down over hers so seductively, it was hypnotizing, lulling her deeper into him with every swipe of his tongue. She went up on her toes, craving more, and boy, did he give it to her. He didn't just kiss her; he *consumed* her, tongue plunging, hands roving, hips grinding, drawing every ounce of her into their realm. Her limbs tingled, and her knees weakened. She was dizzy with desire, clinging to him as reality spun away and she lost herself in their world of erotic sensations.

"*Whoa!*"

They broke apart at the sound of Kellan's voice, and Dare moved in front of her, just as he'd done with Cowboy all those years ago. Kellan was smiling victoriously.

"Hey, man," Dare said calmly. "We were just…discussing something."

"Like if she needed a tonsillectomy?" Kellan laughed.

Billie glowered at him.

He looked right at Billie. "Bad matchmaker my ass. I *called* it. Do me a favor—bring in another case of Guinness when you're done *discussing*."

As Kellan walked out, Dare pulled her back into his arms, grinning. "Good luck keeping it off the gossip vine now."

"This is *not* funny. I have to manage him." Although she was smiling too, because never in her life had she imagined being caught in a compromising position at work. But ever since Dare dropped out of the sky, it was like the world was pushing them together. Was this another of Eddie's signs? Or was this just where they were always meant to be?

"Want me to have a talk with Kellan?"

"Hell *no*. I can handle my own business, but I do need to get back out there."

He held her tight and palmed her butt, making her warm all over again. Did she really have to go back to work?

"Just one more kiss to hold me over until I get you in my bed tonight," he said in a low, husky voice.

"And what exactly would you like to do to me tonight?"

As he lowered his lips to hers, he growled, "Everything."

IT TOOK FOREVER to get to closing time, and Dare must have been on a mission to keep Billie all revved up, because he didn't miss an opportunity for furtive glances, stolen touches, and dirty whispers under the guise of ordering a drink. Looking forward to being with him felt almost as incredible as it felt to actually be with him.

By the time she closed the bar, she was ready to tear his

clothes off in the parking lot. But she wasn't going to chance getting caught in that kind of compromising position, so she followed him to his cabin, where they came together like ravenous animals, stumbling through the front door in a tangle of messy kisses and greedy gropes.

"I'm sweaty from work," she said between kisses.

"I like you salty."

She smiled into their kisses, enthralled by his unrelenting passion, but she needed to rinse off the night's grime before she let him put his mouth on her. "Does that mean you *wouldn't* like me naked in your shower?"

He growled, and the carnal sound pounded through her as he took her in more mind-numbing kisses and they made their way to the master bathroom, which looked nothing like it had years ago. It was just as rugged and unique as Dare, with slate floors, marble walls in hues of blues and browns, dark wood cabinets and black countertops. They stripped each other naked as the shower warmed.

The slate was cold beneath her feet, but her body was hot as fire as they stepped into the enormous shower. Warm water rained down them as he drew her into his arms, devouring her mouth again. His scruff abraded her cheek, and she reveled in it. She was addicted to his kisses, to the heat that blazed between them every time they were together. His body was enticingly slick and deliciously hard. When he drew back with fire in his eyes and reached for the body wash, she instantly missed his mouth and the feel of him against her. But those warm feelings were iced over at the sight of *several* bottles of pink-green-and-gold body wash on the ledge. "How many women have you had in here?"

"None, why?"

She nodded to the bottles.

"Those are from *Birdie*. She shows up every few weeks with all this shit and says I need to use it or my skin will be like leather. I've got about a half dozen bottles of lotion, too. She gets them from some chick named Roxie in Upstate New York. I feel bad if I don't use them."

She breathed a sigh of relief, and he drew her into his arms again and kissed her cheek. "You're not *jealous*, are you, Mancini?"

"*No.* Just curious."

"Mm-hm." He kissed her softly. "I like you jealous."

"Put your ego away before you kill the mood," she teased.

He moved one hand between her legs, his thick fingers sliding through her slickness. "It doesn't *feel* like I'm killing it." He leaned in, teasing her most sensitive nerves as he spoke gruffly into her ear. "It feels like you want me."

He continued applying pressure in exactly the right place to make her lose her mind. His arousal brushed against her, and her mind sprinted down a dirty path, recalling all the luxurious pleasure that monstrous appendage could bring, heating her up from the inside out. He must have felt a shift in her energy, because he moaned into her ear and quickened his efforts between her legs. She clenched her teeth against the pressure mounting inside her. *"Dare."*

He ran his tongue around the rim of her ear. "Tell me you want me, Mancini."

She panted out, "*Fuck.*"

"We'll get to that." His hand stilled.

She rocked her hips, urging him to move.

"*Say it*," he demanded.

The low timbre of his voice was just as intoxicating as his

touch. "*I want you—*"

He covered her mouth with his, his fingers moving at breakneck speed, taking her right up to the edge of ecstasy—and holding her there, fingers and tongue slowing. It was the most glorious torture she'd ever endured. When he quickened his pace, intensifying their kisses, need pulsed hot and insistent inside her, gathering force and heat from her fingertips to her toes, until it swelled and burrowed in her core, drawing needier, greedier moans. He broke the kiss—*No! Come back!*—gritting out, "I'm going to enjoy every second of this." His scruff scratched her cheek as he sank his teeth into her earlobe, sending bolts of lightning between her legs, shattering the last of her restraint. She cried out, clinging to him as pleasure exploded inside her. Then his mouth covered hers again, kissing her roughly and somehow also sweetly, slowing as she came down from the peak, breathing his air into her lungs.

"*Jesus, Dare,*" she said breathily. "I may never shower alone again."

A low laugh rumbled out as he poured body wash into his hand. "My evil plan is working."

"Two can play at this game." She held out her palm, and he poured body wash into it.

Their eyes locked as they bathed each other. His rough hands moved across her shoulders and down her arms, and she did the same to him, reveling in the firm dips and hard ridges of his muscles. Neither one spoke as they explored each other's bodies in this new and different way, the silence broken only by the sounds of water cascading over them and their heavy breathing. Her hands moved over his broad chest as his traveled down her sides, slowing at her waist, and squeezed her hips. She inhaled sharply, running her fingers over his nipples, caressing, teasing, and tweaking them. His muscles tensed and heat flared in his eyes, sending lust straight to her core, amping up her desire to bring him even more pleasure, to see him gritting his teeth as he was now, as her hands moved down his stomach, and feel his restraint as she touched him so close to his cock it jerked.

She'd thought their connection had hit its height, but she hadn't expected this new type of intimacy. He put more body wash in his hands, still holding her gaze as he bathed her breasts, giving her nipples the same attention she'd given his, sending ripples of pleasure all the way to her toes.

"I want my mouth on you," he said through gritted teeth.

She fisted his cock, stroking him tight and slow. "I was thinking the same thing."

His lips quirked, but when she ran her palm along his hard length and over the broad head, that grin turned to clenched moans, desire intensifying in his eyes. "*No* mouths," he commanded, pulling her tight against him.

His arousal pressed temptingly into her belly, and she tried to reel him in. "You *know* you want to kiss me."

"I want to kiss you, fuck you with my mouth, and have your mouth wrapped around my cock until I come so hard I can't move."

Her body shuddered with anticipation. *Yes, please...*

"But we're not doing any of those things, because I don't want you to come again yet." He groped her ass, his thick fingers sliding between her cheeks as he squeezed so hard it stole her breath. "Feel that clench deep inside you, Wildfire?"

She answered with something between a moan and a whimper.

His hands slid down the backs of her thighs, sending pinpricks down both legs. "*That's* what we're going for. I want you so turned on, you can barely speak."

Before she could get a word out, he turned her around so her back was against his chest and snaked one strong arm over her shoulder, cupping her breast. The other slid slowly down her stomach, teasing her clit, and her breathing hitched again.

"I thought…" She sighed, lost in the exquisite sensations moving through her like waves. "You weren't going to make me come."

"I'm not." He sucked her earlobe into his mouth. *"Yet."*

He put more body wash in his hands, and as they slid over her breasts, she closed her eyes, surrendering to his sinful seduction. He soaped her body, groping and *taking*, growling dirty things in her ear every time she clenched or moaned. He palmed her breasts, squeezing her nipples so hard she went up on her toes. "One day I'm going to come on these tits." An illicit sound, somewhere between *yes* and *oh God*, pushed from her lungs. His hard length ground into her flesh as his hands moved over the tops of her legs, making their way to her inner thighs and sliding up, brushing over her sex. "And all over this pretty pussy."

She could barely fill her lungs for the desires swelling inside her with those promises. She rocked her hips, reaching back to touch him, but he pressed himself tight against her, continuing his relentless pursuit of bringing her to the brink of insanity. He unhooked the showerhead, rasping into her ear as he messed with it. "Ready to *play*, darlin'?"

She tried to clear the lust from her mind to figure out what he meant, but one of his hands snaked around her middle again, caressing her breast, and he turned the concentrated showerhead between her legs. Her eyes slammed shut at the titillating sensations racing through her, and sparks flew behind her closed lids. *"Ohmygod."* She pressed her palms to the cold, wet tile for support, and he didn't miss a beat, still fondling her breasts and using that tantalizing water wand to make her eyes roll back in her head. He pushed his cock between her legs, rubbing along her sex, causing toe-curling friction.

"Squeeze your legs together."

His demand collided with the feel of his thickness stroking and sliding between her legs, the water working like a dozen tongues to perfection, and his hand wreaking havoc with her breasts. She squeezed her shaky legs together as hard as she could.

"Jesus," he gritted out. "I want to fuck you so bad right now, Wildfire."

She tried to catch her breath, scintillating sensations coming from all angles. "Oh God, *yes!*" She looked over her shoulder, their eyes colliding with such passion, she swore she felt the earth move, and had trouble finding her words. "I'm...*protected.* Birth control."

"Fuck, baby. Hold this, and don't you *dare* move it from between your legs." He handed her the showerhead and grabbed her hips. "Better hold that wall with your other hand, dar-lin', 'cause once I'm inside you, I'm not gonna be able to hold back. We're going hard and dirty."

"You'd *better.*"

A low growl erupted from his lungs as her palm hit the wall, and he drove into her with one hard thrust. They both cried out, their indiscernible sounds echoing. He didn't slow down, pounding into her, taking her with the power of the tsunami she'd always known him to be, sending electric currents through her in gusts and waves. She couldn't think, could barely breathe, and dropped the showerhead to grip the wall with both hands, trying to steady herself in their dizzying world. The showerhead flailed on its long tail, hitting the wall and spraying their legs as their orgasms took hold, and they spiraled into oblivion, bodies jerking, curses flying, their all-consuming passion taking everything they had to give. The pleasure went on and on, until her legs gave out, and Dare wrapped his arms around her, kissing up her spine.

"I lose my mind when I'm with you, darlin'. I didn't hurt you, did I?"

How could he think that, when she was the one who had asked for it? She shook her head, unable to speak, and he turned her in his arms, the love in his eyes making her head spin anew.

"You've got nothing to be jealous of, darlin'. Other women might have had my body, but you're the only one who's ever had my heart."

She swallowed hard, surprised that he was still thinking of her comment about the body wash and wishing she had the ability to be as open with her words as he was. She didn't know if she could ever be that girl, but he made her want to try.

Chapter Ten

MOONLIGHT STREAMED THROUGH the windows, casting a sexy glow over Billie as she poked around Dare's kitchen wearing only his T-shirt. Dare wasn't big on having people in his house, but in some strange way, it had always felt like Billie was there with him. He used to enjoy having people over, but that had changed after Eddie died and Billie had shut him out. He hadn't wanted anything to disturb the memories they'd created there, but *man*, he could get used to seeing Billie padding around bare-legged and happy. For as long as he'd known her, she'd been a nighttime snacker. When they were teenagers, if he lost track of her at a party, he could usually find her nosing around the kitchen looking for food. He'd found it cute, and was glad to see it hadn't changed.

He wrapped his arms around her from behind as she opened a cabinet and kissed her neck, breathing in the scent of his body wash. It smelled a hell of a lot better on her than it did on him. "If you're looking for a snack, you're looking in the wrong place."

She turned her head with a sexy smile. "Didn't you have enough in the shower?"

"I'll never get enough of you." He nipped at her earlobe. "But I was talking about food. I think you'll find what you're looking for on the top shelf in the cabinet on the other side of the fridge."

She opened the cabinet and went up on her toes, reaching for a package of Oreos. His shirt rode up, exposing the curve of her ass, and he couldn't help giving it a little slap. She *squeaked* in surprise, and half scowled, half smiled, and he had to laugh.

"There are barbecue chips up there, too, if you want them."

She eyed the cabinet. "I don't see chips. You just want me to reach up again."

"Do I?" He arched a brow.

She tugged a chair over from the table and climbed up to get the chips.

"Now we're talkin'." He moved behind her, running his hands over the fronts of her thighs as he kissed one ass cheek and sank his teeth into the other.

"Dare!" She turned around, bringing him eye to eye with his favorite snack. He stole a lick before she climbed down, clutching the bag of chips in one hand and holding her other hand palm out. "Stay there. I need to eat before *you* do."

He grabbed his junk. "I got some sausage for ya."

She rolled her eyes, and he hauled her into his arms and kissed her. "I'm kidding. Why don't I make you something real to eat?"

"These *are* real." She tore open the bag and shoved a chip into her mouth as she reached for the Oreos. "Do you have any—"

"Right here, darlin'." He pulled two Capri Suns out of the fridge and handed her one.

Her eyes widened. "No *way*. You still drink these?"

"Hell yes. I'm a loyal motherfucker, and these will forever be the best snacks known to man."

"Damn right they will." She bit into an Oreo, but as she ate it, the light in her eyes dimmed, and her brows knitted as she opened the straw for the Capri Sun.

"What's wrong, darlin'?"

"Do you ever feel guilty for being happy?"

"You mean because of Eddie?"

She nodded.

"I did at first, but not anymore. Are you feeling bad about us because of everything that happened?"

"Not bad, just a little guilty. I love being with you, and I'm happy for the first time in years. But is it *fair*? I mean, we get to live our lives, and he never even got to make that *unforgettable* movie he was always talking about."

He knew talking about this was difficult for her and that she might shut down if they dug too deep, so he treaded lightly. "Do you really think Eddie wouldn't want you to be happy?"

"No. He wasn't a selfish person. Did you know that he didn't think I'd accept his proposal?"

"No. I never knew he was going to propose. What makes you say that?"

"I talked to my dad earlier, and he said the proposal was Eddie's last-ditch effort to see if I was all in and that he knew I didn't love him the way he loved me, but he loved me too much to break up with me."

"Now, *that* sounds like Eddie. Loyal to the end. But don't you see what he was doing?" He moved in front of her and reached for her hand. "He knew it wasn't your responsibility to love him in that way, and he must have felt like he was holding you back. He was giving you an out. Setting you free in the only way he knew how. He wasn't strong enough to let you go, so he needed you to be. Doesn't that tell you that he wanted you to be happy, even if it wasn't with him?"

She looked down and stayed like that for a full minute, maybe two, before meeting his gaze with a small smile. "I didn't know what to make of it when my father first told me. It was a lot to take in, but I think you're right about Eddie wanting me to be happy, and I agree with what you said about responsibility." Her eyes twitched, as if she was overthinking something. "When I broke up with him, I *knew* I was doing the right thing for both of us. I mean, I knew it like I know my own name. People break up all the time. But I must have shut that belief down when he died. I've been looking at the whole situation from the standpoint of it being my fault because I couldn't—or maybe I didn't want to—see it any other way. I felt so guilty for ending our relationship."

"That's not uncommon after something so traumatic, and realizing where the guilt comes from is the start of healing."

Her brows knitted. "You must think I'm a nutcase."

"Why? Because a man you loved was ripped from your life and you did your best to survive him?"

"Because it shouldn't take this long to figure things out."

"Babe, grief doesn't have a timeline. Some people go their whole lives and only realize their truths on their deathbed. And don't be surprised if you try to talk yourself out of what you just realized in an hour, or tomorrow, or next week. That's the thing about PTSD. The effects may seem like they go away completely, but our minds play tricks on us, and we still think about what we've gone through for a long time, and for some people, forever."

"Oh good, something to look forward to," she said solemnly. "You think I have PTSD?"

"I think we both have it on some level. It's not a bad thing. It's just what happens to some people." He kissed her softly. "It's okay, babe. As you explore and share your feelings, you'll begin to see what happened and the years since more clearly, and you'll learn how to navigate the slippery slopes when they pop up."

"Do you still have slippery slopes?"

"Not as often as I used to, but it took me a long time to get here." He put his arms around her. "I know you don't love talking about your feelings, but you're not alone in this, and if you told your dad, then that makes two of us who can help you through those slippery times."

"Now you sound like a therapist."

"I am a therapist. A therapist who loves you and wants to help you heal."

"I want to say thanks, but I'm afraid it'll go to your head and you'll think you can use your psychobabble on me all the time."

He knew she was just teasing, and he was grateful she hadn't shut him out. "Would I do that?" He leaned in and kissed her.

"I'm serious, Whiskey," she warned. "Don't think just because you sexed my brain into submission you can get me talking about my feelings all the time."

"I know you better than that. Grab your Oreos, Mancini. I've got something to show you."

"If we're going to the bedroom, I want whipped cream."

Damn, I love you. "We're going to the living room, but from now on my fridge will be stocked with whipped cream. In fact, I'll get a mini fridge for the bedroom."

He snagged the chips and she smacked his ass—*hard*—and

ran out of the kitchen laughing. Hell yeah, he could get used to this. He sauntered into the living room and found her grinning like a fiend. What a glorious fucking sight that was.

"Paybacks are hell, Mancini."

"I'll just keep my butt to the wall."

He laughed. "Sit down and get comfortable. We're going to be here awhile."

She sat cross-legged on the couch, eating Oreos and watching him curiously as he connected his laptop to the television. "If you're turning on porn, we could probably make a movie ten times better than the crap that's out there."

That piqued his interest. "Good to know my Wildfire has a kinky side." He slid her a wink. "But this isn't porn." He grabbed the remote and sat beside her. "I've wanted to show you this for a long time."

"What is it?"

"Eddie's unforgettable movie. He made it. He just never had a chance to share it with us."

Her heart stumbled. "Seriously?"

"Yeah. His parents gave me access to his hard drives so I could get copies of pictures and videos, and it was on there. The last time it'd been opened was the morning of the accident." He put his arm around her, pulling her closer. "Do you think you can handle watching it? It might be hard at first, because it's Eddie, alive and in action." He paused, giving her a minute to think about it. "We don't have to if you're not ready."

"I WANT TO" flew from Billie's lips. Her heart was racing, but her mind wasn't. She didn't know what to expect, or how she'd react, but she *wanted* to see Eddie and the movie he'd worked so hard to create.

Dare held her a little tighter as he turned it on.

Music played as images of the three of them as young kids enlarged one by one in rapid succession, making them appear to get closer to the camera. She watched her young self, bright-eyed and skinny-limbed, riding her dirt bike over a jump and sticking her tongue out, Dare looking fierce, doing a heel flip on a skateboard, and Eddie hanging upside down from a rope swing, getting ready to flip into the lake below, his arms flailing, shaggy blond hair sticking out everywhere. As those pictures flew off the edges of the screen, a zoom shot of THE UNFOR-GETTABLE DAREDEVILS appeared at an angle across the middle of the screen in bold red-and-gold letters, with flames coming off the first *D* in *Daredevils*, and just below, in plain black letters, was BASED ON A TRUE STORY.

Her throat thickened. She cuddled tighter against Dare's side as the title screen faded and a shot of the old dirt bike trails where they used to race appeared. Eddie swaggered onto the screen, tall, tanned, and supremely handsome, his shaggy blond hair as tousled as always. His mischievous baby blues lit up, bringing out the boyish charm she'd adored as he spoke to the camera. "What you're about to witness is the birth of two fast-talking, unforgettable daredevils and one devilishly handsome, sometimes-daredevil cinematographer. Sit back and enjoy the ride. I know I have."

Tears burned Billie's eyes, and Dare kissed her temple.

Music played as another picture from when they were little appeared. The three of them were running along a fence at the ranch. Dare was holding his cowboy hat on his head and laughing. Billie ran beside him, determination written all over her face, and Eddie led the pack, his chin held high, grinning with the magnificence that only a six-year-old could exude. The music dimmed, and from off camera, Eddie said, "It started with races and dares." The camera zoomed in on another picture of them skiing, knees bent, bodies low, and once again Eddie was out front.

"He was always so fast," Billie whispered as a picture of the three of them racing on dirt bikes appeared. Their fathers were standing at the sidelines, arms crossed, chins low. Dare and Billie were neck and neck, and Eddie took up the rear. Eddie's voice rang out as more pictures played. "On foot, there was a *clear* winner." His face appeared on-screen again, and he flashed a cheesy grin that made Billie smile. "But give those two daredevils a set of wheels or wings, and they were unbeatable."

A tear slipped down her cheek as Eddie said, "They were each other's biggest cheerleaders and harshest critics. All in the name of excellence, of course." A picture appeared over his shoulder of Billie around eight years old, hair tangled, arms crossed, scowling at Dare as he crouched on a skateboard, his hand on the back of it, mouth open, like he was telling her how to do a trick. He always used to correct her, and it helped her go faster, get more air, or otherwise hone her skills, but that didn't mean she liked it.

She put her hand on Dare's leg, and he covered it with his own.

"When it was just the three of them, these mini daredevils weren't out for notoriety. It didn't matter who won or who did a stunt better," Eddie said. "Because at the end of the day, they always knew that the *right* person had taken first place, and that wasn't true only of stunts and activities. They helped each other study for spelling bees and make projects for science fairs. They were the best of friends and had each other's backs through thick and thin."

She heard the change in Dare's breathing and knew he was smiling as pictures of them cheering each other on, hugging, and high-fiving at finish lines of races popped up, giving way to a picture of Billie flanked by Eddie and Dare, the three of them arm in arm, all dirty knees and pointy elbows, beaming at the camera with goofy eight-year-old grins. That picture morphed into one of them as teenagers sitting on a blanket by the lake where they used to swim. Billie wore a yellow bikini, sitting between Eddie and Dare in their swim trunks, their youthful bodies just beginning to broaden, bronzed from the sun, lazy smiles on their beautiful faces.

"As the years passed," Eddie said, "their innocent grins were replaced with rascally smirks and their stunts got bigger and riskier. But nothing could steal the fire from the two unforgettable daredevils' eyes, and one great cinematographer caught it *all* on camera."

Billie's heart squeezed, and she looked at Dare, catching him watching her. "What?"

"I was just making sure you were okay, and I got a little lost in you."

"Don't get all mushy and weird on me, Whiskey." She kissed him. "I'm really glad we're watching this. Now stop looking at me and watch the movie."

They turned back to the movie, and Eddie's face was *right* in front of the camera in the dark. He was obviously lying down, and he was whispering, "We're camping in the woods for Billie's thirteenth birthday. Check out what Dare gave our girl." He tilted the camera to show a piece of paper that had *Happy birthday, Billie. One day I'm going to build you a great motocross track. Daredevils for Life! Dare Whiskey* scrawled above a drawing of a very detailed motocross track.

She still had that card hidden away. "It's a good thing you included your last name," she teased, to try to stave off her tears, and Dare hugged her against his side.

Eddie whispered, "Check this out." The camera panned left to Billie lying on her side facing Eddie, her hand in his. Dare lay behind her, his hand resting on her hip. Eddie's smiling face appeared again. "Daredevils forever, baby!"

Longing sliced through her.

The darkness transitioned to a video of Dare jumping out of the tree house in Eddie's backyard. He rolled when he landed and shot up to his feet as Billie scrambled up the ladder, yelling, "Get me in the video, Eddie!" Eddie turned the camera on himself and said, "As if I ever miss a thing." He turned the camera back to Billie, catching her jumping out of the tree house, shouting, *"Daredevils rule!"* After she landed, she and Dare argued about who had jumped higher.

Dare whispered, "Remember that day?"

"Mm-hm." She leaned into him. "I jumped higher."

They both chuckled. Eddie had taken that video camera everywhere, and he used to say it was a good thing he did, because she and Dare bickered all the time about who did this or that better and the videos showed them the truth. He was the peacemaker. *Right up to the very end,* she thought with a pang of missing him.

"Sometimes we broke the rules," Eddie said from off camera as a video played of Dare trying to walk across a homemade tightrope tied between two trees. He held a big stick with both hands for balance. He fell the first two times, cursing and climbing right back up. The third time he stayed on the rope for a few feet.

Billie remembered how excited she was for Dare and how much she wanted to try it, too.

He was about halfway across when the camera panned to the right and caught Tiny storming toward them, hollering, "Boy, what did I tell you about that?" From off camera Dare yelled, "Oh shit!" and then there was a thud. The camera whipped around, catching Dare and Billie sprinting away. Eddie chased after them, the camera bouncing as they laughed hysterically. He cut to a video of the three of them mucking stalls, sweaty and dirty, cracking up as they taunted each other, pretending they were readying to throw rakes of manure at each other. Threats flew, and more laughter ensued.

"You had to muck stalls for weeks because of that tightrope, remember?" she asked quietly. She and Eddie had helped him the entire time.

"It didn't stop me." He smirked.

"Nothing could stop you. You were a maniac about that tightrope. You thought you were going to be the greatest tightrope walker on earth and walk between skyscrapers in New York City." He was going to be the best at every stunt he'd ever tried.

"I would have if I didn't get sidetracked with BASE jumping."

She laughed, and they watched videos of her and Eddie horseback riding while Dare did tricks on the back of his horse. There were videos of Dare and Billie bungee jumping, cliff diving, hanging out at birthday parties, barbecues, and Friends-givings at the ranch and a montage of the three of them watching firework displays, their ages progressing in each one.

They'd never missed watching them together until they lost Eddie, and she'd stopped going. It was one of the things she missed most. She realized she had a lot of those *missed most* things.

They cracked up at a video of Billie lying on the hood of Dare's Chevelle wearing cutoffs and a bikini top, while he washed it. Eddie must have set up a tripod, because he'd caught himself dumping a bucket of sudsy water on Billie, who shrieked and sprinted after him, jumping on his back and taking them both to the ground, while Dare sprayed them with the hose. When a video came on of her and Dare skydiving, their colorful parachutes bright against the clear blue sky and Eddie on the ground filming them, she remembered the picture in Dare's workshop and realized Eddie must have set up a tripod that day, too. Eddie turned toward the other camera and said, "Look at them up there, having the time of their lives. I envy their fearlessness." He turned his attention back to them as they neared the ground and hollered, "I love you guys! You're awesome!"

Billie's chest constricted, and tears stung her eyes.

Dare and Billie appeared on the screen wearing jeans, leather jackets, and boots and carrying motorcycle helmets. They climbed onto their Harleys, and Eddie turned the camera on himself and said, "Hold on to your hats, folks. It's just past dawn, and the amazing Dare Whiskey is going to blow you away as he takes Hope Valley by storm with his death-defying motorcycle stunts."

Billie knew exactly what stunts were about to play out, and her pulse sped up.

Dare must have felt her tension, because he leaned closer and said, "You know nothing bad happens."

She nodded, but it didn't stop the goose bumps from prickling her arms as Eddie zoomed in on Dare's determined face. "Dare, how are you feeling right now?" Dare hiked a thumb at Billie and said, "Like I want you to get your ass on the back of her bike so we can go have some fun!" Billie yelled, "Come on, Eddie, let's roll!" Eddie turned the camera on himself again. "You heard it here first, folks. Dare's excited and ready to go."

In the next scene they were speeding down an empty highway, and Eddie was filming from the back of Billie's bike as Dare pulled his legs up, crouching on the seat, and swung his feet up and over the handlebars. A few seconds later, he pulled his legs back and kicked them out behind him, his body flying above the bike, parallel to the road, doing the Superman stunt. From there he sat back down and did a wheelie, and then he brought his feet up and stood on the seat, flying down the highway on one wheel.

Billie's hands were sweating, a mixture of anxiety and excitement coursing through her.

The movie went to her last professional motocross race. She was decked out in her racing outfit and holding her helmet as Eddie announced, "You haven't seen a race until you've witnessed the one and only Billie 'Badass' Mancini, the fiercest woman to ever ride—"

"*Person* to ever ride," Billie corrected him on-screen.

"She's right, folks," Eddie said with a laugh. "Mancini is the fiercest, and most beautiful, motocross racer the sport has ever seen, and she's going to walk away with the trophy."

Dare's face appeared over Billie's shoulder, and he said, "Damn right she is!"

The camera zoomed in on Billie, and off camera, Eddie said, "What are you waiting for, Billie? Get out there and show the world what you've got." He cut to the race, and as she watched, Billie could still feel the adrenaline rushing through her, still hear the roar of her engine and the pounding of blood in her ears. She was neck and neck with two other racers, and as they neared the finish line, she crouched lower, giving it everything she had as she flew past them, taking the win. The camera panned to Dare, fists shooting up as he hollered, "*Way to go, Mancini!*" and took off running toward the track. Eddie was on his heels, filming and cheering, "That's our girl!" as Billie climbed off her bike and whipped off her helmet, shouting, "*Daredevils rule!*" Dare swept her into his arms and spun her around. She beamed at the camera, waving Eddie over as Dare shouted, "Get in here, Daredevil!" Eddie filmed the three of them from arm's length, hugging and laughing, their faces going in and out of the camera as he pressed his lips to hers and said, "Congratulations, baby!"

Tears slid down Billie's cheeks, and Dare held her tight as Eddie said, "Not all stunts went as planned, but that's the risk you take when you're a daredevil."

Outtakes played in rapid succession: Billie falling off her bike after a jump, doing a flip off a rope and landing in a belly flop in the lake, and stealing Dare's cowboy hat and sprinting away, only to trip on a rock and land with her face in a puddle.

Billie laughed. It was just like Eddie to inject humor at the perfect time.

She watched Dare skydiving into a tree, trying to do a trick on a horse and falling on his ass, and being chased across the grass by Doc and Cowboy for Lord only knew what. Eddie had caught her and Dare dancing on the Roadhouse bar, laughing hysterically as her father fumed at them to get down. There were clips of Eddie waving his hands, backing away from a cliff where Dare and Billie were going to BASE jump and twisting his ankle on a rut in the dirt, and one of him losing his balance over a ski jump, sending him flailing in the air and landing in a heap in the snow, and another of him walking away from a party at Billie's parents' house, talking from behind the camera as he panned the yard. "Where have those two Daredevils gotten off to?" Billie and Dare ran into the camera's line of sight about thirty feet away from Eddie, heading for Dare's Chevelle.

Oh my God, Eddie. No. She squeezed Dare's hand.

"There they are," Eddie said. "Let's go see what kind of trouble they're getting into." Just as Eddie said it, Cowboy stepped in front of him, stopping him in his tracks, and blocking the camera with his hand. "Dude, come on!" Eddie complained, wrestling the camera away and turning it on Cowboy's stoic face, as Cowboy's deep voice vibrated off the screen. "We need you in the backyard with that thing. Some-one's doing a flip off the roof." The camera shook as Eddie said, "*What?* Someone's crazier than Dare?" He turned the camera on himself as he hurried away and said, "Mission aborted. We'll catch up with those two troublemakers later. Hopefully they won't get in over their heads."

Billie watched in stunned silence as the song "Good Rid-dance (Time of Your Life)" came on. The movie faded back to Eddie swaggering onto the screen at the old dirt bike trails where the movie had begun, and he said, "Legend has it, if you pinkie swear in a barn on a hot summer's day, you're friends for life. I was lucky enough to have been near the right barn at the right time, so here's a piece of advice. If a pretty, smart-assed girl and a tough, big-mouthed boy tug you into a barn and say, *You're gonna be our best friend,* take the risk and say okay. It doesn't matter if you're an only child from a quiet household and you have no idea how you'll keep up, because once you pinkie swear, those ballsy kids will always have your back. This movie is dedicated to the two daredevils who have always had mine." As lyrics rang out about collecting memories and something unpredictable being right, his expression turned thoughtful. "While you're out there thinking about the tattoo we never got and the stunts yet to come, make the most of every minute, because as you two taught me, we can never get them back. Be happy, mad, ridiculous, sad. Be whatever you need to be, and never stop having the time of your lives. I know I am, thanks to the two of you." He patted his chest over his heart, and his fist shot up toward the sky as he hollered, "*Daredevils rule!*"

Tears flowed down Billie's cheeks, and she swiped at them as the credits rolled, naming Eddie Baker as the writer, director, and producer, followed by a note that said, THERE ARE NO ACTORS TO NAME, BECAUSE NONE OF US WERE ACTING. Beneath that was UNFORGETTABLE DAREDEVILS: BILLIE "BADASS" MANCINI AND DEVLIN "DARE" WHISKEY.

Dare turned off the movie and reached up to wipe her tears. "You hate crying."

"No shit," she mumbled to try to thwart her emotions. "Ever since you dropped out of the sky and into my life, it seems like all I do is cry." She sighed heavily and rested her head on his shoulder. "What are you doing to me, Whiskey? That was…"

"Emotional overload?"

She nodded. "I feel so much, and everything conflicts."

"Do you want to talk about it?"

"No." She grabbed an Oreo and bit into it. "It's just that back then, there were times when I was nervous when we did stunts, but it was more heightened anticipation than fear. But did you *see* the things we did?"

"I've watched it a hundred times."

"We were *reckless*."

"We were fearless," he countered as she finished her cookie and snagged another.

"They go hand in hand. I wish we could go back and start over so Eddie was still here, but at the same time, I wouldn't want to have missed any of that, except..." *Eddie's accident.* "Well, you know. We had the greatest time. We always thought we were invincible. That was the problem, wasn't it? Eddie thought he'd go out there and do that flip on the bike and maybe come out with an inflated ego or a broken arm."

"Of course he did, darlin'. He probably thought he'd do the flip and come back and gloat, rub it in my face, show you what you were missing. All the normal stuff guys do when they're hurt and don't know how to handle it."

"You mean some guys don't party too much for two years and ride bulls?"

"You heard about that, huh?"

"Everyone in Hope Valley probably heard about you riding the wildest bull on the Carlson ranch. *You're* the one with a death wish." She tilted her head, giving him a serious stare, but he kissed that seriousness away.

"No death wish, darlin'."

She gave him a *yeah, right* look, tabling that topic for another day, and grabbed the bag of chips, shoving one in her mouth. "And Cowboy? What was *that* about? Was he protecting Eddie's feelings? Protecting my reputation? Protecting you in some way?"

"Yes, to all three. It's Cowboy, the great protector. That's what he's always done."

She sighed, feeling wiped out and invigorated, as if watching the movie had opened several doors inside her, and all these questions and feelings were coming out. "Eddie was *really* talented, and funny, wasn't he?"

"Yeah, he was. Remember how we used to tease him about bringing all his camera equipment everywhere we went, and he'd say he had to be organized because you and I wouldn't remember to bring our heads if they weren't attached to our bodies?"

She laughed. "Steady Eddie was always prepared, and thank God he was. Look what he made. I can't believe he put all that together and did it so well. I mean, I *can* believe it. He was determined. But to think that he put all of that thought and time into making *us* his first big project." She teared up again. "First and last. We'll have that forever. Can you make me a copy?"

"I made you one years ago."

That tugged at her heart. She always said Eddie was so good, but Dare was just as good and loyal and loving. "How could I turn my back on you for so long? How could I turn my back on the three of us like that? I let that horrible day over-shadow all of those memories and everything we had together. I can't believe I did that. I'm so sorry."

He pressed his lips to hers. "It's okay. You're here now, and you're not running from the memories, and hopefully you won't get sick of me and kick my ass to the curb."

"If you keep snacks on hand, I might stick around longer." She held up a chip for him to eat. As he leaned forward, she popped it into her mouth. He tackled her onto her back. "The cookies!"

He reached beneath her and pulled out the package of Oreos, setting them on the coffee table. "So I've got to feed you snacks, do I?"

"Only if you want me to hang around."

"So if you bug the hell out of me, all I have to do is empty my cabinets and you'll be gone?"

She grabbed his butt. "You're losing your touch, Whiskey. No comment about your *built-in* snack?"

A husky laugh rolled out, and he rocked his hips.

"Slow down, Daredevil." She ran her hands up his back, loving the look in his eyes. He was always in a good mood, but she'd seen an undercurrent of worry in his eyes for so long, she'd forgotten how they'd glittered before she'd pushed him out of her life. It made her happy to see them clearing up, and she wondered what else she might have forgotten. "Can we watch the movie again?"

"Really?" He went up on one elbow, his gaze moving slowly over her face.

"Yeah. It was overwhelming, but it made me happy seeing the three of us having so much fun together." As they sat up, she said, "I have a feeling it'll take a while to process everything the movie makes me feel, and I might need a stiff shot of Whiskey or two to help me along, but I'd like to watch it one more time."

He hooked his arm around her, pulling her closer. "I can help you with a stiff Whiskey as many times as you need it." He kissed her smiling lips. "As for the rest of it, you're not alone. I'm here to help you through it if you'll let me."

She snagged the cookies and put them on her lap, handing him one and taking one for herself. "Thanks, but can I play therapist for a minute?"

"Be my guest."

"I think you might want to schedule a few sessions with Ezra or Colleen, because if you didn't get scared off by six years of my attitude, you've definitely got a screw loose in that big head of yours."

"Oh, you think so, do you?" He nipped at her lips.

"You're a glutton for punishment, obviously." She giggled and bit *his* cookie. "But I kind of love you for sticking around."

"I'll give you *kind of*."

He pulled her into a hard, passionate kiss, making her body sizzle and spark. When their lips parted, she pulled his mouth back toward hers. "Get back here, Whiskey. I'm not done with you yet."

Chapter Eleven

BILLIE LAY WITH her eyes closed, trying to hold on to the last threads of her dream, in which she, Dare, and Eddie were riding horses along Blackfoot Trail, where they'd ridden when they were younger. She could still hear the guys' banter and laughter. She used to love listening to them crack jokes. When the last of her dream flitted away, she opened her eyes, feeling a little euphoric. She'd slept fitfully for so many years, her dreams nothing more than unmemorable blurs interspersed with nightmares of ghosts she couldn't escape, she'd initially been rattled by how deeply she'd slept the last several days. Especially since she hadn't even been in her own bed. But she'd come to appreciate it, and she had the man beside her to thank for that.

Her gaze moved slowly over Dare's rugged face, and she welcomed in the fluttery feeling in her chest. It felt good to allow herself to be happy.

She had him to thank for that, too. Between his persistence and patience, and the movie Eddie had made, which they'd watched two more times in the four nights since they'd first watched it, she'd come to accept that it was *okay* to be happy. Not that their relationship had suddenly become perfect or easy.

She and Dare weren't perfect or easy people, and never would be. To most people that might be a problem, but for her and Dare, it was probably a saving grace. They'd get bored with perfect and easy.

Dare's lips twitched, and that fluttery feeling intensified.

It would take time to deal with the feelings she'd suppressed for so long, and it would surely be one of the biggest challenges she'd ever faced. But if this was what it felt like to *really* breathe again, to start to live without walls around her heart, it would be worth all the tears she hated to cry.

Dare's eyes opened, and just like the previous four mornings, his dark eyes gleamed even before his lips tipped up, as if he were thinking, *There's my girl.* That's how she felt every time she saw him. Last night he'd come to the Roadhouse with a number of other Dark Knights after church, and he'd stood at the bar flirting with her for most of the evening. She was sure everyone knew they were seeing each other. There was no missing her ridiculous smile, which Bobbie had said was like a neon sign announcing, THAT'S MY GUY! It wasn't like they were hiding their relationship. She was just trying to keep a modicum of professionalism at work. But it was getting harder to maintain even that distance.

He splayed his hand on her back, tugging her against him, and kissed her. "Morning, darlin'."

"Hi." She traced the wings of the tattooed bird on his neck.

"What are your plans for your day off?"

"I have *big* plans." She stretched, and his hand pressed more firmly on her back, keeping her close. "I'm going for a run, then doing laundry and taking care of a few errands."

"Think you can get it all done by noon?" he asked hopefully.

"Probably. Why?"

"It's going to be a beautiful day. I've got to meet with Kenny and two other clients this morning, but then I thought we'd go riverboarding."

Excitement zipped through her. He was just as spontaneous as he used to be. "You know I love riverboarding, but I haven't even been kayaking in years."

"Then we'll start with kayaking." He rolled her onto her back, shifting over her. "*After* we limber you up for your run."

"Is that what we're calling it now? Last night it was *wearing me out* so I'd sleep better." Not that she was complaining.

"And we did a hell of a job, didn't we?"

As his lips covered hers and their bodies came together, she couldn't think of a better way to start her day.

BILLIE GOT MORE excited about kayaking as the day wore on. When Dare picked her up, she was practically bouncing off the walls. During the hour ride to the river, he asked her if she remembered how to handle the rapids and basically gave her a Kayaking 101 lesson, going over all the things she already knew by heart.

When they arrived at the river, the crisp air and the scents of damp earth and *freedom* called out to her, but they also brought a hint of trepidation. As they put on their safety gear, she reminded herself that they weren't reckless kids. They were adults, she'd done this more times than she could count, and they were taking all the necessary safety precautions.

"Are you okay, Mancini?" He eyed her as he put on his life

vest. "Nervous?"

"*Dare*," she warned, eyes narrowing.

He held up his hands. "I know you've done it before. Sorry."

She felt bad for her knee-jerk reaction as she put on her life vest. "I'm sorry. I know you're just watching out for me, and I appreciate it, even if I'm not used to it."

"And you hate to feel *less than* anyone else."

"Yeah, that, too." He knew her so well, but maybe he needed to know who she was *now* a little better. "It's just that I might be rusty, so I am a little nervous."

He came to her with a thoughtful smile and began adjusting the fit of her vest. "Was that so hard, sharing your feelings with me?"

She rolled her eyes. "No, and I'm not *that* nervous. I *want* to do this so badly I can taste it. I just have a teeny, tiny bit of nervousness in the back of my mind."

"Kind of like the first time you saw the enormous viper in my pants."

"*Dare!*" She laughed, glad for the levity. "Get your ass in the water before I deck you."

"That's the Mancini I remember."

They put their kayaks in the water, and as they paddled down the river, snaking between rocky riverbeds, surrounded by dense trees and massive boulders, Billie was overcome with a rush of adrenaline. She welcomed it, letting it feed the sleeping parts of herself that she'd been ignoring for far too long.

Dare looked over his shoulder, flashing a sexy grin. "You're doing great, Mancini!"

His encouragement bolstered her confidence, and as they paddled downriver, the current growing stronger, he continued calling out to her, just like all those years ago, unexpectedly bringing out her competitive side. She didn't even try to fight it. She paddled faster, her muscle memory as strong as her love of the outdoors.

Dare eyed her as she pulled ahead. "*Game on*, Mancini!"

They raced downriver, laughing and giving each other crap, and as the water became rougher, Dare eased back.

"Don't treat me with kid gloves, Whiskey. I'm good."

He glanced over with a serious expression. "You *sure?*"

"You be the judge." She paddled harder, pulling ahead and entering the rapids before him. The front of the kayak tipped up and smacked down, spraying her with water, and she shrieked with joy.

She and Dare hollered back and forth as they rode the rapids, navigating around rocks and the dips and curves of Mother Nature. It was even more exhilarating than she remembered. She felt powerful and confident, and she soaked in the beauty of the river, the sun shimmering off the water, the swirls and falls that seemed to come out of nowhere. How could she have gone so long without *this* in her life? This was what fed her soul. She needed it as much as she needed the air she breathed.

When they hit a stretch of calmer water, Dare pulled up beside her, his joyful eyes glittering. "Rusty, my ass, Mancini."

She laughed, but inside she was celebrating. She'd been sure of her own skills, but she hadn't known if that hint of trepidation would hold her back. Her heart was full, knowing she wasn't tethered by fear, and if they could share *this*, they could hopefully share other adventures again, too.

"Stop lollygagging, girl, and show me what you're made of." His paddle hit the water, and he was gone in a flash.

She paddled as fast as she could as they raced toward more

rapids—and the future she hadn't ever expected to have.

DARE WAS RIDING high when they got back to the ranch that evening. He hadn't been sure Billie would go to the river with him, much less fall right back into being the competitive girl he'd known so well. He'd been on the water with Rebel and Flame and a handful of other friends, but nobody was as much fun as Billie. Their energy and connection made everything more exciting, and he knew it was because he was doing it with the person he loved most. Billie might not be one to tell him she loved him more than in a confession, but she didn't have to. It was apparent in the way she looked at him, even when she was scowling.

He pulled into the parking lot of the main house and saw Birdie's '78 yellow T-top Camaro Z28 he'd restored and given her for her twenty-fifth birthday. He wondered what she was up to.

"What are we doing here?" Billie asked as he parked.

"I've got to pick something up. Come in with me."

She looked down at her wet top and shorts. "I'm wet."

"I like you wet." He slid his hand over her thigh, waggling his brows.

She laughed softly, shaking her head.

He'd always been sexual, but with Billie he was *insatiable*. She brought out a playful intimacy and intense desire to love that had only ever existed around her. When they were in bed, he wished time would stand still, and when they were out, he wanted to experience everything with her. He could only hope that as they got to know each other better for who they'd become and their relationship deepened, she'd continue to open up to him, and he'd continue to gain her trust and bring out the parts of *her* that had only existed around *him*, like the spontaneous, zany girl who would climb on the bar to dance.

"I guess you're not the same girl who used to raid the kitchen in her bikini. My mistake."

She gave him a deadpan look.

He threw open his door. "Get your beautiful and *spankable* ass out of the truck, Mancini. You're my girl, and I want you with me."

"Well, if you put it *that* way." She pushed open the door and climbed out.

He came around to her side and slung an arm over her shoulder, pulling her into a kiss. "I'm glad you have tonight off."

"Me too. I hope Dwight has leftovers. I'm starved."

Little did she know, she was having something better than leftovers tonight.

All the teens were in the great room, and Dare was glad to see Kenny playing a video game with another boy. Dwight was sitting at a table, deep in conversation with two other teens. He nodded at Dare.

Dare took Billie's hand and headed into the kitchen, where they found Birdie leaning over a counter, wearing shiny black above-the-knee boots and a too-damn-short miniskirt attached with a silver hoop to a skintight white cropped tank top. "What the hell are you wearing?"

Birdie spun around with her cheeks full, a half-eaten hunk of pie on the counter. Her eyes filled with surprise, and she swallowed with a dramatic *gulp*. "Billie? What are you two—"

Her gaze moved to their joined hands, and she gasped. "You're *together?* Please tell me you're together." She looked at Billie. "I mean, if I were you, I'd have gone for Kellan, with those dreamy dimples and bedroom eyes, but he's totally not your type, so I get it."

"*Birdie*," Dare warned.

"I'm kidding! I'm so happy!" She squealed and ran over, throwing her arms around both of them. "More Kellan for me. Yay!"

He glowered at her.

"Why are you guys *wet?*" Birdie raised her brows. "*Ohhhh.* I don't want to know about *that.*" She took Billie's hand, dragging her toward the counter. "But I want *all* the details of how you two went from frenemies to getting *wet* together." She pushed the rest of the pie toward Billie. "You have to try Dwight's Oreo mud pie. It's so good!" She handed Billie a fork, then shoveled a ridiculously big forkful of pie into her mouth.

Dare walked over to them. "You mean the pie he made me and Billie?"

Birdie's brow knitted, and she hunched sheepishly. "Oops." She wiped her mouth. "Sorry."

"He made it for us?" Billie asked.

"Yeah. I wanted to surprise you with your favorite dinner and dessert, and he's a hell of a lot better of a cook than I am. He made chili, too. I thought we'd light the fire pit and eat on my patio."

Billie's eyes softened in a way he hadn't seen before, but before she could get a word out, Birdie said, "Aw. That's *so* romantic. The love potions finally worked!"

"Love potions?" Dare asked.

"The body wash and lotion I got you from Roxie Dalton,"

Birdie said. "She puts love potions in them. Everyone in Sugar Lake, New York, swears by them. Just don't tell Cowboy and Doc." She put her finger over her mouth, nodding.

He wondered if his sister was going off the deep end.

"You picked the right guy after all, Billie." Birdie leaned on her palm. "Tell me *everything*."

Billie was still looking at Dare. "I don't know, Birdie. He dropped out of the sky and into my life, and now I can't get rid of him."

Damn, he adored that love-drunk look in her eyes, like getting rid of him was the last thing she wanted to do.

As if she caught herself going soft, she cleared her throat and dug the fork into the pie. "With pie like this, I'm not complaining." She shoved the forkful into her mouth, eyeing him teasingly.

I love you too, Mancini.

"Sasha told me about his skydiving mission," Birdie said. "I want somebody to do a grand gesture like that for me. Heck, I'd take a guy doing a tiny gesture."

"No one's going to be doing anything for you, because you're not leaving the house in that getup." Dare waved a hand at her outfit.

She planted her hands on her hips. "I'll have you know this is an iconic outfit from *Pretty Woman*, and I am leaving the house in it because you are *not* the boss of me, and I'm meeting Sasha and Quinn at Bar None for ladies' night." Bar None was a hot pickup spot in Allure.

"The hell you are," he growled. "The woman in that movie was a *hooker*."

Birdie patted his arm like he was a child. "But I'm *not* a hooker, so who cares? Right, Billie?"

"Don't put me in the middle of this." Billie ate another bite of pie.

Dare pulled out his phone and thumbed out a text to Cowboy and Doc. *Birdie's heading to Bar None dressed like a hooker.*

"What are you doing?" Birdie peered over his shoulder as he typed out, *Can one of you get there?* "God, you're a pain in my ass." She looked at Billie. "He's making my brothers show up at the bar. I changed my mind. You *should* go for Kellan."

"This girl does *not* need a bodyguard, whether she's wearing a hooker outfit or not," Billie said. "All she's got to do is start rambling in ten different directions, and the guys who are just looking to hook up will walk away."

She was right, but guys could be persistent assholes. He was pocketing his phone when Dwight walked in.

Dwight eyed the pie, Birdie's angry face, and Billie's amused expression. "Let me guess." He pointed at Dare. "You pissed off Birdie, so she ate the pie?"

"*No.* I ate the pie not knowing it was for *him*," Birdie insisted. "But now I wish I'd eaten the whole thing."

Billie put her arm around the pie, pulling it closer, and Dare chuckled.

Dwight waggled a finger at Billie. "You, young lady, are a welcome sight in this kitchen. It's been far too long since you've been in here poking around. Now get over here and give me a hug."

Billie picked up the pie, watching Birdie out of the corner of her eye, and handed it to Dare. "Protect this. She's a vengeful little bird."

They all laughed.

Billie hugged Dwight. "Thank you for cooking for us."

"Don't thank me. Thank the big guy over there." He nodded to Dare as Birdie finished her slice of pie.

"I guess I'll have to think of a worthy way to thank him." She sauntered over to Dare with a challenging and vixenish look in her eyes, and he slid an arm around her waist, leaning in for a kiss.

"Keep *those* details to yourself. I'm heading out." Birdie put her plate in the dishwasher and snagged her bag from another counter, glowering at Dare. "I'm mad at *you*, but I want to hang out with Billie. Why don't you cancel my *other* bodyguards and come with me? It'll be fun."

"I'll keep dinner warm for you, and if Birdie's not here, the pie will be safe." Dwight winked at Birdie.

"I haven't been in a bar other than the Roadhouse in years." Billie looked hopefully at Dare, and he turned their backs to the others so they could talk.

"Don't let her pressure you."

"I'm not. I know you and Dwight went to a lot of trouble to give us a special night, and I'm excited for that. But I'd also *really* like to dance with you someplace other than where I work. I know it sounds weird, but..."

"It's not weird. Who wouldn't want to dance with me?"

She smiled. "We could go for a while and hang out with your sisters, which I also haven't done in forever, and then we can have our special night when we get back."

Now, that's the girl I used to know. "I'm in, darlin'."

"Yes!" She went up on her toes and kissed him. Then she turned to Birdie and said, "Let's do it."

"Do you want to change out of those damp clothes first?" she asked.

"No," Billie and Dare said at the same time, sharing a laugh.

"And there you have it, Dwight. The lowest maintenance

couple on the planet," Birdie said. "Let's go, weirdos."

DARE TEXTED HIS brothers and told them they were off the hook, and he and Billie spent the next two hours dancing, stealing kisses, and talking with Birdie, Sasha, and Quinn in the dimly lit bar. He'd wondered if Billie would keep her distance in front of his sisters and was glad that she didn't. Not that she was all over him—that wasn't Billie's style. But she didn't rebuff his kisses or his arm when he put it around her, and when they were on the dance floor, she was smokin' hot, rubbing against him and matching his dirty dance moves with that sexy, challenging look in her eyes.

He gave the girls space to talk with guys, but when he didn't like the way a guy looked at them, he shot warning glances and noticed Billie doing the same. He liked that she was just as protective of them as he was. They snacked on appetizers, and Billie laughed more than he'd seen her laugh in ages. The girls begged them for details on how he'd won her over, but Billie was her snarky self, saying, *I wouldn't go counting your chickens. I'm still on the fence about this one,* to which he'd thought, *Sure you are, darlin'.*

They had a great time, and when Billie whispered, "This has been great, but I'm ready to be alone with you," he didn't hesitate. They said their goodbyes and headed back to his place.

They stopped at the main house and picked up their dinner and dessert and ate by the fire pit, just as he'd planned. Only this was better because Billie's smile was even bigger and brighter than it had been earlier, and there was a new sense of peace around her.

"I *love* Dwight's chili." She wiped her mouth. "Thank you for planning all this and for getting me out on the water again and taking me dancing with the girls. I had an amazing day."

"You kicked ass on the river, Billie. Have you really not gone out on the water recently?"

She shook her head.

"How did it feel?"

She sighed and looked up at the sky for a long moment before those gorgeous eyes found him again. "Do you remember when we were in elementary school, how it felt after summer break to go back and see all our friends?"

"Hell yeah. That trickle of nervousness and the thrill of seeing everyone."

"That's what it was like. I wasn't sure what to expect, but once we were out there, it was like I'd never stopped. It was exhilarating, like I stepped back into my old body. And tonight was *so* fun. I haven't danced like that in I don't know how long. You *know* Eddie couldn't dance."

He laughed. "He had two left feet."

"But not you. You've got better moves than Magic Mike."

He leaned in and kissed her. "Thanks, darlin'."

"I missed feeling like this."

"Happy?" he asked.

"Yes, and excited about what's next. I've been so bogged down with guilt for so long, I woke up every day fighting myself. I'd see you at the bar and have this fleeting moment of *There's my bestie*, and then I'd remember the accident and the guilt would hit, and I'd shut all the good feelings down. I'd convinced myself that I was fine living that way. But I was miserable. I've missed *this*. Hanging out with you, doing spurof-the-moment things, and having fun with your sisters."

"I've missed it, too."

She was quiet as they finished their chili, and when she set her bowl aside, she said, "But I'm not the only one who's changed, you know. You're different from the way you were, too."

"I am? How?"

"I don't know exactly. I just feel it. You talk a lot more."

"I've always talked enough for both of us."

"Yeah, but it's different now. You don't blatantly push as much, and you listen and ask leading questions, which can be annoying, but it's also kind of nice."

"You're going to give me a hard time about being a therapist, aren't you?"

"Not right now, but maybe later," she teased. "Do you like being a therapist?"

He took a drink of his beer. "I love it. I get to help people, and with some, like Kenny, I can try to make a difference before things get too bad."

"Is he doing well?"

"I think so. He's been here for a little over a week, and we had a great session today."

"What happened?"

"I can't really talk about specifics because of client confidentiality, but I think he's finally realizing he can trust me. He's opening up more and figuring out where his issues stem from and talking more instead of getting angry. That's a breakthrough in my book."

"That sounds like me, doesn't it?"

"Sounds like all of us at different points in our lives."

"Do you work with a lot of teenagers?"

"Sometimes, but I work with a mix of teens and adults."

"I bet you're good at it. I remember hearing something about you working outside while you talk with your clients. Do you?"

"I do. It's easier to get people talking if their hands and minds are busy."

"Is that *really* why? Or is it because you like working with your hands and can't sit still?"

He laughed softly. "A little of both, I guess. What about you? Do you still love working at the bar?"

"I do. It's crazy, and guys can be dicks, but I love it. I like knowing I'm carrying on my grandfather's legacy, and I love working with Bobbie when she can come in and my parents." She stared out at the darkness. "But I miss not caring what people think."

"Come on, Mancini. Nobody scoffs at bullshit like you do."

"That's not what I mean." She looked at him thoughtfully. "I love working at the bar, but it was definitely more fun when I wasn't the boss and could just be myself."

"Do you miss riding the mechanical bull? You used to be damn good at it."

"Sometimes."

He steeled himself before asking a more difficult question. "How about motocross?"

Her expression turned serious. "Sometimes."

"What do you miss about it?"

"That feeling of being one with the bike. Knowing it's totally up to me if I win or lose. That rush of *wanting* to push myself to the limit. Nothing else mattered when I was on the bike."

"You were a force to be reckoned with, and if you'd stuck with it, you'd have been the best for years to come."

She lowered her gaze, rubbing the toe of her sneaker over a crack in the patio.

"Do you regret giving it up?"

She looked up. "It doesn't matter, does it? I can't go back and change it."

"Your feelings matter to me even if the past can't be changed."

"I don't know if I regret it. I couldn't have ridden after we lost Eddie. I was traumatized. It scared me."

"I know. It scared me, too. Does it still scare you?"

She shrugged. "I don't know."

He pushed to his feet and took her hand, bringing her up with him. "Let's take a walk. I want to show you something." He put the grate over the firepit, then went to the utility box on the back of the house and hit the button. Garden lights illuminated a path before them, leading into the woods.

"Whoa," she said. "What kind of secrets are *you* hiding?"

"I'm about to show you."

He slung an arm over her shoulder, and they walked along the path and through the bordering trees. When they got to the other side, he stopped by the brick column that housed a utility box and opened the control panel, flicking another switch. Spotlights bloomed to life, illuminating his five-acre motocross track, complete with a starting gate, berm turns, double and triple jumps, step-ups, tabletops, whoops (a long set of evenly spaced, few-feet-tall bumps that, if done right, riders skim the tops of), rhythm sections (continuous bumps that riders double, triple, or quad jump through), and other obstacles.

"Holy shit." Her jaw gaped. "Did you build this?"

"Nah. Some asshole built it when I was sleeping."

She bumped him with her shoulder. "Dare, this is amazing."

"It's a great track. Come on, let's check it out."

As they walked around the track, she *ooh*ed and *ahh*ed about everything, her voice escalating excitedly. "Do you ride it often?"

"Pretty often. Some of the guys ride with me occasionally. You're welcome to join me sometime."

She tightened her hold on his hand. "I don't know about that."

"No pressure." He drew her into his arms. "This is your track, baby. Ride it whenever you'd like."

Her brows slanted, confusion rising in her eyes.

"I promised I'd build you one."

She teared up. "But *why* would you, when you knew I gave it up?"

"Because you were grieving, and I thought you might give it a try again one day. Even if you didn't, I wanted to keep the promise I made to the thirteen-year-old girl who had practiced her ass off, won trophies, and showed *me* that I could achieve anything if I tried hard enough."

Tears slipped down her cheeks.

He took her face between his hands, brushing away her tears. "I hope those are happy tears."

"They are, but I hate that I spent so many years being bitchy to you, while you were fixing my bike, making this track, and watching out for me."

He gazed into her beautiful eyes and knew her tears carried tremendous pain, but that pain was coming out, which was a hell of a lot better than seeing her hold it in. "I fell in love with a stubborn girl who hates to cry, and I never saw your attitude as malicious. It's your armor, and you wouldn't be you without it."

Chapter Twelve

BILLIE SHOVED HER hair dryer under the sink and rushed out of Dare's bathroom Saturday morning, grabbing her underwear and cutoffs and pulling them on as fast as she could. They'd slept until eight o'clock, which neither of them *ever* did, and then they couldn't keep their hands off each other in the shower, making her even later to meet her mother and sister for brunch at Grandma's Kitchen, a diner in town. She quickly put on her bra and snagged her T-shirt from a chair by the dresser, willing herself not to look at Dare as he dried off from their shower. But that was like asking a starving woman not to eat, and she couldn't resist stealing a glance. Her ridiculously needy body whimpered in desperation as he dragged the towel down his abs, biceps flexing. A slow grin appeared, and he stretched his arms out to his sides, giving her a full-on view of the orgasm master between his legs, which had turned her into a total nymphomaniac. Every time they were close, she wanted to be closer.

He reached down and gave his pleasure wand one slow tug, waking up the sleeping beast. She bit her lower lip. *So unfair.*

He raised his brows. "You could skip brunch."

"I can't. I promised my mom I'd be there. We don't have breakfast together very often, like your family does, and after what my dad told me about how my pulling away from everyone affected them, I don't want to let my mom down."

"Babe, it's okay. I think you should go. I was only teasing, or wishing out loud, even though I know you need to see your mom."

She pulled on her shirt and hurried out of the bedroom, scanning the living room for her boots as she plucked the clothes she'd been wearing last night off the floor. Dare had stripped them off her the minute she'd arrived. She looked under the couch and glanced in the kitchen but didn't see them anywhere. "Dare, do you know where my boots are?"

He came out of the bedroom wearing only a pair of worn jeans that hugged him in all the right places. "You kicked them off, and one hit the fireplace, remember?" He walked over to the fireplace and pulled her boot out from behind the fireplace equipment. "Found *one*."

"Thank God." She ran over to grab it and spotted her other boot behind a pillow on the couch. She snagged it and reached for the one Dare was holding.

He held it high out of her reach, and she glowered at him. "I just want a kiss, darlin'."

It was hard to be mad when she wanted one, too. She went up on her toes, giving him a quick kiss, and sat down to put her boots on.

"I wish you were riding with me today," he said.

He was going on a motorcycle ride with some of the guys. She *loved* riding motorcycles, but she'd given that up, too. She wasn't afraid of them, but she wasn't ready to jump on one again, either. "Maybe one day I will. You're coming by the bar later?"

"Absolutely. I want to see you, and I'm meeting my father and brothers there after my ride."

"They're not riding with you?"

"No, they have shit to do. It's just Rebel, Flame, Taz, and a few other guys."

"Cool. Where are you riding?" She pushed to her feet, grabbed her keys from the coffee table, and went to grab her phone from the bedside table.

"Up to Stone Edge. Rebel's buddies are bringing in six buses so I can practice my jumps."

She stopped cold, a chill trickling down her spine. She turned to face him with her heart in her throat. "You're jumping buses today?"

"Just six, they couldn't get a seventh. Maybe next time." He cocked his head, eyes turning serious as he came to her side. "Are you okay? You look like you've seen a ghost."

"Maybe that's because that might be all I see of you after today. I can't believe you're jumping buses. *Why* are you jumping buses?"

"Because it's cool and fun, and I want to beat the world record eventually."

She knew that, but somehow now that they were together, it felt different. *Real.* And there was no holding back her anxiety. "But why would you do that when you know it's more dangerous than what Eddie did? Do you want to end up dead?"

"No. *Jesus*, Billie. I'll be fine. I've been doing this for years."

"All it takes is *one* mistake. You know that." Her voice escalated, heart slamming against her chest. "You were there when Eddie died. Have you forgotten what it was like to see our best friend lying lifeless? To see him carried away? Buried in the ground?"

His jaw clenched. "You *know* I'll never forget that."

"But *that* could happen to you! It doesn't matter how many times you do something. Eddie had ridden bikes a million times."

"He'd never done a *flip* on one, and it was stupid of him to try when he was pissed off. But he didn't deserve to die because of one fucking mistake. If anyone deserved to die out there, it was *me*. So don't think you have to remind me of what *can* happen, because I think about it every damn day."

"Is that why you've been doing crazier stunts ever since? Climbing out of a moving biplane and strapping yourself to it? Riding the Wall of Death? Testing fate every chance you get? Because you're waiting for your turn to die?"

"*No*," he gritted out. "I'm doing it because this is who I *am*, Mancini. It's who I've always been."

"I don't know if that's true," she said shakily. "You've always done crazy shit, but jumping over *buses* on a motorcycle? That's not like skydiving or riding the scariest bull at the Carlsons', which was also terrifying, but your chances of survival were a lot higher than jumping buses or *running* with bulls in Spain."

His eyes bored into hers. "You never had a problem with the way I lived my life before."

"Yeah, well, I guess this is the *new* me," she said angrily, hating the fear and anxiety consuming her as much as she hated the things she was saying to him. "The me *after* I lost a man I loved." She tried to rein in her emotions, but she was shaking. "We *just* got together, Dare, and I don't want to lose you."

"You're *not* going to lose me, Billie."

"You don't know that." Her head was spinning. She crossed

and uncrossed her arms, feeling scared and out of control. "I *hate* this. I hate worrying. I hate the fear that's eating me alive right now, and I hate saying all this to you. I sound like someone I *never* wanted to be."

"You sound like someone who lost a friend during a stunt, and you're allowed to be worried about me," he said vehemently, putting his hands on her upper arms and bringing her eyes up to his, his expression softening. "This is who I am, Billie. I know you're scared, but I want to live my life, not live it in fear."

"I don't *want* you to live in fear. I've done enough of that for both of us, and I don't want to *change* you. But I don't know if I can handle worrying every time you decide to up your game."

His jaw tightened. "What are you saying? If I do this, we're done?"

"*God* no. I'm not going to make you choose between me and something you love doing. Even if we weren't together, I'd still worry about you. I barely took a breath when you were off doing that damn Wall of Death."

"Then what *do* you want?"

"I don't *know!*" She exhaled loudly, shaking her head. "To *not* have all this stuff in my head."

He reached for her hand. "Then let's talk about it."

"I can't. I'm late. I have to go. *Just...*" She went up on her toes, holding his gaze. "I love you, Whiskey. Please don't die." She kissed him and hurried out the door before he could see tears of frustration trickling down her cheeks.

By the time she got to town, she'd thrown out open-ended threats to the universe—*So help me, if you let anything happen to him*—and dozens of silent prayers to keep Dare safe. Her tears had stopped, but she felt like she'd eaten a plate of lead. Usually just driving past the cute brick shops in her quaint small town brightened her spirits, but that sinking feeling wasn't budging.

She drove past the fountain in the center of town and around the corner to the iconic '50s style diner where she was meeting her mom and sister. It was decked out with red vinyl seats and checkered floors, served drinks in mason jars, and was known for its comfort food. Billie questioned the sense of that term—*comfort food*. She was so stressed, she felt like she could throw up.

She took a deep breath as she stepped out of her truck, throwing out another silent prayer and trying to think of an excuse to tell her mother and sister about why she was late other than sleeping in, having sex in the shower, and then fighting about shit she didn't want to think or talk about.

I lost my keys.

The old excuse she and her sister had used when they'd missed curfew because they didn't want to stop kissing a boy they were with or they were having too much fun with their friends would work perfectly.

As she passed the window of the diner, two of her father's Dark Knights buddies waved from inside, where they were eating breakfast with their wives. Billie smiled and pulled open the door.

"There's Hope Valley's superstar," Flo said from behind the counter.

Flo was in her midfifties, with thick dark hair that she wore twisted into some sort of bun and trapped under a scarf when she was at work and loose and wild when she wasn't. The diner had been in her family for generations, and they'd been hanging up pictures of locals' claims to fame for practically as long.

When Billie had hit the pro-motocross circuit, the town had thrown a freaking parade. She, Eddie, and Dare had ridden on a float down the middle of the street. They'd done the same for Dare when he'd broken the world record for the Wall of Death, although she hadn't attended that parade.

Billie glanced at the picture of herself above the bar. She was riding her motocross bike at her first professional race. A photographer for the newspaper had taken it, and Flo had asked her to autograph it. She'd scrawled BILLIE "BADASS" MANCINI, DAREDEVIL FOR LIFE. She felt a pang of longing, but it was pushed to the side by that morning's frustrations. "That was a long time ago, Flo."

"You'll always be a hero in my eyes, sweetheart. Your mama and sissy are right back there. I'll bring you a cup of coffee." She motioned to a booth in the back of the diner, where they were drinking coffee and chatting.

"Thanks, Flo." As she weaved around the customers eating at tables, waving to the ones she knew, she realized her mother and Bobbie were sitting beside the picture of Dare riding the Wall of Death. *Great.* He'd signed his picture the same way she had—DAREDEVIL FOR LIFE. When she'd first seen the picture of him doing the stunt, and his signature, it had sent her heart into a full-on tizzy. The three of them had signed everything that way, from schoolwork to birthday cards, but she'd stopped after Eddie died, and she'd been shocked to see that he hadn't.

Billie's thoughts returned to the motocross track Dare had built for her, and her chest constricted. How could she feel so many conflicting things at once? She tried to push those thoughts away as she plopped down in the booth beside her sister, who looked cute in a pink blouse and white miniskirt. Her long blond hair was loose and wavy, and she wore a smirk that Billie wasn't in the mood to decipher.

"Sorry I'm late." Billie picked up a menu and stared absently at it.

"That's okay, honey," their mother said cheerily.

"Trouble finding your *keys?*" Bobbie mused.

"More like trouble with Whiskey," Billie mumbled to herself.

Their mother reached over and lowered the top of the menu so she could see Billie's face. Alice Mancini was a rare mix of strong-willed and lovingly sweet, and even though Billie knew her mother was often baffled by her, she had always known their mother would walk through fire for her. She had fair skin, wavy shoulder-length blond hair that was always a bit tousled and frizzy, and she never wore much makeup. Bobbie had once asked her why she didn't take more time to pretty herself up, and their mother had said she had enough *real* things to spend her time on to worry about that. She had been naturally beautiful when she was younger. Now she had fine lines around her eyes and mouth, her hair was thinner, her waist thicker, but she was still pretty, especially when she smiled, and Billie thought her not-so-perfect style suited her to a T.

"Do you want to talk about it?" their mother asked.

"Not really. I don't even want to *think* about it," she said as Flo arrived with her coffee.

Flo looked at Billie curiously as she set the mug in front of her. "Word around town is that the Daredevils have been *canoodling.*"

Billie stopped herself from rolling her eyes. "Gotta love small-town gossip."

"I remember when you, Dare, and Eddie—*rest his soul*—would pop in here all hyped up and sit at the counter yammering about skiing or racing dirt bikes, drinking milkshakes and stealing each other's fries." Flo glanced at the picture of Dare on the wall and turned a warm smile on Billie. "I swear you used to look at those boys like they'd hung the moon. But there was always a little extra spark in your eyes for Dare. I always wondered when you kids would figure it out. You're a lucky girl, Billie. Those Whiskey boys turned into good men, and we all know they're the hottest bachelors in town with all the good they do out there at that ranch. Now we've got to find a nice young man for this beautiful lady." She smiled at Bobbie.

"Why don't we see how Billie's love life pans out first?" Bobbie set that smirk on Billie again.

This time Billie *did* roll her eyes.

They ordered breakfast, and after Flo left, their mother said, "I had lunch with Wynnie yesterday, and she mentioned that you and Dare have been spending a lot of time together. I'm glad you're mending that fence. You were such good friends for so long, and we were all heartbroken when you drifted apart."

Billie knew she was just being kind by implying she and Dare had both actively put distance between them. *That was all me, and I didn't just drift. I put myself behind bars.*

"I still want to know how he got the chip off your shoulder," Bobbie pushed. "Not that I'm complaining. I've had the house to myself every night this week, and it has been *heavenly*."

Billie gave her a sister a *thanks a lot* look. She hadn't even had a chance to tell their mother that she and Dare had been seeing each other, although she was sure her father probably had.

"Well, then, I guess you have your answer, Bobbie," their mother said with a smile. "It sounds like our girl has been getting some good lovin', which was long overdue, in my opinion."

"Can we *not* go there?" Billie asked.

"I'm just saying that it explains a lot," their mother said. "Kellan said you've been less snappy at work and smiling more. So you must be happy about it, despite whatever's got you upset this morning."

"I *am* happy about it."

"Then why do you look like if you don't go for a run, you're going to start breaking things?" Bobbie asked.

"*Bobbie*," their mother chided. "She said she didn't want to talk about it. Billie, honey, how is Dare? What's he up to today?"

"The thing I don't want to talk about," she grumbled.

Her mother and sister exchanged a concerned glance, and Billie thought about what her father had said about her moods. She might not like to talk about things, but she owed it to her family to try.

"He's jumping over buses on his motorcycle. *Six* buses, to be exact." Even saying it brought a wave of worry.

"Oh goodness. I'll have to stop by and see Wynnie after breakfast," their mother said. "She must be worried sick."

Bobbie looked at Billie compassionately. "You're worried, too, aren't you?"

"Of course. Aren't you now that you know?"

"Yes, but I'm not in love with him," Bobbie said.

Billie was stunned into silence. She and Bobbie were fairly close, but while Bobbie would lay her heart on the table and label every feeling and nuance of her love, Billie had always kept hers under wraps.

"Don't look so shocked, honey," their mother said. "Just like Flo said, it's been written in your eyes since you were a little girl trying to outdo his every trick."

She wasn't even going to try to deny it. She was tired of hiding her feelings, but she didn't want to pick them apart, either, so she circumnavigated. "Do you have any words of wisdom for me about him jumping over buses? How am I supposed to watch him do something so dangerous? I don't want to stop him from doing what he loves. *I* love that he's fearless and driven and wants to be the best at everything. But I can't..." Tears stung her eyes, and she turned away, willing them not to fall.

Bobbie touched her hand. "It's okay to be worried about him."

"I can only tell you how I got through it with you," their mother said. "It's not easy supporting someone you love when they're doing things that terrify you, and I had to learn how to handle it when you were just a toddler."

"A toddler? That has to be an exaggeration," Billie said.

"I assure you, it's not. Let me give you some examples. When you were two, you climbed over every gate we ever put up, including the one at the top of the stairs. At three, you asked me for a bowl of ice cream just as the mailman arrived, and I said I'd give it to you after I gave him a package. In the few minutes it took for me to do that, you'd pushed a chair over to the kitchen counter, climbed up, and somehow opened the freezer. To this day I don't know how you did it, but when I came in, you were hanging from the top of the freezer door by one hand, with a half gallon of ice cream in the other, grinning from ear to ear like you hadn't just given me a heart attack."

Bobbie laughed. "Sounds like Billie. She's always hungry."

"That was just the *start*," their mother said. "That same year, she climbed the curtains and hung from the curtain rod because she wanted to be in the circus, and a few days after her fourth birthday, she carried a baking pan up the stairs while I was in the bathroom and proceeded to sled down, running headfirst into the wall."

"Jesus." Billie was amused and astonished. She was coming to understand why she confounded their mother so much.

"Obviously I got the brains in the family," Bobbie teased.

"That was when I realized how fearless my little girl was, and short of putting you in a puppy crate, there was *no* stopping you."

"Thanks for not putting me in a crate," Billie said. "What did you do?"

"To be honest, I was a mess. I wasn't prepared to be such a fierce little girl's mother. When other little girls were playing with dolls, you were racing around or diving off things. I was sure you'd end up with a head injury, and it was my responsibility to keep you safe. But it was also my responsibility not to hold you back from becoming the person you were meant to be. Even if I didn't understand who that was. It wasn't easy figuring out how to do both, but your father and I talked about it, and we came up with a plan. We talked with you often about the dangers of what you were doing and tried to give you other options. Your father put up bars for you to climb on out back that weren't as high as the curtains, but you refused to use them because you said they were for babies."

Bobbie stifled a laugh.

"We instituted more time-outs, but you'd sit and stew, and I swear to you, Billie Jean, you spent that time concocting your next endeavor. So, we padded the corners of furniture, fortified the curtain rods, and I made a padded mat for the bottom of the stairs. If I took you girls to a park, I brought a high schooler with me to help me keep an eye on you. But as you got older, our worries got bigger. Your father and I couldn't watch you every second, and if we'd told you that you couldn't ride dirt bikes or climb to impossible heights, you'd have been even more determined to do it. By then, you, Dare, and Eddie had become like this." She crossed her fingers. "Those boys were blessings in our lives. Their parents were going through the same things we were, and we shared the burden of keeping tabs on our riskier kids while we had our others underfoot. We helped each other, and we learned everything we could about the things you kids did, so we would understand the dangers, and it helped us to understand how the activities were good for you, too. It was a relief knowing we weren't in it alone, and Tiny had Doc and Cowboy watching out for you kids, too, although that presented its own problems. Dare was not happy about that, and he was always finding ways to sneak away."

"We all did," Billie said.

Tiny had been tough on his boys when they were younger, drilling into them the need to watch out for their siblings and for others and teaching them to always try to do the right thing. He wasn't shy with his opinions, either. He'd given Billie, Bobbie, Eddie, and plenty of their other kids' friends talking-*tos* about the same things.

"But don't get me wrong," their mother said. "You kids weren't bad children; you just liked doing different things than other kids. But the three of you self-regulated. Eddie was just careful enough to make you and Dare think twice about some things, and as wild as Dare was, he was *always* looking out for you, and you would get furious at him for it. He'd tell you to watch him do something so he could let you know if it was too hard for you, and you'd stomp ahead and do it first."

"Darn right I did. I wasn't going to be told what to do by a boy."

"Here's a news flash," Bobbie said. "You don't like to be told what to do by *anyone*, and neither does Dare."

"I know, but he could get seriously hurt or *die*," Billie pointed out.

"When I used to tell you that, you'd say you could get hurt walking across the street," Bobbie reminded her. "So where's the line between what's okay and what's not? Do you want him to stop doing everything that's dangerous? Parachutes fail. Does he have to stop skydiving? What about driving his motorcycle? They're more dangerous than cars. How about cliff diving? He could land wrong and—"

"I *get it*, Bobbie," Billie snapped. "I don't mean those types of activities. We went kayaking, and I loved it."

"You did?" their mother asked. "That's wonderful."

"I know. It felt great, and it kind of made me want to try doing some of the fun things we used to do again." She surprised herself with that statement but didn't slow down to explore it. "It's just the over-the-top stunts I'm having trouble with. The ones where it seems like Dare has a death wish."

Bobbie held her gaze, her expression warming. "You won't want to hear this, but have you considered that maybe you've changed too much to be with him?"

"Of course I have. But I *want* to be with him. I *love* being with him, and I like who I am when we're together. I just don't want to lose him." She bit back the emotions clawing at her and looked at their mother. "Did you know he has my old racing bike?"

"Yes," his mother said. "You wanted us to get rid of it, and he asked if he could have it. I didn't think you'd mind."

"Did you know about the track he built?"

"I knew he built a motocross track," their mother said. "Why?"

Billie shook her head. "No reason."

"Oh my gosh, *Billie.*" Bobbie looked at her imploringly. "Your thirteenth birthday card. He built it for you, didn't he?"

Tears sprang to Billie's eyes so fast, she didn't know what hit her.

"Oh, Billie." Their mother's brows knitted. "That risk-taking man loves you with everything he has, doesn't he?"

"Okay, *stop.* You're not going to make me all emotional."

"Are those tears I see?" Bobbie teased.

"Don't." Billie exhaled loudly, trying to pull herself together. "Mom, did you tell me all those things about when I was little to show me that there's nothing I can do about my situation with Dare?"

"No, honey. I was trying to tell you that everyone is different. Some people are wired to crave extra thrills, and after everything you've been through, it's only natural that you're afraid of losing Dare. But I think Bobbie has a point. If you're going to be with Dare, you have to accept who he is and support him the best you can, no matter how scary it might be. You know, when I met your dad, he wasn't a biker who went to meetings every Tuesday or on motorcycle rides with Tiny and the guys for hours at a time, and he certainly had never picked up anyone from prison or detention centers, like the Dark Knights do. He was a low-key guy, and we had hopes of opening a bookstore and coffeehouse one day. But when your grandfather offered him the bar, I saw something in your father's eyes that I'd never seen before, and I realized that if we'd followed through with our plans, I might never have seen the extra light he still carries. As you know, your father has faced some tough cookies at the bar and through the club. But that club has become our family, and we've both loved every minute of working at the bar, and now you're carrying on our legacy."

"Thank *God* you didn't open a bookstore," Billie said.

"I would love to run a bookstore and coffee shop. Maybe when Daddy retires, he and I can open one," Bobbie suggested.

"Now, that's an interesting idea. Maybe you should plant that seed with him." Their mother reached across the table and touched Billie's hand. "Honey, I know you're in a difficult place, but I can't give you the answers you're looking for. Only you can decide what you're willing to accept. Maybe it's time to think about talking to someone about everything you've been through."

"I am. I've been talking to Dare."

"That's wonderful," their mother said. "But I mean someone you can tell things to that you might not want to share with us or Dare. I bet you could talk to Colleen at the ranch, or Wynnie can get you the name of someone in town."

"I don't know, Mom." Talking to Dare was helping, but she wasn't crazy about the idea of sharing her innermost feelings with anyone else. "I'll think about it."

Flo brought their breakfasts, and as her mother and sister began eating, Billie said another silent prayer to keep Dare safe. She speared a piece of her waffle with her fork, but she couldn't eat.

"Bobbie, honey, Wynnie and the girls want to get together four weeks from tomorrow to go over plans and schedules for Festival on the Green and the kickoff of the Ride Clean campaign. Can you make it?"

While she and Bobbie talked about their plans, Billie's mind traveled back in time. When they were little, their mother brought them to her planning meetings for Dark Knights events, and Billie had hated it. She'd felt like a caged animal, sitting in a room with her and Dare's moms and their sisters, while Dare and Eddie were running around outside. But her parents had instilled in her and Bobbie that they were a Dark Knights family, and it was important to do their part. Billie had always enjoyed helping out at the events, but the planning part had never been her thing. She'd gotten out of it as a teenager by being stubborn—at least until she was nineteen, when Bobbie, who had always loved planning anything and everything, had asked her to go. Dare had been away at school, and it had made her feel a little more connected to him to be with his family. She'd enjoyed the time with the girls and had continued to help with the planning each year until Eddie's accident.

She was starting to realize how much shutting people out of her life had really cost her. She'd not only missed out on time with Dare and worried her family, but she'd missed out on that time with her mother, sister, and Dare's mother and sisters, too.

"Mom," she interrupted. "Sorry. I'm just wondering if you think it would be okay if I tagged along to the planning meeting?"

Their mother pressed her lips together, looking as though she might cry. "I think that would be marvelous."

"You *want* to go?" Bobbie asked.

"Yeah, I do."

Bobbie pulled out her phone.

"Who are you texting?" Billie asked.

"Dare, to tell him to keep doing whatever he's been doing."

"Gimme that!" Billie tried to grab her phone.

"Okay, okay!" Bobbie laughed, setting it on the table. "I'm

glad you're going. It's always more fun with you there."

"Really?" She was surprised, because Bobbie had never called her fun before.

"*Yes.* You're fun when you're not acting like a fire-breathing dragon." Bobbie bumped her with her shoulder, softening the truth.

"This is going to be so exciting," their mother said. "Let me tell you what I'm thinking..."

Billie wasn't so sure about it being exciting, but it would be nice to start crossing the ravine she'd caused between herself and Dare's family. Her mind tiptoed back to Dare's dangerous stunt, and as she'd been doing all morning, she silently begged for his safety.

SEVERAL HOURS LATER, *Please keep him safe* was still playing in her mind like a mantra as she served drinks at the bar. It was a busy afternoon, and she'd been watching the door like a hawk, praying she'd see Dare walk through it. His father and brothers had just arrived, and she took that as a good sign. If something had happened, wouldn't someone have contacted them?

Doc and Tiny were talking as they headed for a table. Doc pulled out his phone, showing something to his father, his biceps straining against his Redemption Ranch T-shirt, colorful tattoos on full display. Tiny wore his cut, as usual. Billie could count on one hand how many times she'd seen him without it. He was as proud of the Dark Knights as he was of his family and the ranch. Cowboy walked behind them, clothes stretched tight over his bulbous muscles, his cowboy hat firmly planted on his head, and those ever-watchful eyes moving around the bar. He was built like a bodybuilder.

Or a bodyguard, she thought, recalling what he'd done in Eddie's movie.

Cowboy lifted his chin in her direction, and she whispered *Thank you* in her head. Doc and Cowboy had always kept tabs on Dare, but Cowboy had been a little harder on him, giving him grief for the crazy shit he'd done and making sure he'd stayed on task to the point of annoyance. She wondered if he'd done it because he'd feared for his brother's safety or because it was expected of him. Did he feel as much at a loss as Billie did today?

"Where's your boy toy?" Kellan asked, pulling her from her thoughts.

"*Kellan*," she warned. "He's out riding. Why?"

"Just curious since the guys are here. Aren't you going to serve your father- and brothers-in-law?"

"Don't *you* work for *me*?" She was just giving them a minute to get settled in.

He flashed a dimple-bearing grin. "Yes, but you don't want me out on the floor where women can paw at me and slow down my service."

"You just like having the best seat in the house to scope them out."

"Well, there is that, but now that you and *lover boy* are an item, I don't want to cramp your style."

She rolled her eyes and went to take the Whiskeys' orders. They watched her approaching, his father's face as serious as always. Did he know what Dare was up to today? If so, why wasn't he there with him?

Doc smiled, giving her a curt nod, another Whiskey greeting she knew well. She thought about what Dare had said about the time he'd given Johnny Petrone a black eye. *I'd have done more than that if Doc hadn't stopped me.* She wondered if he'd told Doc why he'd done it.

"How's it going, sweetheart?" Tiny asked.

"Pretty well, thanks. You?" He'd been kind to her throughout the years, despite how cold she'd been toward Dare, and now that she was trying to be more introspective and not suppressing her feelings, his kindness stirred all sorts of emotions. But she was too high-strung from worrying all day to think about any of that and stuffed it down deep to dissect another time.

"I'll let you know when I hear from my boy." Tiny looked at his watch and uttered a curse.

"So you *know* he's jumping buses today?"

Tiny nodded.

Cowboy's jaw clenched.

"We know," Doc said. "Crazy bastard."

Something inside her snapped. "Then why aren't you *with* him? Something could happen, and you won't be there."

Tiny tipped his bearded face up, eyes narrowing. "I reckon it's the same reason you're not there."

"I didn't know until this morning, and I had plans with my mom," she said lamely, knowing that even if she hadn't had plans, she couldn't have watched him do that dangerous of a stunt.

Tiny nodded. "I hear ya, sweetheart. I love my son, but that doesn't mean I like everything he does. I can't stop him from chasing his dreams, but I don't have to watch him do it."

Some part of her wanted to say, *What about all that stuff you taught us about loyalty and brotherhood? Doesn't that mean having his back no matter what?* But how could she say that when she didn't have Dare's back, either?

"I'd have gone, but I had to do surgery on a horse this morning," Doc said.

"I had to run a crew on the ranch," Cowboy said. "I asked him to reschedule, but it's not that easy when buses are involved."

Her heart beat faster, thinking of Dare getting into trouble and none of them being there. It made her sick to her stomach, just thinking about it. "I just hope he's okay."

"I've got to believe he will be, darlin'," Tiny said with a nod. "As long as no one gets him riled up before the jump."

The words cut like knives as she realized *she'd* probably gotten him riled up by getting so upset. *Shit.* Her mind reeled. *How could I have done that to him?* Her nerves were fried, and her heart felt like it was being crushed. She quickly took their orders, feeling like she was going to cry or scream or both. But as she turned to walk away, her thoughts returned to the things her mother had said, and she had to ask, "Is Wynnie okay? My mom said she was going to see her this morning."

"Our mother is strong," Doc said. "She's been through this type of thing time and time again with Dare. But what about you, Billie? How are you holding up?"

My nerves are shot, and I'm terrified that something horrible is going to happen.

"I'm fine," she said as convincingly as she could. "I'll bring your drinks right over." She went to fill their drinks, throwing extra prayers out to the universe to make up for her big fat lie.

DARE LED THE pack of motorcycles down the street, the roar of their engines as comforting as the sight of the neon ROAD-HOUSE sign as he pulled into the parking lot, conflicting emotions pummeling him. He parked by his father's bike, telling himself he'd done the right thing as he climbed off his bike and locked his helmet.

He fell into step with Rebel, Flame, and Taz, following the other guys as they headed inside.

Flame clapped him on the back. "Great ride, man. You doing a'right?"

Finn "Flame" Steele had grown up a few towns over in Trusty, Colorado. He and Dare had met several years ago, when he'd prospected the Dark Knights, and they'd hit it off. The smoke jumper thrived on risks, and he'd come from a big family, like Dare's. He was a good guy, despite his twin sister, Fiona, dubbing him the *evil* twin.

"I'm cool." It was a lie. He wouldn't be cool until he and Billie worked their shit out. He'd worried about her all day.

They walked inside, and all eyes turned toward them. But Dare's gaze was riveted to Billie as she spun around behind the bar. Her eyes went wide as saucers, and she launched herself *over* the bar and sprinted across the room, throwing herself into his arms, her legs wrapping around him like Velcro. *What the...?*

"*You'reokayyou'reokayyou'reokay.*" She took his face between her hands and planted a kiss on his lips, earning whoops, whistles, and cheers from around the bar. This was a far cry from the girl who was afraid to kiss him at work a week ago.

"Damn. Where can I get one of those, bro?" Flame teased,

earning laughs from the others. "Come on, let's let these two have their *moment*."

As the guys filed past, Rebel said, "When you're done making out, we'll have a round of beers, but you'd better get that *baby* some milk."

"Fuck off, Rebel," Dare gritted out as Billie's feet hit the floor.

Rebel chuckled and walked away.

"I'm sorry for getting so upset this morning," she said quickly. "I shouldn't have acted like that when you were on your way to do something so dangerous."

"It definitely fucked with my head." He guided her away from the entrance. "But that's okay. Don't ever apologize for telling me how you feel. I want to know what you're thinking, even if I don't like it. I was an ass for springing it on you. I've never had to think like a couple, and I need to work on that."

"Maybe that would help, but we said Daredevils for life, and I didn't have your back today. I'm so glad you're okay. I don't want you to change, and I won't ever try to stop you again. We only get one life, and you need to live yours the way you want to, but I don't think I can watch you do some of your riskier stunts, like jumping over buses."

He couldn't believe his ears, and he pulled her into his arms, holding her tight. "Thank you." He drew back and kissed her. "But I didn't do the jump."

She blinked several times. "What happened?"

"I got ready to do it, but with what had gone down between us, I wasn't feeling it. That's why Rebel made that comment about milk."

"Oh *no*. I suck. I'm so sorry I screwed it up for you."

"No, darlin', you're amazing. You're trusting me enough to

open up, and that's so much more important than me making a jump. We're going to have a lot of things to figure out, and this is just one of them. I rescheduled for about a month from now. That should give us time to deal with some of these feelings and give you time to get used to the idea."

"Okay," she said softly.

"And, babe, I already have tickets to run with the bulls in Spain, so I think we should spend some time talking about that, too. I've wanted to do it for years."

"*Oh boy*," she said exasperatedly, but then she squared her shoulders and lifted her chin, her eyes serious. "Okay. I'd better start buying preparations."

"Preparations?"

"I'm thinking about massive, inflatable stunt pads all around the buses in case you miss and full-body armor for running with the bulls. Do you think they sell that on Amazon?"

He laughed and hauled her into a kiss.

"You think I'm kidding, Whiskey?"

"*No*, Mancini, and I love you even more for it."

"I need to get back to work. I'll bring you guys a round of drinks."

He kept her in his arms and couldn't stop looking at her. Did she have any idea how much what she said, and what she did, meant to him? "You realize you just claimed me in front of everyone in here, right? I'm pretty sure Kellan was one of the guys whistling."

"Don't make me regret it," she warned teasingly.

"Baby, I'm going to make you wish you'd done it sooner." He lowered his lips to hers, earning more hoots and hollers. They came away laughing, and he swatted her ass as she headed back to the bar.

She glowered over her shoulder as Dare went to join the guys.

"What kind of bullshit is this?" Rebel said before Dare even reached the table. "You didn't do the jump, and you *still* got the hottest girl in town?"

"That's because Dare's the *man*," Flame rebuffed.

"He's packin' a magic pecker, unlike your pinkie package." Taz barked out a laugh.

Rebel scoffed, and as they joked around, Dare took a seat by his father and brothers.

His father clapped a hand on his back. "Good to see you, son. Did you call your mother?"

"I will in a minute." *I need a second to process what just happened.*

"Dude, what'd you do to Billie to get that kind of greeting?" Cowboy asked.

"Pissed her off."

"No, you didn't." Doc held his gaze. "You scared her."

"Yeah, that too." He hated that he'd worried her, but he was determined not to let fear rule his life.

"You really didn't do the jump?" Cowboy asked.

Dare shook his head. "I wasn't feeling it."

"Why not?" Doc pressed. "You've never stopped short of doing a stunt, especially one that required that much preparation."

Dare met his steady gaze. "Why do you *think*?"

"Did she tell you not to jump?" Doc asked.

"No. She would never do that."

"Interesting." Doc narrowed his eyes. "Well, I'm fucking thrilled that you didn't do it. I'm not ready to lose you to some dumbass stunt."

"If I'd known that was all it would take to get you to back down, I'd have bribed her a long time ago," Cowboy said.

His father chuckled, sharing a knowing glance with Dare.

Dare watched Billie heading their way with a tray of beers, giving him a half smirk, half smile that said, *Yeah, I claimed you, Whiskey. Don't make a big deal out of it.* "She wouldn't have taken a bribe."

"How do you know?" Cowboy asked.

He turned back to his brother. "Because I know my girl better than you know your left hand."

Everyone cracked up.

"Are you boys gonna behave this afternoon, or do I need to get my whip out?" Billie asked as she handed out their drinks.

"I don't even know what that word means," Rebel said.

"Yeah, beautiful, I can't make any promises," Taz added.

She rolled her eyes and set the last drink in front of Dare. "Can I get you all anything else?"

"I can think of a few things I'd like, but not with these nitwits around." Dare winked.

"Keep it in your pants, Whiskey." She turned on her heel and strutted away.

The guys laughed.

"She loves me," Dare said. "And by the way, I'm doing the jump next month."

"You can't be serious." Doc glared at him. "You're going to put her through that? Soul mates come around only once in a lifetime, bro. I strongly suggest you rethink your priorities."

Dare felt bad for Doc, who had never gotten over the daughter of a prominent asshole he'd fallen for when he was younger. But Dare wasn't Doc, and Billie sure as hell wasn't

Juliette. "Back off, Doc. That's between me and Billie. She doesn't want to change me. It's just going to take some time for her to get used to who I am again now that we're together."

"You were always a stubborn little shit," Cowboy said with as much ferocity as amusement. "Now you're a big stubborn shit. No wonder you and the teenagers who come through our programs get along so well."

"You know you love me, douchebag." Dare flicked Cowboy's hat off and chuckled as he fumbled to catch it. "How'd my boy Kenny do today?"

"He was great. He's learning respect, and he's talking more with the other guys. He's turning into a hard worker, and when he gets too big for his britches, all it takes is one look to get him back on track." Cowboy put his hat back on. "Touch it again and I'll kill you with my bare hands."

Dare laughed. "You can try."

"Dare," his father said, drawing all of their attention. "How do *you* think Kenny's doing?"

"He's getting there, opening up, starting to see his actions for what they really were. We're working on communication, learning to say what he feels instead of just getting pissed off. Another couple of weeks and hopefully we can bring his parents in for a group session and see how that goes."

His father nodded. "Good. I've noticed him saying hello and being more respectful."

"That's because you scared the shit out of him that morning at breakfast," Cowboy interjected.

"It had to be done," their father said. "Nobody messes with my queen, and it fixed the problem in general."

The men nodded in agreement.

"I'm thinking it's time to bring in a game of paintball and

let Kenny and the other kids get some energy out," Dare suggested.

"You know I'm all for that," his father said. He was known for dragging people who were having an especially rough time out to the paintball field to work off some steam.

Cowboy thrust his fists up toward the ceiling and hollered, "*Paintball!*"

All the guys cheered.

"I'll work out the details." Dare pushed to his feet. "I'm going to call Mom and let her know I'm still around."

His father nodded, and Dare headed out front to call her.

She answered on the first ring. *"Dare."* The relief in her voice was palpable.

"Hey, Mom. I didn't do the jump."

"Oh? Why not?"

"I sprung it on Billie and she wasn't thrilled."

"Do you blame her?"

"No. I get it." He paced the pavement. "Part of me thinks she's crazy to be with someone like me, but another part of me thinks if Eddie hadn't died, she'd be doing these things right along with me."

"But Eddie *did* die, honey, and she may never be the care-free daredevil you remember again."

"I know, but I see more of that girl coming back every day. She may never go full throttle, but she's definitely got her foot on the gas."

"I'd love to see Billie get back to smiling more, but just make sure it's her foot on the gas and not yours."

"I'm not pushing her to *do* anything other than support my choices." He paced, thinking about the question that had been eating away at him all day. "I've got to ask you something. With all that she's been through, am I doing more harm than good by being with her?" He couldn't imagine his life without Billie in it, but he needed to know her opinion.

"That's something only you and Billie know the answer to, but, Devlin, sweetheart, I know *you*. If you thought you weren't good for her, you'd have stopped trying a long time ago. There's a reason you're still in each other's lives."

"Right. Thanks, Mom. I'd better get back inside. Love you."

After he ended the call, he headed back into the bar wondering if his mother was right or if he was too damn selfish to even consider giving up the only woman he'd ever loved. He saw Billie talking with his father at the table, and his heart did a fucking flip. There was no way in hell he'd ever be able to give her up. And maybe Eddie was the better man, because he didn't want to give her an out, either.

He made a beeline for her. "Hey, darlin'. You flirting with my old man?"

"So what if I am?" she taunted.

The guys chuckled.

"Get over here." He pulled her closer, and she stole a glance at the neighboring table. "The way you were all over me earlier, I'm pretty sure they all know we're together."

She whispered, "Just one kiss. I've got my manager hat on."

"I'll take one now, but you have to make up for the ones I'm missing later."

"That'll be my pleasure, Whiskey." She kissed him. "By the way, I told my mom I'd help plan the events with her and Wynnie this year."

"*What?*" He was beyond shocked. "Who *are* you?"

"Shut up." She lowered her voice. "I don't want to feel like an outsider to your family anymore."

"That makes me happy, darlin', and I think what I'm about to say will help you feel like part of the family again. What night are you off this week?"

"Thursday. Why?"

"We're planning a paintball game—"

Cowboy hollered, "*Paintball!*" causing a ruckus at the table.

Dare shook his head. "I'm thinking about having a barbecue and bonfire afterward. Interested?"

She arched a brow and said, "Shooting you in the ass? Heck yeah, I'm in," full of hot-as-sin attitude, earning a round of jokes from the guys as she spun on her heel and strutted away.

"You've got your hands full with that one," his father said as he sat down.

"I sure do, and I wouldn't want it any other way."

Chapter Thirteen

AS THE SUN set Thursday evening, the paintball battle was in full swing. The field, located just beyond the main house, was at least twice the size it had been years ago, when Billie had joined their games. There were several sandbag bunkers, new stone walls, barrels, enormous upright tires that were pinned to the ground, and other obstacles and barriers. Ground lights illuminated the dark field, and the sounds of heavy footfalls, paintball guns shooting, and hollering filled the air. They'd split into teams, and between Dare's family, the ranch hands, and their clients, there were about two dozen paintball-gun-wielding people running around in camouflage suits and helmets. Even Gus had joined them, in his tiny neon-yellow suit, so everyone could see him and be sure *not* to shoot at him.

Billie peered out from behind a barrel, trying to spot Dare as Birdie sprinted across the dirt and dove behind a wall. A paintball hit Birdie's foot, and Doc bolted past her, cracking up. Birdie flipped up her mask and hollered, "Damn it, Doc! You freaking ninja!"

Billie laughed. She had forgotten how stealth Doc was. He didn't often show his competitive side, but on the paintball field, he was out for blood.

Birdie pulled out her phone and grinned for a selfie. She shoved her phone into her pocket, pulled her mask down, and took off running.

Gus was G.I. Joe crawling across the middle of the field. Sasha, who was on Billie's team, ran by and scooped him up under her arm like a football, earning loud giggles as she carried him behind a tire.

Ezra crept by the barrel behind which Billie was hiding, and Billie lifted her gun to shoot him, just as she felt the nose of a gun pressed against her back.

"Turn around slowly and lift your mask, darlin'."

Dare. Her pulse quickened and she turned, meeting his mischievous gaze. She lifted her mask. "Are you going to shoot me?"

He wrapped his arm around her waist, tugging her against him. "Does it feel like I want to shoot you?" He lowered his lips to hers in a kiss that started slow and sensual but quickly turned fierce and passionate.

"Christ Almighty, *Billie*," Cowboy grumbled. "You're kissing the *enemy*."

Billie tried to break away, but Dare held her tight as Cowboy lifted his gun, aiming for Dare, and Kenny sprinted behind him, yelling, "Take this!" shooting Cowboy in the back.

"That's my man!" Dare hollered.

"I've got your back!" Kenny shouted as he took off running.

Just as Dare turned back to Billie, she broke free from his grasp and *shot* him.

He stumbled backward, holding his chest. "I'm in love with a traitor!"

She and Cowboy high-fived and ran off just as Gus ran out

from behind the wall, yelling, "I'm gonna get you, Dad!"

Sasha ran after him. "If Gus doesn't get you, I will." She aimed for Ezra, who leapt over a barrel and ducked down behind it. Tiny popped up from a sandbag bunker aiming at Sasha as Wynnie ran past and shot him, laughing the whole way.

"Bet you forgot how fun this was, huh?" Cowboy said as he and Billie darted behind a wall.

"Yeah, it's been too long."

"I haven't forgotten!" Simone yelled.

They turned, and Simone pegged them both from behind a bunker, cracking up as she darted away.

The game went on for a long time, and when they finally came off the field and took off their gear, everyone was smiling and talking at once. Dwight had opted not to join the paintball game and had prepared a feast of grilled chicken, hamburgers, hot dogs, vegetables, and a host of side dishes, all of which were waiting for them to devour. Everything smelled delicious. Dare and Doc went to start the bonfire, while a bunch of the guys set up chairs and Billie and the others put the gear away.

"That was the coolest thing I've ever done," Kenny said as they came out of the equipment shed.

Tiny put a hand on the boy's shoulder, and she heard him ask quietly, "Cooler than stealing a car?"

"Way cooler," Kenny said, eyes bright.

"Attaboy."

Hyde walked by with two of the other teenagers in the program and said, "Kenny. Let's eat, buddy."

Kenny looked at Tiny, seeking approval.

Tiny gave a nod, and as they walked off, Tiny joined Billie while she waited for Dare. "Good to have you back in the game, sweetheart."

"I had forgotten how much fun it was," she said as Cowboy walked by with Simone, complaining that she'd shot him awfully close to his *junk*. "I've missed nights like this, being around everyone."

"We've missed you, too." He nodded toward Dare. "And I've missed seeing my son this happy."

"Dare is always happy."

"He was a downright mess after losing Eddie."

A pang of guilt sliced through her. "I know I made it worse by shutting him out of my life. I'm sorry for doing that."

"Don't sweat it, darlin'. We love you just the same. You did what you needed to, and Dare found his footing again. But it's been far too long since I've seen him as happy as he's been since you two got the burrs out of your britches. A big ol' piece of him has been missing for quite some time. Don't get me wrong. He's good on his own, but he's a hell of a lot better with you. Always has been."

"I'm glad, because I'm happier with him, too. But I know there are moments when I'm a thorn in his side, like with the buses." She and Dare had spent the last few nights talking about his jumping over buses and her fears. He'd pointed out that he wasn't trying a *new* stunt he wasn't qualified to do, like Eddie had. He was honing the skills he'd already spent years perfecting. She was still worried, but not quite as much.

"You didn't say anything we haven't all thought," his father reassured her. "But you know Dare. There's not much of a chance he'll be changing his ways anytime soon."

"I don't want him to stop doing the things he loves. I remember what it was like to find a new mountain to conquer. It's a rush like no other, and I don't want to take that away from him. I just don't want to lose him."

"Neither do we, darlin'. Neither do we."

Dare came up behind her and wrapped an arm around her. "Is my old man giving you hell for shooting me?"

"Something like that." She shared a knowing glance with Tiny and put her arm around Dare. "I'm starved."

"I figured as much. Come on, let's get some grub."

They filled their plates and joined the others sitting around the bonfire as they ate. It reminded her of when they were younger.

"Look at Doc's smug expression," Birdie said, looking adorable in a funky palm-leaf-print crop top and wrap-around shorts. She'd changed out of the sneakers she'd worn for paintball and into suede fringed knee-high boots. "He's gloating."

"What's that, sore loser?" Doc took a bite of his burger and handed pieces to Sadie, his Irish setter, and Pickles, his husky-shepherd mix.

Billie chuckled.

"Hey, Doc, you should've invited Mandy tonight," Cowboy said.

"We're not seeing each other anymore." Doc took a swig of his beer.

His siblings all exchanged glances. Sasha put down her plate and picked up her guitar, strumming out the tune to "Another One Bites the Dust," and Dare and Cowboy began singing the chorus, making everyone crack up.

Gus ran over to Sasha. "I wanna play! Will you teach me, sugar?"

"*Gus*, what did I say about calling her sugar? Let's give Sasha a break." Ezra got up to fetch his boy.

"It's okay. I don't mind." Sasha patted her lap, and Gus scrambled onto it, beaming at his father. "If any guy can call me *sugar*, it's this one." She ruffled Gus's hair.

"My son, the woman whisperer," Ezra said as he sat back down.

Billie loved listening to the banter and laughter around the fire. Dare's family included her as if she'd never missed a single barbecue. On one hand, it *felt* like she hadn't missed anything, since she'd seen them at the bar and at Dark Knights' events. But even at the events she'd avoided Dare, and in turn, had avoided deep conversations with his family. Now that her guilt was lifting and she could see herself and her actions more clearly, she was realizing this life she had wasn't a penance. It was a *gift*, and she—*they*—had already lost too many years. She was done wasting time or worrying about what other people thought.

Dare put his arm around the back of her chair, and she moved it closer, earning one of his sweet temple kisses. What was it about those tender kisses that brought butterflies?

"Love you, darlin'," he said in her ear. "I'm glad you're here."

It wasn't the kisses that brought those flutters. It was *him*.

"I'm glad, too." She leaned in, whispering, "I love you, too," and kissed him.

Wynnie was watching them with a warm expression. "It makes me happy to see you two together again."

"Did you guys break up and get back together or something?" Kenny asked.

"Something like that," Dare said in a tone that put an end to that line of questioning.

"Kenny, do you have any idea who Billie is?" Birdie asked.

"Dare's girl," Kenny said.

"Yes, but she was also a professional motocross racer for years," Birdie explained.

"Birdie, that was a *long* time ago," Billie said.

"So what?" Birdie exclaimed. "Seriously, Kenny. If you looked up Billie Mancini on the internet, you'd see she was one of the *best*. She could have been *the* best if she didn't stop racing."

Kenny's eyes widened. "No *way*. Do they even let girls race in motocross?"

"Are you freaking kidding me?" Billie asked. "Do you live under a rock? Girls have been racing motocross for years."

"She was better than most of the guys," Dare bragged.

"Better than you?" Kenny asked.

Dare looked at her, and the love in his eyes made her warm all over. "A hell of a lot better."

"That's wild," Kenny said. "Why'd you stop racing, Billie?"

Dare held her a little tighter, and she tried to figure out what to say. She could feel everyone's empathetic gazes on her, and she knew they wouldn't mind if she told a white lie, but while she didn't want to talk about what had happened, she no longer wanted to hide from it or the feelings it brought.

"I lost a friend, and it sucked the joy out of it for me." She waited for an onslaught of emotions and was surprised when it was a trickle rather than a rush.

"Oh, man, that sucks. I'm sorry," Kenny said compassionately. "Do you think you'll ever race again?"

"No," she said, relieved that he hadn't pushed for details. "I'm too old to race now."

"Yeah, I guess you are kinda old for racing," Kenny said, earning chuckles around the bonfire.

The competitor in Billie wanted to argue that point, but she had a feeling a teenager would tell her to prove it, and she *wasn't* going there.

"I would love to do something as cool as that and show everyone I'm good at something," Kenny said. "What other cool stuff have you done?"

"They've done it all," Cowboy said. "These two have been doing extreme sports since elementary school."

"You're looking at two of the coolest daredevils Hope Valley has ever seen," Doc added.

After all the times Cowboy and Doc had come after them for their dangerous stunts, Billie was shocked by the pride in their voices. His parents and sisters joined in the conversation, telling Kenny about all the stunts they used to do and raving about how good they were. It was inspiring and made Billie wish she was still that girl. She looked at Dare, the *only* person she'd want to be that girl with, and wondered if he wished it, too. She wanted everything with him, but when it came to stunts and extreme sports, she didn't know what she was emotionally capable of doing anymore.

There was only one way to find out.

She leaned closer to him, whispering, "Maybe we could try riverboarding sometime."

His eyes lit up. "Yeah?"

"Maybe...?" She shrugged.

"Baby, I'm up for anything with you." He kissed her again and pulled her tight against his side.

They listened as Birdie told Kenny about Dare beating the record for the Wall of Death and explained to him what that meant.

"*Dang*," Kenny exclaimed. "And here I thought Dare was

just a badass biker and a pretty good therapist."

"Pretty good?" Billie objected. "This guy got me to admit all my secrets, and he's not even my therapist."

"That's because he's sneaky," Kenny said. "He gets you talking while you're working, and the next thing you know, you've told him stuff you didn't even know you were thinking. I guess he's pretty good at what he does, but I don't like mucking stalls."

The guys laughed.

"You know, Dare wasn't always so good at talking," Wynnie said.

"That is *not* true," Doc insisted. "Dare has always been almost as much of a talkaholic as Birdie."

"I'm not a talkaholic," Birdie said. "I just have a lot to say. Which reminds me, Cowboy, I forgot to tell you that you need to come to one of my yoga classes. I found you a girl, and I think she's *wife* material."

Cowboy sighed. "I told you that I'm not looking for a wife, Birdie. Why don't you bother Doc? He's older than me."

"It's not about age," Birdie protested. "It's about being ready to settle down, and you exude all the qualities of a guy who needs a wife."

"*Christ.* Here we go again," Cowboy muttered.

"Her name is Lucy. She's blond, super cute, and *really* good at yoga. I mean, the girl is a living pretzel," Birdie said.

Cowboy smirked. "Now you've got my interest."

Birdie told them all about *Limber Lucy*, and as the night wore on, they chatted about everything from Festival on the Green and the kickoff for the Ride Clean campaign to music and a new café opening by Birdie's chocolate shop. The girls were excited that Billie was going to join them for their planning day a week from Sunday, and she was excited, too.

Ezra left to put Gus to bed, Kenny and the ranch hands turned in, and a long while later, the rest of them said their good nights. Sasha hugged Billie and asked if she'd be joining them for breakfast in the morning.

"I don't know. I might get a hankering to steal a truck," she joked, and everyone laughed.

"We'd love to see more of you, honey." Wynnie hugged her. "You know our door is always open."

"Thanks." She took Dare's hand. "I think you'll be seeing a lot more of me."

DARE DIDN'T THINK it was possible for him to feel more for Billie than he already did, but tonight had shown him otherwise. As juvenile as it sounded in his own head, he'd fantasized about kissing her during paintball hundreds of times when they were younger. He'd imagined cornering her during a game and dragging her into the equipment shed or behind a stone wall. *Nothing* had been off-limits to his teenage imagination, but even that one stolen kiss on the field today had shown him that nothing came close to the real thing. And that wasn't all that had his emotions on overdrive. He'd been damn proud of her for telling Kenny the truth about losing a friend, and being with her around his family in the way he'd always longed for—as a couple—did something to him.

He wanted to show her how much it meant to him. To get her in his arms and love her like she'd never been loved before. But his mother and sisters were still gabbing with her.

"Hey, Dare." Doc sidled up to him with his pups in tow. "Got a sec?"

Dare petted Sadie. "Sure. What's up?"

"I wanted to apologize for being hard on you the other day at the bar about planning your jump after everything Billie's been through. I was out of line. That's not my call."

"That's okay. You're worried about her, and I appreciate that. Besides, I'm used to you calling me on my shit. It's not such a bad thing, Doc. You got me thinking, and we've been talking about it. She's cool with me doing the jump, but she's not going to come watch."

"Do you blame her?" Doc reached down to pet Pickles.

"Not even a little." Dare glanced at Billie, heading their way, sexy as hell in cutoffs and a Roadhouse T-shirt that hung off one shoulder. "Can you do me a favor?"

"Anything."

"When I do the jump, can you be with her? Just in case."

Doc's brows slanted. "I don't even want to think about that."

"Well, she will be, and I need to know there's someone with her. Can I count on you?"

"Yes, of course."

"Thanks, man." He lifted his chin as Billie approached. "Hey, darlin'." He reached for her.

"Oh, no you don't," Doc said. "It's been a long time since *this one's* hung out with us. Get in here and hug me, racer girl."

"Hug a hot vet? That's not a hardship." She walked into his open arms.

Doc looked at Dare over her shoulder with a smug expression.

"Get your hands off my woman." He tugged Billie to his

side. "See you tomorrow, asshole."

"Later, douchebag."

As everyone went their separate ways, Dare and Billie headed across the field toward his house. "Did you have fun?"

"I had a *great* time. I liked meeting Kenny and the others, and I can tell you're having an impact on him by the way he looks up to you."

"Thanks, babe. He's a good kid. I'm really glad you came tonight."

"I've missed nights like this, spending time with people who knew us as bratty kids and love us anyway."

"What's not to love? We're awesome."

She giggled. "Some of the stories your family told made it feel like I was right back there with you and Eddie, doing all those fun things. I miss so much of what we had, Dare." She turned to him, her eyes full of hope and love. "I miss being out here under the stars and doing whatever we feel like."

He tugged her into his arms. "And what do you feel like doing?"

She went up on her toes and whispered, "*You.*"

He crushed his mouth to hers in a deep, passionate kiss, and she pressed her body against him, awakening the hunger that was always lurking just beneath the surface. She grabbed his head, rising onto her toes again, as if she'd never get enough of him. Their kisses went on and on, her sensual sounds making his body ache for her.

When their lips parted, she looked as drunk on him as he felt and whispered, "*More.*"

"God, I love you." He reclaimed her mouth, fierce and rough, kissing her until they were both moaning and writhing. He pushed his hands down the back of her shorts, grabbing her ass. She whimpered, rocking against his cock, and he growled, "I need to fuck you, baby."

She drew back with a bold look in her eyes. "Come on." She took his hand and ran into the barn. "Remember our first kiss?"

"I remember you *taking* a kiss." He backed her up against the wall and nipped at her neck. "Then calling me names." He yanked open the button on her shorts and unzipped them, pushing his hand into her panties, his fingers delving into her wetness, earning a sexy sigh.

"Because you didn't like my kiss," she said breathily, her hands snaking under his shirt, teasing his nipples.

"Fuck." He pushed his fingers inside her, and she closed her eyes, a needy moan escaping. "I was confused by the kiss." He brushed his thumb over her clit, and she went up on her toes. "But a few years later, your mouth was *all* I wanted."

"We were both dummies then." Her eyes opened and narrowed. "I'm so glad we've finally smartened up." She tugged his shirt up and dipped her head, teasing his nipple with her tongue.

He gritted his teeth and tugged his shirt off with one hand, working her faster with his other.

"Yesss."

The kisses were desperate as they stumbled toward a pile of hay, kicking off their sneakers and stripping each other bare, bodies grinding, hands groping, hours of pent-up desire igniting between them. She pushed him down to his ass, standing before him completely naked and fucking fantastic, heat blazing in her eyes as she straddled him. "Do you know how many times I've thought about doing this with you?"

"Not nearly as many times as I've fantasized about it." He grabbed her thighs, squeezing as the head of his cock rubbed against her entrance. "But in mine, the hay wasn't prickling my ass."

She laughed. "Stop complaining and kiss me."

Their mouths collided with the heat of a volcano, and that was exactly what he felt like as she sank onto his cock, her tight center gripping him. He grabbed her hips, and she clung to his shoulders, riding him slow and so fucking perfectly, lust pounded and swelled inside him, until it felt as though it would seep from his pores. He fisted a hand in her hair, tugging her head back, and sank his teeth into her neck. She cried out, her thighs gripping his body as she rode him faster, fingernails carving into his skin, sending pain and pleasure whipping through him.

He lowered his mouth over her breast, sucking the nipple, and she clenched tighter around his dick. Sparks seared through his core, exploding like fireworks. "You feel so fucking good." He sucked it again, *harder*, thrusting faster as her inner muscles squeezed him like a vise. He moved his mouth to her other breast, continuing the exquisite torture. She arched back, greedy sounds streaming from her lips. He reached between them, using his fingers to send her over the edge.

"*Dare—*" flew loud and untethered from her lungs.

He tugged her mouth to his, tongues thrusting to the same frantic pace as their hips as she rode out her pleasure. Pressure mounted inside him, her sex pulsing madly around his shaft, nearly drawing the come right out of him. But he wasn't done with her yet.

He tore his mouth away and gritted his teeth, doing mental math to stave off his release as he clutched her hips, slowing her down. "You're *mine*, Mancini." He kissed her again, slowly, *languidly*, moving her even slower along his shaft. She whimpered into their kisses, and he felt tension mounting in her, too, her thighs flexing. He drew back, drinking in his girl, so lost in them, her eyes were almost closed. "I fucking love you, Billie." He trailed kisses down her neck and grazed his teeth over her nipple.

"*Dare*" fell pleadingly from her lips.

"My name will be the *only* one you'll ever say that way again, because I'm never letting you go." He wrapped one arm around her, gyrating, keeping himself buried deep as he licked and kissed her neck, chest, and the swell of her breasts, earning one impossibly sexy sound after another. Her every noise and the way they fit together, so tight and hot, amplified the intensity of their every move. He needed to thrust, but the feel of her body growing slick and trembling with need was too perfect to resist. He nipped at her flesh, sucking the swell of her breast, marking her as *his*. He made his cock jerk inside her, and she mewled, her sex clenching greedily.

"*More...*" she begged. "*Please.*"

He reached between them again, using the arm around her to control their movements, sliding her painfully slowly along his shaft. She inhaled quick, sharp gasps.

"*Faster.*"

He gritted his teeth against the need to *move*. "Tell me your sexy body is mine," he said gruffly. "Tell me *you're* mine, Wildfire."

Her eyes opened, flames blazing in them. "I'm *yours*, Dare. *All* of me. But if you keep this torture up, I might change my mind."

He wrapped both arms around her, grabbing her hair with one hand and tugging her lips a whisper away from his. "No, you won't. You can't. Neither of us can."

"I wouldn't even if I could," she said it like a threat, making her proclamation even sexier.

He pressed his lips to hers and turned them over, gathering her beneath him, her beautiful love-filled eyes getting him all twisted up inside. "I love you, Mancini. Always have and always will."

He covered her mouth with his, and his love for her turned fucking into lovemaking. Her soft curves melded to his hard frame as their bodies took over, finding the rhythm that bound them together. They pumped and ground, greedy pleas filling the air, hands groping, teeth nipping, fingernails biting into flesh, their frantic hearts beating as one. As her climax gripped her, the world spun away, and he surrendered to his own powerful release.

HOURS LATER, DARE awoke to an empty bed. He rolled over and glanced at the clock, *3:05*, then at the bathroom, which was dark. He sat up, bleary-eyed. "Billie?" Answered with silence, he muttered, "Fuck." They'd showered when they'd come back from the barn, itchy from the hay, and she'd been even more loving than ever before. But when they'd gotten into bed, she'd been restless. Maybe all their love talk, his family, and telling Kenny she'd lost a friend was too much for her after all.

He sat up and scrubbed a hand down his face, needing to see if his truck was still there. He pulled on boxer briefs, and when he climbed out of bed, he saw Billie's clothes in a heap on the floor. Hopefully that meant she was still there. He headed into the living room, which was empty, and then outside. His truck was there, moonlight shining on the windshield. But it was the glow of the garage light reflecting off the side of the rear bumper that had him heading in that direction.

The interior was dark, save for the lights spilling in from the shop in the back. He listened as he made his way through the garage, hoping she wasn't in tears. But there was no noise at all. When he reached the entrance to the shop, he couldn't believe his eyes. Billie was sitting on her bike, staring absently at the wall in front of her, and it was the most glorious sight he'd ever seen.

"Damn, darlin', you look *fine* on that bike," he said as he went to her.

She startled. "Did I wake you?" She was wearing one of his T-shirts, gripping the handlebars.

"No. How does it feel?" He passed the half wall and noticed her feet were bare and she wasn't wearing pants.

She shrugged, eyes lighting up, and shook her head. "When I sat on it, I got this rush, you know, like before a race. Then Eddie's accident came back to me, and I couldn't move. I was scared and sad."

"I'm sorry, baby." He rubbed her back.

"It's okay. I sat here thinking about Eddie and about the movie he made and just…who he was. He would have given me hell for quitting. When you were away at school, he'd try to push me the way you did." She laughed softly, her eyes tearing up. "He was so bad at that. He just wasn't a pushy guy."

"But he tried because he loved you and he knew how much you wanted to be the best."

She nodded and wiped her eyes. "If he were here right now, he'd ask me what I was waiting for and hand me my helmet."

"I'll get your helmet."

She lifted her hand, the helmet dangling from her fingers. "I found it in the office."

She'd gone looking for it. If that wasn't progress, he didn't know what was. "Do you want to take her for a spin?"

She shook her head. "No. But I like sitting on it, and as bizarre as it sounds, I think Eddie would like it, too."

"I know he would." He ran his hand through her hair. "When I woke up and you weren't there, I thought I'd scared you off with all that possessive love talk."

"You didn't." She climbed off the bike and set the helmet beside it. She put her arms around him, resting her head on his chest as he embraced her. "You've worried about me forever. I still don't know why you didn't leave me in the dust."

"Daredevils for life, darlin'. You're a part of me. The best part of me."

She tipped her face up with a small smile. "You don't have to worry about my love for you. That's as solid as the ground we're standing on." She went up on her toes and kissed him. "I love you, Whiskey. And I love us, so don't die, okay?"

He nodded, his chest aching. He tried to lighten the mood, really wanting to circle back to her love of biking. "You know I can't die, darlin'. I'd have to come back and haunt the next guy who got you in his arms."

"As if anyone could compare to you?" She shook her head. "Not a chance."

She looked longingly at the bike, and he knew it was the perfect time to ask her for the favor he'd been mulling over since the bonfire. "I know you're not ready to ride, but would you consider teaching Kenny?"

"Kenny?"

"Yeah. You saw how excited he got at the bonfire. I've been thinking about it. If you and I didn't have our bikes and all the other stuff we did, we could have easily ended up getting into trouble trying to catch the highs we needed."

"Our dads would have whooped our asses."

"Forget our dads. Doc and Cowboy would have tied us to trees." That earned a bigger smile. "What do you think? You wouldn't have to ride, just guide him so he learns to ride properly. Teach him about safety and sportsmanship."

"You don't need *me* for that."

"He sees enough of me. I think it'd be good for him to spend time with you. Besides, a pretty woman makes everything better."

She ran her fingers down his cheek, and he leaned into her touch. "Mr. Whiskey, are you flirting with me just to get your way?"

"Just being honest, darlin'. What do you think? Can you help a kid out? You could make a big difference in his life, and he obviously admires you."

Her jaw tightened. "When would I do it? He has therapy and works with you guys during the day."

"We'll make the time whenever you can fit it in. It wouldn't take more than an hour or two a week." He kissed her forehead, hoping she'd agree. "I think it would be good for both of you."

Worry lines appeared on her forehead. "What if he gets hurt?"

"Then we'll get him fixed up. He's not going to be doing flips, Billie. I just want you to teach him to ride. He needs an outlet and something to make him feel good about himself. You heard what he said at the bonfire. He wants to prove he's good at something, and I think it has to be something other than the work he does here. I thought about showing him the ropes course, but that won't be enough for him. The thrill of the ride might be enough, and if it's not, you're the best there is. You'll know if and when he's ready for more."

"You're *serious?*"

"Absolutely. I mentioned it to Cowboy and my dad, and they both thought it was a great idea, if you're up for it. I'll need to clear it with his parents, but I think it'd be a fantastic reward for him, and it will give him a sense of confidence and achievement."

"He needs gear."

"I've got gear that will fit him."

"What if I decide to do it but then freak out or something?"

"Then I'll step in and take over. I'm not trying to pressure you, babe."

She looked at the bike again, and rolled her lower lip between her teeth, a flicker of light sparking in her eyes. "Just an hour or two?"

He nodded.

"If his parents are okay with it, I guess I could try it."

"Yes!" He hugged her. "That's my Wildfire."

"I said I'd *try* it. I might hate it."

"You might love it." She was smiling, and he took that as a good sign.

"I might freak out."

"It's okay if you do. At least you will have tried, and I'll be right there with you."

"You have an answer for everything."

"And you always want the last word. Come on, sweet thing. Let's go back to bed."

He swatted her ass, and she glowered at him. "You can

scowl, but I know you still love me."

"Careful, Devlin. There's a thin line between love and hate," she teased.

He pulled her into his arms, feeling higher than any stunt could ever make him feel. "It doesn't matter how thin it is or what side I'm on, as long as you're on it with me."

Chapter Fourteen

BILLIE BOLTED UPRIGHT, startled from sleep by Bobbie's shriek Saturday morning. She ran out of the bedroom and found Bobbie standing in the hallway in pink pajama shorts and a white cami, covering her eyes with one hand, her other arm extended, warding off a naked Dare, who looked amused, standing in the bathroom doorway with his hands covering his privates. *Great.* Billie stifled a laugh.

"I'm *sorry.*" Dare looked at Billie. "I didn't mean to wake you, darlin'. I didn't expect her to be awake so early."

"I had to pee!" Bobbie complained. "It's *my* house. Why are you guys even here? You always sleep at your place."

Dare cracked a grin. "Billie has better toys here."

"Dare!" Billie glowered at him.

"*Ew!* Is that what I heard in the middle of the night?" Bobbie put her fingers in her ears, but her eyes fell to Dare's hands covering his dick, and she spun around. "Put that thing away! I'm scarred for life!"

Dare chuckled. "I didn't *scar* you, Bobbie. I just ruined your expectations of the male race."

"Ohmygod." Billie laughed, because he definitely did, but

she grabbed his arm, tugging him toward the bedroom. "Get *in* there." She gave him a shove and closed the bedroom door behind him, turning to her sister. "The coast is clear. You can turn around."

Bobbie's face was red, and she whispered angrily, "A little *warning* would have been nice."

"Sorry! We were…" *Wanting a little fun.* "We just stopped to pick up some things, but we got a little frisky, and one thing led—"

"*Stop!* I don't want details!"

"Sorry!" Billie hadn't worked yesterday, and she and Dare had gone riverboarding. They'd had a blast and had spent all afternoon either on or by the water. They'd stopped for dinner on the way home and had ended up knocking around that town. Then they'd gone to a park where they used to hang out and talked about when they were kids until after midnight. They'd been on such a high, they'd decided to get a little adventurous and pick up her *toys.* When they'd gotten to her place, Bobbie was asleep. One thing had led to another, and they'd played with every toy she had. Not that she had a huge collection, but she had a few good ones. She hadn't known *just* how good until Dare had gotten his hands on them. Boy, did he know how to use them. Her *entire* body had vibrated long after Dare, and the toys, were done. She shuddered with the memory.

"If you're going to stay here, at least make him wear clothes when he's not in the bedroom. He needs to put a *bell* on that thing!"

Billie laughed. "Well, you always said you wanted me to be more open about my personal life."

"I didn't need to *see* it." She leaned closer, whispering, "But he *did* ruin me. I mean…" She mouthed, *Wow.*

"I'm a lucky girl." Billie narrowed her eyes, wagging her finger. "And *you're* going to wipe your memory clean. Got it? Forget what you saw, or I'll burn all of your books and smash your ereaders. He's *mine.*"

Bobbie giggled. "Well, well, look at the green-eyed monster coming out."

Billie rolled her eyes and reached for her bedroom doorknob.

"*Wait,*" Bobbie said.

Billie turned.

"Good luck today. I know you'll do great." Bobbie hugged her.

"Thanks." Today was Kenny's first motocross lesson, and Billie was more than a little nervous about it. She and Dare had stopped in at the main house the morning after the bonfire, when everyone was eating breakfast. Kenny must have been thinking about all the things Dare's family had told him about her, because he couldn't stop talking about how cool it was that she'd been a pro racer. She hadn't stayed for breakfast, desperately needing to go for a run—even more so after seeing Kenny's excitement. He didn't even know she'd agreed to teach him to ride. Dare had said it was better not to mention it in case Kenny's parents disapproved. He was right. She remembered when they'd told their parents they wanted to ride dirt bikes. If they'd said no after she'd gotten herself all hyped up to do it, she would have lost her mind. She'd felt good about her decision, but remembering that feeling had made her want to help Kenny even more. That didn't mean she wasn't nervous about it. She was, but it was a good kind of nervous.

"I'm really proud of you for facing your fears," Bobbie said, drawing her back to the moment. "Do you want me to be there with you? In case you get anxious?"

"It means a lot to me that you would do that, but I'll be okay. Dare will be there, and I don't want Kenny to know I'm nervous."

"Good point. You'll do great. Call me after you're done and let me know how it went." Bobbie hugged her. "And keep your naked man to yourself."

"I will call you, and I'd better not hear you saying Dare's name when your door is closed."

Bobbie laughed evilly, rubbing her hands together. "Paybacks are fun."

"So are paybacks *for* paybacks."

Bobbie wrinkled her nose. "Oh yeah, right. Never mind."

Billie smiled as she went into her bedroom and found Dare sitting with his back against the headboard, one hand tucked behind his head and a sexy grin on his handsome face. "Sorry, darlin'. I didn't mean to freak her out."

"What were you thinking, walking out there naked?"

"I was thinking, *Damn, last night was fucking amazing, and I gotta piss like a racehorse.*" He reached for her hand, and when she climbed onto the bed, he lifted her onto his lap, guiding her legs around him. He slid his hands beneath his T-shirt she was wearing, gripping her butt, and rocked beneath her. "I was thinking that I've got the sexiest, wildest lady in this town, and I want you on the back of my bike so the whole world knows it."

She knew how much it would mean to him, because in the biker world, the woman on the back of his bike was *his*. She hadn't ridden on a motorcycle in years, but a thrill darted through her at the prospect of it. But he spoke before she could respond.

"You're the only girl, other than my sisters, who's ridden on the back of my bike. You know that, don't you?"

Emotions stacked up inside her, and she shook her head, stunned. "I didn't know."

"There's only ever been you, darlin'. The back of my bike is sacred. What do you say? Let me show the world you're mine?"

"I think that can be arranged, but no wheelies or crazy shit."

"No wheelies or crazy shit. Hell, I'll drive slow just to show you off." He kissed her. "I am sorry about Bobbie. The last thing I want is for her to see my dick in her dreams."

"Hey!"

They both laughed.

"Don't worry. I threatened to burn her books if she even thought about *my* python."

"That's my girl." He pulled her into a slow, sensual kiss, and she felt him getting hard beneath her. But when their lips parted, his expression was serious. "Do you still want to teach Kenny today?"

She appreciated him giving her an out, but that was Dare. Always watching out for her. "Yes, but I'm still really nervous. I'm not sure why. It's not like I'm riding again."

"It's probably because you're going to be around the thing that has scared you the most for the last several years."

She shook her head and traced the Dark Knights' emblem tattooed on the center of his chest: a skull with dark eyes, sharp brows, and a mouth full of jagged fangs. She and Eddie had gone with him to get the tattoo the day he'd turned eighteen, and Dare being *Dare*, he had modified the skull to his liking, giving it black-rimmed *clear* eyes and green brows. "You were the thing that scared me most," she said softly. "Because all my guilt and secrets were tangled up in you."

"And look how well we turned out. What can I do to help you be less nervous?"

"Nothing. This one's on me. I just have to get out there and do it."

"Well, I know one thing that'll help take the edge off." His hands slid around to her belly and moved up her torso, caressing her breasts.

He knew just how to make her crave more. As she lowered her mouth to his, she said, "I knew there was a reason I kept you around."

A FEW HOURS later, after walking the motocross track to make sure there was no debris on it, Billie was pacing Dare's backyard and giving herself a pep talk, trying to ease her anxiety, when Kenny and Dare arrived on an ATV. Kenny was decked out in unfamiliar black and gold riding gear from the tips of his gloves to the toes of his boots and carrying a helmet and chest pad. She got goose bumps, remembering how indestructible she'd felt in *her* riding gear. Worry flitted into her mind, but she tried her hardest to push it away, because today wasn't about her. It was about the seventeen-year-old boy grinning from ear to ear.

"Pretty awesome, huh?" Kenny looked down at his outfit. "These are Dark Knights' colors. Tiny said he and Dare had these racing suits specially made a few years ago. Everyone in the family has them. Well, not Tiny. He said he'd crush a dirt bike."

She laughed. "It's awesome." She smiled at Dare. "Dark

Knights colors, huh?"

He winked. "Show her the back, Kenny."

Kenny turned around. On the back of the jersey was the Dark Knights at Redemption Ranch logo: a circle with the skull inside, and DARK KNIGHTS written inside the circle above the skull, and AT REDEMPTION RANCH written below it. "Dare said if I keep my nose clean, I can prospect the Dark Knights when I'm eighteen and become a member a couple of years later, like he did."

"Now, *that* is beyond cool." *And brilliant.* Dare had given Kenny a goal. The club was a great incentive for any kid to stay out of trouble or if they went looking for trouble, as Dare had long ago, to remind them there was a better life waiting for them.

"Did you know that Tiny is the *president* of the club?" Kenny asked.

"Tiny isn't just the president; he's the founder," Billie corrected him. "And my dad is the vice president."

"Whoa, really? My dad would never drive a motorcycle," Kenny said.

"That's okay," Dare said. "They're not for everyone, and it sounds like your father knows his limits, and knowing your limits is a good thing."

"Even for daredevils like you guys?" Kenny asked.

"Especially for daredevils," Dare said.

Billie hadn't realized she'd get to see Dare in action as a therapist. He really was good at his job, taking every opportunity to help steer Kenny toward a safer future, while also teaching him to respect other people's decisions. Did he even know he was doing it? Or was it second nature?

"Are you ready to get down to business?" Billie asked.

"Heck yeah!" Kenny held his fists out, rolling them forward and making revving noises.

"Slow down, Speed Racer," Billie said. "First you need a safety lesson and to get familiar with your bike."

Dare put a hand on his shoulder. "You pay attention to everything Billie tells you, you hear?"

"I will. I promise. I'm just excited."

"I am, too," Billie said, and Dare looked at her curiously. She was excited for Kenny, and maybe even a little for herself. "I'm going to put the bike into neutral so you can push it out to the track. On a dirt bike, neutral is between first and second gear. You'll need to disengage the clutch, which is here." She showed him the clutch, then crouched to show him the shifter peg. "When you're sitting on the bike, your foot will be on the pedal and your toes will move over or under the peg, depending on which way you're shifting." She moved the shifter into first gear. "Hear that click? That's first gear. Now listen to the difference when I put it in neutral." A softer click rang out.

"I heard it. That's like a half click."

"That's right." She looked at Dare, who was nodding. "Why don't you give me your helmet, and you can walk the bike out to the track while we talk."

"Is this the kind of bike you drove when you were a pro?" Kenny handed her the helmet.

"No, this is a dirt bike. Motocross bikes are lighter so they can go faster. Maybe one day I'll show you my racing bike."

"Really?" Kenny asked. "Awesome!"

As they made their way to the track, Billie went over the general safety measures, and when she was done, she had Kenny repeat them back to her, to be sure he was paying attention. She knew how it was to be so enamored with a bike, nothing else mattered. But Kenny had paid attention, and he recited everything back to her perfectly.

Once they got to the track, Dare stood back, strikingly rugged in his jeans and cowboy hat as she went over the parts of the bike—clutch, choke, kick starter, throttle, brake, et cetera—and how to use them. Kenny asked smart questions, and after they were done, she had him recite back each part and its use.

"You're doing great," she said. "Climb on, and we'll practice while the bike is stationary. It's important to take your time while learning so you don't learn bad habits."

"Like what?" Kenny asked.

"Clutching the handlebars too tight, bad finger placement, not using your hips to help steer the rear tire, not looking far enough ahead. Believe it or not, there are a lot of little nuances that might feel comfortable to you at first, but they'll bite you in the butt in the long run."

"I want to know everything I shouldn't do," Kenny said.

"You're my kind of guy," she said.

Kenny beamed at Dare.

He practiced shifting gears, proper driving form, foot positioning, and everything else she could think of. "How does it feel?"

"Great," Kenny exclaimed, looking comfortable on the bike. "What's next?"

"I'm going to have you take a trip around the outside lane of the track. But I don't want you going anywhere near the obstacles or jumps. Can I trust you to do that?"

Kenny nodded.

She stood beside the bike, holding Kenny's gaze. "Here's the thing, Kenny. I know just how exciting it is to get on a bike for the first time. You'll want to go as fast as you can. *Don't.* You'll

THE TROUBLE WITH WHISKEY

feel more confident than you should be, and you'll want to go over the obstacles or try a jump. *Don't do either.* A dirt bike is cool and fun, but it's also dangerous. I need to hear you give me your word that you won't try to go faster than I tell you to."

"I promise. I don't want to mess this up."

"Okay, I trust you. Remember what I said about the clutch and the throttle?"

Kenny nodded. "If I give it too much gas, when I release the throttle, the bike will shoot forward and leave me on my butt. And if I let the clutch out too fast without enough gas, the bike will lurch and kill the engine."

"That's right. And if you feel like you're going too fast?"

"Let go of the throttle."

"And the brake?" Billie asked.

"I should try to use the foot brake, because hand brakes can grab and throw me over the handlebars."

"I'm impressed," Billie said. "Okay, hotshot. Let's give her a go. Take her around the track one time, no faster than twenty miles per hour, and remember, stay on the outside track."

"Twenty miles per hour, outside track. I won't let you guys down," Kenny said.

She handed him his helmet and stepped back with Dare as he started the bike. Kenny looked over, clearly proud of himself for not stalling, and Dare said, "Good job," as Billie gave him a thumbs-up.

Kenny started off slower than Billie had expected, but she'd rather see that than have him take off like a bullet train. He rode confidently, shifting a little roughly at first, but he got it.

"You have a knack for teaching. How'd it feel?"

"Incredible. As soon as we started talking, all my nervousness went away. I didn't even think about it again until just now." She laughed softly. "And unless he's really good at bullshitting, I think he truly doesn't want to let you down."

Dare put his arm around her, both of them watching Kenny like hawks. "He doesn't want to let either of us down. I'm so proud of you, darlin'."

"I didn't do anything but talk."

"You did a hell of a lot more than that. You connected with him, and you were thorough and demanded he respect the bike and you. Who'd've thought Badass Mancini was a natural teacher?"

"Obviously you did, or you wouldn't have trusted me to do it."

The rumble of a motorcycle drew their attention, and she glanced around quickly, seeing Dare's parents cruising down the walking path on Tiny's shiny black Harley. Tiny dwarfed Wynnie, who was waving.

Billie turned back to watch Kenny as his father parked. "Your parents are the coolest."

"Not when they drive their bike on my walking path," Dare grumbled. "Jesus, Pop. How many times do I have to tell you not to ride on the walking path?"

Billie glanced at Tiny, who was wearing dark sunglasses and his cut, his beard and mustache lifting with his grin.

"'Bout the same number of times I had to tell you not to ride your freaking dirt bikes on the horse trails," Tiny drawled. He put a hand on Billie's lower back and leaned down to kiss the top of her head. "I'm glad you're out here, sweetheart."

"I am, too," Wynnie said, hugging her. She looked pretty in a purple sleeveless blouse and jeans. "This is a big step for you. How do you feel? Are you holding up okay?"

"I feel amazing. I'm glad Dare talked me into it."

"She managed to put away her snark and let her natural teaching ability come through," Dare said.

Billie narrowed her eyes. "I'll give you snark."

"That's our girl," Wynnie said. "I never doubted you'd be a good teacher. You have to be a patient person to put up with this one." She hugged Dare. "I love our boys, but they're each a handful in their own right."

"How's the kid doing?" Tiny lifted his chin toward the track, watching Kenny come down the other side. "He looks good out there."

"He's doing really well. He's a great listener, and he didn't push any limits, which I know is hard for a teenager." Billie glanced at Dare, catching a flirty spark in his eyes. "But your brilliant son gave him a few goals to work toward, which probably helped keep him in line."

"My brilliant son? Was Doc here?" Tiny teased.

"Jackass," Dare said, eyes locked on Kenny.

Tiny chuckled. "I'm kidding. Cowboy's the brilliant one."

"*Tsk*. Tiny!" Wynnie chided, earning a hearty laugh from Tiny. "What goals did you give Kenny, honey?"

"I told him if he kept his nose clean, he could prospect the Dark Knights when he's eighteen, just like someone did to all of us." He cocked a grin in his father's direction.

Tiny didn't look away from Kenny coming down the home stretch as he said, "You didn't listen too well when you went away to college." He turned to Dare. "But you got your ass in line and turned out to be a damn good man."

Dare put his arm around Billie. "You have Mancini to thank for that."

"Now, that's a story I'd like to hear," Wynnie said.

"Maybe another day," Dare said as Kenny neared, stopping

a few feet away and cutting the engine.

Billie ran over to him as he took off his helmet. "Nice ride, dude. How did it feel?"

"Fuckin—" Kenny looked at her and the others with regret. "Sorry." His eyes lit up again. "It was *freaking* awesome!"

Everyone laughed, and Tiny commended him on the correction.

"Did you feel like you had control over the bike? How comfortable are you with shifting?" Billie asked.

"I had no problem controlling it. Shifting took some getting used to. I think I've got it now. I'm still catching myself wanting to use the hand brake, but I'll work on that." He gripped the handlebars. "That was the best ride of my life."

"That's great. Shifting and braking can be tricky. It'll take practice before you really get the hang of it."

"Can I go around again?" he asked excitedly.

"You sure can," Billie said. "But let's stick with the same speed and stay on the outside track, okay?"

"I will. I promise." Kenny looked at Tiny, Dare, and Wynnie and said, "Thank you for giving me a chance to do this."

Tiny gave a curt nod.

"You earned it," Dare said.

"There's a lot of good, clean fun to be had in this life," Wynnie said. "Sometimes it just takes stepping outside what you know and opening your eyes to new people and experiences to find out what they are. If you're lucky, you'll discover more about who you really are along the way."

"I'm a dirt bike rider for sure," Kenny said, and put on his helmet. As he drove away, Tiny took off his sunglasses and set his serious dark eyes on Billie. "He's following the rules now, but kids get cocky. Don't let him give you any grief."

"Tiny, do I ever let *anyone* give me a hard time?"

"No, I guess you don't. You're a smart girl." Tiny lifted his chin. "But the next time you show up in my house at mealtime, you'd better sit your ass down and visit, you hear?"

Tiny had not been happy that she hadn't stuck around to eat breakfast yesterday morning. She'd forgotten just how important family breakfasts were to him, and she was thrilled to still be considered part of their family. She'd be sure to make it up to him one morning when she and Dare weren't busy doing dirty things to each other instead of getting up early.

Feeling ten years old again, she said, "Yes, sir."

"Cut the *sir* crap. You belong at our table—always have, always will."

"Okay, thank you, Tiny." It suddenly became clear where Dare had picked up his confident possessiveness.

With a curt nod, he clapped a hand on Dare's shoulder. "This was a good idea, son. Maybe Cowboy's not the genius after all."

"Ya think?" Dare shook his head, smiling broadly.

"You boys." Wynnie shook her head. "We have to head back out. Tell Kenny we're proud of him." She gave Billie a quick hug and kissed Dare's cheek. "See you later."

"I'll try not to spin my tires on the way out of here," Tiny said, but behind that promise was a mischievous look that brought a boatload of memories of Billie, Dare, and Eddie spinning their wheels and leaving Tiny hollering at them in the dust.

Tiny and Wynnie climbed onto his motorcycle, and sure enough, Tiny spun out, leaving Dare hollering at him and Billie laughing.

Kenny practiced for another hour, and when he climbed off the bike for the last time, he couldn't stop talking about how much fun he'd had and how it had felt to be on the bike. "That was so cool! Can we do this again?"

His enthusiasm was contagious, and Billie was surprised at how much she wanted to do it again, but that wasn't her call to make. "That's up to Dare."

Kenny looked at him hopefully. "I've been doing all the work Cowboy gives me without bitchin—*complaining*—and I won't mess up again. I won't steal cars or skip school. I won't do anything that's against the law. I promise."

The look on Dare's face told her he, too, was remembering how they'd promised their parents everything under the sun in order to be allowed to ride dirt bikes.

"I'll want to talk to Billie about it first," Dare said. "It's a big commitment for both of you."

"I'd like to," she interjected.

"Yeah?" Dare asked with a hint of surprise.

"Mm-hm. Maybe twice a week for an hour and a half or so?"

Dare nodded. "That works for me."

"Yes!" Kenny did a fist pump and threw his arms around Billie. "Thank you! Thank you so much!"

Billie patted his back, looking at Dare, his unstoppable grin mirroring hers. "It's my pleasure. I'm glad you had fun."

"I did, and I can't wait till next time," Kenny said.

They talked for a few minutes, and as Dare and Kenny headed back down the walking path, she heard Kenny ask how old Billie was when she learned to ride. Dare told him she was six, and Kenny said, "Geez. She really is a badass."

Billie hadn't felt much like a badass lately, although riverboarding was pretty badass. She looked at the bike, feeling its pull like metal to magnet, and couldn't resist sitting on it. She wrapped her fingers around the handlebars, which brought a rush of adrenaline. She closed her eyes, reveling in her thundering heart and the way the bike felt beneath her. She saw the track and felt a flutter of intimidation. Eddie's face appeared in her mind, his blue eyes imploring her, and she heard his voice, as real as the breeze on her cheeks. *What are you waiting for, Billie? Get out there and show the world what you've got.* Her heart thudded faster, and she swallowed hard, opening her eyes, but Eddie's shaggy hair and blue eyes were still there, egging her on. She blinked several times and suddenly she saw Dare's face, too, his loving eyes asking, *What do you want to do, Mancini?*

I want to ride. She eyed the helmet.

Eddie's laughter floated into her ears. *Then what are you waiting for? Get out there and blow everyone away.*

You've got this, darlin', Dare's voice whispered.

She *wanted* to have it. She hadn't realized how desperately she'd wanted it until she had the helmet in her hand and was pulling it over her head. She was wearing jeans and sneakers, which weren't ideal, and she had no pads, but she'd ridden dozens of times like that. The words she'd said to Dare came back to her. *I don't want you to live in fear. I've done enough of that for both of us.* She took a deep breath and started the engine, the vibration bolstering her confidence, awakening the rider she'd always been.

She sat up taller, leaned forward, revving the engine, eyes set on the track ahead, and with her heart hammering in her ears, she cut herself loose.

Warm air whipped over her skin, the movement of the bike as familiar as the sky above her. Something shifted inside her, and the laser focus, which had won her more races than she could count, took over. She rose off the seat, leaning forward, speeding up along the straightaway, her muscles and senses on high alert as she approached a turn. She sat down, leaning into the curve, raising her inside leg high and opening the throttle. As she came out of the turn, she cheered, her every nerve on fire. She went around and around the track and couldn't resist going over the whoops, the kings of all speed bumps. She sped toward the step-up, flying up the jump, heels and legs flexed for a perfect back-tire landing on the tabletop. She nailed it and took the descending jump like the pro she'd been, making a smooth landing and speeding around the course.

Adrenaline rushed like fire through her veins. She felt unstoppable, *fully alive* for the first time in years, and when she hit the booter, the big jump before the finish line, she conquered it, soaring through the air, to a perfect landing, and saw Dare watching her. Her heart felt like it was clawing its way out of her chest to get to him as she sped to the end of the track. His face was a mask of shock as she tore off her helmet, climbing hastily from the bike, and launched herself into his arms.

"Thank you. *God*, thank you." Tears streaked her cheeks as he hugged her, spinning them in a circle.

"You did it, darlin'!"

"I did it!" She kissed him hard, her salty tears slipping between their lips. "I can't believe it!"

They were laughing, and she was crying. Dare looked blown away as he set her on her feet. "What happened?"

"I was standing there, and then I was on the bike, and I heard Eddie egging me on and you asking what I wanted, and I don't know. It just happened, and I'm so *freaking* glad. I feel like I put myself in a prison and you freed me."

"I didn't free you, darlin'. I just asked you to help a kid out. What you just did? That was all you, Mancini, and it was fucking fantastic."

She looked at him, remembering the cute boy who had built her up and given her more confidence than she'd ever thought possible and seeing the man who had stepped willingly into her darkness despite her claws and daggers, and there was no holding back.

"You're wrong, Dare. I'm only me because of you. You didn't just show me the light. You led me to the life I'd lost, to the best parts of myself that I'd forgotten, to the girl who hugged and laughed and wanted to experience everything life had to offer. I'm grabbing that girl, Dare, and I'm grabbing *us* with both hands and *never* letting go again."

Chapter Fifteen

DARE PUT THE grate over the fire pit and wiped his hands on his jeans, glad to be home. He'd had church tonight, and he'd barely been able to sit still knowing Billie had the evening off. His brothers had taken great pleasure in teasing him about being pussy whipped, but he couldn't care less. All he'd wanted was to get back home to see his girl.

Billie came out the kitchen door, wearing his forest-green Redemption Ranch hoodie. It looked like it had swallowed her, hanging past the hem of her cutoffs, making it look like she was wearing only the sweatshirt. Her hair hung loose, a wayward lock covering her cheek. She carried a pack of Oreos under one arm, bags of chips and marshmallows in one hand, and a box of graham crackers in the other. Two cans of soda and a package of chocolate bars were tucked between the crook of her arm and her body, and that incredible smile he'd waited so long to see shined like the North Star. How was it possible for one woman to look so sweetly adorable and like a naughty temptress at once?

"I got snacks." She blew that lock of hair out of her face, but it fell in front of her eyes again.

"You are too damn cute for your own good." He grabbed the sodas and snacks and put them on the table by the lounge chair, then pulled her into his arms. How could so much change in a month? He felt like he was living the best dream of his life.

She wound her arms around his neck. "I don't think I've been called cute since I was a kid."

"That's a damn shame, Mancini. From now on I'm going to tell you every time I think it. You'll hear it a lot tonight, because you're adorable in my sweatshirt."

"I forgot to bring mine."

"You could move in. Then you wouldn't have to worry about that." He hadn't expected to say it, but it had been on his mind.

"Don't say that too loud. Bobbie's already talking about renting out my room."

"All your favorite toys are here," he taunted. They'd brought their sexy *teammates* to his house after he'd accidentally flashed Bobbie.

"*You're* my favorite toy."

"Exactly."

She was grinning, but she looked at him curiously. "What has gotten into you?"

"You have." He touched his forehead to hers, overwhelmed with emotion for the woman who had spent the last few weeks helping a boy learn a sport that could keep him out of trouble and coming into her own in so many ways. She'd made his family's day when she'd joined them for breakfast, fitting in like she'd always been there, with her snarky banter and dramatic eye rolls. Six years of contentiousness couldn't even tear them apart. They'd grown up and changed, and still their soul-deep bond had survived, and now it had strengthened and grown into a love so real and true, he couldn't imagine his life without her.

He gazed into her eyes, knowing there was only so much honest, emotional talk she could take before turning snarky to shut him up, but he had to get it out. "I know you're not ready to move in, and that's okay. If this is all I ever get—seeing you in my sweatshirts and T-shirts, waking up with you every morning, holding you at night, walking into the bar and knowing you're mine, hearing your *insanely* sexy laugh—it's enough for me. *You're* enough for me, Mancini, and I'm so glad I took the chance and jumped out of that airplane."

She looked at him with a mix of awe, confusion, and love.

"I don't expect you to say it back. I just need you to know how I feel." He kissed her softly, taking her hand as he sat in a lounge chair by the fire and pulling her down to sit between his legs. He wrapped his arms around her and kissed her cheek.

She turned so she could see him and put her hand on his cheek, her eyes brimming with emotion. She was as sexual as he was, but she'd only recently started touching him more intimately, with a gentle caress here and there. He basked in those moments, soaking up the love they carried.

She pressed her lips to his, her thumb brushing over his cheek, and whispered, "You're all I want, too, Whiskey."

As she turned around, settling her back against his chest, he wondered how six little words could make him feel like he'd been given the biggest gift of all.

They sat there beneath the stars for a long time, thinking their own thoughts, listening to the crackling fire and chirping crickets. He never imagined just sitting quietly by a fire could make him so happy.

A little while later she said, "Thanks for going running with me this morning. I enjoyed it." They'd gone on a three-mile run but had taken a break after two miles to make out like horny teenagers.

"Me too."

"You liked making out in the field." She ran her hands over his. "I have to admit, I did, too."

"That was the best part of the run. Want to go skydiving this weekend?"

She cocked her body at an angle so she could see his face again. "You're doing a really scary jump soon. How about if we table skydiving until sometime after that?"

"You said you were cool with my jump."

"I said I'd never stop you, and I support you doing it. But *cool?*" She held her hand up and wobbled it from side to side. "I'm getting there. I'm still gearing myself up for it."

His chest felt a little tight. "Okay, we'll table skydiving."

"You know what we could do instead? Take that motorcycle ride you've been mentioning. We could ride out to Silk Hollow for the day."

"Is my girl getting the itch to cliff dive?"

She leaned her head back, smiling. "I have Saturday off."

"*Seriously?* Babe, that sounds amazing." He kissed her, ecstatic. "Let's do it. I guess you weren't kidding about grabbing that girl with both hands."

"I've been thinking a lot about all the things I gave up, and that was always one of my favorite things to do with you. Hiking up to the rocks, diving, lying out in the sun, and..." She traced his kneecap with her fingers. "There's that cave we used to play in."

"You know what I used to do in that cave?"

"I'm not sure I *want* to know."

He nuzzled against her neck. "I used to make up scenarios in my head about you dragging me in there like you dragged me into the barn to kiss me, only I was a teenager, so my fantasies were a lot dirtier than kissing."

"I think we had the same fantasies."

He loved hearing that and hugged her.

"I've been thinking about Eddie's parents a lot the last few weeks."

"You have? Why didn't you say anything?"

She shrugged. "I was trying to figure things out, and I didn't want to bother you."

"Darlin', talking to me about things you're having trouble with isn't bothering me. It's leaning on me. That's what I'm here for."

She turned with a sweet smile. "You mean you're not just here for my sexual pleasure?"

"Your pleasure will be even more intense when you trust me enough to ask for help."

"I'm working on that. It's not about trusting you. It's just…I've always wanted to stand on my own two feet."

"And you do. You've proven how strong you are. You've held up under pressures the rest of us can only imagine, and it won't make you weak to lean on someone you love. Letting people in makes you stronger."

She was quiet for a minute, and he could tell she was think-ing it over. "You're right. I'm definitely stronger since opening up to you. Can I tell you why I've been thinking about Eddie's parents?"

"Of course. I'd like to know."

"Because I've realized how unfair it was to push everyone away, mostly *you*, but I feel horrible about pushing them away, too. They were always so good to me, and we lost our friend, but he was *their son*. I was so swamped with grief, I lost sight of that."

"They know you were grieving, and they understand."

"Have you talked to them about me?"

"When I see them in town, if they ask about you. Is that okay?"

She nodded. "Yeah, it's fine. But since I'm in a better place now, and it feels good to get back to living my life instead of trying to avoid it, I realized I can't fully move on until I apologize to them."

"I think that's a good idea. I'll go with you if you'd like."

"I want you to, because I could use your support. But it might be hard telling them the truth about that awful day and also telling them that we're together."

"I understand, but it's a small town, Billie. I'm sure they know by now."

"You're probably right. I'll think about it. I also want to run it by our moms on Sunday when we get together for our planning day."

"That's a great idea. Look at you, asking our moms for help."

"Shut up," she said with a laugh, and sat up. "I said I was running it by them, not asking for help. I'm hungry—are you?"

He waggled his brows. "Just for you, baby."

"As enticing as that is, I want something chocolate first. What should we have, s'mores or Oreos?"

"Why don't we melt some chocolate, grab the whipped cream, and have each other instead?"

Her eyes widened. "Dare Whiskey, you are definitely the most brilliant brother in your family."

"Ya think?" He brushed his lips over hers.

"Mm-hm. And the sexiest." She kissed him.

"Best endowed, too."

She giggled. "I haven't seen the competition to judge that."

"And you never will," he growled, and lowered his lips to hers.

Chapter Sixteen

"PINK FROSTING. MY favorite!" Birdie picked up a chocolate cupcake with pink frosting and a white cupcake with chocolate frosting and put them on her plate beside the cinnamon-chip cookies she'd already snagged, a mountain of pasta salad, half a roast-beef sandwich, and a handful of chips.

It was Sunday afternoon, and they were in a meeting room at the ranch with their mothers and sisters to discuss arrangements for Festival on the Green and the kickoff for the Ride Clean campaign. Billie eyed Birdie's petite figure, which she was amply showing off with a yellow crop top, denim shorts, pink paisley suspenders, and pink cowgirl boots with hearts on the sides. "There is no way you're going to stuff all that food into your little body."

Birdie scooped pink frosting off a cupcake with her finger and licked it off. "*Watch me.* I'm carbo-loading."

"Why?"

"Because I love carbs. *Duh.*" She giggled. "I'm really glad you're here. It's all Mom and Sasha could talk about this morning." She went back to eyeing the massive amounts of food Dwight had prepared for them.

Billie carried her plate to the table, feeling a little nervous. But she and Dare had taken his motorcycle up to Silk Hollow yesterday, and they'd had the best day cliff diving, eating lunch on the rocks, and just being together. If she could do that—and beat Dare around the motocross track three times in the last few days—she could do this. She sat next to Bobbie, who looked seriously cute with a deep tan, wearing green linen shorts, and a white T-shirt that had a stack of four books on it with DON'T BOTHER ASKING, MY WEEKEND IS BOOKED written down the spines. Their mothers were talking quietly while they ate. They looked happy and casual. Her mother wore a navy T-shirt and little makeup, while Wynnie wore a white blouse with bright yellow flowers and matching gold necklaces and earrings. It made sense to Billie that her mother was a little more subdued than Wynnie, since she'd carried the weight of Billie's attitude for years. As she watched them, she realized she owed them the truth about why she'd kept everyone at arm's length, and she hoped it would lift a weight off her mother's shoulders as it had hers.

"Are we ready to start?" her mother asked.

"It might be quicker to pull up a trough for Birdie," Billie answered.

"*Birdie*, are you going to join us so we can start?" Sasha flipped her hair over the shoulder of her silky pink tank top. She was just like her mother: organized, punctual, and *always* well put together. Her denim skirt had flecks of pink in it, as did her sandals.

"You guys can start." Birdie bit into a cookie. "I'm only here for Dwight's feast and the camaraderie."

"You're not interested in helping plan this year?" Billie's mother asked.

"I *totally* want to help." Birdie shoved the rest of the cookie in her mouth and sat at the table beside Sasha. "But I have to run the chocolate shop during the festival, so I thought you might not want my input."

"Even if you can't help with the event, we still want to hear your opinions," Wynnie said. "You're always so creative."

"I hear ya, Mama." Birdie winked and made a clicking sound with her tongue as she pointed at her mother.

"You're so weird." Sasha ate a forkful of salad.

Wynnie pushed her empty plate aside, moving a thick folder in front of her, her smiling eyes moving around the table as she spoke. "Before we get started, I just wanted to say how glad I am that you girls made time to do this with us. I remember when you were little, begging to be involved, and Alice and I would set you up at the table with coloring books, pads of paper, and a plateful of cookies. Birdie would eat all the cookies, while Sasha and Bobbie did their best to *plan*, and Billie would take all the empty chairs and create a fort or an obstacle course, which she'd then send Birdie racing through." She set a warm gaze on Billie. "It's so good to have you back with us."

"It's good to be here. You know, when we were little, I felt like a trapped animal when we came to your planning meetings," Billie confessed. "I wanted to be outside running around, but I've been looking forward to spending this time with all of you. Thanks for letting me back in."

"Oh, honey, you were never *out*," Wynnie said. "Life changes, and we deal with the ups and downs as best we can. But I think I speak for your mom and all of the club wives when I say that you'll never lose your place at the table."

Birdie threw her arms around Billie. "I love you, big sister."

"If you were my sister, Dare would be my brother."

"*Ew*, you pig." Birdie howled with laughter, making everyone else laugh, too.

"Mom, do you guys worry that we'll stop helping?" Bobbie asked. "We love the Dark Knights and the ranch."

"We know, honey, but lives and interests change," her mother said.

"As long as you have food, Birdie will be here," Sasha said, and Birdie nodded in agreement, her mouth full. "Billie's racing around the track again and making out with Dare, and Bobbie and I love planning, so I think it's safe to say we'll be sticking around for a while."

Billie's mother's jaw dropped. "You're *riding* again? I thought you were just helping someone learn to ride."

"I was, but something happened that first day, and I climbed on the bike. I've been riding a number of times since. I'm sorry I haven't mentioned it to you. I didn't want you to worry."

"Oh, honey." Her mother pushed to her feet, tears brimming as she went to Billie.

Billie stood, and her mother embraced her so tightly she could barely breathe.

"My fierce girl is coming back," her mother said through her tears.

"You're not afraid that I'll get hurt or that you'll lose me?"

Her mom took a wad of tissues Bobbie was waving at her and wiped her eyes. "I used to be scared that you'd get hurt, but when you gave up everything you loved and pulled away from all of us, I found out what fear really was. It's watching your child suffer year after year and not being able to help. We all lost you, Billie, but we're blessed that you're coming back to us."

Billie teared up.

"Tissues," Wynnie said, stretching an arm across the table to Bobbie. Sasha and Birdie were grabbing for them, too.

"Why is everyone *crying?*" Billie asked, wiping her own eyes. "This is why I don't hang out with girls."

Everyone laughed.

"But you are hanging out with girls. You're here now," her mother pointed out, giving her another hug before going back to her seat.

"Well, don't make me regret it with all these tears," Billie said as she sat down.

"Everyone, stop crying. No more tears," Bobbie ordered, making them all smile.

"Wynnie and I have been close forever, and we always hoped you girls would share the same kind of close-knit friendships, where you can tell each other anything."

Billie had never really had *that* kind of best friend until now, with Dare. When they were kids, they had shared everything, but as teenagers, they'd kept their crushes, and most details of their relationships with others, to themselves. That was probably normal, but she felt like she could tell him anything now, and even if she didn't always do it, she knew she could. As much as she loved Bobbie, Sasha, and Birdie and wanted them to know how happy she was to finally be with Dare, she didn't have the urge to tell them *everything*, the way other girlfriends did. She wondered what that said about her. Maybe it didn't say anything negative about her. Maybe it said something wonderful about her and Dare.

"We'll always be close," Bobbie said emphatically.

Birdie and Sasha agreed.

But Billie was busy mulling over something else. "Mom, if

you and Wynnie tell each other everything, then, Wynnie, why didn't you tell my mom I was riding again?"

"That wasn't my news to share," she said kindly.

Bobbie touched Billie's arm. "I'm so happy you're riding again."

"Me too." Everyone was looking at her like she was holding puppies or something. She squirmed in her seat. "Can we stop talking about me? Aren't we supposed to be planning or looking at schedules or something?"

"*Aaand* she's back," Bobbie teased.

They discussed schedules, itineraries, flyers, and brochures and went over the activities that would be held at the Ride Clean kickoff—paintball, tractor rides, horseback and pony rides, a bouncy house, and several others. Wynnie went over the social media and other marketing efforts Maya was handling, and Birdie and Bobbie had great suggestions to add to it.

An hour and a half later, as they were wrapping up their discussion, Wynnie said, "I almost forgot, Cowboy is going to be offering pony rides at Festival on the Green this year, and Dare got clearance from Kenny's parents to see if he wants to help."

"That's wonderful," Billie's mother said. "It will be good for his confidence and will show him how good it feels to help others."

"Exactly," Wynnie said.

"He's been great with the horses," Sasha said. "I think he'll do well if he wants to do it."

"If Cowboy needs another volunteer, I'd love to help," Bobbie said.

"I think he'd appreciate all the help he can get," Wynnie said.

"If you're looking for more ideas to boost Kenny's confidence, I have one," Billie said.

"What is it?" Wynnie asked.

"He's doing really well on the bike, and he's passionate about the sport. Dare and I gave him a few motocross magazines, and he read them cover to cover," Billie said.

"Sounds like a few other kids we knew," her mother said.

"He reminds me of us, too," Billie said. "Except we had each other, and from what I can gather from our talks, he doesn't have any friends around here other than the people on the ranch. He really looks up to Dare and Cowboy. He talks about them a lot. Anyway, I was thinking that he's doing so well, maybe at the Ride Clean kickoff, he could do a short exhibition ride. I remember how proud I was when I did my first exhibition. He'd have a few months before the event to practice, so he should be more than ready."

"I think that's a great idea," Wynnie said. "But there are a lot of pieces that would have to fall into place to make it happen. He's been here a little more than a month, and Dare is getting ready to schedule a meeting with his parents. He thinks he's almost ready to go home, in which case I'm not sure what will happen with his riding."

"You mean he might just stop?" Billie asked.

"We hope not, but it's a possibility. That will be up to his parents to decide," Wynnie said.

A kernel of panic burned in Billie's chest. "That would be a mistake. Kids like him need an outlet, and he's already connected to the sport."

"I have to agree with Billie," Bobbie said. "We see that with kids at school a lot. If they have a sport or activity they love and their parents can't afford it or can't get them to practices, and they have to drop the sport, the kids rebel."

"I know, honey," Wynnie said. "One of the hardest parts about working on the ranch is letting our clients go out into the world to use the skills we've taught them." Wynnie looked at Sasha, who was nodding in agreement. "If Kenny's learned strong enough communication skills, maybe he can convince his parents to let him continue to ride. I think it would be a good idea for you to bring your concerns, and the idea about the exhibition, up with Dare. He's the one who will be speaking with Kenny's parents."

"If Kenny goes home and his parents agree to let him continue, would you allow him to ride on Dare's track with me?" Billie asked.

Wynnie nodded. "Of course. We always welcome our clients back."

"Okay, then I'll talk to him."

Billie's mind raced throughout the rest of their meeting, but when they were done, her thoughts circled back to what she'd come there prepared to talk to her mother and Wynnie about, and while she was doing that, she might as well tell them the truth about the day Eddie died.

She hung back while the other girls hugged everyone like it was the last time they'd see them for a year. Birdie rushed out, talking a mile a minute on her phone, and Sasha and Bobbie started walking out together, but they stopped by the door, turning to her.

"Billie, want to walk out with us?" Bobbie asked.

"No thanks. I'm not ready yet."

"Okay, I guess I *won't* see you at home again," she teased on their way out, giggling as she walked down the hall.

Alone with her mother and Wynnie, Billie's nerves prickled.

"Mom, Wynnie, can I talk to you for a minute?"

"Sure, honey," her mother said.

"We should probably sit down." *I can do this...*

"If you're pregnant, just spill it," her mother said.

"*Mom. I'm not* pregnant. Geez."

"Darn it," she and Wynnie said at once, and giggled like schoolgirls.

Billie half laughed, half scoffed. "You two have issues."

"We just miss babies, that's all," her mother said.

"If you thought I was a handful, can you imagine what a kid with mine *and* Dare's genes would be like? We'll need a dog crate for sure."

They laughed.

"What do you want to talk about, sweetheart?" her mother asked.

She took a deep breath. "A couple of things. I've learned a lot over the last several weeks, thanks to Dare. I think he's the only person who could have ever gotten through to me. He helped me see so many things more clearly about myself, him, Eddie, and the three of us together. He taught me about what forgiveness really means, and to be honest, you guys taught us a lot, but he showed me what relationships should be like. I always thought I needed to hold my ground alone, like the queen of the mountain, but I've recently realized that I never did that. I could hold my own in races, but that was because I had him and everyone else cheering me on, supporting me, and building me up."

She looked at Wynnie, who for years had been like a second mother to her, and she got choked up again, but she refused to let that stop her. "I want you to know how special he is and how sorry I am for the way I treated him and for avoiding your family for so long. It wasn't fair to any of us, and I'll never do that again."

"That's okay, honey," Wynnie said compassionately. "We all love you."

Billie nodded, trying not to let her emotions get the best of her. "I'm really trying to forgive myself and move forward, but there are two things I need to do. I want to go see Eddie's parents. I owe them an apology for how I've acted, too. Do you think it's okay if I do that? I don't want to cause the Bakers any more grief."

"Oh, sweetheart," her mother said. "I think it's a wonderful idea. Mary asks about you every time we see her. Would you like me to go with you?"

Billie shook her head. "I think I have to do this myself."

"I agree with your mom. It's a wonderful idea," Wynnie said. "But you might want to reconsider your mom's offer or think about asking Dare to go with you. I have a feeling the visit might be tougher than you imagine."

"I deserve tough," Billie said softly.

"No, honey, you don't," her mother said. "You've had it tough enough for long enough."

Billie swiped at the tears that were spilling down her cheeks. So much for holding in her emotions.

Her mother got up and grabbed a stack of napkins from the other table, putting it between them and handing her some.

"Thanks, Mom." She wiped her eyes and took a deep breath. "The other thing I wanted to tell you is what happened the day Eddie died." She let it all out, telling them everything, from the reason she'd accepted the proposal to the last thing he'd said to her before he'd gotten on that bike. With every word, Billie felt more pieces of her sorrow and guilt chipping away. They listened intently, asking questions, hugging her, crying with her, *for* her, for Eddie and Dare, and all that the three of them had lost, and then they reassured her in all the ways her father and Dare had.

They dried their tears, sitting quietly for a few minutes, and in the silence, Billie's body became heavy. She'd thought she'd feel lighter, but she felt like if she closed her eyes, she could sleep for a week.

"I'm so glad you told us," her mother said. "It makes me sad that you've held it in for so long, but now we understand what you were going through."

"Do you feel better now that we know?" Wynnie asked.

"Yes, but I feel like I just ran a marathon."

Her mother took her hand. "You did, sweetheart. The longest marathon ever run."

"And I have more to go, with Eddie's parents." She sighed.

"Maybe you should give yourself a few days before you do that," Wynnie suggested.

"I will. I have Tuesday night off. I'm thinking of going while Dare's at church."

"I'm taking Bobbie's shift Tuesday night, because she has a date," her mother said. "But if you decide you want me to go with you, let me know and I'll get someone to cover for me."

"Bobbie has a date? She didn't mention it to me." For some reason, that bothered her like it never had before.

"You've been a bit preoccupied with your own special someone," her mother pointed out.

"I have, but it's time to make more of an effort with everyone."

DARE SAW KENNY saddling up horses with Cowboy near the hay barn and headed in that direction. When they were kids, before Doc and Cowboy had outgrown doing fun shit, the three of them had driven their parents crazy racing through the barns and over the hay bales. A couple of years before Doc went away to college, they began using the wooden beams that ran along the ceiling of the barn like monkey bars, racing across them. They came home so often with hands full of cuts and splinters, their father had installed short poles with handgrips on all the beams so they could hang from them, and they'd dubbed the hay barn the monkey bars barn.

His brothers had gotten so serious, that seemed like a life-time ago. He missed those times with them sometimes almost as much as he'd missed hanging out with Billie.

Cowboy looked over as Dare approached and lifted his chin in greeting. He'd been teaching Kenny to ride horses, and in Kenny's spare time, if he wasn't practicing with Billie, he could be found in the barns, helping with grooming, tack, or whatever else needed to be done, or hanging out with Sasha while she worked with the rescue horses. He'd come a long way from the boy who hated the smell of horses and was afraid of them. He'd even started wearing the cowboy hat Wynnie had given him. Kenny looked up from beneath the brim, his eyes no longer shadowed with anger, a smile playing on his lips. It was a damn good sight. He'd gained a little weight, too. The kid had started eating like there was no tomorrow, and in his jeans, cowboy boots—also a gift from Wynnie—and T-shirt, he fit right in.

"Hi, Dare," Kenny said.

"Hey, buddy." Dare glanced at Cowboy. "What's going on?"

"We're going on Kenny's first trail ride," Cowboy answered. "I'm taking him out to Blackfoot."

"That's great. Mind if I borrow him for a minute first?"

"Sure." Cowboy took the saddle from Kenny.

Kenny looked him in the eye as he led him away from Cowboy. "What's up?"

"I've got something for you." Dare reached into his pocket and pulled out Kenny's phone, handing it to him.

"What's this for?"

"I think people use it to communicate," Dare teased.

Kenny gave him a *no shit* look. "I get to use it?"

Dare nodded. "Sure can."

"For how long?"

"It's yours, buddy. However long you want. I'm real proud of the work you've been doing here, and I don't mean just physical labor."

Kenny smiled bashfully and lowered his eyes, but quickly met Dare's gaze again. "Thank you."

Dare nodded but said, "You should thank yourself. You did the hard work. How would you feel about helping some little kids out with Cowboy at Festival on the Green? It's a few weeks away, but we're lining up our men for their jobs, and I'd like to count you in."

He grinned proudly. "What can I do?"

"Cowboy's going to be giving pony rides. He needs someone to help with the ponies and keep the kids from climbing on the corral. He may have you walk the horses around the corral with the kids on them. But you'd have to be really careful and go slow."

"I can do that," he said excitedly.

"And you can't curse."

He shrugged. "I'm not allowed to curse around girls or your mom anyway. I *want* to do it."

"Do you want to think about it for a day or two?"

"No. I love working with the horses, and Cowboy is almost as cool as you."

Dare chuckled. "A'right, cool. I'll make it happen. I also think it's time to schedule a meeting with your parents and try to mend those fences. How would you feel about that?"

Worry rose in his eyes. "Will you be there?"

"Yes."

He looked at the grass, kicking at it with the toe of his boot, his mouth pinching.

"What are you worried about, buddy?"

He looked at Dare, eyes serious. "Well, I got help, but they didn't. I learned to tell them what I'm thinking without getting mad, but they're going to treat me the same as they always have."

"Actually, they have been talking with a family counselor in town. They love you, Kenny. They've been working just as hard as you have to make things better, and hopefully you can go home soon and be with your family."

He took a step back, wariness shadowing his eyes. "What if I don't want to go home?"

"Why wouldn't you want to go home?"

"Because there's nothing to do there, and I have no friends. Here I have all of you, and everyone talks to me, and we eat together. At home there's only silence, unless I'm getting yelled at."

"I'm sure you'll make friends. We talked about ways to do

that, remember?"

"Yeah," he said sullenly.

"And your parents are working on not yelling and taking a more active part in your life. With your help, it can all get better. You can bring up all the things you're worried about when we meet with your parents, and I'll be right there with you."

"But I love working with the horses with Cowboy and Sasha, and I really want to keep training with Billie. She's awesome, and she doesn't get mad if I mess up or don't understand. She shows me what I did wrong, like you guys do, and then shows me how to do it better. She said I'm a natural on the bike, and if I stick with it, I can probably compete one day. Maybe not as a pro, because they start training really young, but who knows."

"We'll talk with your parents about that, too. I know they'd like for you to get a job. Maybe they'll let you work here a few hours each week, and when you're done working, you can train with Billie."

"They'd have to drive me here. I don't have a car."

"I'll tell you what, why don't you sit down later or tomorrow and write down all your worries, and I promise you, we'll address them with your parents."

"Okay," he said sullenly. When he lifted his face, his jaw tightened, as if he were steeling himself against something. "Are you kicking me out when they come? Because you can tell me. I'd rather know now."

"No. Absolutely not," Dare said emphatically. "But it's important to start working on getting you home, so you can finish school and figure out your next steps." He put a hand on Kenny's shoulder. "You're part of the Redemption Ranch family now, and that means you will *always* have a place here. Understand?"

Kenny's face brightened, and he gave a curt nod. "Yes."

"So what's our game plan?"

"I'll write down the things I'm worried about, and we'll talk with my parents about them."

"Are you cool with that?"

"I kind of have to be. It's not like your parents will adopt me."

Dare grinned, because he'd heard similar statements from several other people who had come through the ranch. "You don't want to be adopted, Kenny. You have great parents, just like they have a great son. The thing is, parents don't get handbooks on how to parent, the same way teenagers don't get handbooks on how to make the shift from kid to teen. That's why it helps to talk to people who have been through it and get new ideas. You and your parents are lucky that everyone cares enough to try to better themselves. Come on, let's get you back to Cowboy to take a trail ride."

"Can I ask you something first?"

"Sure."

"The other day Billie told me the friend she lost when she quit motocross was one of your best friends, too."

He was surprised to hear that she'd confided in him. "Yes, that's right."

"I just wanted to say I'm sorry. I'm sure that sucked, and I'm glad you and Billie have each other."

"Thanks, Kenny. That means a lot to me."

"Don't do anything stupid to hurt her. She's the coolest girl I've ever met."

"I'll try not to, but I'm good at *stupid*."

Kenny shook his head. "I'm serious. I've never seen couples like you. You act like best friends. Tiny and Wynnie do, too, but I've gotta tell you, your father is a mean-looking dude."

"I know. Has he been mean to you?"

"No. He's been stern a few times, but to be fair, I probably deserved it. He's nice to me. He just looks like he'd be mean."

"He looks tough, but he's got a big heart."

"He doesn't just look tough. He *is* tough. He told me how he met your mom, that he and his brother were on a motorcycle trip, and he took one look at her and said he was going to marry her. He said he started working on this ranch, which her father had owned, and never went back to Maryland. That takes courage."

"Yeah, it does." Dare wasn't surprised that his father had shared that story. He was proud of it, and it showed everyone he shared it with that love at first sight was possible.

"Know what else he told me?" Kenny asked.

"What?"

"That he'd take a bullet for your mom, and the way she's always touching him when she walks by and saying nice things about him, I bet she'd take one for him, too."

"She would. We all would. That's how it should be when you love someone. That's called loyalty, Kenny, and I think your parents would take a bullet for you, too."

"Probably. That's what parents do."

"Unfortunately, not all of them. We should consider ourselves lucky."

Kenny looked down at his phone, and he handed it to Dare. "Here, I don't need this."

"You don't want to call your old girlfriend?"

He shook his head. "We never had what you guys have. We

were just really good at making out."

"That's awfully mature of you to say."

"Well, it's true. Billie said I'll know I've met the right girl when I smile like a fool every time I think about her. She said that's how it was for her with you. She said she fell in love with you when you were kids."

"What did you do? Give my girl truth serum?"

Kenny grinned. "No, we just talk sometimes while we're walking the track or checking the bike over. It was never like that with Katie. It was never that easy."

He had mentioned that before, and they'd talked about it. "Sounds like Billie gave you good advice. Why don't you hang on to the phone in case you want to call someone else."

They headed back to Cowboy, who was now talking with Doc, and Kenny said, "You know you could talk to someone about being good at *stupid*. I hear they've got pretty good therapists here."

Cowboy smirked. "The kid's got a point, but I'm not sure anyone can get through that thick head you're hiding under that hat. Probably hit it too many times doing all those crazy stunts."

Doc chuckled.

"Don't be jealous of my big brain and athleticism," Dare countered. "It's not my fault you have tree-trunk legs that make you slower than a three-legged horse."

Cowboy scoffed. "I could take you any day. While you're yapping away, I'm out here building the big guns." He flexed his bulbous biceps and massive thighs.

"Dare, he probably *could* take you in a fight," Kenny said, looking warily at Doc. "Don't let them fight. He'll get hurt."

"Dare doesn't fight unless he has to," Doc said. "He's too smart for that."

Kenny looked at Dare, confused.

"What did I tell you about fighting?" Dare asked.

"That it's for weak people who have no other skills," Kenny recited verbatim.

"That's right. Fists don't fly unless there's no other choice."

"He learned long ago he's no match for me." Cowboy flashed a shit-eating grin. "Remember that, little brother?"

Oh yeah, he remembered. Dare had been home for summer break after his freshman year of college, when he was partying too much. Someone had told Cowboy that Dare was partying at the creek, and Cowboy had marched his big, pushy self down there and found Dare shit-faced, making out with two college girls he'd met in town. They were just passing through and looking for a good time, and well, he was fucking great at showing chicks a good time. But Cowboy had hauled him out of there and handed his ass to him for being an idiot, lecturing him the whole damn time about being irresponsible. In his inebriated state, Dare had actually thought he could take on his mountainous brother and had quickly learned how sorely mistaken he was.

"Yeah, I remember. You got a few cheap shots in when I was three sheets to the wind." Dare had a hankering to wipe that grin off his brother's face. He was in a great mood. The woman he loved was by his side every night and finding her way back to all the people she loved, and Kenny was doing phenomenally well and was on a good path for a better future. Yup. His stars had aligned. It was the perfect day to put Cowboy in his place. "How about you put your money where your mouth is? Fifty bucks says my thick head can beat your ridiculous tree-trunk legs in a race."

Doc shook his head. "Oh boy, here we go."

"What? A race?" Kenny's gaze bounced between Cowboy and Dare.

Cowboy's eyes narrowed.

"You and me, just like old times. First one across the monkey bars, *over* the tractor, and *over* the hay bales wins." Dare whipped out his wallet and handed Kenny fifty bucks. "Hold on to that. You'll be giving it back to me in a few minutes."

Kenny looked at the tractor and the enormous round hay bales. "*Over* them?"

"That's right," Dare said, eyes locked on Cowboy. "Unless he's afraid to race."

"Game. *On.*" Cowboy pulled out his wallet and handed it to Kenny.

"This is gonna be awesome!" Kenny exclaimed.

Doc scrubbed a hand down his face. "Come on, guys. You both have big dicks. Now can you back off?"

"Mine's definitely bigger," Dare said.

"You wish." Cowboy sneered.

"Jesus, you're like teenagers," Doc grumbled.

"Spoken like the true owner of the smallest pecker in the family," Dare teased.

"Holy shit," Cowboy said. "That's the reason no girl ever lasts with you, isn't it, Doc?"

Doc gritted his teeth.

"Are you gonna let them talk smack about you?" Kenny asked.

"Yeah, old man. Show us how big your balls are," Dare taunted.

"You know what? Fuck both of you." Doc threw his wallet into Kenny's hands and pointed at his brothers. "You're both going down."

The three of them stood shoulder to shoulder outside the barn doors.

"Y'all are going to eat my dust." Dare tossed his hat to the grass, and they got into their running stances, knees bent, one foot back, ready to propel them forward.

"Shit, I'll beat you on one leg," Cowboy said.

"You're both idiots," Doc grumbled.

"I'm gonna say ready, set go, okay?" Kenny stood by the barn doors, excitement dancing in his eyes.

"Yeah," they said in unison.

Dare lowered his chin, mentally mapping out his route.

"Ready, set, *go!*"

They took off, and Dare used a rectangular hay bale for a step, launching himself up to the bars and nimbly racing across them. He saw Cowboy in his periphery and Doc right behind him and pushed himself harder. Just as Cowboy reached for the last bar, Dare flew off his and sprinted to the tractor, leaping onto the tire, and up to the hood, doing a front flip off of it—earning cheers from Kenny—then landing with a *thud* as Cowboy and Doc scrambled up the other side. He booked it over to the round hay bale, launching himself to the top of it and landing on his hands, knees bent. His feet hit the top of the bale as his hands left it, and he did another flip, calling out, "*Hurry up, losers!*" and landed on his feet just as Cowboy shouted, "*Fuck!* Damn you, Dare! I split my pants!" They cracked up as Cowboy shoved Doc out of the way and leaped to the top of a hay bale, but Doc was right behind him and pushed him off. Cowboy grabbed Doc's arm, taking them both down to the ground, the two of them wrestling and laughing. Dare dove on top, and Kenny cracked up, as applause rang out.

"Uh-oh! Guys! Stop!" Kenny warned.

They rolled off each other, still laughing as they looked for the source of the clapping, and Billie's laughter floated into Dare's ears.

Like a heat-seeking missile, his gaze found her as she headed his way from the far side of the barn with their mothers, smiling brightly. "It's okay, Kenny. We're not in trouble," Dare reassured him as they pushed to their feet, trying to quell their laughter, and Cowboy bitched about ruining his favorite jeans.

"Did you see them?" Kenny shouted to the women. "That was awesome! I want to do that!"

Doc shoved Cowboy, and Dare made a beeline for his girl.

"Some things never change," his mother said.

"You're right. I won," he said proudly, leaning in to kiss Billie.

"Of course you did," Billie said. "How about you take on someone who can actually keep up?"

He wrapped his arms around her, *madly* in love with the challenge in her eyes. He hoped that meant things had gone well with the girls and when she'd talked to their mothers. "You want to take me on, darlin'?"

"Any day of the week."

"How about *every* day of the week?" he kissed her, and as his brothers shouted, "Get a room!" he flicked them off and deepened the kiss.

Chapter Seventeen

BILLIE SAT IN her truck Tuesday evening outside Eddie's parents' house, feeling like she was going to throw up. She'd parked around the corner for nearly an hour before calming herself down enough to drive the rest of the way. She should have taken Dare up on his offer to come with her, but she wasn't sure how Eddie's parents would react to the news she was bringing, much less to her and Dare's relationship. He'd been so supportive, giving her tricks to calm herself down if she got too anxious, but as the speech she'd mentally prepared ran through her head, she couldn't even remember what those tricks were. She thought about texting him, but he was at church, and she didn't want to bother him there.

Besides, she'd caused this rift. She needed to be the one to fix it.

She rested her head back, staring absently at the roof of the truck and breathing deeply. *I can do this. They've known me since I was a kid. They love me.* She looked at the house again, but her anxiety spiked.

Why was this more difficult than getting on her bike?

Because bikes don't talk. Bikes don't cry or blame or look at me like I'm the biggest jerk on the planet.

Dare and their parents had forgiven her, but these were *Eddie's* parents, and they'd lost their only son. They might see what really happened the same way she'd seen it, and they had every right to. When she'd called to say she wanted to stop by, Eddie's mother, Mary, had sounded surprised and a little cautious despite her kind words. *I'm so glad you reached out. We would love to see you.* It was one thing to be kind on the phone, but another when the only person who really knew what happened that day was standing in front of them.

She rested her head back again. "I hope I don't screw this up, Eddie. The last thing I want to do is cause them more pain."

But she knew there was no way around causing them pain. In an effort to help her prepare for the worst, Dare had played devil's advocate and had told her that the fact that she'd broken up with Eddie might be heartbreaking for them. They'd talked about omitting that part, but it was exhausting carrying the secret, and they deserved to know the truth even if it took them all to their knees.

"I'd ask you for a sign, but there's no place for Dare to land with a parachute." She thought about how that morning had set so many changes into motion. "Thank you for that, Eddie," she said just above a whisper, knowing he'd hear her whether or not she said it aloud. "I will always love you."

The front door opened, and her heart nearly stopped as his parents stepped onto the porch.

"Seriously, Eddie? As if I needed more pressure?"

What're you waiting for, Billie? Get out there and show the world what you've got.

"It's not the *world* I'm worried about, but I get it. I'm going. Thank you for being with me today."

Billie managed a smile, or at least she hoped she did as she forced herself to climb out of the truck and make her way to them. His mother wore her blond hair shorter than she used to, just above her shoulders, but her natural waves still flowed, just like Eddie's had. Her floral peach blouse was tucked into a gray skirt that fell just below her knees. His father was tall and broad-shouldered, like Eddie had been, with thinning salt-and-pepper hair. He wore a short-sleeved dress shirt and slacks, just like always. It was unfair how it seemed like nothing changed, and at the same time, everything had.

Her stomach knotted up, and tears stung her eyes. *Don'tcrydon'tcrydon'tcry.*

"Billie, sweetheart, it's so good to see you." His mother came off the porch, blinking rapidly, as if she were holding back tears, too.

Billie's throat thickened. "Thank you for letting me stop by."

"We've missed you, honey," his father said. "You were like a daughter to us, and it's good to have you home."

He opened his arms and embraced her, his words and his embrace unleashing a flood of tears. She'd forgotten how they'd always referred to their house as *home* for her and Dare. They'd spent less time there than they had at the ranch or at Billie's, but when they'd have dinner with his parents, they'd always said it was nice to have *all their kids* around the dinner table. That memory cut like a knife. She'd stolen *herself* from them, too.

"I'm sorry," Billie choked out as his mother pulled her into her arms, both of them crying.

"It's okay, sweetheart. It's been a long time, but I always knew you'd come see us when you were ready." His mother drew back and reached into the pocket of her skirt, handing Billie a small cellophane package of tissues.

"Thank you." Billie pulled out a few and handed the package back to her.

"That's for you." She pulled another package of tissues from her other pocket. "I thought we might both need them. Why don't we go inside and have some iced tea while we chat?"

Billie nodded as she wiped her eyes, and they headed inside.

The house smelled just like it always had, like sunshine and roses. The cozy living room had the same tan sofa and love seat she, Dare, and Eddie had sat on hundreds of times, eating his mom's cookies and talking with his parents, while giving each other secret glances that said, *Have we been social enough? Can we go have fun now?* Eddie smiled down from a picture on the mantel, standing between his parents at their high school graduation. He was so handsome in his cap and gown, with his sun-kissed skin, his shaggy hair curling around his ears, and that contagious smile lighting up his eyes.

"Make yourself comfortable, and I'll get us some tea." His mother headed into the kitchen.

Billie sat on the love seat, trying to rein in her emotions, but there were pictures of Eddie on the walls and bookcases, and she had the strange thought that he might come down the hall and say, *I'm glad you're here. We've been waiting for you.* As her gaze passed over pictures of him from childhood to adulthood, with his grandparents and parents, with her and Dare and their families, she realized he'd already said that to her. He'd just done it without words, by giving her the courage to walk inside. A lump lodged in her throat. She looked at the pictures on the bookcase. In most, he was holding a video camera. She'd seen all the pictures before, but they hit deeper now. This was all that was left of their son, of one of her best friends. Tears spilled down her cheeks, and she pulled out more tissues, swiped at them, trying to pull herself together.

"It's okay, honey," Eddie's father said.

She'd forgotten he was in the room. "Sorry."

"There's no need to be sorry when you're shedding tears for our boy," his father said. "We know how much you kids loved each other. You three running around and causing mayhem was the best thing this quiet little town has ever seen."

A soft laugh tumbled out along with more tears. *Did she have an endless well of them?* "We had a lot of fun."

"Yes, you did," his mother said affectionately as she came into the room with a tray of glasses and a pitcher of iced tea. She set the tray on the coffee table and poured them each a glass, handing one to Billie.

"Thank you." She tried again to pull herself together as his mother sat on the sofa beside her husband.

"We've kept up with how you're doing over the years through your family and the Whiskeys, but we'd love to hear it from you," his father said.

Billie took a deep breath. "I'm doing well, but if you'd asked me that two months ago, my answer would have been very different."

"Honey, you wouldn't have let us get close enough to ask you anything two months ago," his mother said gently.

"I know, and I'm so sorry. I've hurt a lot of people, myself included. But I've been spending a lot of time with Dare, and he's helped me to see things more clearly, and I'm trying to make amends with the people I've pushed away. That's why I asked if you would mind talking with me today. I want to tell you the truth about the day we lost Eddie."

"The truth?"

She nodded and somehow managed to tell them everything. The ugly truth about the breakup, how she and Dare had tried to stop Eddie from getting on the bike, and all the things she'd felt since then, her heart breaking anew for all of them. "That's why I've been avoiding you and everyone else. I'm so sorry. I loved Eddie, and if I'd known he was going to be so upset that he'd try that stupid stunt instead of filming us, I never would have broken up with him." She held their sorrowful gazes. "I won't blame you if you never want to see me again."

As they wiped their tears, his father said, "You couldn't have known what he was going to do, and he wouldn't have wanted you to hold in your true feelings. We know you and Dare did everything you could to stop him from getting on the bike. You might not remember because it was so traumatic, but you and Dare told us that the night of the accident. So please don't think his death was your fault. You kids were young, and our son was a bright, strong-willed young man. When he got on that bike, he knew the risks."

His mother nodded in agreement, sniffling. "We know how much you loved him, and we would never blame you for his decisions. We don't even blame him, honey. It was a tragic accident."

Relief swamped Billie. "Thank you," she said just above a whisper, fresh tears falling. But that was only the first hurdle. She still had two more to go, so she gulped a breath, wiping her eyes, and sat up taller. "There's something else I need you to know. Eddie wouldn't take back the engagement ring. He said he wanted me to have it. But it didn't feel right to keep it, so I put it in the casket at the wake. I wanted him to have a piece of us with him."

"We know," his mother said. "They check for things that have been left behind after wakes, and they found it. They asked us what we wanted to do with it, and we told them to put it exactly where you'd left it."

Billie was too emotional to speak, so she nodded, wiping her tears. She took a few deep breaths as they all pulled themselves together, and when she finally stopped her tears, she said, "There's one last thing you should know. Dare and I are seeing each other."

His parents smiled, and his mother said, "We know that, too, honey. The whole town is talking about how happy they are for you and Dare." She took her husband's hand, gazing thoughtfully at him, before turning a sweet smile on Billie. "We're happy for you, too. You're so well suited for each other."

"Thank you." She wiped the tears that caused.

"But, honey," his mother said, "Dare has been scaring the heck out of everyone with the stunts he's been pulling off the last several years. Maybe you can take on Eddie's role of reining him in before he gets hurt."

"I don't think anyone can rein him in like Eddie did, and to be honest, if losing Eddie didn't slow him down, I don't think anything will."

"And you're okay with that?" his father asked carefully. "We've heard that you're riding your bike again and doing some of the things you used to, and we're happy for you. But jumping over buses on his motorcycle?"

"That scares the heck out of me, too," she admitted. She hadn't thought about it this way back then, but she'd come to realize and accept that loving a Daredevil came with risks that were greater than the stunts themselves, and any heartache that came from it was on her.

They talked for a long time, reminiscing about Eddie, the good old days when the three of them were together, and chatting about how talented he was and his "Unforgettable Daredevils" movie. It was after nine when they finally walked her out.

"Thank you again for letting me come by *and* for not hating me."

"We could never hate someone we love." His father drew her into a warm embrace.

"I love you, too," Billie said, and she was surprised at how easily those words came.

"It was devastating to lose Eddie, but I feel like he will always be a part of you and Dare, and that makes me happy." His mother hugged her. "I'm so glad you came to see us, and I hope we'll see more of you."

"You will, and that's a promise." She headed for her truck on that starry night, feeling the last tethers of guilt falling away. She knew she was forever changed and would never be the *utterly* carefree girl she'd once been. But as she drove toward home, with the windows down and a cool breeze coasting over her skin, she felt like a butterfly breaking free of its cocoon, and she couldn't wait to celebrate those feelings with Dare.

DARE SAT AT a table in the Dark Knights' clubhouse surrounded by the sounds of billiard balls, darts, and the brotherhood he had always counted on. But not one of them could help ease the worry eating away at him. He tried to focus on the discussion going on between his father, brothers, Ezra,

Rebel, and Manny, about the reopening of an old missing persons' case from nearly two decades ago his father had announced during the meeting, but his mind was miles away, on his dark-haired beauty. Billie was facing one of the most difficult times of her life, and she'd wanted to go it alone. He loved her autonomous streak, but she'd been so nervous the last few days, he regretted not pushing her to let him be there with her.

Rebel rose to his feet. "I'm grabbing a beer. Anyone want one?"

"Sure," Doc and Ezra said in unison.

"No thanks," Cowboy said, studying the flyer his father had handed out about the case.

"How about you, Evel Knievel?" Rebel asked.

"Nah, I'm good, man." Dare pulled out his phone for the millionth time to see if Billie had texted and uttered a curse at the blank screen.

"Still no word?" his father asked.

Dare gritted his teeth, shaking his head. "It's been *hours*. I should've heard from her by now. Manny, have you heard from Bobbie or Alice? Have either of them heard from her?"

Manny shook his head. "No, son. We're all waiting on pins and needles, just like you."

"The Bakers are good people," Doc said. "Billie's going to be fine."

"And what if she's not? You know how she shuts down." Dare didn't even want to think about that, but he knew it was a very real possibility.

Cowboy put a hand on Dare's shoulder. "That's why she's got you. She trusts you, man, and for good reason. She's not going to shut you out again."

"I hope not, but if this goes south, talking about it with me might be too much for her."

"If she wants to talk to someone she's *not* sleeping with, you know I'll make time," Ezra offered.

"I appreciate that, and I've suggested she talk to someone else, but she's not into it." He couldn't sit still a minute longer and rose to his feet. "I'm going to step outside and call her."

He weaved around the other members and headed out the doors as he made the call. He heard a phone ring in the parking lot as he put his phone to his ear. It rang again in his ear and in the parking lot. He scanned the darkness, spotting Billie leaning against his motorcycle, and closed the distance between them as she answered his call, practically purring in his ear, "Hey, Whiskey."

She looked like a million bucks in tight snakeskin pants, a sexy black halter, the choker he loved, and a gorgeous smile that unfurled the knots in his gut. He pocketed his phone as she pushed from the bike. The energy radiating from her was lighter and different than it had been in years, and he knew things had gone well.

"*Damn*, Mancini. You in that outfit…" He drank her in and drew her into his arms. "*Mm-mm.* I'd like to bend you over that bike and take you right here and now."

She raised her brows. "I was hoping you'd have that reaction."

"Does this mean it went well with the Bakers?"

"Even better than I'd hoped. I told them everything, and we cried a lot, but by the time I left, I think we all felt better. I'm so glad I went, and I never would have gotten the nerve if it weren't for you."

He held her tighter. "And this outfit is your way of thanking me?"

"Only the part I can show you in public." A taunting grin curved her lips, and she wound her arms around his neck. "I was hoping you'd take me to the Roadhouse to celebrate."

"Are you sure you want to celebrate where you work? Where's your truck? How'd you get here?"

"It doesn't matter how I got here. And yes, I'm sure. I know I've got to be a boss, but I'm also a woman who is madly in love with the hottest guy in this town, and if I want to celebrate with him in *my* bar, that's what I'm gonna do. Fuck 'em if they don't like it."

There it was, the difference he'd noticed, shining as bright as the dawn of a new day, and hell if he didn't want to stay right there and fucking revel in it for the rest of his damn life. "God, I love you."

As he lowered his lips to hers, she said, "I love you, too."

He kissed her greedily, and she went up on her toes as he took the kiss deeper. *Jesus.* Even their kisses felt different. Hotter and more electrifying, lighting up his entire body. His hand moved into her hair, angling her mouth beneath his, taking the kiss impossibly deeper. He heard something in his periphery, but her hands slid down his back and she grabbed his ass, obliterating his every thought beyond wanting *more.*

"That better be my daughter's hands on your ass, Whiskey, or you're not going to have an ass to be grabbed," Manny growled.

Their lips parted on grins, and Dare kept her close, turning to see their fathers, his brothers, and a handful of guys, who all cheered and whistled.

"Guess things went okay with the Bakers, sweetheart?" Manny asked.

"Yeah, Dad. They did." She was grinning from ear to ear and slid her arm around Dare's waist.

Dare looked at his beautiful girl and said, for her ears only, "Are you up for a big celebration with the guys?" The joy that sparked in her eyes as she nodded had his heart stumbling. He turned around and hollered, "Party at the Roadhouse!"

"That's what I'm talking about!" Rebel shouted, and more cheers rang out. "I'll get the others!"

There was a flurry of activity as Rebel headed into the club-house and guys went for their bikes.

Manny came over to hug Billie, and Dare stepped away to give them privacy.

His father lumbered over. "Feel like you can breathe again, son?"

"Yeah. I was so worried." He looked at his father and noticed that he looked lighter, too. "You?"

He nodded curtly. "She's been like a daughter to me and your mother since she was a sassy little thing romping around in cowboy boots and your hat. She's been hurting for a long time, and so have we. She's got that look she used to get when you two were younger and getting ready to do some crazy-ass stunt." His father cracked a smile. "I reckon you're in for a hell of a wild night."

"I'm looking forward to it. Aren't you coming?"

"I wouldn't miss it for the world, and neither would your mom. I'm going to pick her up. We'll see you there"

"WILD HEARTS" BY Keith Urban blared from speakers, and

people practically shouted to hear each other, but there was only one person Dare needed to hear, and he was twirling her on the dance floor. They'd been dancing on and off for nearly two hours. The Roadhouse was packed with Dark Knights, their families, and a handful of other customers. They were so busy, Manny had joined Alice and Kellan, serving behind the bar. It wasn't a coincidence. Dare knew damn well his father and Manny had spread the word that Billie "Badass" Mancini was celebrating. After all, it's not every day the feistiest girl in Hope Valley, who had gone from being a Daredevil and professional motocross racer to living behind walls so thick Dare didn't know how she'd breathed, to joking around with everyone and dancing like she deserved a spotlight.

And she fucking did.

Cowboy and Bobbie were dancing a few feet away, as were Doc and a tall redhead. Their parents were dancing, too. They didn't often get to see their parents out on the dance floor, but nobody was holding back tonight. Especially not his girl, who was dancing like the music flowed through her veins.

When the song ended and "Take My Name" by Parmalee came on, Dare tugged her into his arms, slowing them down. "Are you enjoying torturing me with all your sexy dancing, in that fuck-me outfit, Mancini?"

She draped her arms over his shoulders, running her fingers along the back of his neck. "Why, yes, Whiskey. Yes, I am."

"I don't *care* if you don't know how to dance," Birdie said loudly as she dragged a complaining Hyde past them, followed by Sasha and Taz.

"She's such a pest," Dare said. "Hyde hates dancing."

"Let your sister be, and focus on *me*," Billie said.

"Baby, my focus is never off you. Do you know how happy

I am right now? Seeing you dancing like this?"

"Well, I'm about to make you even happier."

He held her tighter, brushing his lips over hers. "Now we're talking."

"Keep it in your pants for a little longer, Whiskey." Her expression softened. "I decided to watch you jump the buses next weekend."

He was dumbfounded. "Are you sure?"

"Yes. I've been thinking about it, and when we said Daredevils for life, I *meant* it. If something happens to you, and I pray it doesn't, but if it does, I want you to know that I'm there supporting you and cheering you on, just like you've been cheering me on. I'm in this with you, Dare, no matter where it takes us."

Overwhelmed and beyond happy, he touched his forehead to hers, trying to find words big enough to describe how that made him feel, but his heart must be drawing all the blood from his brain, so he went with "You can't imagine how much that means to me."

"Yes, I can. Now kiss me, Whiskey."

He did, slow and deep, holding her tight as the song came to an end, and "Man! I Feel Like a Woman!" came on.

Birdie and Sasha squealed. Birdie grabbed Billie, and Sasha grabbed Bobbie, and the four of them started dancing together. "Mom!" Birdie waved their mother over, and Bobbie hollered to Alice, who came out from behind the bar to dance with them.

Dare loved every second of it and headed over to the bar with his father and the guys.

"Your gal sure is something tonight," his father said as Manny came over to serve them.

"Yeah, she is, and so is yours. Look at Mom out there,"

Dare said as their mother shimmied with the girls.

"I haven't seen my wife and daughters dance like that in years," Manny said. "That's all you, Dare, and I sure do appreciate it."

"I didn't do anything but open a door. Billie's the one who had the courage to walk through it."

"Well, thanks for opening it, son," Manny said. "You've been on that dance floor all night. You ready for a cold one yet?"

"Nah, I'm not drinking tonight. I've got our girl on the back of my bike. How about some ice water?"

"You've got it." Manny took the other guys' orders and went to fill them.

Dare couldn't take his eyes off Billie. It wasn't just her sexy moves or how incredible she looked in that slinky little outfit. It was the joy and freedom she exuded that held his rapt attention.

"Man, it's good to see her out there with the girls again, isn't it?" Doc said.

"You have no idea how good."

Manny brought their drinks, and they talked while the girls danced. When "Country Girl (Shake It for Me)" came on, the girls squealed again and continued dancing, except for Billie, who made a beeline for Dare.

"Make a hole, boys," his father said loudly. "Let the lady through."

The guys stepped aside, but Billie didn't go to Dare. She *winked* at him, took two big steps, and hoisted herself onto the bar, causing everyone to cheer as she started dancing. Dare cheered the loudest.

Billie pointed at him and crooked her finger. "Get your ass up here and dance with me, Whiskey!"

"That's my girl." He climbed onto the bar, matching her sexy moves one for one, earning more cheers, hoots, and whistles. He heard someone ask Manny if he was going to kick them off, and Manny said, "Not on your life. We've been waiting years for this."

When the chorus came on, Billie threw her hands up, turning in a circle as she danced, and the whole bar joined in singing the song.

As Dare sang the last chorus to Billie, telling her to shake her body for him, she didn't just shake it. She *worked* those luscious curves, rubbing and grinding against him, driving him out of his fucking mind. When the song ended, he dipped her over his arm and kissed her. The bar erupted in cheers, whistles, and applause.

When their lips parted, Billie was beaming. "Take me home, Whiskey. I'm done giving these people a show. Now it's your turn."

She didn't have to ask twice.

As they climbed down from the bar, she pointed at Kellan, who was laughing and shaking his head. "I'm still your boss, and you still have to respect me."

His face went serious. "I've got more respect for you now than ever."

"You damn well better, dimples," she said.

They said their goodbyes and left the bar arm in arm, kissing on their way across the parking lot. It was a beautiful, clear night, and as Dare drove toward the ranch, with Billie warming his back, her arms wrapped around him, he didn't think life could get any better. They stopped at a red light, waiting for the green turning arrow, and she put her hand between his legs. *Soon, baby.* He put his hand over hers, giving one firm squeeze, and lifted it, pulling her arms tight around him and pressing her hands to his stomach. The light changed, and he turned left. He was halfway through the intersection when he saw headlights speeding toward them on the road he was turning onto. He veered right, trying to avoid the car, but it clipped the back of the motorcycle, sending Dare airborne—*Billie!*—his body flipped head over heels, and he landed *hard* on the grass beside the road, tumbling and skidding to a stop. His ears were ringing as he tore his helmet off, hollering, "*Billie!*" He gritted his teeth against the stabbing pain in his chest and tried to sit up. His entire body screamed in pain as he searched the ground, spotting her lying by the bushes a good distance away. "*Billie!*" He tried to stand but crumpled to the ground, pain searing through his leg as he gasped for air. "*Billie!*" She wasn't moving. He dragged himself along the grass, shouting. People were running from their cars toward her. "*Billie!*" Tears blurred his vision as he dragged himself farther, fighting off people who were trying to help him. Billie's leg and arm were cocked at horrible angles, her helmet was gone, and his beautiful girl, his love, his *life*, lay lifeless and bleeding. "*Nononogodno.* Don't you leave me!" He scooped her body into his arms, telling the people who were saying not to touch her to *fuck off*, as he cradled her against him. "*Billie. Wake up, baby, wake up. Come on, baby. Wake up, Mancini.*" Agony raged through him, and he buried his face in her bloody hair, "*Nooooo!*" bled from his lungs as two people pried him away from her, and he struggled to break free. "Leave me the fuck alone! I gotta be with her!"

"*Dare,* we've got her. She's breathing. It's me, Hazard."

The cop's face came into focus. Hector "Hazard" Martinez, Maya's brother, a Dark Knight. "She's..." Excruciating pain seared through Dare's chest.

"Yeah, man. She's alive but unconscious. The paramedics are with her. We've got to get you to the hospital. You're in bad shape."

"I don't give..." He tried to drag air into his lungs. "A fuck." *Gasp.* "Need to be...with her." He tried to throw himself in the direction of the paramedics loading Billie onto a stretcher, but Hazard held him back as more paramedics appeared and started pawing at him. "Get...*off* me...Help her."

A paramedic crouched before him, getting right in his face. "Listen to me, man. They've got her, but we need to help *you*. Your leg is broken, and you've got a chest wound. Now lie the hell down and don't make my job harder than it needs to be."

Chapter Eighteen

COWBOY AND DOC stood on one side of Dare's hospital bed, his parents on the other, and his sisters and Rebel by his feet. Many of the Dark Knights and their wives had shown up, but he'd sent them upstairs to be with Billie's family in the ICU. The doctor had said they were lucky they were turning a corner and not driving full speed when they were hit, or things could have been a lot worse. Dare had a concussion, three broken ribs, his left leg was broken and casted, and his right shoulder was fractured. His right arm was in a sling/shoulder immobilizer. He had a bandage over a stitched-up chest wound, and he had so many other cuts, abrasions, and stitches, he felt like a freaking pin cushion. His body and head hurt like a son of a bitch, but it was his heart that felt like it had been put through a meat grinder. Manny had given them an update on Billie about an hour ago. She had broken her right arm, left leg, collarbone, and ribs. She had a punctured lung, a body full of stitches and abrasions, and she was still unconscious. They were running more tests, and damn it, he needed to be up there.

Birdie looked at her phone. "Bobbie said there's still no word. But don't worry, Dare. She's going to be fine."

He gritted his teeth, knowing she meant well, but if one more person told him that Billie was going to be fine, he would lose his mind. They were checking for swelling and bleeding in her brain. *Christ. Her fucking brain.* He couldn't lose her, not after all they'd been through. She didn't deserve that. Her parents didn't deserve that. *Fuck.* He didn't deserve it, and he sure as hell wasn't going to lie there doing nothing. He threw his blanket off and tried to sit up, wincing in pain.

"Whoa, buddy. You need to lie back down," Doc said.

"The hell I do. I need to get up there."

"You can't see her yet," Cowboy said sternly. "They're still running tests."

"I don't give a rat's ass," he gritted out through clenched teeth. "I need to be where she is, to be with her family and make sure they're okay, and to see the doctor's face when he comes out, so either help me or get out of my fucking way."

"A'right, *settle down*," his father said sternly. "Rebel, go get him a wheelchair."

As Rebel left the room, Doc said, "This is *not* a good idea. You can't do anything up there. The best thing you can do is rest until we know something, and then we'll bring you to see her."

"You have three seconds to put those fucking side bars down or I'm gonna start swinging."

Doc looked at their father imploringly.

"You heard the man," his father said, and his brothers cursed as they lowered the protective metal bars.

Dare grimaced through the pain as he sat up and swung his legs over the side of the bed.

"Oh, honey. Are you sure about this?" his mother asked.

"I'm *fine*, Mom."

"No, you're not, but I know better than to argue with you," she said. "I'm going with you."

A few minutes later, Rebel pushed a wheelchair into the room. "Are you sure this is a good idea? The nurse gave me shit when I said it was for you."

"I'm wondering the same thing," Sasha said as his brothers helped him into the wheelchair. "You suffered a major trauma, and your body needs rest to heal."

"*Geez*," Birdie said exasperatedly. "He wants to be there for Billie. He *loves* her. Don't you want a guy who will drag his broken body to you regardless of the consequences?"

"Yes, but—"

Dare started rolling the wheelchair toward the door with his good arm, gritting his teeth against the pain.

"Honey, let me do that." His mother wheeled him out.

Dare heard his brothers bitching at his father about *what ifs*, and a minute later the rest of his family and Rebel caught up to them near the elevator.

"I'm not changing my mind," Dare warned.

"No shit, you stubborn ass," Cowboy said. "We're going with you."

"I don't need a babysitter," Dare snapped.

"Shut up before I knock that chip off your shoulder," Cowboy warned. "We're going to be there *for* you, not to hold you back. We just didn't want you getting all worked up and hurting yourself when you should be resting."

Dare swallowed hard, appreciating the support.

"When they're done running tests, if Billie hasn't woken up and they keep her in the ICU, they'll only let two people in to see her," Doc said.

"Her parents," Dare relented. He needed to see them. To

apologize.

Doc nodded. "I know an ICU nurse. I'll see what I can do."

"Thanks, man. I appreciate that. I'm not trying to be a dick. I just need to see her."

"We get it," Doc said. "But while you're worrying about Billie, someone's got to worry about you."

Doc went to the nursing station as the rest of them filed into the ICU waiting room. Billie's family looked as devastated as Dare felt, bringing back that awful afternoon when they'd lost Eddie and all their parents had shown up at the same time as the ambulance, frantic and shattered, gutting him anew. Bobbie's eyes teared up as his sisters went to her, the three of them embracing.

Alice's gaze moved over him in the wheelchair, and she covered her mouth, tears spilling from her eyes. "Oh, *honey*."

"I'm fine. Have you heard anything about Billie?"

"Not yet, but they said the tests would take a while," Manny said, putting his arm around Alice. He looked like he'd aged ten years in the past few hours. "Billie's strong. She'll pull through this."

"The strongest." Dare bit back the fear gnawing away at him. "I am *so* sorry. I tried to avoid the car. If I'd only gone—"

"Don't you dare take responsibility for this," Manny insisted. "The guy who hit you was high as a kite. They arrested him, and this is *his* fault, not yours."

"I know, I just...We can't lose her. That should be *me* in there, not her." Struggling against the emotions swamping him, he clenched his jaw and turned his face to wipe a stray tear. Her parents didn't need to see him break down.

"Don't say that," Alice said. "It wouldn't be any better for anyone if it were you. We just have to believe she'll be all right."

"She will be. She has to be." Dare couldn't sit still while the love of his life was lying unconscious. He needed to get up and move, but when he tried, his father put a heavy hand on his shoulder, not so gently shoving him back down. Dare glowered at him.

"I let you come up here, but you're going to keep your ass in that chair," his father said as Doc returned and headed for Dare.

A short, stout, balding man in a white lab coat came through the double doors and headed for the waiting room. Dare's pulse raced, and it felt like everyone in the room held their breath as the man said, "Mr. and Mrs. Mancini?"

"Right here," Manny called out, and the crowd parted as they went to him.

Dare tried to get up, but his father shoved him down again. When his father didn't push the wheelchair to follow them, Dare glared at him. "What the—"

"Stay put out of respect for her parents" was all his father said.

Dare cursed under his breath, even though he knew his father was right.

Doc put a hand on his other shoulder and said, "I pulled some strings. You'll get a chance to see her, and so will Bobbie."

"Thanks, man." Dare tried to read the doctor's expression, but he didn't like what it said as he motioned toward the hallway.

As Manny and Alice followed him out of the waiting room. Manny stopped and looked at Dare. "Come on, son. You should hear this, too."

Thank fucking Christ.

His father pushed his wheelchair over to them. Cowboy and

Doc stayed behind.

The doctor went over the litany of injuries that had already been reported, and then he said, "She's still unconscious, but we didn't find any swelling, bleeding, or bruising on her brain, which is good news."

Thank God. He was cautiously relieved.

"She's breathing fine on her own, and we're watching her closely," the doctor said. "We opted not to put her on a ventilator so we don't have to sedate her."

"Why hasn't she woken up?" Manny asked.

"When *will* she wake up?" Alice asked.

"Unfortunately, there's no road map for this. Everyone's brain reacts differently to trauma. I can't tell you when, or if, she'll wake up, but we'll know more in the next twenty-four to forty-eight hours."

Dare gripped the arms of the wheelchair to keep from growling, *She'll wake up. She fucking has to!* His father's hand landed on his shoulder again. *Twenty-four to forty-eight hours? What happens after that? Is that the minuscule window of hope?* He didn't ask. He didn't want to know the answer.

"You'll be able to see her soon," the doctor promised.

"Will she be able to hear us talking to her?" Alice asked anxiously.

"Yes, and it's good to talk to her. Familiar voices may help stimulate her brain and speed up her recovery. The nurse will be back shortly to take you to see her."

The doctor smiled for the first time, and that made Dare feel like that last comment was the first true sign of hope. He would talk to her until he ran out of breath. He'd do whatever it took to get through to her and bring her back.

Manny gave the group a quick update, and there were

murmurs of relief and worry. A little while later a tall, brunette nurse explained that they were making an exception in visitation policies, and she escorted Manny, Alice, and Bobbie to see Billie. Dare threw more silent prayers up to the powers that be for Billie to wake up and be okay, making deals with the devil and anyone else who would listen. His father and Cowboy stood a few feet away, their feet planted firmly on the floor, arms crossed, watching him like a hawk. He tried to stand, forgetting about his fucking cast and broken ribs, and sank back down with a curse.

"What do you need?" Doc asked.

"For Billie to *fucking* wake up."

"I know, man. She *will*. She's strong, and she loves you. You know she's fighting tooth and nail to come back."

God, I hope so. "I need a crutch. Can you find me one? If I sit here another minute, I'm going to lose my shit. And can you swing by my place and get me some clothes later and a replacement phone? Mine broke in the crash."

"Sure."

As Doc went to find a crutch, Dare called Cowboy over. "I want to know everything there is to know about the guy who hit us."

"Hazard's already on it. His name's Crew Hendricks. Jilted groom, went for a night of partying. This was his first offense. He'll probably get jail time and a hefty fine, and there'll likely be some sort of victim restitution."

"No amount of restitution can make up for what he's done to Billie."

"Hey, as long as he ends up behind bars, he's not your problem."

"Right. Thanks. I need to talk to Ezra before my brain stops working. It hurts like a motherfucker."

With a nod, Cowboy went to get Ezra, and Dare closed his eyes, trying to get his head to stop feeling like it was going to explode.

"You need me, Dare?" Ezra asked.

Dare opened his eyes. "Yeah. I need you to handle my clients."

"Sure. Whatever you need."

"This'll shake them up, but I'm mostly worried about Kenny because of where he is in the program. This is probably going to freak him out, so be careful not to scare him. He needs to know what happened and that I can't meet with him tomorrow and Billie can't ride with him. It could totally derail him."

"I won't let it," Ezra promised. "Dwight and I will keep a close eye on him. I'll make sure he's supported, don't worry."

"I know you will. Let him know I'm *fine* and I'll see him as soon as I can. We have a meeting with his parents next week. Have Maya put that off until we figure things out. I need to be with him for that. Do you have time to take over our sessions for now? I'm not sure my mom will be up to it. I doubt she'll want to leave Alice and Manny."

"I'll make time for him and whichever other clients you need me to take over, too."

"Thanks. Work it out with Maya, but make sure you get Kenny. I think he'll relate to you better than Colleen. He might see her as too much of a maternal figure. I can catch you up to speed in the morning. I can't concentrate right now."

"No problem. I'll head back to the ranch now to nip this in the bud. I'd tell you not to worry about work, but I know you too well. Just know we've all got your back, so it's okay to put your work thoughts on hold."

"Thanks, man. I appreciate that."

A little while later, Manny, Alice, and Bobbie returned, red-eyed, the little color that had remained in their faces gone, and Dare hobbled on a crutch down the hall beside the nurse on his way to see Billie.

"Thanks for letting me see her."

"Sure. I'd do anything for Doc." She smiled in that way that told him just how fond of his brother she was. She stopped outside Billie's room, speaking gently. "Not too long, okay? I made sure the other nurses know to let you in however long she's here."

"I appreciate that."

"Be positive, and talk to her like she can answer. It helps."

Dare nodded and went into Billie's room. His heart clawed its way into his throat. Her cheek was bruised and bandaged, as was her forehead. Her leg and arm were casted, and her casted arm was in a sling. She had an IV, and there were tubes snaking out from under her gown. This wasn't the end. It couldn't be. The woman who'd been ready to take the world by storm couldn't go out in the blink of an eye on a simple fucking ride home. Dare wanted to get his hands on the motherfucker who did this to her.

The tears he'd been holding back burned free, sliding down his cheeks as he went to her. He set his crutch against the bedside table and pressed a kiss to her forehead. "I'm *sorry*, baby. I'm so fucking sorry. I'd give anything to switch places with you. But you're going to be okay. The doctor said your head looks good, and everyone is here waiting for you to wake up." A tear fell from his cheek to hers, and she didn't flinch, didn't move a muscle. Her stillness brought more tears. "You *will* wake up, Mancini. I know you will. We have a life to build together, and I *know* you want it." He carefully took her hand between his. "Daredevils for life, *baby...*" His voice trailed away, an onslaught of tears rushing in as reality slammed into him. He never wanted her to be in the position he was in right now, crying over the person she loved, willing to sell his soul to bring her back to life.

He gritted his teeth. "I won't scare you with crazy stunts ever again. That's a promise." Her voice whispered in his head, *Don't make promises you can't keep, Whiskey.* It was so real, he felt himself smiling. "I didn't say we wouldn't go cliff diving, skydiving, or skiing, and do other fun things, but I won't push the limits anymore, baby. I don't need to jump over buses or run with the bulls. Fuck breaking records. All I need is *you*, darlin', and I'm not leaving this hospital without you. So you get whatever rest you need, and know that when you're ready, I'll be here waiting to take you home."

Chapter Nineteen

DARE FELT LIKE he'd spent the night in a trash compactor, but he was sure that was due to the accident and his aching heart rather than his sleeping quarters. He'd argued with his parents and the nurses last night about going back to his room, but they'd finally accepted that he wasn't budging and let him sleep in a recliner in the ICU waiting room, just as his parents and Manny, Alice, and Bobbie had. As promised, Doc had fetched him clean clothes last night, and he'd finally showered. It hurt like a son of a bitch, and he'd needed a damn bag around his cast, but he was glad to get out of that awful hospital gown. When he'd returned to the waiting room, Kellan had been there, out of his mind with worry. He'd told Manny he'd take care of the bar, and Rebel and several other Dark Knights were going to fill in as long as they needed them. Colleen had assured Dare and his parents that between her and Ezra, their clients would be well cared for. His father and Manny had sent the club families home, but Dare had seen a number of them milling around in the early hours of the morning. He knew they'd continue to be around to support their families at the hospital and to support his siblings at the ranch, since they had to go back and do their jobs. He was thankful for them, because no matter how strong their families were, nothing could have prepared them for this.

It was Wednesday evening, and although his siblings and dozens of others had come by to check on him and Billie, he hadn't seen any of them. He sat in the chair beside Billie's bed, holding her hand, where he'd been since early morning, promising her the sun, moon, and stars if she'd just wake up. His mother had brought him the new phone Doc had dropped off, and he'd touched base with Ezra about Kenny. He was glad to hear that although Kenny was worried, it hadn't pushed him over the edge.

That was a good thing, because Dare would be no help to anyone right now. All he could think about were the doctor's words about the next twenty-four to forty-eight hours, which felt like a ticking time bomb, as if after forty-eight hours a door would close, never to open again. The hours moved painfully slowly, and he'd spent every second trying to figure out how to draw Billie out of this new, unfamiliar darkness. He couldn't use any of his usual tactics. He couldn't flirt with her or tempt her with things she loved. He couldn't egg her on with a challenge or get under her skin by touching her.

He'd tried *everything*, and he'd never felt so helpless in his life.

"I need you to wake up, Mancini." He rubbed his thumb over the back of her hand. "You've made your point, and whatever you want, whatever you need when you come out of this, I'll do it, build it, or buy it. I've promised you everything I can think of, and I know you don't want any of it. All you want is us and your family, and we're here, baby, waiting for you to come back from wherever you've gone." He kissed the back of her hand, his tears falling on her skin. He watched her intently, but her eyes remained closed, her body still. "I'm going to keep bugging you until you hear me, so you might as well wake up."

The door opened, and he wiped his tears as his mother walked in with a cup of coffee and a sandwich. He didn't know what kind of strings Doc's friend had pulled, but they owed her big-time. The ICU usually allowed only two visitors per day, and they'd not only allowed Bobbie to go in *with* her parents and allowed Dare to see Billie last night, but they were allowing Billie's and Dare's families to visit as long as no more than two people were in the room at the same time.

"I brought you some dinner," his mother said, but her smile quickly faded. "Oh, sweetheart." She set the sandwich and coffee on the table and went to him, touching his cheek, his hand, his arm.

"I'm fine," he lied, getting even more choked up with her affection.

"It's okay not to be fine, honey. Your love is lying in a hospital bed, and I know she's trying to come back to you."

More tears fell, and he swiped at them. "I've cried more in this room than I have in my entire life other than…" He didn't need to say *when Eddie died.*

"No, honey, it just feels that way." She pulled up a chair beside him and took his hand. "You don't remember when you were little and Billie told you she didn't want to be your friend anymore. You cried all day. You also picked fights with your brothers, hurt your little hand punching a wall, and kicked anything that got in your way. And then you snuck out on our ATV to go see her, scaring the daylights out of us."

He dried his eyes. "I remember that. I was pissed. I felt like I'd been duped. Like I had this best friend who called me names whenever she was mad, but I called her a stupid girl *once* and she abandoned me."

"Do you have any idea why she was so hurt?"

"Because she's Billie, the most competitive female on the planet, and she didn't like to be called names."

"Nobody likes to be called names, but that's not the only reason. You called her a stupid *girl*. You didn't like something about her that she couldn't change."

He scoffed. "I *loved* her then, and I love her now. I didn't know what to do with all those feelings. That's why I said it. Even as a little kid, every time I saw her, I wanted her to be *mine*. I didn't even know what that meant, but I had no way to stop it. It was bigger than I was."

"I know, sweetheart."

"I can't lose her, Mom." More tears fell. "I don't even know who I am without her."

She put her arms around him, and he let it all out, crying years' worth of tears that he'd never let himself shed. "It's okay, honey. She's going to be okay."

Dare sat back, forcing himself to pull it together. His mother didn't need any more stress. "I hope so. I keep trying to figure out how I can draw her out of wherever she is. Where do people go when they're unconscious? Into a void of nothingness? Is she dreaming?"

"If she is, those dreams are of you."

He managed a smile, hoping that was true.

"She'll wake up, and things will go back to normal. You'll see."

"I don't need *normal*. I just need her to wake up, and whatever happens, whatever she needs, she'll have it. And I will never put her—or you and everyone else—in a position where you might be sitting by my hospital bed like this."

His mother's brow knitted. "What are you saying?"

"I promised Billie I won't push the limits anymore. I was selfish wanting her to support me jumping over buses and running with the bulls. What the hell was I thinking? How could I not see the pressure and fear that put on her and everyone else? I'm an idiot. You guys should've beaten some sense into me."

"Your brothers tried for many years." She patted his hand. "Honey, you wouldn't listen to us any more than Billie would when she pushed everyone away. You two are wired in a way that only the two of you understand, and although I'm thrilled to hear that you'll temper the need to scare the daylights out of us, you need to know that you're not an idiot. You're just Dare, and she's just Billie. Two relentless Daredevils who are loved wholly and completely for who you are."

Struggling against tears, he said, "Thank you, but I'm still sorry for putting everyone through it, and without her, there is no me. She's the *only* thrill I need."

AN HOUR AND a half later, after Manny, Alice, Bobbie, and Tiny had cycled through Billie's room, Dare was alone with her again. The male nurse who was on shift tonight peeked in and said, "Visiting hours are over in five minutes."

"I don't suppose I can buy another hour for a hundred bucks," Dare offered.

"I wish I could let you. Sorry."

"It was worth a try."

The nurse shut the door, and Dare pushed himself up to his good leg and gazed down at Billie's beautiful, marred face. "What're you really dreaming about, gorgeous? Are you out there in the *in-between*? I know you feel me waiting for you, so whatever you're doing, can you please hurry it up and get back here?" He looked up at the ceiling, brushing his thumb over the back of Billie's hand, and he did something he hadn't done in years.

He called on the best friend they'd lost.

"Hey, Eddie, if you can hear me, Billie told me about what happened that day and why she broke up with you. I'm sorry, man. I'm sure it hurt like a son of a bitch. But I didn't know she was into me. There was nothing going on behind your back. So if you don't hate me, I need a favor. Our girl needs a push. It's not her time yet, so if you have *any* pull, could you send her back to me? Just show her the way, man. I think she's lost, and I really need her. I know that makes me a selfish motherfucker, but she is the blood in my veins, the air that I breathe. She *is* the very heart of me." He gritted his teeth, and the door opened again.

The male nurse came into the room. "I'm sorry, but I have to ask you to leave."

Dare nodded and leaned down to kiss Billie, stopping just shy of her lips. "I have to leave your room, but I'll be right outside your door when you wake up. I love you more than life itself, Mancini." He pressed his lips to hers and felt her fingers move. Hope soared inside him. "She moved her fingers!"

The nurse looked at her hand, which had stilled. "It was probably involuntary. That's not uncommon."

"No, man. I'm telling you she did it." He squeezed her hand, but there was no response. "Come on, baby. You can do it." He lowered his face closer to hers. "I know you can hear me, Mancini. Move your fingers if you can hear me." Her fingers closed lightly around his. "*See? She's moving. Look at her hand!*" Her eyes fluttered open with a look of bewilderment, and Dare's heart leapt. "She's awake!"

The nurse hurried over and pushed a button, talking into the intercom as Dare spoke to Billie. "Hi, darlin'. I'm right here. I knew you'd wake up."

"Where am I?" she asked softly.

"In the hospital. We had an accident. Don't you remember?"

She stared at Dare, shaking her head. "Who are you?"

Dare's stomach plummeted. "It's me, baby, Dare."

"I don't know you." She shrank away from him as the doctor and a female nurse rushed into the room.

"It's me, Billie. *Dare.*"

"I don't know him," she repeated, her voice threaded with fear, and then the doctor was pushing Dare out of the way, and another nurse was shoving his crutch under his arm and escorting him toward the door.

"*Wait!* Why doesn't she remember me?" The doctor blocked his view of her, and panic flared in his chest. "She needs to see me so she can remember who I am!"

"We need to assess her, and we can't do that with you here. We'll take good care of her," the nurse reassured him.

"Let me talk to her, *please!*" He struggled to get back to Billie, but the male nurse was now helping to force him out the door.

"Mr. Whiskey, if you fight us, you *won't* be allowed back in," the nurse said. "I know you're worried, but you need to let us do our jobs."

DARE HAD THOUGHT every minute was treacherously hard before Billie had woken up, but waiting for the doctor to come out of Billie's room was excruciating. The nurse had told them that it wasn't uncommon for patients who have been unconscious to have trouble remembering certain things and that the doctor would be out as soon as he was done assessing Billie. But she was *awake*, and it felt like the biggest fucking miracle on earth. They were all elated about that and hopeful after what the nurse had said, that not recognizing Dare was just a blip from waking after being unconscious for a day. Dare was so anxious to see her, his entire body felt tight and ready for a fight, which didn't fare well with his injuries. But he didn't give a damn about the pain he was in. All he cared about was getting back to Billie.

When the doctor finally appeared, they rushed toward him. "How is she?" Alice asked at the same time Dare said, "Why didn't she remember me?"

Just like last night, the doctor's expression remained serious. "She was a bit disconcerted and agitated, but that's to be expected. She's sleeping comfortably now, but she appears to have retrograde amnesia."

"What does that mean? She doesn't remember anything?" Manny asked.

"It means she's lost the ability to recall events that happened before the onset of amnesia, or in Billie's case, before the accident, but she's able to make and retain new memories," the doctor explained.

Alice gasped, and tears filled Bobbie's eyes. Manny put his

arms around them. Dare steeled himself against the emotions suffocating him as his mother's tears slipped free. His father put a hand on his uninjured shoulder and took his mother's hand.

"In most cases patients lose recent memories but they're able to recall older ones, like their childhood, for example. In Billie's case, she remembers who her parents are and that she has a sister, but she doesn't remember her sister's name." The doctor looked at Dare. "Unfortunately, she doesn't remember you, either, and she can't recall any other details of her past."

"Goodness gracious," his mother said, wiping her tears.

His father's gaze was locked on Manny. "We'll get through this." He looked at the doctor. "Will she eventually remember more?"

"We hope so. In some cases, retrograde amnesia resolves fairly quickly, within twenty-four hours or so, and we'll be watching her closely," the doctor promised.

That fucking timeline brought another wave of fear. This time Dare needed to know what they were facing. "What happens after twenty-four hours?" His voice sounded as ragged as he felt.

"Everyone is different. Why don't we worry about that if and when the time comes?" the doctor suggested.

Dare wanted to slam him against the wall and demand answers, and his father must have felt that, because he tightened his hold on Dare's shoulder and said, "What can we do? Are there specialists we can bring in who can help her to regain her memory?"

"The best thing you can do right now is to gently remind her who you are and tell her things about her life," the doctor said reassuringly. "Sights, smells, and tastes can also help spark memories, but try not to overwhelm or put pressure on her.

Answer her questions, but don't push. She's been through a lot, and her brain is already working hard to try to fill in the gaps, so she'll probably tire easily."

"Does she remember how to do things?" Bobbie asked.

"Yes. This type of amnesia involves facts rather than skills," the doctor explained. "For example, someone with retrograde amnesia might forget that they own a bike and what kind it is or where they bought it, but they remember how to ride."

They all breathed a sigh of relief.

"When can we see her?" Manny asked.

"She's sleeping now, and she will likely be out for the night," the doctor said. "I suggest you go home and get some rest and come back in the morning."

Dare wasn't going anywhere. As the doctor walked away and the others talked, he went into battle mode, coming up with other ways to help make Billie's memories bigger and stronger than her bastard opponent.

He stepped to the side and called Cowboy.

"Hey, man. What's up? You okay?" Cowboy asked.

"Yeah. Billie's awake, but she has amnesia. I need a favor..."

Chapter Twenty

BILLIE LOOKED AT the dozens of framed photographs covering every surface in her room, even the tray where someone had left her breakfast. There were pictures of her family and of people she didn't recognize. Groups of people. Other families maybe, and guys on motorcycles, and dozens of pictures of her and two boys on skateboards, snowboarding, riding bikes, and doing other activities. There was a laptop on the bedside table, too. None of the pictures or the laptop had been there last night when the doctor had explained that she had been in a motorcycle accident and had something called retrograde amnesia. That was why she hurt all over and couldn't remember anything. The person who'd brought her breakfast had said her family had probably brought in the pictures and laptop while she was sleeping to help her remember her past.

She picked up a picture from the bedside table and studied it. She looked young, and so did the two boys she was with. They were all sitting on bikes, and she was in the middle. One of the boys was blond. The other looked like the dark-haired guy who was in her room last night and had said his name was *Dare*. He looked younger in the picture, and he was wearing a cowboy hat, but there was no mistaking those eyes. They'd rattled her last night. When she'd first woken up, his eyes were the first thing she'd seen, and in the space of a second, she'd felt those intense dark eyes as if they could see into her head, into her *heart*, as if they were searching, exuding energy so intense, she'd felt herself spiraling into them, and she hadn't been able to separate from that feeling. She felt like she *should* know who he and the other guy in the picture were, like all the information about them was on the tip of her tongue, but she couldn't get it to fall off. It was like looking at the world through a foggy lens that she desperately wanted to wipe clean but was unable to.

It was a little terrifying to think that other people held her secrets, while she was kept in the dark. The door to her room opened, and her mother peeked in. Relief washed over her.

"Good morning, honey. Is it okay for your father and I to come in?"

"Yes." She put the picture facedown in her lap. She didn't remember much about her parents, but she *knew* them and she felt safe around them. Her father's warm smile hit in a way that told her they must have been close. He carried a bag in one hand, and his other hand rested on her mother's back as they came to her bedside.

"How are you feeling, sweetheart?" her mother asked.

"I'm okay." She didn't want to worry the only people she knew in this world.

Her father tilted his head, eyes narrowing, an expression that also felt familiar. "You sure about that, sweet pea?"

The endearment brought another pang of happiness. "I'm trying to be okay," she confessed.

"Maybe this will make you feel a little better." He opened the bag and withdrew a can of root beer, watching her curiously as he opened it and handed it to her.

"That's our thing, isn't it? Drinking root beer? I remember that."

"You do?" Her mother's eyes were wide and hopeful.

"Yes, but I don't know *why* it's our thing."

"I can tell you that," her father said thoughtfully. "Your sister, Bobbie, is younger than you, and after she was born, sometimes I'd bring you to work with me at our family's bar when I opened for lunch, and we'd have lunch together to give your mother a little break. One day you were mad about something or other, and you saw me serve a customer a beer and talk to him about a problem he was having. You asked me for a beer and got mad when I wouldn't give you one."

"We own a bar?"

"Yes, and you love managing it," her mother said. "You kind of grew up there, doing homework while we worked."

She *wanted* to remember everything they were telling her. It felt like she could almost remember it, but it was just out of reach. "How old was I when the root beer thing happened?"

"Almost four," her father answered.

Almost four. "Was I a pain?"

"No," he said with a smile. "But you've never liked being told you couldn't have or do things, and you sat at the bar pouting. Only you didn't pout like a whiny kid. You glared at me, and if looks could kill, I wouldn't be standing here right now."

She laughed softly. "I *was* a pain."

"No, honey," her mother said. "You were fierce, and we love that about you. When I came to pick you up that day and saw how mad you were, I suggested that we give you a *special* beer."

"Root beer," Billie said.

"That's right. Only once you had it in your hands, you wanted to sit at the bar and tell your father what you were so mad about when you'd gotten there, like the customer had."

She looked at her father. "Do you remember what it was?"

"I'll never forget." Amusement rose in his eyes. "Bobbie was about seven or eight months old then, and you said you'd been thinking about it, and you didn't want a sister. You wanted us to send her back and get you a brother."

"I hope Bobbie doesn't know that story. What did you say?"

"I told you that we loved your sister very much, and we would no sooner give her back than we'd give you back." Her father smiled. "You got even madder, but we talked for a while, and by the end of our conversation, you said having a sister wouldn't be that bad and asked if we could order a boy next time."

"I love my sister, don't I? I feel like I do."

"Yes, honey. You love her very much, and she adores you," her mother said. "She's here if you'd like to see her."

"I would like to."

"Okay, but first how about you take a sip of that root beer and tell us how you're really feeling?" her father suggested.

She took a sip, and the sweetness stirred something inside her. Not specific memories, but the sense of times like the one they'd just told her about and a feeling of happiness.

"That smile is a welcome sight," her mother said.

"The root beer makes me happy."

"Are you in much pain?" her mother asked.

"I kind of feel like I was dropped from the roof of the hospital."

Pain worked its way across her parents' faces. "I'm sorry, honey," her mother said.

"Should we ask for more painkillers?" her father asked.

"No. I'm kind of glad I can feel something other than numb from not remembering who I am or what I've done in my life."

Her mother touched her hand, and that brought more happiness. "The doctor said there's a good chance your memory will come back. You just have to give it time."

"I hope so."

"The doctor said you might tire easily. Why don't we get Bobbie for you?" her mother suggested.

"We love you, sweet pea." Her father leaned down and kissed her cheek, and then her mother kissed her, too, and they headed for the door.

"Wait," Billie said anxiously. "Can I see you later?"

"We'd love that," her mother said. "They're going to move you out of the ICU today, and then you'll be able to see all of us together, as a family."

Billie looked forward to that after they left the room, and she studied the picture again, until her sister walked in. She was pretty, and she had their mother's smile.

"Hi," Bobbie said softly, her eyes tearing up.

Her tears made Billie uncomfortable. "Hi."

"How are you feeling?"

Billie looked down at her casts. She was covered in stitches and abrasions, and she had broken ribs and a tube in her chest from a collapsed lung. The doctor said the tube would come out soon. She had the strange thought that she'd lost her breath and her memories at the same time. She looked at her sister and said, "I hope I've had better days."

Bobbie laughed softly, and it made her laugh, too.

She winced and wrapped her good arm over her ribs. "That hurts."

"I'm sorry. I won't make you laugh anymore."

"It's okay. I'm sorry I don't remember anything about you or us." She hated feeling so lost and thought of the story her parents had told her. "Were we close?"

"That's a hard question to answer. I want to tell you yes and make up a story about how close we were with hopes of it coming true, but the nurse said to be as honest as possible. We were close in some ways. We've lived together for a few years in a great little house, and we get along well. You've always been protective of me, and I've always looked up to you."

Tears slipped down her sister's cheeks, and Billie looked away to try to escape the discomfort those tears brought.

"*Sorry.*" Bobbie quickly wiped her eyes. "You've always hated it when I cry."

"I did? I'm sorry," Billie said, feeling bad.

"It's okay. I've always been more emotional than you."

The way she said it made Billie wonder what she meant and what kind of a person she was. "Am I a *bitch*?"

Bobbie smiled. "No, but you've had your moments."

"I *was* a bitch. I can tell by the way you said it."

"No, you weren't. I promise."

"Then why did you say we were close in *some ways* and not just that we were close?"

"We're just different." Bobbie sighed. "You like to be in control and to keep things to yourself, whereas I tend to wear my heart on my sleeve. We have different interests. I would drive you crazy talking about hair and makeup, or clothes and boys, and you weren't into anything like that."

She tried to understand what she was saying. "Am I into girls?"

"No. You're definitely into guys. We just have different

interests and personalities. You're much tougher than me. I admire that about you."

"Thank you."

"To be honest, there were only two people you've ever been *really* close to."

"Who are they?"

Bobbie looked around the room and went to the window-sill. She picked up a picture and handed it to Billie. "We were teenagers, and that's a lake we all used to go to."

Billie studied the picture. She was on the shoulders of the guy she believed to be Dare, and Bobbie was on the shoulders of the blond boy who was in the other picture she'd been looking at. Billie got that feeling again, like she knew his name but couldn't put her finger on it.

Bobbie pointed to Dare. "That's Dare Whiskey. His real name is Devlin, but when you guys were younger, you started calling him Dare because you could dare him to do anything, and he'd do it." She pointed to the blond. "That's Eddie Baker. You used to call him Steady Eddie because he was always careful and prepared for anything. You could always count on both of them, but you knew Eddie would take the safe route and Dare would take the riskiest. You three were best friends and did everything together."

Billie ran her fingers over their faces.

"Dare is the one who brought all these pictures in to help you remember."

"Devlin 'Dare' Whiskey and Steady Eddie Baker."

"Do their names ring any bells?" she asked hopefully.

Billie shook her head. "No."

"Dare hasn't left the hospital since you got here. He loves you very much."

"He loves me. It's strange to hear that about someone I don't know. Did I love him?"

Bobbie nodded, quickly wiping at the tears trickling down her cheeks. "*Sorry.* I'm trying not to cry, but you loved him so much, and he made you incredibly happy."

"Did I love Steady Eddie?"

"Yes, very much."

Billie thought about that for a minute. "I loved them both? How did that work?"

"I think the difference was that you loved Eddie, but you were *in love* with Dare. Would you like to see Dare and ask him these questions?"

She mulled that over because of how the way he'd looked at her last night had made her feel. Every iota of her being had *willed* her to get lost in him, despite not being able to put the pieces together of a single day of her life or their relationship. Bobbie was right. She didn't like feeling out of control. But if everything Bobbie was saying was true, then Billie owed it to herself, and to Dare, to try to remember.

"Yes," she finally answered. "But can I ask you a few more things?"

"Anything."

"Is Eddie here, too?"

Bobbie's face blanched. "No. I'm sorry, Billie, but Eddie died in an accident several years ago."

"Oh, that's so sad. I don't remember him or the accident." She was so frustrated. She hated knowing she'd lost someone she was close to and couldn't even honor him with a single memory.

"That's probably a blessing. We were all devastated."

"Was I good to him?"

"You were wonderful to him. You and Dare were his best friends."

"I have this weird feeling that I'm not a good person, and I don't know why or what it means." That made her sister cry, and Billie feared it meant she wasn't.

"You're a *great* person, and we all love you very much."

Billie was quiet for a long moment, thinking about everything her parents and her sister had said. Bobbie was sweet and obviously loved her very much, and Billie wanted to try to get closer to her, if that was even possible. "Dad told me a story about how when you were little, I wanted them to trade you in for a brother, but I don't think I ever really wanted them to get rid of you."

"I bet you did at times. I was a pest. When I was little, I tried to follow you around, and as we got older, I borrowed some of your sexier clothes without you knowing, but they never looked as great on me as they did on you, and you always found out anyway."

"You're beautiful. I bet you turn heads everywhere you go, with or without sexy clothes. You're also nicer than someone who *has her moments.*"

"Thank you. I know you don't love hugging, but can I hug you if I do it carefully?" Bobbie's eyes teared up again. "I was so scared that we might lose you."

Billie's throat thickened, and she nodded. Bobbie embraced her, and her lemon-scented shampoo brought a rush of the same warm, happy feelings she'd gotten with her parents.

"I love you," Bobbie said softly.

"I love you, too." For some reason that made Bobbie cry harder. "What can I do to stop you from crying?"

Bobbie laughed and wiped her tears. "Nothing. I'm built

this way, just like you're built to be tough. I'll go get Dare."

"*Wait.*" Billie caught her hand. "It's strange knowing any-one can lie to me and say they know me, or we did things, and I won't know the difference."

"That is a scary thought."

"Is there anything I should know about Dare?"

Her gaze warmed. "*Yes.* He would never lie to you."

"Because he loves me?"

"Because that's the type of man he is, and you should know that when you two were in the accident, he crawled more than fifty feet with a broken leg, a fractured shoulder, broken ribs, *and* a chest wound to get to you."

"*Wow.* He sounds a little crazy."

"He's definitely crazy about you, and maybe a little of the good kind of crazy, too, just like you."

"What do you mean by that?"

"Just that I've always admired your fearlessness. I'll get Dare."

Billie looked at the two photographs in her lap while she waited, trying to puzzle together the boy in them and the man who had filled her room with dozens of pictures and had crawled fifty feet despite his own injuries, just to get to her. He sounded too good to be true.

The door to her room opened, and Dare's worried face appeared. "Mind if I come in, darlin'?" He was wearing a cowboy hat, an oversize black tank top, and cargo shorts and using a crutch under his left arm. A backpack was hooked around his left wrist. His left leg was casted below the knee, and his right arm was in a sling and strapped to his very broad chest. His face was all scratched up, and he had a bandage above his left eye. His neck, shoulders, and chest were covered with tattoos. And those dark eyes were as intense as they were thoughtful.

She had the urge to snag that cowboy hat off his head and put it on her own, and the way he said *darlin'* made her heart beat faster, but it was the energy buzzing in the air between them as he held her gaze that had her voice sounding strange and a little breathy as she said, "Sure."

"How are you feeling?" He set the backpack on the floor and leaned the crutch against the bedside table.

"Probably about like you are, except my brain doesn't work and yours does."

"Your brain works, Mancini. It's just tired from getting knocked around."

The way he said her last name made it feel special. "Why do you call me that?"

"Because you're *my* Mancini."

He said it matter-of-factly. Like it was a truth she simply couldn't remember, and then he smiled, and *holy cow*. He was already handsome, with his scruffy cheeks and chiseled jaw, but that smile made her insides go hot, which was silly, because even though they apparently had a long history together, he was still a stranger to her.

THE WARY LOOK in Billie's eyes was about the only thing helping tamp down Dare's urge to climb onto her bed, take her in his good arm, and profess his love for her until she remembered every little thing about them. But he was determined not to make this harder for her, no matter how torturous it was for him. *Gentle reminders*, his mother's voice whispered. She'd spent the last few hours drilling it into his head.

"You might not remember this," he said casually. "But you call me *Whiskey* a lot."

"I do? Why? Because it's your last name?"

"I'd like to think it's because you like how I taste, but the truth is, you've called me that since we were kids. I think it made us more like equals. You would never let me get one up on you. If I beat you in a race, you wanted to race over and over again until you won. But we were never equals, Billie. You've always blown me away."

She smiled a little bashfully and looked down at the pictures she had on her lap. "Thank you for bringing me all these pictures."

"I hope they help you remember how great your life has been."

She looked at him thoughtfully. "My sister said you dragged yourself over to me after the accident. That must have hurt."

"Baby, I love you so much, nothing could hurt as much as the thought of losing you." He bit out a curse. "I'm sorry. I don't mean to pressure you."

"I don't feel pressure. I'm sorry it's awkward. Bobbie said we loved each other."

"*Love.* We *love* each other. That doesn't change because of an accident. You might not remember that you love me right now, but our love is like no other. It's lasted since we were kids, and I'll spend every day for the rest of our lives giving you reasons to fall in love with me. I'm not giving up on you, Mancini."

Her eyes teared up.

"I'm *sorry.* I didn't mean to upset you."

"You didn't. I just wish I remembered us. We must have meant the world to each other for you to say those things. I feel bad for you because I'm so broken."

He leaned closer, wanting her to hear every word he said. "You're not broken, Billie. We were in a horrible accident, and we're lucky to be alive. Your mind just needs time to catch up, and there's no rush, no pressure." Even as he said it, that time bomb kept ticking in the back of his mind.

"You really are a good guy."

"I'm a pushy son of a bitch, but I also try to be a good person. Is there anything you want to talk about? Anything you'd like to know?"

"I want to know about all these pictures. It looks like we had fun." Her gaze fell to the pictures in her lap, and her smile faded. "But Bobbie told me about Eddie."

"She did?"

She nodded. "I don't remember him, but I'm sad that he died."

"We loved him very much. How would you feel about watching a movie? I have one that will give you a pretty good idea about all these pictures and our lives together before Eddie's accident."

"I'd like that."

"Do you think I can fit on the bed with you? No hanky-panky, just to share snacks and watch the movie?"

She smiled. "You're funny. I only have one root beer, but you can share it with me."

He picked up the backpack. "I've got everything we need."

He carefully settled onto the mattress beside her and reached into the backpack, pulling out a pack of Oreos, barbecue chips, and two Capri Suns.

"Do I like those?" she asked.

"Let's put it this way. Cookie Monster has nothing on you." Her face pinched.

"What's wrong?"

"It's just frustrating. I feel like I know who Cookie Monster is, like I've heard the name a thousand times, but I can't picture it."

Dare rested the laptop on his lap and pulled up a picture of Cookie Monster.

Her eyes lit up. "I know him! I remember. *Sesame Street*, right?"

"That's right!" He leaned in to kiss her, and she drew back. "Sorry." *Fuck.* "I just got carried away. I'm really sorry. It's just instinct with you."

"That's okay."

"No, it's not. I don't want to make this harder or mess this up for you."

"I have news for you. It's already a pretty messed-up situation."

"I know, but we're going to make the most of it. You're going to fall in love with me over and over again, and when you get your memory back, you'll just love me even more."

She studied him, eyes narrowing. He could practically hear the gears in her head churning, picking his words apart. That was okay. He had nothing to hide. Especially not from her.

"You really don't give up on people, do you?"

"Not usually and definitely not where you're concerned."

"What if I don't fall for you?" she asked carefully.

"That's not going to happen. You once told me I made it impossible for you to love anyone else."

She picked up an Oreo, those gears churning again, and bit

into it. Her whole face brightened. "I *like* these." She grabbed
the package, tucking it against her other side. "You can eat the
chips."

He laughed, then grabbed his ribs, stifling a groan from the
pain. "Are you serious, Mancini? You won't even give an injured
guy one cookie?"

"You can have *one*," she said sassily. "But you have to let me
try the chips."

"So you can find out you like them and steal those, too?
Hell no," he teased, and handed her the bag of chips.

She tucked them into her other side with a mischievous
smirk. "Are you going to start the movie or what, Whiskey?"

She may not have her memory, but she definitely hadn't lost
her spunk. He navigated to the movie and settled back against
the pillow. "I'm going to put my arm around you so we have
more room, and you can lean against me, but please move
slowly."

She carefully leaned against him, and they both winced.
"We're quite a pair."

"We're a perfect pair. You'll see."

As they watched the movie, Dare watched her expression
changing from knitted brows to smiles. She asked dozens of
questions about how old they were and the things they were
doing. She ate chips and cookies and drank both of their Capri
Suns. They laughed and regretted it, both groaning in pain.
Dare kept waiting for that light bulb moment that would bring
her back to him. But it never came.

When the movie ended, she rested her head against his chest
with a heavy sigh. She was pressing on his wound, but he didn't
dare move, wanting to soak up every moment she was willing to
share. He wanted to ask her if she remembered anything, but he

was trying not to pressure her, so instead he said, "What did you think of the movie?"

She tipped her face up to look at him, tears glistening in her tired eyes. "I wish I could remember all of it. Eddie seems wonderful, and the three of us sure had fun, didn't we?"

"There was nothing we couldn't do. We were unstoppable." *We still are, babe. You'll see.*

She ran her fingers lazily over the tattoo on the underside of his forearm. "You have a lot of tattoos. Do you have one for the three of us?"

"Yes. We were all going to get them the summer after we graduated from high school, but Eddie chickened out, and you said if he wasn't getting one, then you weren't, either. I can't show it to you right now, because it's on my back. It says DAREDEVILS with flames coming off the first *D*."

"Like at the beginning of the movie," she said sleepily.

"Yeah. Do you want to see the one I got for you?"

Her brows knitted. "Okay."

He lifted his chin and touched the tattoo that covered the front of his neck. "It's a phoenix, the symbol of immortality, because my love for you will never die."

Her gaze softened. "That's a big commitment. When did you get it?"

"The year after we lost Eddie. You were grieving, and you did your best to push me out of your life."

"That's awful. We were such good friends in that movie."

"There are no closer friends than us. But that was a complicated time."

"How did we end up together if I pushed you away?"

He smiled, remembering the look on her face when he'd parachuted into her running path. "I'm pretty irresistible."

"Well, you *do* have the best snacks."

That sounded so much like his girl, he had to remind himself she still didn't remember him. "And I have the *best* friend."

She yawned. "Sorry. I don't know why I'm so tired."

"The accident took a lot out of you." The last thing he wanted to do was climb out of that bed and walk out the door, but he knew she needed to rest. "I'd better let you sleep." He kissed the top of her head, moved everything to the bedside table, and carefully climbed off the bed, grabbing his crutch. "Do you want me to close your curtains?" It wasn't even noon yet.

"No thanks. I'm so tired, I think I could sleep through an earthquake. You're probably supposed to be resting, too."

"I'm fine." He wouldn't rest until she came back to him.

"Thank you for everything."

"My pleasure, darlin'."

She smiled, and it tugged at him, making him want to draw her into his arms. "I like when you call me darlin'. Can I see you later?" she asked hopefully. "Unless you're too busy or tired."

"I told you last night that I won't leave this hospital without you by my side, and I meant it."

"I'm sorry. I don't remember that," she said softly, yawning again.

"You hadn't woken up yet. But I still meant it. Close your eyes and let that beautiful brain of yours rest before they come to take you to your new room."

"They'd better move all these pictures with me." She looked around. "You forgot your laptop and backpack."

"I'll move the pictures myself once you're assigned a room, and I left the laptop in case you want to see the movie again. All you have to do is open it and push play."

"What about your backpack?"

"There are more snacks in it in case you get hungry at night. You usually do." That earned another sweet smile. "Don't worry. I've got you covered, darlin'. Get some rest."

"Okay," she said sleepily, settling back against the pillow and closing her eyes.

He took one last long look at her. *I'm going to make you fall in love with me every day for the rest of our lives, Mancini. Whether you get your memory back or not.*

Chapter Twenty-One

"OH GOOD, YOU'RE awake," the nurse said as she entered Billie's room.

Billie held her finger over her lips, shushing her, and pointed to Dare, fast asleep in the recliner in the corner of the room. It was Thursday evening, and they'd moved her out of the ICU several hours ago. Dare and her family had moved all the pictures he'd brought, and dozens of vases overflowing with beautiful flowers had been delivered throughout the afternoon. Once she'd settled in, Dare's family had visited, and she'd really enjoyed *meeting* them. They were funny and kind and had told her dozens of stories about her and Dare ranging from childhood to the night of the accident, when she had apparently gotten up on her family's bar and danced with Dare. *On. The. Bar.*

She was putting the pieces of her life together little by little, and from what she'd learned so far, she was an okay sister, but she could, and wanted, to do better. She was fun and liked playing sports and taking risks, and she was also a bit of a smartass. She wondered about those *moments* her sister had mentioned, and when she'd asked Dare's family about it, they'd stumbled a bit, and his mother had finally said, *We all have our moments, honey.* Billie felt like there was more to her moments than theirs, but she couldn't back that up with anything more than a feeling.

"I brought your pain medication," the nurse whispered, handing Billie a little paper cup with pills in it and a glass of water from her tray. She looked thoughtfully at Dare as Billie took the medication. "I still can't believe he hasn't left your side. That's the type of chivalry romance novels are made of."

"I don't know anything about romance novels, or much of anything else beyond Oreos and chips," Billie whispered as the nurse checked the monitors. "But it's easy to see why I would have fallen for him." And it wasn't just Dare. She had a feeling she'd been in love with his family, too. They were so loving toward her today, even his brothers, and they seemed to know her so well, it made her lack of memory even more aggravating. She hated relying on other people. At least the nurse had taken out her catheter and IV. Even though she was uncomfortable and had to ask for help getting to the bathroom, she was glad to have a little control over *something*.

"Have you remembered anything more?"

"Just the flashes, or moments, I mentioned when Dare's family was here, but nothing I can hold on to. I hate this feeling. It's like all this information is out there, but I just can't grasp it." The doctor had been very encouraging and hopeful when she'd told him the types of things she was remembering, despite feeling like they were only fleeting moments. She recalled some memories from her childhood, but they were just flashes of everyday things, like running through a field with Dare and Eddie, the smell of horses, breakfasts with her family.

"I know it's frustrating, but those are very good signs," the nurse whispered. "You're making progress. You have a lot of people who love and support you, and hopefully the more you learn about yourself, the more you'll remember. You and Dare have taught me something in just the short time you've been on my floor."

"What?"

"That it's time to break up with my boyfriend. That man is my new standard." She smiled. "Can I get you anything before I go?"

"I'm okay, and sorry about causing you to want to break up with your boyfriend."

"Don't be. It's been a long time coming. You guys did me a favor."

"Well, I didn't do anything. It was all Dare. Thanks again for letting him stay tonight."

"Letting him? He made it known to every nurse out there that he wasn't taking no for an answer." She winked. "I'll check on you in a bit. Try to get some rest."

Billie felt like all she'd been doing was sleeping because she got mentally exhausted so quickly. She hoped *that* wasn't permanent. She'd hate spending half her life sleeping. But she wasn't tired now. She was restless and hungry.

She looked at the additional snacks Dare had brought in the backpack, which were now on the table beside her—containers of cut-up vegetables and sliced apples, crackers, peanut butter, chocolate bars, root beer, Capri Suns, and a bag of nuts. She couldn't remember which ones she liked, but she'd loved the ones she'd already tried and knew she'd love the rest, too, because Cowboy had told her that Dare had given him a very specific grocery list of all her favorite snacks. His youngest sister, Birdie, who had bounced from one subject to the next so fast,

Billie had trouble keeping up, had brought what she'd said was Billie's favorite pizza for dinner. It had ham, pineapple, green olives, and mushrooms. Billie had eaten four slices and had loved every bite. She liked knowing the kind of foods she preferred and felt lucky to have so many people who knew her so well.

She grabbed the apple slices and peanut butter and put the laptop on the bed beside her. She sat back and watched the movie, dipping the apples into the peanut butter and loving the taste of them. She studied Eddie. His movements, his voice, and that effervescent smile were so familiar, they felt like they were a part of her. Even his voice was familiar.

You haven't seen a race until you've witnessed the one and only Billie "Badass" Mancini, the fiercest woman to ever ride—

Person to ever ride, she corrected him in the movie.

She wondered if that snarkiness was what Bobbie had meant about her having her moments. It didn't feel like it. She watched herself winning a motocross race, and Dare doing a fist pump, yelling, *Mancini!* as he ran toward the track. Eddie ran, too, filming and cheering, *That's our girl!* as she climbed off her bike and whipped off her helmet, shouting, *Daredevils rule!* Dare swept her into his arms and spun her around. She beamed at the camera, waving Eddie over. He filmed the three of them from arm's length, hugging and laughing, their faces going in and out of the camera as he pressed his lips to hers and said, *Congratulations, baby!*

Baby...

A flash of Eddie down on one knee careened into her mind, stealing her breath. Another flash of him, wearing different clothes. A different day? Hurt and anger blazed from his eyes as her voice traipsed through her mind. *"I'm sorry. It's not you. It's me. I love you, just not like I should to marry you."* She was trembling, gulping breaths, as the movie on the screen was obliterated by the one in her head. *She was pulling off an engagement ring, trying to give it to him, but he was shoving her hand away, saying, "I bought it for you. I want you to have it."*

"But we're not getting married."

"It doesn't matter. I'll always love you."

"And I'll always love you."

"Just not the way you should." He spoke low, his voice raw and tortured.

"I'm sorry! I never meant to hurt you."

His eyes narrowed, his anguish pinning her in place. "It's Dare, isn't it? It's always been Dare."

She opened her mouth to deny it, but she couldn't.

Eddie was enraged. He stalked away from her, heading back toward Dare, who was way across the field, but then he cut right, heading for the bikes, and ran to them. Billie ran after him, trying to catch up, but he was too fast, the distance too great. He grabbed a bike, leveling her with his words. "I'll show you how to do a damn flip."

"No!" she yelled, tears streaming down her face as the movie in her mind played on.

Dare ran toward Eddie. "Don't do it, man," Dare begged. "You're not ready for a flip."

"Eddie, please don't! You'll get hurt!"

Dare grabbed Eddie's arm, but Eddie shoved him away and took off on the bike toward the ramp.

"No! Eddie—"

Billie held her breath as he went up the ramp and soared into the air. The bike flipped, and she thought he had it—but he lost his grip, plummeting to the ground as the bike sailed forward.

"No! Eddie—"

She and Dare sprinted toward him. Her lungs burned and tears blurred her vision. Dare reached him seconds before her and spun around, trying to push her back the way they'd come. "No, Billie! You're not going over there." They were both crying, shouting, and he grabbed her around her waist as she flailed and fought to get to Eddie, and then she saw him lying on the ground, his head bleeding, his neck and limbs bent at impossible positions, unseeing eyes and lifeless mouth open, and she crumpled to the ground screaming.

"Billie! Billie, you're okay. It's me, Dare!"

She startled, trying to see through her tears as Dare's face came into focus. Her heart was racing, and she realized she was fighting him and screaming.

"You're okay, darlin'. You're in the hospital. We had a motorcycle accident, and you lost your memory."

"*I know*," she choked out. She was shaking all over. "I saw Eddie. I remember the day he—" Sobs stole her voice.

Dare carefully drew her against his chest. "I'm sorry, baby. That was a long time ago."

A nurse ran into the room. "Are you okay, Billie?" She put a hand on her back.

Billie nodded against Dare's chest.

"She remembered our friend's accident," Dare explained. "I told the doctor about it. It should be in her records."

"It is," the nurse said. "Billie, why don't I give you something to help you calm down?"

She lifted her face and looked at the nurse. "I don't want to calm down. I want to remember, even if it hurts."

"Do you want to rest, and we can talk about it later?" Dare asked.

"*No.* I want to talk about it now, while I have a chance of remembering."

He looked at the nurse. "Is that okay?"

"Let me take her vitals and make sure she's okay. Billie, I want you to sit back and try to relax." She checked Billie over, and when she was done, she said, "Everything looks good. I'll update the doctor, but you should try not to get too worked up."

"Thank you." Dare turned back to Billie as the nurse left. "What can I do? Do you want a drink of water?"

She shook her head. "I just want to talk. Will you stay here and sit with me?"

"It would take an army to get me to leave your side. But I want you to lie back, so your body can relax." He cleaned up the food she'd dropped on the blanket and moved the laptop to the bedside table. Then he sat beside her, tucking her beneath his good arm, like he had earlier.

"Were Eddie and I engaged?"

He nodded.

"I broke up with him because I loved you?"

"Yes, but I didn't know that until recently."

"How long ago did he die?"

"Six years."

"I remember the funeral and how sad we all were." She gave in to her tears, drawing them from Dare, too. He handed her the box of tissues from the bedside table. She sniffled, wiping her nose. "I loved him so much. I still feel it."

"And he loved you, baby."

"Did you and I talk about this? I feel like we did."

"We have, a few times."

"That's why you said I pushed you away. I remember now. I

pushed everyone away, didn't I?"

He looked pained. "Yes."

"That's what Bobbie meant by me having my moments. I can feel it." She looked at the phoenix on his neck. "But you never gave up on me."

"And I never will. But you never gave up on yourself, either. You're the strongest person I know, Billie."

He told her about how she'd tried to blame herself for Eddie's death and how after years of punishing herself and keeping her distance, she'd finally let him in and realized it wasn't her fault. They talked for a long time, and as he reminded her about her talk with their mothers and her visit with Eddie's parents, those memories came back to her, too, along with other recent memories. Like riding her bike again, teaching Kenny to ride, going running, kayaking, spending time with his family, and making love with Dare.

"You're blushing."

"I remember us...*you know*."

A slow grin curved his lips, and those brows went up. "Pretty great memories, huh? You were never a blusher."

"Shut up." She turned her face away. "It's like seeing you naked for the first time."

"Look at me, Mancini." When she did, his dark eyes were so full of love, it felt like an embrace. "That blush looks good on you, and I can assure you that you liked what you saw the first time, too."

She remembered that, too, but it still felt a little weird with the gaps in her memory. "Tell me more."

"I believe you said something like, 'Damn, Whiskey. I thought I'd imagined that glorious creature.'"

Her cheeks burned hotter. "I meant more about other

things we've done, not *that*."

"Sorry, darlin'. My mistake."

"That smile tells me you're not so sorry."

"Okay, you caught me. I said I was going to make you fall in love with me all over again, and letting you know what you have to look forward to can only help."

With his loyal, caring nature, she didn't think he needed any extra help.

He went on to tell her about more places they'd gone and things they'd done, and the more he shared, the more memories trickled in. They weren't complete, and many were fuzzy at best, but it was a start, and as the pieces of those years came back to her, so did her love for Dare. It didn't hit her all at once or steal her breath. It snuck up on her a little at a time. It was a whisper of lightness at first, a flutter in her chest, a smile in her heart, a longing in her loins, the sense of safety in his touch. Those and other sensations trickled in until she felt a fullness she couldn't name. It felt so right, and so good, she had the overwhelming sense that together they really were unstoppable, and it gave her hope for the missing memories.

It was a strange feeling to pick up all those broken pieces and feel her heart sewing them back together, but it was also a relief to not feel so lost anymore. She closed her eyes, listening to him talking about her in a way nobody else had. He was painfully honest, expanding on Bobbie's description of her being tough, telling her she could make biting remarks to people who deserved it—and to people who didn't deserve it when she'd pushed everyone away. He said she'd needed to do that, and he explained why. He sounded proud of her strength and in love with her despite all that. He described her sensitive side and the way sometimes late at night when she thought he was asleep, she'd press a kiss to his chest and whisper *I love you*. She kind of remembered that.

He said she didn't like to talk about her emotions, and she'd told him only a few times that she loved him, but he said that was okay, because he knew it and didn't need to hear it. She wondered about that, because it sure felt good when he said it to her. He spoke thoughtful and low, as if he treasured the moments he spoke of, and she realized why nobody else had tried to tell her who she was in such detail.

She might be missing years of memories, but she didn't need them to be certain of one thing. Devlin "Dare" Whiskey knew her better than anyone else, and she knew in her heart that the unstoppable Daredevil who had inked his love for her on his neck for all the world to see always would.

Chapter Twenty-Two

DARE SAT ON his front porch with Cowboy and Kenny, listening to the giggling and chatter coming from inside, where his and Billie's mothers and sisters were helping her get ready for their date. Hearing his girl laugh was one of the greatest sounds in the world, right up there with when she said *I love you* and whispered those sinful pleas when they were close. They'd been home for almost a month, and Billie's memories had mostly returned. Every now and then she experienced fogginess around a memory the first time it was brought up, but those times were few and far between. She'd been staying with Dare since they'd left the hospital, and their families had rallied around them, helping her shower and dress, while Dare stubbornly did those things himself, preparing meals, taking them to medical appointments, and pampering the hell out of them. He appreciated everyone's help, but the next few weeks couldn't pass fast enough. There was only so much caretaking a guy could take before he lost his mind. He was looking forward to getting their casts off so they could go back to doing things on their own and having a little more privacy.

He was looking forward to having Billie all to himself for a few hours tonight. It was the last night of Festival on the Green, and they'd been bummed to have missed the weeklong event, but it would've been difficult hobbling on crutches and each having the use of only one arm. But Dare wasn't about to let her miss the fireworks show. Especially since they'd missed them on the Fourth of July. They needed this. Neither of them was used to relying on others or taking it easy, and they'd been edgy because of it. Dare was seeing clients again, and that helped. Although he still held sessions outdoors, he missed working with his hands. Billie had been right about him having a hard time sitting still. He was having almost as hard of a time with it as she was.

Billie desperately wanted to get back to work at the bar. That was out of the question for a few more weeks, but she'd been spending more alone time with Bobbie, and he'd noticed they'd both been happier because of it. Bobbie had taken her to the Roadhouse during the lunch shift a few times, and that time at the bar seemed to feed Billie's spirits almost as much as her lessons with Kenny did. She'd insisted on continuing to work with Kenny, and Dare made sure he was at every lesson, as did Doc. They needed at least one non-injured adult present. Kenny had even gotten Doc to ride with him a few times, and it made Dare immensely happy to see his oldest brother cutting loose a little.

"I still can't believe I get to do an exhibition ride at the Ride Clean kickoff," Kenny said for the tenth time in as many minutes. They'd cleared the idea with his parents and had given him the news right before the girls showed up to help Billie get ready.

"You'll have to practice a lot, so you're not too nervous when the time comes," Dare said.

"I'd practice every day if you'd let me," Kenny exclaimed.

Cowboy arched a brow. "When would you ride horses if you ride that bike every day?"

"Where there's a will, there's a way," Kenny said with a very Whiskey-like nod.

Everyone had raved about how great a job Kenny had done helping Cowboy with the pony rides at the festival. He'd become so enamored with horses the last few weeks, he'd been talking with Sasha about becoming an equine rehabilitation therapist. Dare couldn't be prouder of him, and he looked forward to seeing where his passions lay as time passed. They'd had a great meeting with his parents, and Kenny would be going home this week. His parents had agreed to let him work at the ranch for a few hours several times a week until school started and continue training with Billie even after school began, as long as he kept his grades up and stayed out of trouble. Dare would be meeting with his family weekly to keep a pulse on things and help with any issues that might arise.

Cowboy lifted his chin in Dare's direction. "How are you doing over there? Need anything?"

"Yeah, think you can hurry the girls up? I'm ready to rock and roll."

"They'll come out when they're ready," Cowboy said. "Nervous about your big date?"

"Yeah, actually, I am. It's hard to make moves on a girl when you've both got broken bodies." He winked at Kenny, who laughed. "I just want tonight to be perfect for her. I want to see that smile that hits me right here." He pounded his chest with his fist and winced. His chest wound was mostly healed, but if he caught it just right, it smarted.

"I guess it'll be a while before you can jump buses or run

with the bulls," Cowboy said.

"Didn't I tell you I'm not doing those higher-level stunts anymore?"

"Yup. I just didn't believe it."

Dare held his gaze. "I meant it. I can't stand the thought of Billie, or any of you, sitting by my hospital bed, or worse."

Cowboy straightened his hat, eyes serious. "You realize your accident happened from just driving down the road, right? No fancy stunts needed."

"Yeah, and you realize Billie and I are still going to do fun shit, right?"

"I assumed as much." Cowboy's lips quirked. "You two wouldn't be who you are if you let life scare you into submission."

"There's only one thing I submit to, and that's the gorgeous brunette who's probably sick of being pawed at in there. I'm going to rescue her." Dare grabbed his crutch and stood.

Cowboy leapt to his feet. "Sit your lame ass down. I'll get her."

"And if I don't?"

"She'll be sitting by your hospital bed because of this." Cowboy waved his fist.

Kenny laughed.

"Don't encourage him." Dare sat down. "The guy's got a savior complex bigger than this state."

"It comes from growing up with a younger brother who thinks he's indestructible." Cowboy opened the door and hollered, "Get your clothes on, ladies. I'm coming in."

"I still think you lucked out," Kenny said as the screen door closed behind Cowboy. "You and your brothers have great relationships."

"They're a pain in my ass," Dare teased.

"You're a pain in mine, but I still like hanging out with you."

Dare chuckled. "I like hanging out with you, too, buddy. Are you ready to go to the festival? Got everything you need?" Cowboy was driving them to see the fireworks, and Kenny was going to hang out with Billie's and Dare's families and the other Redemption Ranch clients, who had already left for the festival with Dwight, Hyde, and Taz.

Kenny picked up his cowboy hat and settled it on his head, giving Dare a curt nod. "I'm all set."

The door flew open, and Birdie ran out, looking as bright and happy as her purple overall shorts, which she wore with a white tank top and a funky pair of platform boots that made her about five inches taller. Her hair was braided into two thick plaits, and she wore glittery purple eye shadow. "Dare! Close your eyes!"

"Birdie." He just wanted to see his girl.

She crossed her arms. "It's not every day that Billie has an entourage to help her get ready."

"Sure seems like it," Dare teased as he grabbed his crutch, put on his hat, and stood up.

Birdie rolled her eyes and began straightening his shirt, a plaid peach-and-rust sleeveless and collarless button-down, which she'd brought with her tonight, along with tan cargo shorts, and insisted Dare wear. She said he should dress nicely for his and Billie's first post-accident date. The clothes were comfortable, and everyone had complimented him, but it was Billie's reaction that had convinced him to keep them on. She'd bitten her lower lip, and the heat in her eyes had told him she'd done it to keep from saying the dirty things going through her mind in front of his sister. They'd managed to keep their hands to themselves the first few days while they'd rested, but they'd since found creative ways to use their hands, mouths, and battery-operated teammates to fulfill their desires.

"*There*," Birdie said, and stepped back, admiring Dare. "You look really handsome."

"Thanks, Bird."

"Billie looks *amazing*, too." She bounced on her toes. "Bobbie did her hair, Sasha did her makeup, and Alice, Mom, and I helped pick out her outfit and accessories. I can't wait for you to see her!"

"Accessories?" Billie didn't accessorize. She was probably going as nuts as he was.

Cowboy hollered from inside the house, "Close your damn eyes, Dare! You're the one who made me hurry them up."

Dare closed his eyes and heard a flurry of hushed whispers, footsteps, and Billie hobbling onto the porch with her crutch, while their mothers fawned over her.

"Okay. Open your eyes!" Birdie exclaimed.

He opened his eyes and literally lost his breath. Billie's hair was luxuriously glossy, and her eyes were smoky and sexy. He was glad they hadn't covered up the scars on her face, because he loved her as she was, and he didn't want anyone making her feel like she had to hide any part of herself. She wore a light blue spaghetti-strap dress with lace cutouts that started at her waist and formed an upside-down V at her sternum, although her sling covered half of it. The top of the dress clung to her curves, but the skirt was loose, with a tiny ruffle a few inches higher than the hem, which was just above her knees. She wore several gold bangles around one wrist and three gold necklaces. The black choker she'd worn like a brand had been cut off after the crash. He looked forward to the day he could take her to pick out a new one. The shortest necklace she was wearing had a small diamond charm. He recognized it as the one her parents had given her as a high school graduation gift. He'd given her the middle-length necklace with the gold *D* charm for her seventeenth birthday, and his heart beat a little faster remembering that day. The longest necklace had three connected circles hanging from it. He didn't recognize that one. She wore white sneakers that had been bedazzled with gems to match her dress, and he knew that was all Birdie's doing. Her cast, like Dare's, had been signed by practically everyone they knew.

"Holy fu—*dge*," Kenny said, jerking Dare from his reverie.

"I know, right?" Cowboy hiked a thumb at Billie. "This one cleans up *nice*."

"Jesus, darlin'. I don't think I've seen you in a dress since high school prom. You look gorgeous."

"You went to prom?" Kenny asked.

Billie smiled, eyes locked on Dare. "I went with Dare and Eddie."

"Yes, you did." Dare felt that tug in his chest that had hit every time she'd recalled a memory for the first time since their accident. "And you were the prettiest girl there."

"You and I didn't want to go," she reminded him.

"That's right, but Eddie wanted to."

"I remember." She looked down at the dress, and when she met Dare's gaze, her eyes narrowed seductively. "So you like it, huh?"

"I'll like it better on our floor later, but yeah, you look sexy as hell." He remembered Kenny was standing there and winked, hoping he'd think it was a joke.

"*Christ*," Cowboy gritted out. "Only you two would be

thinking of *that* with your casts and broken ribs and slings."

Everyone laughed.

"Young love is a beautiful thing," his mother said.

Alice looked at Billie and said, "And it only gets more beautiful with time."

Dare leaned in to kiss Billie. "Shall we go, Mancini?"

She plucked his hat off his head and put it on. "Yup."

"Wait!" Birdie shouted. "I want a picture!"

After Birdie took about a hundred pictures, Billie, Dare, and Kenny climbed into Cowboy's dual-cab truck, the others piled into Alice's car, and they headed for the festival.

A short while later they drove beneath a FESTIVAL ON THE GREEN banner hanging across the road in the center of Allure, a quaint small town with brick-paved roads, old-fashioned streetlights, and brick storefronts with ornate iron fences, all of which were decorated for the festival. Crowds of festivalgoers were heading down to the green. Couples walked hand in hand, and balloons danced from long strings tied to children's wrists.

Happiness shimmered in Billie's eyes. When Dare had first brought up the festival before she'd been discharged from the hospital, she'd remembered going to it but hadn't been able to place all the little things they'd done there. Dare had reminded her and promised that next year they'd go every day of the week. He intended to keep that promise and made it his goal to ensure tonight was as unforgettable as she was.

AS COWBOY PARKED by the edge of the green, Billie looked out the window at the sea of tents being taken down and booths being packed up. There were masses of people sitting on blankets, kids running around, and couples dancing by the stage, above which was a banner announcing a local singer, Kaylie Crew. Billie liked her music and rolled down the window to hear it. It was then she saw a horse-drawn hay wagon in the grass a short distance away. The wagon had twinkling lights along the sides, and the horses were decked out with ribbons in their manes and tails.

"Look, Dare. Someone brought horses. Maybe they're doing hayrides."

"Let's go see." He climbed out of the truck with his crutch.

When he turned to help her, Cowboy muscled his way in front of him. "Move over, bro. I've got her." He leaned closer to Billie. "Put your arms around my neck."

"Why?"

"Just do it," Cowboy said sternly.

"You're pushier than your brother." She did as he asked, and he cradled her in his arms.

Cowboy smirked. "Better lookin', too,"

"Dream on, muscle head," Dare said.

"Cowboy, you can put me down. I can walk with my crutch."

"Not tonight you can't." He looked at Kenny, and Kenny grabbed her crutch from the truck.

"Dare, tell him to put me down." She'd been doted on for three and a half weeks, and as much as she was enjoying a closer relationship with their families, she was tired of feeling helpless.

"He will, darlin', as soon as we get to our wagon."

"*Our* wagon?"

"You didn't think I'd let you sit on the hard ground to-night, did you?" Dare flashed a sexy grin. "I had the guys put a blow-up mattress in the wagon so you'd be comfortable."

Her heart skipped. "You did that for me?"

"I'd do anything for you, babe."

She knew he would. While everyone else was helping her with physical things, Dare had become her emotional caregiver, helping her to remember the good times and the bad, and when she was in pain, he held her, telling her stories about their lives or jokes to distract her from the aches. But he'd been taking care of her head and her heart well before the accident, and she thanked her lucky stars for that.

As they neared the horses, she saw that their ribbons were gold and black and that Dare hadn't just put a mattress in the wagon. There were blankets and pillows with rose petals strewn across them. Beside the mattress there were crates with champagne, bouquets of red roses, and one of those insulated warmers for food. It was the most romantic thing she'd ever seen. She felt like she might cry. That had been happening a lot since the accident. As if the impact had jarred her emotions free. Or maybe Dare's assessment was right the other night when she'd mentioned it, and he'd said she was just so happy, she didn't care what anyone else thought anymore.

"*Dare...?*" Her heart caught in her throat.

"You've been through the wringer, baby. I wanted tonight to be so special, you'd never forget it. I had dinner brought in from that restaurant you used to like here in town."

"Barkley's?" She had no idea where the answer had come from. It had just appeared in her mind, so different from the way she'd struggled to remember other things early on. She wondered if she'd analyze that feeling forever. She had a feeling she would, because losing her memory had made her cherish them even more.

He grinned, nodding. "You remember."

"Yeah. They had that carrot cake that I loved."

"I got that, too. But I can't take all the credit. I made the arrangements, but I had a little help putting it all together."

"Bobbie, Sasha, and Birdie decorated the horses and wagon," Kenny said as he set her crutch in the wagon. "And Doc and Tiny brought the horses and wagon out and got them ready."

"Your father picked up our dinner and champagne and made sure we had everything we needed," Dare said.

Everyone had gone to so much trouble for them. No wonder the girls were so excited to dress her up.

"How about we talk about the details after we get Billie comfortable," Cowboy suggested as he set her on the blankets and helped her get situated with her back against the pillows.

Dare stood by the tailgate fluttering his lashes. "I'm next, big boy."

Kenny laughed.

Cowboy glowered at Dare, but he offered a hand anyway.

"Get outta here. I've got this." Dare grimaced as he hoisted himself into the wagon and scooched up beside Billie. He reached into the crate and pulled out battery-operated candles, turning them on as Cowboy and Kenny climbed into the driver's seat.

"Candles, too?" Billie couldn't believe it. "When did you get so romantic?"

"I told you I was going to give you reasons to fall in love with me every day for the rest of our lives, and I meant it."

"I don't need reasons. I love you with everything I have, Whiskey, and I know I always will." Their connection was stronger than ever, and after everything they'd been through, she knew it was unbreakable.

"I love you too, darlin'." He leaned closer and kissed her as Cowboy hollered for them to hang on and began driving the horses across the lawn.

"Where are they taking us?"

"To our spot to watch the fireworks."

"*Our spot*," she whispered, the memory of their spot coming to life in her mind. "I love our spot." She snuggled closer as the horses climbed the grassy hill to *their* knoll, stopping by a small group of trees. She, Dare, and Eddie had watched the fireworks from that very spot right up until the year he'd died. She hadn't been back since, and now, as they were serenaded by the music from the festival and surrounded by glorious views of the mountains in the distance and festival lights below, she was glad she hadn't. She liked that their spot wasn't marred by those stressful years. Now it held only the happy memories of the three of them and any new memories she and Dare made.

Dare poured them champagne and handed her a glass. When he handed her a plate from the warmer, she saw that all the food was already cut into bite-size pieces. "You thought of everything."

"I thought of you, and I want to give you everything, so it was easy." He held up his champagne glass and said, "Here's to us, baby."

"To us." They clinked glasses, sipped their champagne, and kissed. She looked for Cowboy and Kenny, but they must have been standing in the shadows.

They kissed and talked as they ate dinner, sharing from each other's plates, just like they always had. They toasted to just about everything and gobbled down the delicious carrot cake for dessert. The music ended as they finished eating, and they set their dishes aside to lie on the blankets and wait for the fireworks to start.

Billie put her head on Dare's shoulder. "Do you hear that?"

"What? The hum of voices from the festival?"

"No. The silence around it. Nobody's asking if we need something."

"It's fucking bliss, isn't it? I'll deny that if you ever mention it in front of our families."

She laughed softly. "Your secrets are always safe with me. I love our families, and I know we couldn't have made it this far without them, but it's nice to just be alone with you."

"I feel the same way."

"Do you ever wonder what would have happened if my memories didn't come back?"

"No. We'd just make new memories, and we'd still be right here, looking up at the stars, waiting for the fireworks to start."

She loved that he was so confident in *their* love.

"Do you think about it?" he asked.

"Sometimes. Mostly because it was scary not knowing anything about my life. But I have a feeling you're right, and we'd be right here doing this." She turned her face toward him and found him watching her. She remembered looking into those dark eyes when they were kids and never wanting to look away. "You really do make it impossible to love anyone else. You know that, don't you?"

"So do you, Mancini, and that's because we're meant to be."

She touched her necklace with the *D* charm that he'd given her when they were teenagers. "Do you remember giving me this necklace?"

"For your seventeenth birthday. I told you the *D* was for *Daredevils*, but it was really for *Dare*."

She smiled. "It was *not*."

He raised his brows. "Knowing I've loved you since we were kids, do you *really* think I wouldn't try to brand you as mine in the only way I could?"

"Oh my God. You *totally* did." She laughed, because that was so very *Dare*.

He pressed his lips to hers in a tender kiss. "Where did you get the necklace with the three circles? It's pretty."

"Eddie gave it to me when you went away to college. I was missing you so much, I drove him nuts about it. One day he gave it to me and said it signified the three of us, and that no matter where we were, we'd always be together."

"Nice. I love that. I don't remember seeing you wear it."

"I wore it for a few days, but you know I never wore jewelry when I raced. I must have put it in my jewelry box and forgotten about it. The girls said I should wear jewelry tonight, so Bobbie brought my jewelry box with her. Your mom said I should pick my three favorite necklaces. I thought three was a lot since I never wear them. But I'm glad. These three necklaces are special, and now Eddie is with us tonight, too."

"He's always with us, watching out for us." He looked up at the sky, and she did the same. "If you could have one wish come true, what would it be?"

"That Eddie had never gotten on that bike."

"Me too. What if you could have two wishes?"

She looked at him again, and he turned with a smile. "I'd wish that nobody ever has to go through an accident like we did."

"I love that about you."

"What?"

"Your beautiful heart."

"You love my body. My heart is just a sidebar," she teased.

"Yeah, you're right." He kissed her just as the first fireworks went off. "You light up my world, Mancini."

She laughed and kissed him again. "What would you wish for?"

"That you'd marry me."

Fireworks burst above them, showering the sky with color, and she pressed a kiss to his chest. "You know I'd hobble into the courthouse with you tomorrow."

"The courthouse? That's not nearly enough fanfare for two Daredevils."

She couldn't stop grinning. "What are you imagining? Saying vows while we're skydiving or something?"

"Something like that."

"You're *crazy*."

"You know you love me."

"More than you can ever imagine, Whiskey."

"That's what I'm counting on." He reached beneath one of the pillows and withdrew a small black velvet box.

Her heart raced, and she looked from the box to him as he awkwardly shifted onto his knees and then onto *one* knee. *Oh God. Are you...?* She sat up, but he didn't say anything. The silence magnified between them. "Dare, *what* are you doing?"

"I'm trying to propose, but I'm so damn nervous, I can't remember what I wanted to say."

She laughed, tears burning her eyes.

"Fuck it. I'm just gonna wing it." He swallowed hard, his brows knitting, serious eyes gazing deeply into hers. "I have never known fear like when we were thrown from the bike. My only thought was *Where's Billie? I need to get to her.*"

Tears slipped down her cheeks.

"Baby, you are my whole life, my entire world, and I don't want to waste a minute of this second chance we've been given. I don't want to wait for the perfect time, because every minute with you is *our* perfect."

There was no stopping her rivers of tears.

"I have loved you since we were kids, and I will love you as we get wrinkled and gray, and long after the day we join Eddie on the other side. I want to wake up to your beautiful face every day and leave trails of clothes to our bedroom every night. Eventually, when we're ready, I want to raise snarky little girls with your gorgeous eyes and sharp-witted tongues and pushy boys who won't take no for an answer and give their hearts to one girl and one girl only. I love you, Mancini. What do you say we make this thing permanent? Will you marry me?"

She could barely see through the blur of tears. "Yes, Whiskey. *Yes*, I will marry you." She grabbed his shirt with one hand, hauling him into a kiss. "I love you so much."

"I love you too, baby. More than life itself." He opened the box, revealing a stunning ring with a simple white-gold band with two flames outlined with white diamonds, the centers filled with dark orange stones.

She'd never seen anything so beautiful in her life. "Twin flames," she whispered, remembering how she'd worried about her scars at first, and Dare had kissed every one of them and said, *We're twin flames, baby, and the scars in our hearts are proof of our mirrored souls.*

"That's us, baby." He slid it onto her finger. "The stones inside the flames are cognac diamonds. I know you don't love wearing jewelry. I hope it's not too much."

The diamonds were small, not flashy, and the flames didn't sit high enough to catch on things. "It's absolutely perfect."

Tears slid over her lips. "I'll never take it off."

"Don't make promises you can't keep, Mancini. You know you won't want to wear it when you ride your bike, and that's okay. I know you love me, and I know you're mine."

He pressed his lips to hers in a sweet kiss, leaned back, and shouted, "*She said yes!*"

Loud cheers rang out as their families and friends ran up the hill toward them. Billie couldn't stop laughing and crying as they surrounded the wagon, calling out congratulations and popping bottles of champagne. Dare looked happier than she'd ever seen him.

"Everyone knew?" she asked.

"I was so excited, I think the whole town knew. You're lucky I didn't blow it and tell you, too." He handed her a champagne glass and picked up his. "Here's to us, baby. Daredevils for life."

"Daredevils for life and *your* Wildfire *forever*." While she touched her glass to his, his loving eyes were trained on her. They each took a sip, and then he kissed her, tasting of champagne, happiness, and the only future she ever really wanted.

Chapter Twenty-Three

SEPTEMBER BREEZED INTO Hope Valley like an artist, painting the hills and valleys with broad strokes of vibrant fall colors, creating a gorgeous backdrop for the kickoff of the Dark Knights Ride Clean campaign at Redemption Ranch. Billie and Dare had fully healed and completed physical therapy, and as much as they appreciated their families, they were thrilled to be able to take care of themselves and focus on building their life together. Dare's brothers had moved Billie's things in the week after he'd proposed, and strangely, it hadn't felt like a milestone to Dare. It had felt more like she'd finally settled into the place she'd always been in his heart. She'd come *home*. Dare was glad to be working alongside his clients again, and Billie had gone back to work at the Roadhouse. As soon as she'd been able, she'd gotten back on her bike, which had thrilled Dare to no end. He'd worried fear might hold her back, but they'd talked a lot about it during their healing weeks, and Billie was determined not to close herself off again from the things she loved. While he and Billie had been going on motorcycle rides again, and they were planning to hit the slopes this winter to ski, snowboard, snowkite, and snocross, and they were excited to get back to skydiving and other fun activities together, Dare hadn't had the urge to break any more records. Life with Billie, and enjoying activities in and out of the bedroom together, was enough for him. Sometimes he wondered if Billie had been right, and pushing the limits to the extreme had been his own self-inflicted penance for surviving Eddie. Or maybe he was just a crazy motherfucker who liked to defy death.

He had a feeling it was a little of both, and he was okay with that, as was his beautiful fiancée, who looked insanely sexy in cutoffs and a black Ride Clean/Dark Knights T-shirt, with a flannel shirt tied around her waist and the new choker he'd given her around her neck. She and their parents were cheering Kenny on as he sped around the motocross track.

Dare pulled Billie closer and kissed her cheek.

She leaned into the kiss, but her eyes remained trained on Kenny. Dare didn't mind. She'd worked hard to help Kenny succeed, and they'd honored his hard work. The Dark Knights had opened the event with a welcome speech from Dare's father and Manny and had kicked off the festivities with Kenny's exhibition ride. All the club families and hundreds of others from Hope Valley and nearby towns came to support the campaign and were gathered around the track watching him.

Kenny was doing great, and his parents had a front-row seat. He'd been living at home for almost two months. He and his parents had hit a few rough patches, as was to be expected, but together, and sometimes with Dare's help, they'd found peaceful resolutions. Kenny was back in school and keeping his grades up, and his parents were allowing him to continue working at the ranch and train with Billie two afternoons a week and one weekend day. Kenny was still excited to prospect the Dark Knights, and he was on the right path. He'd surprised

Dare when he'd told him that he'd apologized to the neighbor whose car he'd taken on a joyride. He must have really made an impression, because that family had come to watch him ride today. Their daughter, Mariah, was a cute blonde with a mischievous gaze, and there was no hiding the mad crush she had on Kenny. Dare knew how much girls could influence boys Kenny's age, and he was keeping tabs on that, too. Although he had a feeling Mariah's urging Kenny to take her parents' car had just been her way of getting Kenny's attention.

The crowd gasped as Kenny rode over the rhythm section and cheered wildly as he nailed the last jump, flew down the home stretch, and came to a stop before them.

Kenny took off his helmet, beaming at his parents as they, and a mass of other people, went to talk to him. They'd prepared Kenny for that, and from the whoops and applause coming from Dare's and Billie's parents, he knew they were just as proud of Kenny and Billie as he was.

Dare squeezed Billie's hand. "You did good with him, babe."

Billie was smiling from ear to ear. "He's amazing, isn't he? He's a natural."

"He sure is," Dare's father said. "And so are you, sweetheart."

"Thank you, Tiny, but my time in the spotlight is over." Billie glanced at Kenny, who was surrounded by people as he answered questions and talked to little kids. "Kenny's time is just beginning, and he has so much to look forward to."

"So do you, honey," her mother said. "You've got a wedding to plan and a honeymoon in Spain to enjoy." They'd decided to go to Spain for their honeymoon next July and *watch* the running of the bulls.

"And we couldn't be happier about all of it." Billie looked at Dare, their secret twinkling in her eyes. They hadn't wanted to wait to get married, but their parents were so excited to throw them a wedding, and their sisters were over the moon about planning it with Billie. They hadn't wanted to disappoint anyone, including themselves, so the week they'd gotten their casts off, they'd snuck over to a courthouse three towns away to apply for their marriage license and had secretly sealed the deal the following week with just the two of them, and Treat Braden, the son of one of their father's oldest friends. Treat was a real estate mogul who lived in Weston, Colorado. He was ordained, and more importantly, a master secret keeper. He'd married Billie and Dare at midnight in the barn where they'd shared their first kiss. But they were still looking forward to having a real wedding, and Dare couldn't wait to see his beautiful bride walk down the aisle.

"I've been thinking that maybe your time in the spotlight isn't over," Tiny said.

"Believe me, Tiny. I'm an old lady by pro-circuit standards. I can't race anymore."

"I'm not talking about racing, darlin'." Tiny eyed Manny, who nodded, and Dare wondered what they were up to. "You've done so much for Kenny's self-esteem, I thought you might want to consider taking on more students. Maybe kids from the ranch who show an interest."

"Or kids from nearby towns," Manny added. "Who knows where it might lead."

Dare couldn't believe his ears. "Are you shitting me?" He shook his head.

His father glowered at him. "No, son, we're not. We think Billie has what it takes to run her own program."

Billie looked at Dare with a furrowed brow. "You don't think I do?"

"No, baby. I *know* you do. What kid wouldn't want to train under Billie 'Badass' Mancini? But I thought I had an original idea, and I'd hoped to surprise you with it *tonight*." He pulled the folded piece of paper out of his pocket and handed it to her.

"What's this?" she asked as she unfolded it.

"The sketch of the clubhouse I want to build, and the entrance from the main road I want to put in on the other side of the track, so you'll have a place to teach and take on students without having to bring them through our yard."

"Are you…?" Billie's eyes teared up, and their mothers' did, too. "But I've only taught *one* person."

"And you helped change his life," Dare pointed out. "I know you love managing the bar, and I'm not suggesting that you give that up. But, baby, you light up when you're around the track, and you're a gifted teacher. We *all* know what you're capable of. The only question is if it's something you'd like to do. If you want this, we'll build it. If you don't, that's okay, too."

She looked at him, and at their parents, her eyes damp but brighter than the sun. "Of course I want it! Thank you!" She threw her arms around him. "I *love* this idea." She looked at their fathers. "Thank you all for believing in me."

"You make it easy, sweet pea." Her father hugged her.

Dare's father eyed him. "Don't you think you should've clued me in on your plans, son?"

"I didn't think I needed to until I knew if she wanted it or not." He cracked a grin. "Besides, you're a softy for my girl. There's no way you'd have an issue with it, and since you tried to steal my thunder, I believe I was right."

Everyone laughed.

"Great minds, Pop." Dare winked. "Although there is one more thing I should mention. Billie and I have been tossing around the idea of expanding the ropes course. It's a great way to work off frustrations for kids and adults."

Manny nudged his father. "Why do I have a feeling this is just the beginning of an overarching Daredevil plan?"

"Because you know our kids." Dare's father said with joy in his eyes.

"Well, I think they're *both* wonderful ideas," Alice exclaimed.

"Me too," his mother said. "But now we have a lot to coordinate. It'll take time to build the clubhouse and put in the entrance, and you'll probably want a fence to keep riffraff off your property, and you'll need a business license."

"And a name for your school," Alice added. "There's so much to do, and we want to be sure to have enough time to plan your wedding…"

As their mothers went on a planning spree, their fathers shook their heads and headed back up to the festivities. Billie stepped in front of Dare and wound her arms around his neck. "You never fail to amaze me, Whiskey."

"I'm just looking for extra nookie points."

She laughed, and he kissed her.

"Hurry *up*, Mickey. Mancini is *right there!*"

They both turned to see who the chirpy voice belonged to.

A little blond girl, who looked to be about six or seven years old, was stomping toward them in cowgirl boots and leggings, dragging a dark-haired boy behind her. The little girl looked up at Billie with wide brown eyes. "Are you Billie Mancini? We want to learn to ride motocross, and that boy on the bike told us to talk to you."

"I am Billie," she said sweetly. "Who are you?"

"I'm Eddie, and this is—"

"Your name isn't *Eddie*," the boy said. "It's Edelyn!"

Dare and Billie stifled laughs.

Eddie's eyes narrowed, and her lips pinched. "Call me that again, and I'll give you a knuckle sandwich, Mickey."

"Whoa, darlin'." Dare put a hand between the kids. "There'll be no knuckle sandwiches on this ranch."

"How about we go find your parents and talk to them about riding bikes?" Billie suggested.

"Okay. Come on, Mickey!" Eddie took Mickey's hand, and they took off running.

Billie grabbed Dare's hand. "Let's go, Whiskey. You're getting slow in your old age."

"I'll give you slow." He pulled her into a kiss.

"Hey!" Eddie hollered. "You two comin', or what?"

Dare and Billie laughed.

"We're coming!" Billie yelled.

"Reminds me of a pushy little girl I once knew. Let's go, Mancini." He slapped her ass, and she took off running and laughing with Dare on her heels.

BY MIDAFTERNOON THE event was in full swing. Kids were running around with cookies and hot dogs while adults trailed behind them, mingling as they went from one activity to the next. The lawn was covered with tables of food and drinks prepared by club families and Dwight, all of which were being sold to support the campaign efforts. Throughout the morning, Dare and several others had given brief talks and answered questions about struggles they'd faced as kids, what it was like to be a Dark Knight, and the work they did on the ranch. Birdie made a brief announcement offering a flyer with coupons for free chocolates at her shop. Everyone took turns overseeing the activities, and between the Dark Knights and dozens of volunteers, there were plenty of people to help.

Dare and Billie were on pony-ride duty. He lifted a little girl off a pony, and she ran to Billie, waiting by the gate. He watched Billie talking animatedly with the little one as she walked her out. Billie was a natural with little kids, just as she was with Kenny. They were in no rush to have a brood of their own, but Dare looked forward to the day they would.

Billie looked up as she closed the gate behind the little girl, and the love in her eyes hit him square in the center of his chest. She mouthed, *I love you*, and he winked, feeling like a king as he went to get the next kid.

Gus was at the front of the line, holding Ezra's hand and jumping up and down, his dark curls springing around his face. "It's my turn!"

"Yes, it is, little man." Dare and Ezra shared a laugh as he lifted him onto a pony. "Do you remember what to do?"

"Uh-huh! Hold the horn!" He held the saddle horn with both hands, beaming at Dare and his father.

"Attaboy." Dare nodded at Ezra. "Okay, Dad. See you in a few minutes."

As Dare walked Gus around the ring, Gus shouted, "Look at me, Dad! I'm riding."

"Looking good, Gus." Ezra took out his phone and snapped a picture.

"Sasha! Look at me, sugar!" Gus hollered.

Sasha waved as she walked up to the corral. "Be careful, Gusto. Hold on tight."

"I am!" Gus yelled. "Billie, look at me!"

"You look like a real cowboy," Billie said, falling into step beside Dare.

"I *am* a real cowboy," he exclaimed.

Billie looked seductively at Dare. "I *like* rugged cowboys."

"I believe you mean *a* rugged cowboy."

"*My* rugged cowboy." She leaned closer, lowering her voice. "Is it my imagination, or is Flame looking at Sasha like he wants to eat her for dinner?"

Dare shot a look in his sister's direction and saw Flame leaning on the corral beside her with a flirtatious grin and too-damn-hungry eyes. He sure as hell hoped Sasha had been honest about just being friends with him, because most of Flame's female friends came with *benefits*. "That's *not* happening."

"Oh, I think that's happening." Billie laughed. "Unless a certain someone's daddy has something to say about it."

Dare followed her gaze to Ezra, and hell if he didn't look like he wanted to tear Flame apart. "*What* is going on around here?"

"Maybe Birdie gave Sasha body wash, too." She giggled.

As they finished Gus's ride and walked him back to Ezra, Dare saw Cowboy riding Sunshine up from the lower corral, where he'd been managing the horseback rides with bigger kids. He stopped to talk to Hyde, who was running the hayrides. Hyde swapped places with a ranch hand and ran over to the bouncy house, grabbing Taz, Pep, and Otto, the four of them clapping other Dark Knights on the back and talking jovially on their way up the hill, then spreading out as they each made their way up the lawn in different directions. A group of guys wearing black leather cuts walking determinedly would call attention to whatever was going on, which was why if they got a call during an event, they acted like they were now. Visitors would simply see guys having a good time.

Cowboy was heading for Dare and Ezra, his expression even more serious than usual.

"Good job, Gus." Dare handed Gus to Ezra, Ezra's nod telling him he saw what was going on, too. Dare turned his back to the people waiting in line so he could talk to Billie. "Babe, can you take over for a bit?"

"Sure. What's going on?"

"I'm not sure, but Cowboy's rallying the Knights." Dare walked out of the corral just as Flame and Sasha joined Ezra and Cowboy rode up.

"Hey, Cowboy! I rode a horse, too!" Gus said excitedly.

"That's great, buddy," Cowboy said.

Gus began talking a mile a minute, and Sasha reached for him. "Hey, Gusto, how about we play in the bouncy house and then get one of Birdie's yummy chocolate pony pops?"

"Yeah! Bye, Dad!"

She winked at Ezra and carried him off.

"Hey, guys, what's going on?" Flame asked.

"Tiny needs help carrying some stuff from the main house," Cowboy said. "I'm on my way to grab Doc and the guys from the paintball field."

"I'll let Mom know we're going to help," Dare said casually, so as not to alert nearby families. His mother would alert the rest of the club wives and make sure no attention was brought to the club gathering.

Ten minutes later Dare stood with the rest of the club

members, their attention riveted on his father standing at the front of their largest meeting room. "We've got a situation. A young gal escaped from a cult in West Virginia and was picked up by a trucker who was heading this way. They need a safe haven for her while DNA tests are run and they figure out what's what. Her name is Sullivan Tate, and she goes by the name Sully. She's in her early twenties, and she's tough but scared. She refused to go to a doctor or to the police for fear of being taken back to the cult. We're bringing her to the ranch tonight after dark, where she can undergo therapy and be seen by our doctors. This girl needs *complete* protection. We don't know if cult members are coming after her or not. *Nobody* can know she's here until I get word that it's safe—not even your wives—or you could be putting our entire family, and everyone on this ranch, at risk. Hazard, this needs to be kept *off* the records."

"You've got it," Hazard said.

"Cowboy, you're taking the lead on this," his father said. "I want you to have eyes on her at all times. No exceptions."

Cowboy nodded.

"The trucker who picked her up and his wife are going to a safe house. Pep and Otto, I want eyes on his house from a distance. If you see anyone sniffing around, we need to know about it." When they nodded their understanding, his father said, "When the event ends, take your families home, and then I need everyone who can come back and stick around to do so. We need extra security around the ranch for the foreseeable future. And remember, when you step out of this room, it's business as usual."

After the meeting, Dare walked out with his brothers, Rebel, Hyde, and Ezra. He hated keeping anything from Billie.

She'd grown up in a Dark Knights family, and she understood that he couldn't talk about club business, but that didn't make it any easier.

"Damn, that poor girl," Doc said.

"That's a hefty dose of perspective, right there," Ezra said.

"No shit," Rebel agreed.

"Yeah, while we're dicking around wondering what girl is going to land in our beds tonight, that poor girl's scared for her life." Hyde shook his head.

"Kind of like any girl who ends up in your bed," Rebel said as they pushed through the doors and walked outside, doing just as they were told. Going back to business as usual.

The guys chuckled, but those sounds were heavier, weighed down by their new reality as they shifted gears from club business to upbeat campaign hosts.

Dare scanned the grounds, needing to get his arms around Billie. It didn't matter that there were hundreds of people milling around the property. He was drawn to his girl like lightning to the ground and headed for Birdie's table, where Billie was talking to their sisters.

"Where are you heading?" Doc asked.

"To the one person who can put a smile on my face." He looked at Cowboy. His eyes were hooded, and he looked like he was ready to spit nails. "Dude, you okay?"

Cowboy nodded.

"Better get that look off your face, or you'll scare off the women around here," Doc said.

"Right." Cowboy rolled his shoulders back and cleared his throat. "Better?"

Dare took in his forced smile. "Now you just look like you've got a wedgie."

"Maybe I do," Cowboy said with a laugh. "Asshole."

BILLIE WAS EATING chocolate with the girls by Birdie's table, trying to listen to Gus go on about all the fun things he did today between bites of his enormous pony pop, but she was sidetracked, worrying about whatever the Dark Knights were up to.

"There's Daddy!" Gus shouted.

She saw Dare and the guys come through the crowd. His eyes locked on her, and she tried to send a silent question. *Is everything okay?* He nodded and winked, and she breathed a sigh of relief.

"Dad! Sasha gave me a whole lotta sugar!" Gus waved his pony pop, and the guys chuckled.

Ezra looked at Sasha, a smirk playing at the corner of his mouth.

She laughed and splayed her hands palms up. "What can I say? I have a thing for curly topped little boys."

"How about well-hung big boys?" Hyde waggled his brows. "I'd like some sugar."

"Sasha's saving her sugar for my dad!" Gus yelled. "Right, Sasha?"

The girls burst into hysterics.

Sasha covered her face with one hand, pulled the chocolate pop she'd saved for Ezra out of her pocket, and smacked it against Ezra's chest. "Enjoy."

"You guys, come over here." Birdie ran around corralling the men closer to the table. "Hot guys always bring more single moms and kids. Just stand there and look approachable and talk about how sweet the chocolate is."

"Let's see how sweet it is." Dare hauled Billie into his arms, his dark eyes and coy smile promised all sorts of dirty things.

She held up her chocolate pop. "Want a taste?"

"Hell yeah, I do." He lowered his lips to hers, kissing her so long and deep, she came away tingling from head to toe.

"Come on, Bobbie, let's show them how it's done." Cowboy draped an arm over her shoulders. "Go ahead, offer me some chocolate."

Bobbie held up her chocolate pop, and everyone laughed.

"Oh my *gosh*. Why didn't I think of you two?" Birdie let out an exasperated sigh. "You're *perfect* together."

"Birdie, I was kidding. Bobbie's as much of a sister to me as you are. I actually *wanted* the chocolate." Cowboy took a big bite of Bobbie's chocolate.

"Yeah, Birdie. He's not my type, anyway," Bobbie said. "He's too bulky."

"Bet he's never heard that before," Dare said for Billie's ears only.

"Lucky for me, you're bulky in all the right places," she whispered, earning another delicious kiss.

"Are you freaking kidding me? This isn't bulk." Cowboy lifted his shirt. "These are perfectly defined muscles."

Bobbie's eyes nearly bugged out of her head.

"Put that shit away, Cowboy." Rebel swaggered over. "She's into guys who can rock the boat, not blow it out of the water." He put his arm around Bobbie. "Right, babe?"

Bobbie rolled her eyes, wiggling out of his reach, earning more laughter.

"Good, that means I haven't been wasting my time scoping

out single moms for Cowboy," Birdie said. "See the brunette with the little girl by the ponies? She was at the top of my list. She's a nurse and is super nice."

"I suddenly feel an ache coming on. I think I might need someone to give me a rubdown." Doc cocked a grin, heading in the brunette's direction. "See you kids later."

Birdie rolled her eyes. "Why do you let him do that, Cowboy? She was perfect for you, and you know Doc will date her for a few weeks and break her heart."

"Do yourself a favor, Bird. Take me off your marriage list," Cowboy said. "I'm going to be busy for the foreseeable future anyway."

"But—"

He glowered at her.

"Fine." A mischievous grin curved her lips. "Are you at least using that body wash I gave you, because women don't like guys who stink."

"Yeah. I love that shit. I've got to get Sunshine back to the barn. Catch you guys later."

As Cowboy walked away, Birdie rubbed her hands together. "Perfect."

Dare pulled Billie closer. "Think I should warn him?"

"And ruin Birdie's fun?" She put her arms around his neck. "I can think of better things for you to do with that mouth of yours."

"Careful, baby. Keep talking like that and I'll haul your pretty little ass into the hayloft and make good on all those things."

She shuddered with anticipation. "You can't. There are kids playing in there." She went up on her toes and whispered, "But I hear the tack rooms have locks on the doors…"

Fall in love with Cowboy and Sully
in FOR THE LOVE OF WHISKEY

When Sullivan Tate escaped from a cult, leaving behind the only life she'd ever known, she thought she'd already endured the most difficult things she'd ever have to deal with. She knew she needed to figure out who she was, but she hadn't expected to fall for overprotective and sexy-as-hell Callahan "Cowboy" Whiskey along the way. How can she give her heart to a man who has always known exactly who he is, when she's only just begun figuring that out about herself?

Please Note: You might also enjoy reading THEN CAME LOVE (The Bradens & Montgomerys) featuring Sullivan's sister, Jordan Lawler, and Jax Braden. Jordan's story takes place prior to FOR THE LOVE OF WHISKEY.

Meet Levi Steele, a member of the Dark Knights at Harborside, and fall in love on the sandy shores of Harborside and Silver Island

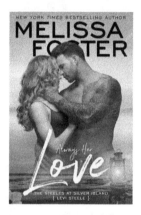

Some fates are too tempting to deny

When single-father Levi Steele offers to help his daughter's beautiful aunt Tara find a home on Silver Island, their intense connection makes it even harder for him to resist the one woman he and his daughter can't afford to lose.

Ready for More Dark Knights?
Meet The Wickeds: Dark Knights at Bayside

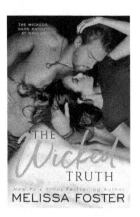

When a mysterious stranger crosses paths with Madigan Wicked, their connection is undeniable, yet neither is open to love. He's on a road to redemption, and she's been hurt before. But love has been known to bully its way into even the most resisting hearts. When the wicked truth of his dark past is revealed, will it be too much for them to overcome?

Get ready to binge read
The Whiskeys: Dark Knights at Peaceful Harbor

If you're a fan of sexy alpha heroes, babies, and strong family ties even to those who are not blood related, you'll love Truman Gritt and the Whiskeys.

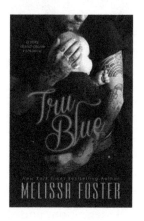

There's nothing Truman Gritt won't do to protect his family—including spending years in prison for a crime he didn't commit. When he's finally released, the life he knew is turned upside down by his mother's overdose, and Truman steps in to raise the children she's left behind. Truman's hard, he's secretive, and he's trying to save a brother who's even more broken than he is. He's never needed help in his life, and when beautiful Gemma Wright tries to step in, he's less than accepting. But Gemma has a way of slithering into people's lives, and eventually she pierces through his ironclad heart. When Truman's dark past collides with his future, his loyalties will be tested, and he'll be faced with his toughest decision yet.

New to the Love in Bloom series?

If this is your first Love in Bloom book, there are many more love stories featuring loyal, sassy, and sexy heroes and heroines waiting for you. The Bradens & Montgomerys is just one of the series in the Love in Bloom big-family romance collection. Each Love in Bloom book is written to be enjoyed as a stand-alone novel or as part of the larger series. There are no cliffhangers and no unresolved issues. Characters from each series make appearances in future books, so you never miss an engagement, wedding, or birth. You might enjoy my other series within the Love in Bloom big-family romance collection, starting with the very first book in the entire Love in Bloom series, SISTERS IN LOVE.

See the Entire Love in Bloom Collection
www.MelissaFoster.com/love-bloom-series

Download Free First-in-Series eBooks
www.MelissaFoster.com/free-ebooks

Download Series Checklists, Family Trees, and Publication Schedules
www.MelissaFoster.com/reader-goodies

More Books By Melissa Foster

LOVE IN BLOOM SERIES

SNOW SISTERS
Sisters in Love
Sisters in Bloom
Sisters in White

THE BRADENS at Weston
Lovers at Heart, Reimagined
Destined for Love
Friendship on Fire
Sea of Love
Bursting with Love
Hearts at Play

THE BRADENS at Trusty
Taken by Love
Fated for Love
Romancing My Love
Flirting with Love
Dreaming of Love
Crashing into Love

THE BRADENS at Peaceful Harbor
Healed by Love
Surrender My Love
River of Love
Crushing on Love
Whisper of Love
Thrill of Love

THE BRADENS & MONTGOMERYS at Pleasant Hill – Oak Falls
Embracing Her Heart

Anything for Love
Trails of Love
Wild Crazy Hearts
Making You Mine
Searching for Love
Hot for Love
Sweet Sexy Heart
Then Came Love
Rocked by Love
Our Wicked Hearts
Claiming Her Heart

THE BRADEN NOVELLAS
Promise My Love
Our New Love
Daring Her Love
Story of Love
Love at Last
A Very Braden Christmas

THE REMINGTONS
Game of Love
Stroke of Love
Flames of Love
Slope of Love
Read, Write, Love
Touched by Love

SEASIDE SUMMERS
Seaside Dreams
Seaside Hearts
Seaside Sunsets
Seaside Secrets
Seaside Nights
Seaside Embrace
Seaside Lovers

SUGAR LAKE

The Real Thing
Only for You
Love Like Ours
Finding My Girl

HARMONY POINTE

Call Her Mine
This is Love
She Loves Me

THE WICKEDS: DARK KNIGHTS AT BAYSIDE

A Little Bit Wicked
The Wicked Aftermath
Crazy, Wicked Love
The Wicked Truth

SILVER HARBOR

Maybe We Will
Maybe We Should
Maybe We Won't

WILD BOYS AFTER DARK

Logan
Heath
Jackson
Cooper

BAD BOYS AFTER DARK

Mick
Dylan
Carson
Brett

HARBORSIDE NIGHTS SERIES
Includes characters from the Love in Bloom series
Catching Cassidy
Discovering Delilah
Tempting Tristan

More Books by Melissa
Chasing Amanda (mystery/suspense)
Come Back to Me (mystery/suspense)
Have No Shame (historical fiction/romance)
Love, Lies & Mystery (3-book bundle)
Megan's Way (literary fiction)
Traces of Kara (psychological thriller)
Where Petals Fall (suspense)

Acknowledgments

The banter and love between Billie and Dare were immensely fun to write, and as you can imagine, the scenes surrounding Eddie's death, Billie's guilt, and Dare and Billie's accident were treacherously heartbreaking. I relied on several people to help me portray the scenarios in this book as accurately as possible, and I always take a few fictional liberties to keep the story rolling at an enjoyable pace. Any and all errors are my own and not those of the people who were kind enough to answer my ongoing questions. While many of my sources would like to remain anonymous, I owe heaps of gratitude to my good friend Maggie Hunter, Director of Admissions and Quality Assurance, Head Injury Rehabilitation and Referral Services. Maggie has more than sixteen years of experience working with brain-injured adults in various capacities, and I am beyond grateful that she was willing to answer my numerous questions. I'd also like to thank Aeryn Havens, author of SPIRIT CALLED, for her patience when answering horse- and ranch-related questions. Aeryn, you are always a godsend.

For those of you who will be reading Cowboy and Sully's book, FOR THE LOVE OF WHISKEY, I'd like to give you a peek into how Sully's and her sister Jordan's stories came to be. I began writing Sullivan "Sully" Tate's story in 2013 as a stand-alone novel, and I set it aside because of other projects and a feeling that it wasn't quite Sully's time yet. When I met Jordan Lawler in HOT FOR LOVE (The Bradens & Montgomerys), I knew in my heart that she was Sully's older sister in Sully's original story and that she also needed her own story. While writing Jordan's story, THEN CAME LOVE (The Bradens & Montgomerys), I finally realized what was missing in 2013: Redemption Ranch. It was the perfect place for Sully to heal. I am excited for you to read Sully's story, and if you haven't read THEN CAME LOVE, you might want to pick it up before Sully's book comes out. It's a fantastic forbidden-love story.

I am inspired on a daily basis by my fans and friends, many of whom are in my fan club on Facebook. If you haven't yet joined my fan club, please do. We have a great time chatting about the Love in Bloom hunky heroes and sassy heroines. You never know when you'll inspire a story or a character and end up in one of my books, as several fan club members have already discovered.
www.Facebook.com/groups/MelissaFosterFans

To stay abreast of what's going on in our fictional boyfriends' worlds and sales, like and follow my Facebook fan page.
www.Facebook.com/MelissaFosterAuthor

Sign up for my newsletter to keep up to date with new releases and special promotions and events and to receive an exclusive short story featuring Jack Remington and Savannah Braden.
www.MelissaFoster.com/Newsletter

And don't forget to download your free Reader Goodies! For free ebooks, family trees, publication schedules, series checklists, and more, please visit the special Reader Goodies page that I've

set up for you!
www.MelissaFoster.com/Reader-Goodies

As always, loads of gratitude to my incredible team of editors
and proofreaders: Kristen Weber, Penina Lopez, Elaini Caruso,
Juliette Hill, Lynn Mullan, and Justinn Harrison, and my *last
set of eagle eyes*, Lee Fisher.

I am forever grateful to my family, assistants, and friends who
have become family, Lisa Filipe, Sharon Martin, and Missy
Dehaven, for their endless support and friendship. Thank you
for always having my back, even when I'm deep in the deadline
zone and probably unbearably annoying.

Meet Melissa

www.MelissaFoster.com

Melissa Foster is a *New York Times, Wall Street Journal,* and *USA Today* bestselling and award-winning author. Her books have been recommended by *USA Today*'s book blog, *Hagerstown* magazine, *The Patriot,* and several other print venues. Melissa has painted and donated several murals to the Hospital for Sick Children in Washington, DC.

Visit Melissa on her website or chat with her on social media. Melissa enjoys discussing her books with book clubs and reader groups and welcomes an invitation to your event. Melissa's books are available through most online retailers in paperback, digital, and audio formats.

Melissa also writes sweet romance with no explicit scenes or harsh language under the pen name Addison Cole.

sidelineflats.com

9 781948 004183